ACE IN THE HOLE

"I don't want to play the piano," I said facing up to him, waving Rosalie away from us with my left hand. My right hand hung close to my gun. Butch had the .45 in his hand, but it wasn't cocked.

Butch gaped at me. "You are mad, ain't you? You're ready to shoot it out over a few tunes on the piano."

Rosalie grabbed at my left arm and I pushed her away. "You better play for them. This is Butch Cassidy you're talking to. Don't say no, Jim! The rest of his boys are downstairs."

YUKON RIDE

White Pass looked like the entrance to hell. A frozen hell. Snow was blowing and Skagway was 20 miles behind. Somewhere on the other side was Lake Bennett, 20 miles away on the downgrade. There the wayfarers built boats and rafts that would take them downriver to Dawson, biggest of the boom towns in the Yukon. Well over half of them sank or were ripped to pieces in the rapids of the Yukon, and unless Saddler could pay his way on a sturdy craft, he might have more to worry about than Soapy Smith or the others trying to get at Judge Phineas Slocum's body before he did.

Saddler Double Editions by *Leisure Books:*
HOT AS A PISTOL/WILD, WILD WOMEN
A DIRTY WAY TO DIE/COLORADO CROSSING

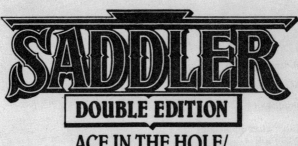

SADDLER

DOUBLE EDITION

ACE IN THE HOLE/ YUKON RIDE

Gene Curry

LEISURE BOOKS   NEW YORK CITY

A LEISURE BOOK®

March 1995

Published by

Dorchester Publishing Co., Inc.
276 Fifth Avenue
New York, NY 10001

Printed in the United States of America.

ACE IN THE HOLE

ONE

The girl squirming under me gave a little yelp when Butch Cassidy came in without knocking and said, "I hear you can play the piano."

That's exactly how it started. I couldn't help it if Butch took a liking to me because I could tickle the ivories, a thing he had always wanted to learn how to do but never had. Me, I picked it up one time working as a bouncer in a whorehouse in El Paso. This particular bordello had a pretty well-behaved clientele so there wasn't much bouncing to do, and since you can screw only so many girls in a day, I'd looked around for something to while away the hours. After I gave up solitaire—all forms of gambling were frowned upon—I started taking piano lessons from the old colored man who showed up early and stayed late. Most mornings were slow and I learned to play such easy tunes as *Streets of Laredo* and the like. Compared to a real musician, I couldn't play a lick. But Butch had an ear of pure tin, so it made no difference.

Of course if Butch hadn't found me he would have

found someone else. I just happened to be in the right place at the wrong time, namely the town of Jackson Hole, Wyoming, on the evening of April 25, 1890. Land up that way was known as Butch Cassidy country then. The law and the Pinkertons and the railroad detectives had been chasing Butch for about a year and hadn't been able to catch him. But that's aside from the point, which is that I had never met the man and never expected to.

This state of affairs changed abruptly on the night I'm talking about. After working for three months as a bodyguard for a rich Englishman, a rancher who had been dodging bullets from bushwhackers, I was on my way south. The Englishman had wanted to fence off the range with barbed wire and the small ranchers didn't like the idea. Up close I was a good bodyguard, but that didn't stop them from busting his head open with a high-powered rifle one day. So I was out of a job and had decided to go on home to Texas, which is more my kind of country than the damp, rainy Northwest.

Jackson Hole was on the way, and I wish I'd never seen the place. I would have passed right through town if my horse hadn't gotten a broken shoe. When I saw the blacksmith was drunk, I asked him how long it would be till he sobered up. He had spotted, yellow skin and a lower lip that stuck out like a dish. "Whyn't you go over to Doxy Milligan's whorehouse and get yourself a poke whilst I take a little nap," the horseshoer suggested, and at the time I thought it was a fine idea.

The Grand Tetons were glorious at sunset, tall and jagged against the deepening blue of the sky, and the wind was cold as it blew down from the peaks. Compared to the majesty of these great mountains, the town was shabby and depressing. I felt like a drink and a woman to help me on my way home.

Not all whorehouses have red lights, but this one did. It was a three-story frame building painted pink, with white trim on the doorframe and windowsashes. It was the best-looking place around. I knocked and was admitted by a hard-eyed gent in a black suit with a daisy in his buttonhole. He carried his gun in a shoulder rig, but it didn't bulge too much. His wary eyes flicked over me, sizing me up as a spender or as a cheapskate, a peaceful man or a brawler. When he decided I wasn't going to try to wreck the place, he pointed me towards the parlor, where Doxy presided over four fair-to-middling whores, aged from 16 to 40 years old. There would be others upstairs. I had already decided on the 16-year-old when Doxy beckoned me with a queenly air.

"We have a visitor, ladies," Doxy announced in a throaty voice. Her bright red hair had come out of a bottle, and it was piled and teased and pinned until it sat on the top of her head like a hen on a clutch of eggs. She had fat cheeks, with a beauty spot pasted close to her mouth on the right side. The beauty spot moved about while she talked.

All the women looked at me and smiled obediently. Doxy patted the couch beside her and told me to sit down. "Might I inquire as to your name, sir?"

"Jim Saddler," I said. "From Jonesboro, Texas."

"A fine state," Doxy said, and of course I agreed with her. It was easy to see why they called her Doxy, for though she was crowding 60-years-old, she might not be too bad if you were hard up. I was glad I didn't have to find out firsthand, though.

Doxy introduced the women and said every one was from a fine family. Everything was fine with her, and it was quite a layout she had there. The carpet in the parlor was rich and red, and so was just about everything else. On the polished piano was a red shawl with gold tassels. A stack of seasoned logs blazed quietly in the fireplace. A sign read, "God Bless Our Happy Home." Idly, I played a few bars of *Laredo* on the piano.

My girl's name was Rosalie, a pretty name, and she was pretty too. Some of the others were pretty enough, but worn around the edges from too many bedroom rides. It would be a few years before Rosalie got that look; at the moment she wasn't long from the farm. She was fresh-faced and brown-haired, with nice rounded breasts. I liked her pale, gray eyes and quick smile.

Now that I had picked out who I wanted, the other women lost all interest in me and went back to their reading and needlepoint. "Have a good time, you two!" Doxy cooed as we headed for the stairs. "Rosalie will see to the arrangements." Doxy was referring to the money. The price was kind of high, but I'd thought what the hell, we pass this way but once.

Rosalie's little room was on the second floor. For a room in a whorehouse it was a nice room, and the furniture hadn't been boot-scarred and cigar-burned as it usually is. Of course the brass bed was a double and the sheets were clean. I like it when my girl is pretty and the sheets are clean.

Rosalie helped me off with my clothes; there was no need to help her because she had nothing on under her dress. I came up hard as a rock when I caught sight of her round, red-nippled breasts and sweet little bush. I admit to liking them young, but no younger than 16, so Rosalie was just right. She got onto the bed and I got on top of her, driving straight into her, because I had been on the trail for a week, and for me that's a long time to go without a woman. She was wet but that may have been pussy-melted vaseline. I won't swear her groans were real, but I do appreciate a girl who throws herself into her work like she did.

I kneaded her firm, young ass as I slid in and out of her, and when she locked her ankles around the small of my back, my balls tightened with anticipation. She squeezed and relaxed her pussy until I was ready to go crazy. There was no holding back with her, not the first time. I shot a week's load into her and she held me tight and looked straight into my eyes while I was doing it. Jesus! I don't know why but that excited me even more, and I kept on coming until I hadn't a drop left.

"Are you having a good time?" Rosalie whispered an hour later, after I had unloaded in her again. "Doxy gets mad if she thinks the guests don't have a good time."

I was limp but she insisted that I stay in her, and it seemed that if you paid for a second ride you got the third one free. Of course Doxy wasn't losing much by that, since for most men two comes inside of an hour are enough. However, I'm different. I like women so much that I can never get enough of them.

By profession I'm a poker player, if you can call that a profession, so I am around hotels and saloons a good deal of the time, and that's where you find women. At times I work at other jobs, if the pay is right, and with the Englishman it was. But even if he hadn't been murdered, I guess I wouldn't have kept the job more than another month. Out there on the high plains, with the wind from Canada blowing day and night, I got lonesome for my women. Hell! What's the point of going to bed if there's nothing in it but you? Late at night I'd lie there listening to the wind and get hopelessly hard just thinking about the women going to waste.

"You're a caution, Mr. Saddler," Rosalie whispered. I liked the way she whispered because you could almost forget that we were whore and customer. "You're just a caution, sir, and someday you're going to make some lucky woman a fine husband. By any chance are you married, sir?"

I guess she was just making conversation while we waited for my hard-on to firm up. "Call me Jim," I said. "By no chance am I married."

"Oh," she said, a little disappointed. I have no way of knowing why it mattered to her. Maybe she was still young enough to be romantic. I wanted to please her though. "I'm not married, but I am engaged to a sweet girl near as pretty as you are. And that's the honest truth."

The nicest thing about Rosalie was that she hadn't been a whore long enough to be bitter about men and about her work. That bitterness might come eventually, but for the moment she was young, merry-eyed and enjoying life. Some young whores have to learn the bed-game; others come by it naturally. I think Rosalie was one of the naturals. The affectionate way she handled my cock made me feel right at home with her.

Soon she whispered, "I'm going to give you a special treat," and she put the head of my cock in her mouth while she held the base of it with both of her small hands. I tried to push it in as far as it would go, but she held it back and sucked only the head. That's the most sensitive part naturally. She knew what she was doing. She sucked it steadily but gently, using her tongue at the same time. Doing that, she made it even more sensitive than it was. Even for me this was a new way of getting a suck-job.

Right away the bulb of my cock seemed to swell up to twice its usual size. It throbbed as she sucked it in that special way. Now and then I tried to re-take control, but she wouldn't let me. After several attempts I gave up and let her do it her way. Her flickering pink tongue continued to tease my enlarged, throbbing cock, sending waves of pleasure all the way up my spine. As she kept sucking and tongue-teasing, I felt little electric shocks in my skull. I wanted to cream in her mouth but at the same time I wanted it to go on forever. I knew the moment I came the feelings would begin to fade.

Rosalie faced me while she sucked and she smiled with my huge cock bulb in her mouth. She had a small, sweet mouth with very red lips and that made it all the more exciting. Then, without warning—the surprise was part of the treat—she sucked so hard she grew pink in the face, creating a tremendous suction. I raised my ass and literally exploded in her mouth. She sucked me dry and empty. I lay there like a man in a trance. Finally I became aware that she was talking to me. Whore or not, I felt a great affection for her.

"What did you say?" I asked her.

"Tell me about your girl," Rosalie asked. "Please tell me about her."

I pieced a girl together for her, the hair of one, the eyes of another. "My girl is, uh, a schoolteacher in, uh,

Jonesboro, West Texas, and her name is Rose of Sharon. Almost as pretty as yours."

Ignoring the last part, Rosalie said, "I think your girl's name is prettier. Maybe I'll change my name to Rose of Sharon. Do you think she'd mind?"

"Rose of Sharon wouldn't mind a bit," I said. "I'll tell her I met a pretty girl in Wyoming who wanted to use her name and I said it was all right." Outside the Wyoming wind tried to shake the house apart. A tree groaned close to the house, a sad sound, and I was glad I was in a warm, clean bed with a pretty girl with sweet tits and a firm ass, and not rolled in my bedroll beside the trail.

I asked her to get my fixins from my vest pocket. For the moment, I didn't have the strength to roll a cigarette and asked her if she could do it. That was just being polite, because all whores are taught that rolling smokes is an important part of the job once the main job is over.

"Here you go!" she said, putting the cigarette in my mouth. She struck a match on the tiled washbasin beside the bed and lit the gasper for me. I sucked in smoke and let it out slowly. There is nothing like a good smoke after a good fuck.

A clock with a painted face ticked quietly on the wall, and Rosalie said, "My, how time flies! We've been here all of two hours. I'll have to be getting downstairs."

I hadn't intended to stay all night, but now it seemed like a great idea. I asked Rosalie if she would stay with me. "Well, it'll cost quite a bit for the whole night," Rosalie said. She named the figure and it was quite a bit; on the other hand I wasn't ready to face the lonesome trail all fucked out as I was. I offered her more than she'd requested. "Oh, that will be just fine!" she said. "But I'll have to tell Miss Doxy, you understand."

"Oh, sure," I said. "You'll find the money in my pocket. You think you can find something to drink? Jack Daniels, if you have it."

"Your wish is my command," Rosalie said, smiling and rolling over me to get off the bed. She looked good standing there in the soft lamplight. It was a very nice whorehouse and Miss Doxy was to be complimented on how well she ran it. Rosalie got into her dress and buttoned it. Her face was pink from all the fucking. "I'll be right back," she said.

Good as her word, she came back with a full quart of Daniels and one glass; in the good houses the whores don't drink, or aren't allowed to drink. She uncorked the bottle with strong, even teeth and poured a drink for me.

"More," I said. "I'm thirsty."

Rosalie laughed. "Well, I wouldn't wonder. Now you just have your drink and I'll give you a fine bedbath." "And after I wash you I'll do myself. That way we'll be clean as new pins and will feel better."

"I'd rather do you," I said.

"Another poke! Right this minute!" Rosalie showed her astonishment. "You think you can?"

"I meant wash you," I said.

"Well, of course, yes, that will be fine," Rosalie said. "But first I'll wash you."

And she did, from head to toe, cock and balls. The water was hot and soapy and she squeezed out a washcloth and began to wash me all over. I groaned when she got to my balls.

Just then the front door banged open and a bunch of men came in downstairs and there was whooping and laughing. I must have tensed up, because Rosalie said, "That's just a bunch of friends. They're all right. Relax and let me finish washing you."

Soon I was done and it was time for me to wash her. She stretched out on the bed and smiled at me. "I feel like royalty," she said.

I didn't feel like royalty, but I felt good. I had two big drinks in my belly and a warm, wet girl under my hands—a naked and pretty girl with her legs open. I washed around in there and, honest Injun, I got hard again.

Her eyes widened in surprise and she said in mock

reproach, "You'll kill yourself, I swear you will."

Fact is, it didn't do me one bit of harm to stick it in her again. We were damp and smelled of soap, and the hair around her face was damp, too. I was just about to come when I heard someone with a heavy tread coming upstairs. The door opened and I knew it was a man. Completely off my stroke, I turned my head to see who the son of a bitch was. At least he could've said, "Sorry, wrong room."

But he didn't say that. He had a cheerful red face and was wearing a derby hat on the back of his head. Rosalie laughed when the man said, "I hear you can play the piano."

"Mister," I said wearily, "you better get out of here before there's a murder. Anything you heard about me and a piano is a goddamned lie. I can't even play the paper and comb. Be sensible now and let me be. Can't you see you're breaking in on a private party. You came in that door and you can leave the same way if you know what is good for you."

I was losing my hard-on and that was making me mad. "Let's get back to work," I told Rosalie, hoping the chunky man had enough manners to take the hint.

Unfortunately he did no such thing. All he did was stand there watching me at my labors. Now it's widely known that there are certain people who like to watch, and there are those who get paid money to be watched. Me, I don't belong to either faction. I advised the chunky man of that fact and suggested that he talk to Doxy about his special needs.

"Talk to Doxy," I said. "She'll fix you up with what you want. New Orleans style, or any old thing your heart desires." There was no sound of a door closing. "You gone yet, mister?"

"No, I ain't gone yet," he answered.

"Why ain't you gone yet?" I asked.

"If you're bashful about this, I'll wait till you get finished," he said. "Anyhow, what's all the brannigan

13

about? A lady photographer who once took my picture told me there's nothing more beautiful than the human body."

"You can't take any pictures in here. One more time, sir, will you take yourself out of here? Be off now before you get yourself injured something awful."

That was my last effort to keep the peace. I got the feeling that it wasn't going to work, and I was right.

For an answer I got, "Ain't you never going to get through whaling that little girl?"

TWO

Now, I've been in a few ridiculous situations in my time, but this one beat all. It was hard to stand on my dignity because I had none. Rosalie kept on laughing until I jumped off the bed, and then she yelled, "Don't hurt him, Butch!"

The name Butch meant nothing to me, and it was my firm intention to hurt him, and not the other way around. I didn't grab for my gun, which was slung over the back of a chair, because the derby-hatted gent didn't look that dangerous. It was just as well I didn't go for my iron. Before I got my hands close to his neck, he reached inside his coat and snaked out a double-action .45 with a shortened barrel.

He grinned at me and said, "Hold on there, soldier. Let's not get hot over nothing. Sorry if I barged in on you at the wrong time. Doxy said you'd be all through by now. Since you ain't, how's about I wait a while in the hall?"

That started Rosalie laughing again. She laughed so

hard the bed shook. "You got a nerve, Butch!" she said, kicking her heels in merriment. "What you think you're doing, anyhow?"

Butch leaned against the doorframe with the stubby revolver dangling from his hand, regarding Rosalie with good-natured interest. "What am I doing, little sister? Looking for a piano player is what I'm doing."

No one else seemed embarrassed so why should I have been? Standing there naked with my limp cock dangling, I asked him, "Is that what you think I was doing? Playing the piano?"

"More like the old trombone," Butch said, sending Rosalie into gales of laughter. "Come on now, soldier. Where's your sense of humor? In case you don't got any, you can forget about that gun of yours. Wouldn't do you any good to try for it."

I turned, feeling like a fool. "I'll be going," I said. "I just want to put on my pants. That all right with you?"

Butch flipped his coat open and slid the short pistol into a well-oiled shoulder holster. "See! I'm putting my gun away, only you won't want to forget I can get it out again just as quick. I said I was sorry for barging in on you."

I didn't know what to make of him. He was all duded up like a cowpuncher on his wedding day, uncomfortable in his stiff, new clothes. But there was more to him than that. The speed with which he handled a gun was proof of that, and the shoulder holster itself was out of the ordinary. A sun squint made a permanent crease between his light blue eyes, or maybe he just needed glasses and was too vain to get fitted. I didn't know him, and didn't want to know him. All I wanted to do was to get out of there.

Would that I had been so lucky.

I knew I'd be looking at his gun again if I tried to take him. It wasn't that important, so I didn't try. You can't trade bullets with every fool who crosses your path. Keeping my hands away from my gunbelt, I dressed quickly and sat down on the edge of the bed to pull on my boots, while Rosalie lay back and looked at me.

"Take it easy, Jim," she said. "We're all friends here."

"That we are," Butch agreed.

I had buckled on my gunbelt under the eye of the derby-hatted man and turned to go when the stranger said with a rough edge in his voice, "Where do you think you're going, soldier?"

"Going out," I said.

That got him mad in a mild-mannered way. It's hard to describe how it got him mad. Everything about him was so good-natured, as if he wanted to be liked and couldn't understand why he wasn't. I guess he wasn't too bright; most good-natured people aren't.

"What's your hurry?" he said, snaking out the gun again. He was very fast with that iron. He grinned at me, the sun squint deepening as he did. "You got an invitation to play the piano downstairs. We're going to have ourself a party."

I looked at the chopped-down .45. "Play it yourself," I said.

"Not friendly, is he?" Butch said to Rosalie, who had pulled a corner of the sheet over her cooze. "I invite him to a party and he gives me a sourball look. That ain't nice, soldier, and I don't like it when people ain't nice. Life is too short for sour looks and hard feelings." He raised the revolver and grinned at me, not wanting to take no for an answer. "I think you better come down and play that piano."

Well, you know how it is. When they push, you have to push back. The path of peace had gone crooked on me, and I was ready to step off.

"I don't want to play the piano," I said facing up to him, waving Rosalie away from us with my left hand. My right hand hung close to my gun. Butch had the .45 in his hand, but it wasn't cocked.

Butch gaped at me. "You are mad, ain't you? You're ready to shoot it out over a few tunes on the piano."

17

Rosalie grabbed at my left arm and I pushed her away. "You better play for them," she said, no longer laughing but breathless and frightened. "This is Butch Cassidy you're talking to. Don't say no, Jim! The rest of his boys are downstairs."

I stared at the most famous outlaw in the country, and he grinned back at me. The man who ran the railroads ragged. The bandit who gave bankers the shits. Cassidy had done all the things they said couldn't be done. They said the Wild West had had its day, but someone had forgotten to tell Cassidy. He ranged the Northwest like a tiger, taking what he wanted and moving on.

I don't know how many lawmen, official and private, were chasing him, maybe a small army. He had broken all the laws and dared them to come and get him. They had tried. Lord knows how they had tried! When they beefed up the guards on the banks, he switched to robbing the railroads. Back and forth he switched, and always got away with it. He was denounced in state legislatures all over the Northwest, and even in the Congress of the United States. Butch was an affront to every honest citizen in the land. But then, in so many ways, so was I.

Butch grinned at me, watching for my reaction to his name. Not getting any, he said, "Pleased to meet you, Saddler." He flipped the gun to his left hand without taking his eyes off me. "Why don't we shake, soldier? I'd like it if you was to shake hands with me."

I shook hands with him.

"Now, why don't we start all over?" Butch said. "I'll go out in the hall and knock."

"This is horseshit," I said.

"Most everything is. That's why you can't take life too serious. I don't."

He went out and when he knocked I told him to come in. Butch was a clown, though a dangerous one. Standing in the doorway, he said, "My name is Cassidy, and I'm looking to hire a piano player for the evening."

"Why don't you try the next house?"

Ignoring that, he said, "I'll pay five hundred for the right man."

Rosalie, buttoning her dress, let out a whoop and her eyes brightened at the sound of $500. I guess mine did too, but I didn't say anything.

"I can vamp a little," Rosalie said. "Lordy! I wish I could play."

Butch regarded her fondly. "So do I," he said. "I love you, Rosalie darlin', but between us we couldn't play 'Chopsticks'."

Rosalie pouted prettily and Butch got back to me, displaying impatience for the first time. "Be a pal, Saddler, and don't make me mad. Me and the boys are here to make an evening of it, so don't get me mad. Come on downstairs and play the fucking piano."

He dug into his pocket and threw a fat roll of bills onto the bed. Rosalie grabbed it and said, "Can I be Saddler's manager, Butch? Singers and musicians always have a manager. I read that in the paper. How much do I get, Butch?"

Somehow that broke the tension in the little, sex-smelling room, and I found myself smiling at both of them. "You get ten percent like all the other managers," I said.

"I'll kick in another ten," Butch said.

Rosalie squealed and threw her arms around him. I guess old Butch had enjoyed her favors a few times, because he squeezed her ass before he let her go. Rosalie peeled off $500, kept $50 for herself, and gave the rest to me. Butch told her to take his ten percent, which came to another $50. There must have been $5,000 in that roll. Butch stuffed it back in his pants without even looking at it.

"I sure hope you can play 'The Cowboy's Lament'," Butch said to me. "That's one of my favorites."

It so happened that I could, and I was glad of it. There was a wildness, a madness about this man that I found myself drawn to. Reckless beyond reason, he seemed to look at the world as through a cracked mirror, taking nothing seriously. I have some of that in me, though not nearly as much as Cassidy, and for the moment, I was ready to go along with him. How it was going to end I had no idea at the time. And if I had known, would I have said no? Of course I wouldn't have because there was no way to say no, graciously or otherwise.

I was glad I'd said yes when we got downstairs and saw the merrymakers I was expected to entertain. Butch had holstered the gun and was singing "The Cowboy's Lament" before we got all the way down. He sang like a bull moose. The house guard was adding bottles to the bottles already on the big table in the parlor. Smiling like a mechanical doll, Doxy was pointing where everything should go. She was eager to please, telling the house guard to fetch more liquor, ice for the champagne, and wood for the fire.

Butch said, "We got ourself a piano player."

Five pairs of eyes regarded me from the parlor. I knew Ben Kilpatrick, known as the Tall Texan, from his wanted posters. Ben was wanted for many crimes in many states and territories, and I had seen his likeness nailed to walls, fences, and trees long before I arrived in Wyoming. It was said that Ben always ordered ham and beans in restaurants because he couldn't read the menu. A stringbean of a man, he was dressed up in new town clothes like Cassidy: derby hat, embroidered silk vest, even a watchchain. The chain was heavy, solid gold, and must have cost its real owner a pretty penny.

For a moment they looked like they were grouped for a photograph, holding themselves in a stiff studio pose; and indeed the members of the Wild Bunch were well known for their fondness for photographs, something that was going to get them all killed. I realized that I had seen all of them before—not in the flesh but in wanted posters. They looked the same, and yet they were different. I wasn't delighted by what I saw.

Butch made the introductions, though there was no need. I got a quick smile and a strong handshake from

Harry Longbaugh, known to the world as the Sundance Kid. They said Harry was from New Jersey, and he was handsome and knew it. After the Kid I traded handshakes with Tom O'Day, a demented Irishman, Harvey Logan, notorious as Big Nose Kid Curry, and an ordinary looking man named Will Carver. I didn't know anything about Carver.

"And last but certainly not least," Butch said, "I'd like you to meet Harry Tracy. Everybody loves Harry and you will too. Come on now, Harry, shake hands with the man."

Some killers don't look like killers. Harry Tracy did. The murderous nature of the man reached out at me. Mostly it was the eyes, as it usually is with killers. They were big and flat and gray, mindlessly hostile and utterly lacking in compassion, humor or mercy. He had a wedge-shaped face the color of a smoked ham, his iron jaw stuck out, and his whole chunky body was like a bunched-up fist ready to strike. Though he was dressed up for a party like the others, his cropped head gave him the look of an escaped convict. The hand that came out to shake mine was dry and hard. He didn't just shake my hand though, he tried to crush it. Our eyes met and Tracy smiled his killer's smile, and it went on like that for a few seconds until Butch yelled at him to let go.

"What the fuck you trying to do, Harry, crush his fingers? The only piano player we got?" Butch yelled again and Tracy let go, not liking it but taking it from Cassidy. Butch was the boss of the gang, but I could see that Tracy had his own ideas about that. The others looked good-natured enough, more or less like Butch himself; only Harry Tracy didn't seem to fit in. But he was there and had been part of the gang for a long time.

Butch clapped his hands and the group photograph came to life. The Sundance Kid asked me what I was drinking and when I told him he sloshed out a full glass of Jack Daniels and shoved it at me. I downed it in two swallows, and Tom O'Day, already half-drunk, allowed I was a scholar and a gentleman and a judge of good whiskey.

"Play!" Butch commanded.

I limbered up by cracking my knuckles and, fired by bourbon, I launched into "The Cowboy's Lament" while Butch sang about 200 yards behind the music. I guess I didn't do too badly because Doxy, nervous until now, began to smile. It began to shape up as a real party, the whores chattering like magpies, the whiskey going down like water. Another drink of Daniels put real life in my fingers, and at Butch's urging I played all the old easy tunes I had learned back in the whorehouse in El Paso. Maybe I wasn't very good, but you'd never have known it from the way Butch sang and applauded at the end of every song.

Inspired by more whiskey, I was able to manage a waltz and everybody but Butch and Tracy got up and danced. Butch was too busy singing to dance; Tracy didn't want to. All Tracy did was drink a lot and stare at me, as if measuring me for a coffin. A few times Butch tried to get Tracy into the mood of the party, but all he did was smile his killer's smile.

I played another waltz and Butch danced with Rosalie, steering her around the parlor like a man pushing a wheelbarrow. He sang as they danced. Butch sang all the time. He couldn't carry a tune in a bucket, and he sang loud if he didn't sing good.

The Sundance Kid admired himself every time he danced past the big mirror over the fireplace. The Kid was the best dancer in the bunch, and he knew it, just as he knew he was the handsomest man in the room. All the whores took a shine to the Kid, even old Doxy herself. A real gentleman, the Kid danced with everybody and had a fancy line of talk that never stopped.

My fingers flew over the keys. I wondered then why a talented musician such as myself had to make his living playing cards and hiring out his gun. Of course I was getting drunk, and as one tune followed another I got a lot drunker than that. No one seemed to mind that I had to keep repeating the five or six tunes I knew, and maybe they didn't sound the same, the way I played them. Only Harry Tracy didn't like the music, or maybe he didn't like me. He drank and continued to stare at me.

Done with dancing, Butch came back and leaned on the piano, and tears came into his mild blue eyes when I played "The Cowboy's Lament" for maybe the tenth time. I did some fancy trilling with my right hand, and Butch couldn't have liked it more. He wrapped his arm around Tom O'Day's shoulder and they sang together, the Irishman in a shaky tenor, Cassidy in a gravelly roar. Outside the night wind whipped against the house but inside all was good cheer—just a bunch of good fellers having a good time.

There was a lot of reward money in that parlor. Butch was worth a fortune all by himself. I don't know why I thought about reward money then, for I had no thought of turning them in, even if I got the chance.

I got drunker but never forgot that Harry Tracy was watching me. I knew he wanted to start trouble and was wondering how to go about it. I knew it would come before the night was over. I guess he wanted to kill me, though I couldn't imagine why. Harry Tracy didn't need much of a reason to kill a man I guessed. Any reason would do. At the time he didn't bother me much, and that shows you how drunk I must have been, for any man in his right mind would have been bothered by Mad Dog Harry.

Like the Sundance Kid, Tracy was an Easterner, a New York Stater. Other than that, the two men had nothing in common. I liked the Kid. I even liked Tom O'Day, who smelled pretty rank in spite of his new suit and boiled shirt. O'Day looked like a confused walrus, with his cross-eyes and straggly mustache.

In the middle of the party, the house guard lugged in a whole mess of food and set it out for the merrymakers. Concerned for my well-being, Butch yelled at me to take a break from playing. By now he was drunk enough to want to play himself. I let him have the stool while I drank whiskey and worked on a fat roast chicken. Tom O'Day waltzed with a turkey drumstick in one hand, singing with his mouth full.

Before he banged out a note, Butch stroked the piano keys like a man stroking a naked woman. His wet, blue eyes were full of love for the instrument he couldn't play. I felt sorry for the poor feller.

The dancing went on without music, and sometimes Harry Tracy watched the Sundance Kid, but his eyes always came back to me. I guess he hated the Kid because the Kid was everything Tracy was not. He was handsome, even charming in a way, and the whores hung all over him. They all stayed away from Tracy. Now and then Doxy said a few words to him, but she gave up in the face of his sinister smile. Sinister was the only word for Tracy. Even now, years later, I find it hard to put him into words. All I can say is that Harry Tracy was the worst man I'd ever met in my life.

Curry and Will Carver were still waltzing and I was still playing, stone drunk now, but happy as a pig in shit. Curry, big-nosed and awkward, danced with two whores at the same time. Tom O'Day sat in a stupor with a bottle in his hand. It was well into the night and the parlor reeked of liquor and cigar smoke. Maybe I shouldn't have winked at Harry Tracy, but I did, and he drew his gun so fast I hardly saw his hand move. It came out smooth as velvet, with the hammer back. The trigger was squeezed tight and only his thumb was keeping the hammer from dropping on a cartridge. Tracy was drunk, but his hand didn't waver.

"Stand up, you stinking spy!" he rasped in his dead-cold voice. One of the whores crashing around with Curry gave out a short scream when she saw the gun. Curry pushed the whores away and stood watching. Will Carver stared at the gun in Tracy's hand, then his eyes flicked over to me. O'Day, half-asleep, didn't even notice what was going on.

"Listen, Harry," Curry said cautiously. "You don't want to wreck the party."

Tracy didn't look at the big-nosed outlaw. "Keep out of it, Curry. Don't get in my way, I warn you. While you been banging around with the whores I been figuring things out. This son of a bitch is a Pinkerton spy. Stand up, sneak, or I'll kill you where you sit!"

I got up as best I could. I was none too steady, though the liquor had started to die in me. Nothing like the threat of death to sober a man up. Tracy smiled again and moved his thumb around on the hammer of his gun. All he had to do was to slip his thumb off the hammer and I'd be dead. I had been sweating from heat and whiskey, but suddenly my sweat turned cold. Curry and Carver didn't do anything but wait.

Watching my eyes, Tracy wiggled his thumb on the hammer, maybe hoping I'd piss in my pants. Tracy's rasping voice had a trace of love in it as he looked at me. The man was in love with death, and suddenly I got it. Harry Tracy was as queer as a three dollar bill and maybe he killed other men because they had something that was lacking in him. Sure as hell, he wanted to kill me.

"Where do you want it?" he said, smiling, his eyes as flat as an animal's. "Lift your right hand, sneak. Your piano-playing days are over."

I didn't raise my hand. I knew I had no chance at all, but I wasn't going to let him kill me by inches. My gun was holstered and I was drunk. Still, I had to try. At least I'd die quickly.

Then Butch spoke from the top of the stairs. "Put the gun away, Harry. Drop that hammer or I'll blast you out of your boots."

Tracy's eyes flickered but he held the gun steady. "The son of a bitch is working for the Pinks. Go back to the whore and let me take care of it."

"I'll kill you, Harry," Butch warned, starting down the stairs.

"We'll both kill you," the Sundance Kid said behind him.

Tracy had the nerve of a genuine maniac. The killing mood was on him and he didn't want to let go, even with two guns pointing at him. For an instant I thought he was going to slip the hammer and take his chances. His thin mouth tightened and quivered and sweat beaded on his forehead, so great was his effort to gain control over his lust to kill. I looked at the muzzle of the revolver. It looked big enough to jump into. I thought I heard a clock ticking loudly though there was no clock in the room. Cold sweat slid down my ribs and a muscle fluttered under my right eye. Then, smiling like the mad dog he was, Tracy pointed the revolver toward the ceiling and let down the hammer.

"You'll be sorry you didn't let me kill the spy," he said. "For that and other things, you'll be sorry."

I wondered why Butch didn't kill him then and there, for the threat was unmistakable, and I figured the tension between the two men had been building for a long time. I sure as hell would have killed him.

But Cassidy had his own way of doing things, as I was to learn the hard way. Now that the moment had passed, Butch was all good humor again, as if nothing much had happened. He spilled whiskey into a glass and folded my hand around it. I drank it down and Butch filled it again. "Don't mind Harry," he said. "It wouldn't be a party if he didn't try to do somebody in. But Harry always sees my side of it. It takes some explaining, but he always agrees with me in the end. That's right, ain't it, Harry?"

This time Tracy made no attempt to conceal his hatred of Cassidy. "That's right, Butch," he said.

I wondered why Tracy had backed down, because clearly he was afraid of no man. True, Butch was fast with a gun, but I couldn't see that he was any faster than Tracy. It had to be something else, something more complicated than that.

"Let's get some life back into this party!" Butch yelled.

Ben Kilpatrick came downstairs buttoning his fly. None too steady on his feet, he made for the table where the bottles stood half-empty. Under Butch's pushing and prodding, I made my way through some tune, but my heart wasn't in it. Harry Tracy had spoiled the party and we all knew it, especially me. Even so, I had a wad of Cassidy's money in my pocket, so I played on as best I could. Butch had sobered up along the way, but now he proceeded to get drunk all over again. Feeling the way I did, so did I.

Soon I felt I was playing the piano with two pairs of mittens on my hands. Butch didn't mind a bit. In fact, he said he'd never heard better music in his life. Tears trickled down his face, so good was my playing, and he said he'd give up everything he had, if only he could play as well as me.

I shouldn't have said what I did then. "There's nothing to learning the piano, Butch. All you do is start with a few easy tunes and go on from there." I think I hiccuped. I drowned the hiccup with another drink. "Hell! Butch, I could have you playing inside of a week." I looked at Butch and his face seemed to float by itself.

Butch wrapped his arm around my shoulder and blew his whiskey breath in my face. I didn't mind the smell 'cause my own breath was just as bad. "You really mean that, Saddler? You're not just bullshitting me? All my goddamned fucking life I have wanted to play the piano. That's crazy, ain't it?"

I had another drink. "You're just musical, that's all," I said. "Only you never got a chance to learn. Here! Let me take hold of your hand. Loosen up your fingers, for Christ's sake! Don't keep your wrist so stiff. Lay your hand down on the keys like I tell you!"

I wasn't able to see too well, but I managed to get Butch to thump his way through part of *"The Cowboy's Lament."* Listening to it, Butch's face broke out in a wide grin.

"I'm playing the piano," he roared. "I'm playing the fucking piano!"

"Nothing to it, Butch." I drank another drink. "All you got to do is find some lady to teach you, maybe a schoolteacher. She'll have you playing in no time."

My head nodded forward and I fell asleep.

THREE

Morning found me roped over the back of a horse and heading deep into the badlands. The sun was full up and Jackson Hole was far behind. I opened my blood-shot eyes and felt sick. I felt sicker when I realized where I was and what had happened to me. I closed my eyes and kept them closed for a while. That didn't do any good, so I opened them again. There were pines on both sides of the trail and the morning air smelled damp. Even if I hadn't known where I was, I could have figured it out from the loud whistling just a few yards away.

The tune was *"The Cowboy's Lament"* and Butch Cassidy was whistling it, or trying to. He couldn't whistle any better than he could sing, but that didn't stop him. Nothing stopped Cassidy when he made up his mind to do something. He must have been waiting for me to wake up. He rode his horse up close and twisted his head to look down at me.

"Shame to lie abed on a fine morning like this," he said. "For a while there I thought you was dead. That'd be a pity 'cause we been toting you a long ways. You ready for some hair of the dog?"

As soon as Butch righted me in the saddle I threw a punch at him, but he dodged it easily. "That's no way to treat an angel of mercy," he said, taking a pint bottle from the side pocket of his wool-lined coat. "Go on now, Saddler, have yourself a big drink and you'll feel better. Then you can have some good spring water to kill the taste."

Grinning at me, Butch didn't look any worse for the wear; his blue eyes didn't have a trace of red in them. Curry and Tom O'Day were roped across their saddles sleeping, but Ben Kilpatrick was more or less awake, and so were the Sundance Kid, Carver, and Harry Tracy. Ahead of us, Tracy turned in his saddle and gave me an angry look. The Sundance Kid, whiskey-sick and bleary-eyed, drank from his own pocket bottle and put it away. He gave me a tired grin and closed his eyes, letting the horse do the work. Ben Kilpatrick looked as hungover as the Kid, maybe more so, and he knitted his brow in pain as Butch let go with more of that goddamned whistling.

"Jesus Christ, Butch!" he complained.

Butch grinned and held out the bottle to me. "Drink hearty," he said. "Plenty more where that came from. Come on now, Saddler, let's see a smile on that face of yours. It's a nice day, the sun is shining, and there's banks and trains waiting to be robbed."

I had to get some of that whiskey down, or I wouldn't have been any good. Usually hair of the dog is a mistake, but I didn't know what else I could do. The Tetons were a lot closer than they had been the day before. I thought of Texas and wondered if I would ever get back there. I tilted the bottle and shuddered as the whiskey burned its way down to my belly. First it was awful, and then it didn't taste too bad. I took another big drink and the world came into focus. The air was so clear that I felt like I was looking at the Tetons through one of those stereo gadgets. A chattering squirrel ran up a tree and looked at us as we rode by. Butch passed me a full canteen after unstoppering it. After the whiskey, the fresh, cold water tasted good. I drank a lot of water and handed the canteen back to him.

Gradually the pain behind my eyes began to ease and I was able to stop squinting. I looked at Butch and asked him what the hell he thought he was doing. "You're wrong if you think I'm a Pinkerton spy. I got nothing to do with the Pinks. I got nothing to do with nothing."

The trail began to climb up through the trees, and from the looks of it, it wasn't used very much. Unless Butch had planned a job for that day, there was only one place we could be going: the Hole in the Wall, headquarters and hideout for Cassidy's Wild Bunch. Like everybody else, I had read about it in the papers. The Hole was where Butch always ran when the rest of the world got too hot for him. More or less the law knew where it was, but knowing wasn't enough. The badlands stretched clear into Idaho, thousands of square miles of the wildest country on earth. Over the few short years of Butch's career, the law had mounted many well-equipped expeditions, all to no effect. The law brought in Indian trackers, but no one had been able to find Cassidy.

Butch took a drink and wiped his mouth. "Who said anything about the Pinkertons? If I thought sure you was a Pink I'd have let Harry kill you last night."

"Then give me back my gun," I said. "Give me my goddamned pistol and let me ride out. You wanted a piano player and that's what you got. A deal is a deal."

"You still got the money," Butch said. "Look in your pocket if you don't believe me. The deal is still good, so what are you complaining about?"

The money was in my pocket, but that didn't mean much, because he could take it back anytime he wanted to. Guessing that he wouldn't do that was no consolation to me. "I *was* going to Texas," I said.

"Texas can wait," Butch decided. "You know what you're going to do, Saddler? You're going to teach me the piano."

"Then let's go back to the whorehouse. You're not

likely to find a piano in these mountains."

But of course I was wrong. And the minute I said it I knew it. Butch's grin showed me how wrong I was. "Got me a nice new piano, one of them half-size jobs," he said. "Found it in a baggage car two train robberies ago. Never been played, it looked like. All crated and so forth. Bound for Pocatello, Idaho, the shipping label said. You could have knocked me over when I saw that dandy little piano. Course it wasn't easy lugging it up and down and over the mountains. But I did it. By Christ, Saddler, I did it. And now you're going to teach me how to make music good as you do.

"Now before you start bitching, think on this. I got a lot more folding money than that first five hundred. Teach me to play good, you gloomy bastard, and you can name your own ticket. Truth is I got more money than I know what to do with. What's the point of having money if you can't spend it on something you like? Can't go too many places with the law chasing me all the time. Now and then I whoop it up at Doxy's. That's only because I grease the palm of the county sheriff."

Butch gave me the bottle without being asked, and I killed what was left in it and the world got a little brighter. What else could I do but level with the man? "Butch," I said wearily, "I'm not a Pinkerton spy and I'm not a music teacher. If you weren't so drunk you'd know what a lousy player I am. What's say I just turn my horse and forget I ever saw you?"

Butch knitted his brow in deep thought. "Well, you could be a spy for the Pinks. Admit it, Saddler, you could be."

"I could be, but I'm not."

"I have to be sure about that."

"You're not usually so careful with spies. Usually you just shoot first and worry later. Why haven't you shot me?"

"Most spies can't play the piano as good as you do."

"For Christ's sake! You don't really think I'm an agency detective do you?"

Butch looked me over as if he hadn't seen me before. "Probably not," he said. "But I have to be sure, and while I'm doing that you can teach me to play."

"Jesus Christ!" I said, smashing the empty bottle on a rock beside the trail. And then I grew silent.

At some time in the past the trail must have been used by miners prospecting in the Tetons. Now it was grown over with grass and weeds and getting fainter as we put distance behind us. Tom O'Day was coming to life and Ben Kilpatrick rode up close to untie the ropes that bound him to the horse. The Irishman slid off and fell to the ground with a crash. Everybody laughed and O'Day laughed, too, when he struggled to his feet and climbed back on the horse.

"That was some party all right," O'Day said, grinning like a fool. He felt in his pocket for a pint bottle and smiled happily when he discovered it wasn't broken. He drank the whole pint, which would have been enough to make another man drunk all over again. But O'Day just wiped his walrus mustache and said he hadn't had a better time in a coon's age.

Butch turned to me. "There, you see! Even Tommy agrees with me. You were the hit of the party, Saddler, and that's just one of the good times we're going to have. Listen to me. You're going to like it in the Hole. You think it's just another hideout? Wrong, my dear friend. All the comforts of home is what we have in there. And women! Why we got plenty of women, if that's what you're worried about. I figure a horny man like you would want to know that right away."

"Then why the party at Doxy's?"

"Now and then I like a change of pussy. A man gets tired of the same old holes. Besides, it's good to get out and see what the rest of the world is doing."

"No offense, Butch," I said, "but I'd just as soon not get tied up with a gang of outlaws. I've bent the law a few times, but I've never robbed any banks or trains. I don't have a hankering to be hunted for the rest of my life."

I was surprised when Butch saw my side of it—at least

he said he did. He pushed the derby hat onto the back of his head and knitted his brow. Butch always did that when there was an important decision to be made. "Nothing much to tie you in to us," he said. "We took you from Doxy's drunk to the world and roped you to a horse. So if anybody asks you can say you were kidnapped. What do you think of that?"

"I'd just as soon they didn't ask."

"Nobody's going to ask you a thing, least of all the law. The thing is, Saddler, you're going where we're taking you, and that's the Hole. How long you stay there depends on how fast you teach me the piano. Last night you said a week? Was that a fact or just the whiskey talking? I don't want to play fancy. I just want to play a little. No bullshit now, how long do you figure?"

"For the easy songs a week. First you learn how to do it, and after that you practice. I can't practice for you."

Without a doubt this was the most ridiculous conversation I had ever taken part in. There I was in the middle of nowhere, talking about piano lessons with the most notorious outlaw in the West. And not just the West, the whole country. He had looted the banks and railroads, yes, and he had killed plenty of men, though most of them were detective agency operatives and railroad thugs, so I couldn't get too worked up about that. Even so, he was a thief and a murderer, maybe the most hunted outlaw in the world, and I was talking to him about piano lessons! Maybe it's hard to believe, but it's true.

"I ride out in a week, is that a deal?" I said.

"You teach me in a week, you can ride out in a week. Of course you got to give your word you won't lead the law back in. Thus far they haven't been able to find the Hole. We'd like to keep it that way."

But even as he spoke those reasonable words I realized that Butch Cassidy's word was not quite as good as gold. The way into the Hole was the sore spot in the whole plan. It was the needle in the haystack, the pain in the

34

ass. Just knowing how to get in and out of the Hole could get me killed.

From a practical standpoint Harry Tracy was right: there was no proof that I wasn't a Pinkerton operative. The Pinks carried no badges, no identification papers, nothing to link them to the agency headquarters back in Chicago. The Pinks were ruthless and clever and often brought in men from hundreds, even thousands of miles away, men who spoke several languages and could pose as just about anything.

The famous Pink operative, James McParland, could have made his fortune on the stage, so skilled was he in mimicry and disguises. One day he was a traveling photographer complete with darkroom wagon, the next he was a Bible-thumping preacher with a Scottish accent. Everybody was afraid of the Pinks, and with good reason. More powerful than the law, the Pinkertons hired men of absolutely iron integrity, meaning that they were cold-blooded, fanatical bastards. So Harry Tracy was right, though I wasn't about to tell him so.

When the talk turned toward the way to the Hole, I thought Butch was going to blindfold me for the rest of the journey. He didn't but that didn't make me feel any better. It could mean that he trusted me—which he had no real reason to do—or it could mean that he didn't intend to let me go. The trouble with Cassidy was that you never knew how to figure him. Mostly he was good-humored. Even so, I was learning to see shifts of mood under the grinning surface, and I guess he grinned harder when he got mad.

In the end I decided to make the best of it. There was no way I could go up against the whole gang. I could maybe take out one or two of them before the others shot me to bits. It was likely that Butch was thinking about such a possibility. To this day I still think he hadn't thought past learning to play the damned piano, though. That was the way he lived, doing everything on the spur of the moment.

On the face of it, taking me to the Hole was a dumb idea, but it would have been unwise to try to explain this truth to him then. Butch had no great ideas about how bright he was, though he was smart enough in many ways. He was more than a trifle crazy, and if he hadn't been a notorious outlaw, he might well have been the head sport in some small town, playing rough practical jokes and cutting up at the dance hall on Saturday nights.

"You don't have to look so glum about it," Butch said to me. "What's the big hurry, Saddler? Why all the hurry to get back to Texas? I've been in Texas and it's not that great."

Harry Tracy was ahead of us on the trail. "What about him?" I asked, ignoring Cassidy's comment. "Maybe others in the Hole will share his opinion of me."

Butch smiled at Tracy's back. "My opinion is the only one that counts. Most of the boys are all right. If Harry gets too rambunctious, I'll just have to kill him. But I'll decide when—I decide everything. It's worked pretty good so far. We take what we need and try not to kill too many people. Of course not including Pinkertons and railroad detectives."

For a moment I saw the killer in Cassidy, and I didn't doubt that he would kill me if he found cause to do so. There was no turning back. For him no amnesty was possible, for he had robbed and killed too many times to plead for mercy. If they trapped him they wouldn't bother to take him alive. He knew he was a walking dead man, though he loved life more than any man I ever knew. There was no great injustice done to him in the past, and he never pretended otherwise. And though he might be taking me to my death, I liked him in an odd sort of way. I hadn't the faintest notion of how I was going to get out of his grasp, but I was going to try like hell.

The badlands began about 20 miles from where we were—wild, raw country cut with deep canyons that sometimes turned back on themselves. The whiskey was wearing off and I didn't want to drink any more of it. We had left the old trail and were winding deep through the dun-colored wasteland. It was hot and dry in the deep canyons protected from the wind. It was rough country where a stranger could get lost in a hurry. Cassidy and the others rode with the easy confidence of men who had been through there many times, who knew every rock and bush and gully. The day wore on and we kept going.

The sun started to slide toward the west and I figured we had come more than 40 miles from Jackson Hole. Butch hummed and whistled a lot. The others were quiet. Tom O'Day drank plenty of whiskey, but he was silent too. I wondered how long it had been since they had pulled their last job. But nothing was said about business.

We kept on going after it got dark, and after another hour, riding by moonlight, we started through a long, turning slit in the rock that provided just enough room for one rider at a time. In places it was almost covered by an overhang of stunted trees. Half-a-mile into this ravine we were challenged by two men squatting behind rocks on both sides.

Butch called out the password, "Pinkerton," and the two lookouts waved us through. There was some laughing at the password, which must have been a new one, and after that we made our way into a small, grassy valley hemmed in by high rock walls. Up ahead there were lights in a scatter of solidly built cabins.

"What did I tell you?" Butch said to me. "We're as snug as a bug in here. Only one way in and that can be defended by just a few men. Even if they find the place, they can't starve us out. Got a fine spring back here and all the food we need for a long siege. Something else you didn't know. We got dynamite planted in about a dozen places. I take good care of my little congregation."

I looked up at the high rock walls outlined against the night sky. "Any way to get in from the other end of the valley?"

"No way in or out from that side. Country on all sides

runs off to nowhere. Don't even think about it, Saddler. You wouldn't stand a chance."

"Thanks for warning me, Butch."

Butch laughed again. Laughter came as easily to him as frowning to a preacher. "I don't want nothing to happen to you, Saddler. In years to come you can tell folks you knew Butch Cassidy. I'll tell you again, soldier. Loosen up and enjoy yourself. You're going to have one hell of a time. Yonder there on the porch stands my lady. Her name's Etta Place, and I guess you've heard of her."

Everybody had. In her way Etta was just as wanted as Butch. I'd seen her picture—the Wild Bunch were the most photographed bandits in the world. But no picture could have done her justice. Some women just don't photograph well, and she was one of them. She wasn't all that tall, but what there was of her was well-built. She was dark-haired, pale-skinned, and tough as nails. The toughness showed in the lift of her strong chin and the defiant stare in her black eyes. Light flooded out onto the porch and I saw the glint of the heavy pistol belted high on her side. While she waited, two more women came out of the cabin and stood beside her. One had a halo of thick red hair. The other was several years younger, not much more than 17 or 18.

Etta Place spoke first in a tough, husky voice that was hard to place. "You took long enough," she said to Cassidy. "One of these days your whores are going to get you hanged."

Butch grinned at her. "In a pig's ass they will. Anyhow, what're you so hot about. I told you, me and the boys was going down there. Etta, my sweet, I'd like you to say hello to Jim Saddler, a lonesome Texasman far from home."

Etta stared at me with hard eyes. "Who the hell is he?"

"A friend of the family," Butch said.

Etta wasn't buying any of Cassidy's blarney, at least not then, "This Saddler, what do you know about him?"

"I know he's going to teach me to play the piano. Where's your manners, Miss Etta? Say how do to the man, for Christ's sake." He said to me, "The other two ladies are Pearl Hart and Laura Bullion."

"Ladies," I said, and tipped my hat.

"You sound like you're from Texas," Laura said, friendly enough. "Pleased to meet you, Saddler," Pearl Hart said.

The Hart girl was prettier than the others, though all were pretty enough. It was plain that Etta Place didn't like what she saw of me. Call me contrary if you like, but I liked her fine. I wondered if all of them belonged to Butch, for anything was possible with him. To tell the truth though, women were not my concern at that moment. After a long, hard day in the saddle I was hungry as a son of a bitch.

As if reading my mind, Butch asked what there was for supper. Looking at Etta, he said, "If there's nothing to eat, I'll eat you."

The other women giggled and Etta said angrily, "Watch your dirty mouth, Cassidy. There's food on the stove if you want to eat it."

Butch clapped me on the shoulder. "In you go, Saddler." Sundance went in ahead of us. Tracy and the other men went on to the other cabins. Etta Place stood aside to let me pass.

It was a big cabin and the main room was well if roughly furnished. A cookstove glowed red-hot and against one wall stood the new miniature piano Butch had been talking about. It was scratched in a few places. Apart from that, it gleamed with wax polish. Etta Place went to the stove and took off a large pot of simmering stew, using a rag to protect her hands. She banged it down on the table and began to dole out plates of meat. After that she set out coffee and tin cups.

The women had eaten, but they sat with us while we dug into the stew. It was good and hot with big, tender chunks of beef. No doubt the beef was stolen, just like the piano.

It seemed as if Butch couldn't take his eyes off that

piano. He positively glowed with the pride of ownership. Etta saw him looking and got angry again, though she had sort of simmered down. She puffed hard on a brown cigarette and blew clouds of smoke at the roof. Getting angrier by the moment, she stubbed out the smoke, then lit another one. Butch, I noticed, had terrible table manners, or maybe he was just trying to annoy the dark-eyed gunwoman even more.

Finally, she said, "Have you gone crazy, Cassidy? Here you have the whole country looking for you, and you bring home a so-called piano player? If that isn't crazy I don't know what is. Who in hell is this man and where does he come from? You're just as bad, Sundance," she said turning to Harry. "Why did you let him do it?"

"Don't blame me," Sundance answered. "You know anybody who can stop Butch when he sets out to do something?"

"You didn't even try," Etta said, still blowing smoke like a chimney.

"Can you really play it?" Pearl Hart said in that girlish voice she had.

"Go on, play it," Laura Bullion said, urging me. "It'll be a change from Cassidy's whistling and bellowing."

Well, what else could I do? I'd eaten all I could eat, and that was plenty. Etta watched me with hostile eyes as I pulled up a chair and opened the lid of the piano.

"Saddler doesn't even need sheet music to play songs," Butch said, as proud of me as he was of the piano. "You should have heard him last night."

"Play if you're going to play," Etta said, staring at me harder than ever. I wondered if she meant to keep up her badmouthing, or if she'd leave off after a few minutes. She was a dangerous woman and would make a bad enemy if she decided to be one. I guess she loved Cassidy for all her tough talk. And maybe she knew what I knew, that Cassidy didn't have that long to live. She was smarter than Cassidy, and maybe tougher as well, and she must have known that the relentless Pinkertons would find a way to run him down. They had scattered the James gang not so many years before, and what they could do to Jesse they could do to Butch.

I only knew a few tunes and I started with the one I could do without getting too many thumbs into the music. Butch grinned at Sundance, enjoying every minute of it.

"I declare, that's very pretty," Pearl Hart said. "Don't you think so, Laura?"

"Pretty as can be," Laura agreed.

Only Etta didn't like my lousy music. She looked over at Butch. "Anybody can play one song," she said.

"Not Saddler," Butch said. "He's got a whole trunkful of tunes."

Of course I didn't, but I did my best, and while I played what I knew I wondered how many members were in the gang. I had seen the two lookouts in the ravine. Unless I was wrong, there would be more than that.

Etta was as good as any man there, and she had her own list of dead men. I had never heard of Laura Bullion, but it seemed to me that I knew something about Pearl Hart. My recollection was that she had come from Colorado or New Mexico. I couldn't be sure about that though. One thing was sure: she was nowhere as famous as Etta. Etta and Butch were always mentioned in the same breath, and in a short time together they had made one hell of a reputation.

I played until I was thoroughly sick of it. Etta frowned as I began to hit more sour notes than sweet ones. Sundance didn't care how I played. He kept looking at Etta and yawning. At last he said, "I don't know about you folks, but I'm going to bed."

Etta stood up and looked at Butch. "You plan to stay up all night, do you?"

Butch yawned too before he gave his attention back to me. "Better hit the hay, Saddler. Too late now to give me a lesson. These two fine young ladies will make you comfortable."

Butch and Sundance went into the only bedroom. Etta followed them and closed the door. I looked at the door and must have showed surprise.

Laura laughed and Pearl joined in. "That's how it is with them," Laura said, shaking her head. "They've got their own special arrangement. Some people are like that. Come on now, Saddler. We'll show you where you're going to sleep."

"I'd just as soon not have to bunk in with any of the men," I said, afraid that they might put me in with Tom O'Day. I'd sleep out in the rain rather than have to smell that rank Irishman all night. I had nothing against the walrus-faced Irishman, but it was like that gent had never heard of soap and water.

Pearl and Laura came up close to me and began to tug at my clothes. Pearl managed to feel my muscles without making it too obvious. Laura admired me too. I began to feel like a stud at a horse auction. Not that I minded all the attention.

Sounds of combat came from the bedroom and Pearl giggled. Winking at me, she went to the door and put her ear to it.

"Hot damn!" she said. "Sounds like a wrestling match in there." She looked at me and licked her lips.

"I'm beginning to get excited," Laura said.

"Me too," Pearl said.

Together they propelled me toward the door.

"It's way past your bedtime, Saddler," Pearl said.

FOUR

"**B**utch wants you to have a good time here," Laura explained as the two lady outlaws led me through the darkness to a small cabin not far from where Cassidy and Sundance were now bedded down with Etta Place. I wondered how they did it with Etta. Did they both take her at the same time, one from the back, and one from the front? It was just an idle thought and none of my business. Like Laura said, they had an arrangement. If they both wanted to sleep with Etta, it was jake with me. My own arrangement was going to be just as uncommon.

Pearl opened the door of the cabin and went in to turn up the lamp. Outlaws or not, they had fixed up the place as only women can. Framed pictures hung on the walls, and the floor had been scrubbed and strewn with clean, white sand. The fire had burned down and Laura threw in chunks of wood. It was a one-room cabin with a double bed against the wall. The bed had a quilted spread and the pillows were the big kind I like. It was warm in the cabin after the fire blazed up and somehow

Wyoming didn't seem so bad after all. We all took off our guns and hung them up, and after that the two women helped me off with my clothes. I was tired but not as tired as I had been, and the more clothes I got off the less tired I became.

"It's very nice of you to be doing this," I said as Laura unbuttoned my pants and took out my cock. It stood up stiff and throbbing as they peeled off their clothes. Both had very good bodies, young and soft, and I wondered if I was going to get any sleep that night.

Pearl was the more ladylike of the two. Both were fine with me though, and I hoped it wouldn't come to killing between us at some point. I will say that I did feel like a man in a dream. I had been on my way to Texas the day before, with every expectation of getting there, and now I was on my way to bed with two lady bandits. My life is like that, I guess, always full of surprises.

Then we were all in bed; the fire was banked, and the lights were turned low. The north wind whacked itself against the cabin, and we were the best of friends. We piled in together and it was agreed that I should do Pearl first because, as Laura explained, she hadn't had a man for a long time.

Pearl was ready and wet for me and when I thrust into her, she gasped with pleasure. That got Laura all excited and she wriggled around until I got my head behind her legs while I was fucking her friend. I tongued Laura until her backside bounced on the bed. One girl excited the other and I excited both of them. I wondered how Butch, Sundance, and Etta were doing over yonder. I held back while Pearl had her come and then she shifted from under me and I pushed myself, still rock-hard, into Laura.

It went on and on like that until the bed creaked and swayed under our weight. All tiredness left me and I worked like I'd never worked before. I was able to hold back because I'd done so much fucking the night before. We went on and on until we were sweating hard in the dim, warm light of the cabin. And then, sated for the moment, they urged me to have my first come, and I was deep inside Laura when I did. Then we all lay back and rested until it was time to start again.

"When he comes he really comes," Laura said to Pearl. "All some men can manage is a little dribble, but this rowdy comes like a stallion with his first mare of the day. You come like a real stud, Saddler," she said to me. "It just shoots out of you, strong and hot. You haven't felt that yet, Pearl, but you will. You won't forget it in a hurry. I can still feel it, the way he volleyed into me."

"I want to feel it," Pearl said. "That's what I miss about not having a steady man of my own. To feel him shooting off inside me. I like to tighten my cunt muscles when a man comes inside me. It's like I can trap his prick inside me and never let it out. All real woman-loving men like that. As long as their prick is in there, in the warm woman-juice, they can get hard again in half the time. Isn't that true, Saddler?"

"It sure is," I said honestly. I felt like a hospital patient being discussed by a doctor and a bunch of medical students. But that's what the women were like in the Hole in the Wall. They were free of shame. That was great for a man like me who loves sexually free women more than anything—more than steaks or whiskey or even poker.

I lay on my back with the two women on either side of me. Laura had just had a tremendous come and she was satisfied for the moment. Pearl had come a number of times, but she wanted more. She played with my cock, coaxing it back to hardness. It didn't take much coaxing. It was starting to come up again, stiff and strong. Pearl massaged it expertly. My balls began to tighten with anticipation of yet another come.

"Men love it when you pull their prick," Pearl said. "I used to jerk off my older brother and he loved it. Then my younger brother—he was fourteen—found out what we were doing and he wanted to be jerked off too. Why not? I loved both my brothers. Odd thing is that it was my kid brother who first put his fingers in me. The little devil knew I wanted him to do it. I guess my older brother was too shy. My kid brother was anything but. In no time at all he had his fingers in me, diddling me while I jerked him off. But that wasn't enough for the little devil. He wanted more. One night when he came to my room to be jerked off, he brought a pad of butter and rubbed it all over his cock. My hand flew up and down his buttery cock and you should have seen the look on that kid's face. It was like he'd died and gone to heaven. He put butter on his fingers before he diddled me. Those were happy times, Saddler. Then my parents died and the family broke up."

The night wore on and to keep me going they fed me drinks from a quart of whiskey they had in the cupboard. Laura drank along with me, but Pearl didn't drink at all. It was well into the night when we called it quits, but instead of going to sleep they talked about themselves and wanted to hear about me.

Snuggling against me, Pearl said she was just 17-years-old but had been an outlaw for more than a year. Her specialty was robbing stagecoaches, and she'd only turned to robbing banks and trains when so many stage lines had gone out of business. Yes, she said, her story was the old, old story of the good girl who had fallen in love with an outlaw.

"Now I'm a bad girl and love it," she giggled, making the bed shake. "My man got caught and sent to prison, but he couldn't have been too good at his job if he'd got caught, so I don't care about him anymore. I love this life and wouldn't go back to the old one if I could. How about you, Laura?"

"Not a chance," Laura said. She had worked at all kinds of lousy jobs, from waitressing in a restaurant to dancing in a saloon. "I feel wild and free, and to hell with the respectable life. When I get old, maybe about thirty,

I'm going to take my money and go to Chicago. That's where I've always wanted to go. But that's years away, and right now I'm having a good time. How about you, Saddler? What are you going to do with yourself?"

"I don't know what I'm going to do years from now," I said.

Laura said quickly, "Does that mean you're not a Pinkerton spy?"

She hadn't reached for her gun, so I was able to answer without any fuss. "Not a chance of it."

Pearl turned in the bed until she was facing me. "You're sure of that, Saddler? I'd hate it if you turned out to be that."

Laura reached down to massage my shaft. "No lousy Pink-spy could ever pleasure a woman—a couple of women—like you've been doing. Butch doesn't think you are, but it is kind of peculiar, you turning up like that in Jackson Hole."

I was getting hard again, but asked them, "Butch asked you to ask me?"

Laura said, "True, he gave us the nod, and I'm glad he did. Butch is good people, Saddler, and I'd hate for something bad to happen to him."

"So would I," Pearl said. "We'd have to kill you if you turned out to be the wrong kind, Saddler. You want me to tell you something else?"

"What's that?"

"Maybe you should decide to stay on with the gang."

"Why don't you?" Pearl urged. "We could have a lot of nights like this. Carrying on the whole night through."

They were urging so hard that I began to get suspicious. They seemed to be telling me there was no way I could leave. They seemed to be hinting that I'd get shot if I tried.

"Butch said I could leave," I said. "He gave his word. We made a deal."

Laura said urgently, "There's a lot of things you don't know about Butch. You'd do well not to argue too hard."

Pearl slipped her hand between my legs. "That's good advice, Saddler. Keep Butch happy and everything will be fine. Go against him and he'll get mad."

"I guess I'd better think about it," I said. "I wouldn't want to make Butch mad." And as I said that I knew I'd better start making some other plan to get out of there. Robbing banks wasn't my life's work and I knew I'd never get used to it. First and last I was a poker player, and a damned good one, if I do say so myself. All I wanted was to get away from the Hole in the Wall and keep on going. It wouldn't be long before the Pinkertons or some other law put an end to Butch and his gang, and I didn't want to be there when it happened.

"Well, there's no use worrying about it right now," Pearl said. "I don't think about what's going to happen tomorrow, and you shouldn't either. You want to have more fun or go to sleep?"

"More fun," I said. "Why think about tomorrow?"

But I was lying. Really I was thinking about nothing else.

"That must be Butch," Pearl said about seven o'clock the next morning. Her voice seemed to come from a distance. Light came in the window and I wanted it to go away. I wanted it to be five hours earlier and dark so I could sleep. Lord knows I needed my sleep. After the night I'd had, my cock was sore.

The doorlatch rattled again. "Anybody alive in there?" Even in my worn-out state there was no mistaking Cassidy's goddamned cheery voice.

Like me, Laura was tired. But Pearl—the kid of the outfit—got up and went bare-assed to open the door. And when she did, a blast of cold, wet air came in. Beside me, Laura sighed and snuffled and finally put her feet on the floor.

"You better roll out, Saddler," she warned. "The bossman is here."

Butch came in as loud as a traveling salesman and

slapped Pearl on her bare ass. "God bless all this fine mornin'," Butch said. I guess he thought he sounded like Tom O'Day.

The cold air was still blowing in and I knew I'd have to get up. With the fire burned down it was pretty cold in the cabin at that hour. I opened my eyes and knuckled the sleep out of them. Pearl was getting stovewood from a box. I looked at Butch and he didn't look one bit tired. Butch never seemed to tire, but I'm mortal and I was tired.

"'Tis a fine mornin' we're having," Butch said, again in what he thought was Tom O'Day's voice. "A shame it would be to lie abed on a mornin' as nice as this one."

I knew it wasn't a fine morning because I could hear the rain on the roof. In the Northwest it rains winter and summer. It can be hot and raining at the same time. Pearl was using the iron lifter to set the stove lid back in place. The dry wood began to pop and, leaving out Cassidy, it was the liveliest thing on the premises.

The bed creaked as Butch sat on the edge of it and regarded me with affection. "Well, did you?" he asked.

"Did I what?"

"Have a good time?"

The girls had worked hard, even if he had set them to spying on me, and I couldn't deny the pleasure I'd had. "Couldn't have been better," I said. "Thanks for thinking of me."

"Don't mention it, soldier. There's a big breakfast waiting for you. Who says you have to drink to have fun—that's what I always say. At one point in the night I thought I'd come over and join you good people."

Jesus! The idea of being in bed with Butch Cassidy!

"Rise and shine," Butch said. "After you get a good feed of steak we'll have our first music lesson. Guess it's been on my mind all night long. Harry and Etta bitched at me for humming in my sleep. It seems they don't have my great fondness for music."

Butch began to whistle tunelessly. Laura and Pearl

giggled and started to get dressed. I guess there was nothing they didn't do in the Hole in the Wall. Nothing was held back; they all took Cassidy's lead and said whatever came into their heads.

I swung my legs off the bed and Butch slung my pants at me. "I'm up," I said. Butch gave me the rest of my stuff: shirt, boots, gunbelt. Suspected of spying or not, I hadn't been deprived of my gun, which seemed to show that Butch thought I couldn't do a thing about my situation.

The girls had washed their faces and crotches and were combing their hair. All in all, it was a very homey scene. The fire snapped in the stove and a few minutes later I was dressed for whatever the miserable day had in store for me. I rubbed the stubble on my chin. Butch had shaved.

Pearl suddenly said to Butch, "I don't think Saddler was sent to work against you."

"Me neither," Laura agreed, with hairpins in her mouth.

Butch handed me my hat. "That's all to the good," he said. "Nothing in this world's worse than a sneak. Come on now, Saddler, you got to get your strength back. Get the wrinkles out of your belly and we'll have a go at the old pianny."

Laura and Pearl were fixing their own breakfast and said they'd be over directly. Laura made a face as she cracked eggs into a fat-sizzling skillet. "Listen to that goddamned rain," she said, letting an egg down easy.

The rain didn't bother Butch. Nothing much bothered Butch. "Good for the crops," he declared.

The smell of food reminded me of how hungry I was. I didn't feel like making music, but all the fucking and sucking of the night before had left me with a hollow feeling in my stomach.

Butch and I ducked out into the driving rain and made a dash for his cabin. Etta had a big breakfast waiting when we got over there and slapped the water off our hats. I'd never seen so much food—steak and eggs, hot biscuits, fried potatoes, and gallons of black coffee. The Wild Bunch might be hunted, but they sure lived high on the hog.

From the dirty look Etta gave me I thought the whole, good-smelling mess might be poisoned. But I was too hungry to worry about that, so I pulled up a chair and tucked in hearty. Butch joined me, though he said he'd eaten a first breakfast earlier.

Etta sat at the table with us, drinking coffee and smoking one strong, brown cigarette after another. You would have to say she smoked in anger, but angry or not she was a good cook.

After a while Sundance came out of the bedroom buckling on his gunbelt. He was wearing a clean red undershirt and pants. No socks, no boots. He grinned at Cassidy and then at me.

"No use trying to sleep once Cassidy is up," Sundance said. Etta shoved the steak platter his way and he heaped his plate.

Sundance said, "You look like you're in a good mood, missy. Why'd you have to get up so early? I was hoping along about now we could—"

"No throwing hot coffee," Butch warned Etta. "Hot or cold, don't throw it. You got to learn to take a joke, girl."

"Save your jokes for your whores." And having said that Etta lapsed into sullen silence, lighting one cigarette from the end of the one before. The door was open and wind-driven rain pattered on the porch. Heaped with wood, the stove glowed red, and another pot of coffee simmered on top of it. The piano stood waiting and I began to hate the goddamned thing. If it hadn't been there, then I would not have been either.

We hadn't finished eating when Laura and Pearl came in, followed by Tom O'Day. Butch made them welcome. There was no sign of Harry Tracy and the others. Plenty of food was left and Etta told O'Day to help himself.

"A shame to have it go to waste," O'Day declared

wisely. "There's poor people starving in China."

Butch said grinning, "They'd be starving worse if you was there."

Laura and Pearl, though invited to dig in, said they were too full to eat another bite. "You don't mind if we sit in for the music?" Laura asked. "Nothing else to do on a day like this."

"Heaven is open to all," Butch said, getting up from the table. "I don't mind a bit, Laura girl."

He looked at me.

"All right," I said. "Let's go to it."

Etta snapped a dishrag at Butch. "Wipe your god-damned hands before you touch that piano." Butch rubbed his hands with the damp rag and bowed in a bad imitation of a man on the stage of a theater.

It was time to face the music.

So there we were side by side, Butch with his sleeves rolled up, his freckled, hairy hands suspended above the keyboard. At first Butch's fingers were like sticks, and I had to tell him he was reaching for his gun to get him to loosen up. I tried to remember all the things that old colored man back in El Paso had taught me.

"Spread your fingers but keep them limber," I said.

They say you can teach anybody to play anything if you have enough time. Looking at Cassidy I wasn't too sure about that. Still, I had to try because I figured that that piano was maybe my only way out of there. Nothing more had been said about me leaving the Hole, and I didn't bring it up because I didn't want to sound like a nagging wife.

We started with "Down in the Valley," and they don't come any easier than that.

"Forget about the left hand," I told Butch. "We'll get to that later. First we work on the melody—later comes the fancy stuff."

I took hold of Butch's hand and brought it down on the keys. Then, pressing down on his fingers, I made him go *dong dong dong dinggg dong*! and his face lit up like it was Christmas. He turned to me, about as grateful as a man could get. You'd think I had just saved his poor old mother from the workhouse. His blue eyes were full of wonder.

"Holy shit! I played that, didn't I!" He let out a whoop. "You old son of a bitch, Saddler! You're teaching me to play."

If I had been an onlooker instead of a prisoner I would have thought it funny to see two big men wearing guns sitting together at a piano.

"You're doing good," I said. "By the time I leave you'll be playing with both hands. When I ride out a week from now you'll be playing the easy ones."

I waited for his response to that.

Well, they say give a man an inch and he'll take a mile. Butch said, "Be nice if I could play more than the easy ones."

That had an ominous ring to it, and I knew damn well that he wasn't going to keep his word. In a way it was something I'd known all along, but then I'm an optimistic galoot by nature. I'd been hoping for the best; now I knew I wasn't going to get it.

A few years back there had been a newspaper story about a crazy Mexican bandit-general who couldn't read but loved adventure books about the Spanish Main pirates and so forth. This madman attacked a town garrisoned by federal troops just so he could carry off the whole library in wagons and oxcarts. Along with the library he took the librarian, some harmless, middle-aged gent, and sentenced him to read aloud for the rest of his life. Ten years later, with a very sore throat I guess, he was still doing it when the federals killed the bandit and the librarian got away.

Listening to Cassidy that's how I felt. I decided then not to hand out any more guff about leaving the Hole. You have to work with what you've got, and what I had was Butch's friendship. Sort of, I did. I had to find a way out of that place. The ravine was well-guarded and hard to get through, and I guessed Cassidy wasn't lying when he said that was the only way in or out. He wouldn't be likely to hole up in a place where the Pinkertons or the law could get at him from the rear. Right then I had no idea what my plan was going to be.

After a rest we did "Down in the Valley" again, and kept at it until Butch was able to do it himself. At last, sick of it, I said, "That's enough for today. You don't want to wear yourself out."

"I don't feel wore out," Butch said.

"Who's teaching here, you or me?" I asked, thinking that if the music wasn't going to be a way to freedom, then I might as well drag out the lessons. Maybe by doing that I'd manage to stay alive. I wasn't forgetting Harry Tracy. I wasn't forgetting him for a minute.

Butch nodded obediently, though he wanted to go on. "You're the teacher. How soon do we start on the left hand?"

"Tomorrow," I decided.

"Why don't we just take a rest and go on with it? I feel so good about this," Butch said.

To show me what he meant, Butch let out a whoop and a holler. "That's how good I feel," he said. "When I'm having a good time I want the whole world to know about it. You got to shake off that hang-dog look, Saddler. Laugh and the world laughs with you. Some newspaper feller said that one time, and he got it exactly right. Course he was just putting my own feelings into words."

"Can't you ever get enough of anything, Cassidy?" Etta said irritably. "God Almighty! Hasn't there been enough racket around here for one day? Give that damn piano a rest so our ears can get a rest."

Butch smiled at her. "Your ears hurting you, Etta? If they are we'll get you to a doctor next time we hit some town. Anything else bothering you besides your ears? Be a shame if a good-looking gal like you had some ailment we don't know about."

That got Etta very mad. "The only ailment I have is you, Cassidy. Why is it you're such a pain in the ass?"

Nobody smiled too hard because now Butch himself was getting mad. He stared at Etta. "There's a cure for what's wrong with you, girl. It's called getting the hell out of this cabin and out of this valley. Works wonders for what ails you. I think maybe you ought to try it. Listen to what Dr. Cassidy is telling you, my sweet."

I wondered why a woman like Etta put up with him. Away from Cassidy, away from the Hole in the Wall, she would have had men hanging all over her with offers of marriage and other things. A woman like that could name her own price. So why did she put up with him? Because she loved the big, roaring bastard, I guess.

Cassidy had to prove his point—that he owned her— in front of the rest of us. I hate to be a party to things like that, but I wasn't calling the shots, so I kept my mouth shut. I guess it was a scene that had been played many times. Still, the others there in the cabin were an interested audience.

"So how about it?" Butch wanted to know.

Suddenly the defiant light in Etta's eyes went out and her fine body went slack. "I didn't mean anything by what I said, Cassidy. Go ahead. Beat on the piano all you want for all I care."

Butch grinned. "Thanks for telling me," he said. "I know you like my piano playing as much as I do." Now that he had won, Butch was prepared to be merciful. Or maybe he knew that he could push Etta just so far. "Maybe Saddler's right about trying to learn too much the first day. That's what you said, ain't it, Saddler?"

"That's what I said. The trick is to learn just so much at one time. That's how all the great piano players do it, I'm told."

Still smarting from Cassidy's humiliation of her, Etta turned her bad humor on me. "What great piano player told you that, Saddler?"

"An old colored man in a whorehouse in El Paso," I answered.

Everybody laughed and Butch let out another whoop.

"That's telling her, Saddler. Course you wasn't suggesting that sweet Etta ever worked in a whorehouse?"

"Gosh no," I said, explaining that the old colored gentleman I spoke of had been a demon at the keyboard. "It's too bad you don't have him here instead of me," I added sincerely.

"I got nothing against the colored people," Cassidy declared, wanting to let us know that he believed in the brotherhood of man. "Next time I'm down in El Paso I'll drop in on him." He winked at Etta. "For piano lessons and a few other things."

Etta flared up again. "You and your poxy whores!"

"Nothing wrong with being a whore, my love," Butch said. "We all have to make our way in the world. You, me, everybody. Especially you."

I was getting sick of Cassidy's grinning cruelty. "We could have another go at the piano," I said. "Just for a while, anyhow."

Butch sensed what I was up to, and he gave me the same kind of grin he'd been giving Etta. "A minute ago you didn't want to go on with it. What's it going to be? Make up your mind, Saddler?"

I was of no mind to be shot. "Anything you want to do is all right with me."

"That's true, ain't it," Cassidy remarked. I think he was pleased with me for reminding him that he was the boss.

So he forgave me, too. "Always agree with me and you'll do fine," Butch Cassidy said.

FIVE

We were all sitting around the table listening to the rain. After thumping his way through the old song a few more times, Butch joined us. Tom O'Day was forking the last of the steak and eggs into his big mouth. Smoking a thin cigar and drinking coffee, Sundance looked like a man with no problems.

Etta looked out at the rain falling from a gray sky and said, "Cassidy, why don't we leave this goddamned place?"

The words came suddenly, but I could see she'd been thinking about the idea for a long time.

"Where would we go?" Butch asked.

"Away from here," Etta said irritably.

"We could go down to the place in New Mexico."

Sundance had been paging through an old *Farmer's Almanac*. Now he looked up. "Too hot down that way, and I don't mean the climate. It was all right for a time. By now I think they're on to it."

Etta said, "I'd like to go someplace."

Butch looked at me. "You look like a man that's been all over, Saddler. Where would you go if you was me and you decided to leave your happy home?"

"Australia," I said. "They tell me it's a lot like the West, some of it anyhow. Big and free and hardly any people. Got deserts and mountains, cattle and sheep country just like here. I once knew a man who found a lot of gold there."

The conversation was taking an interesting turn, one I liked. If Butch went to Australia, I could manage to duck out along the way. I sure as hell wasn't going to play the piano at the bottom of the world.

"They got banks in Australia?" he asked.

"They got banks everywhere."

"How about trains?"

"I thought Etta's idea was for you to give that up."

"I've thought a few times about Canada," Butch said.

"Canada is too close. If you think the Pinks are bad, try tangling with the Mounties. No way to buy off the Mounties. They'll stick to you closer than a dirty shirt."

Butch said, "So I been told. Must be funny law that can't be bought with enough money."

I said, "Not funny law, Butch, the best in the world."

Butch had been rummaging through his mind for a few facts of geography. "I don't know about Australia. Saw a boxing kangaroo one time in a traveling circus. I don't like the thought of going to Australia."

Tom O'Day patted his belly and set his knife and fork in the middle of his empty plate. "Australia is where they hung Ned Kelly," he stated.

The name wasn't familiar to Cassidy. "Who the hell is he?"

"They called him the Robin Hood of New South Wales," the Irishman answered. "Robbed banks for a living, was related some way to my mother. Wore a suit of armor he had some blacksmith make up. Bullets just bounced off it like rain on a shed. Then one day he rode into some town to rob the bank. He fell down and couldn't get up. Kept on firing till all his bullets were gone. That's how they got poor Ned. Like I say, they hung the boy."

"Never heard of him," Butch said.

O'Day went on. "Near as famous as you, Butch. To this day they sing ballads about him."

Butch didn't want any thunder stolen from him. He was vain about his notoriety. "I don't want to hear any more about Australia."

"Then where?" I said.

"Mexico might not be so bad."

"They got the *rurales* down there. Not honest like the Mounties and worse because they're not. Those boys are the President's private police. 'Get rid of the bandits,' he told them a few years back. The talk is that they've been doing a good job of it. When they catch a bandit they don't just kill him. They cut off his head and put it on a spike at the gate of some town. I saw a few heads last time I was down there. Matter of fact, one day coming into some town I saw a head that looked familiar, and when I got up close there was old Dan Flagg I grew up with in West Texas. He'd done his share of bad deeds in West and South Texas before the Rangers chased him south."

"He must of lost his head," Tom O'Day said with a sly grin.

Butch felt his neck, thinking of my story about Dan Flagg. The story was true. I had seen poor old Dan staring down at me with sightless eyes. The head was freshly cut and there were ants and flies all over it.

"That's not funny, O'Day," Butch said. Then he laughed. "I guess it is kind of funny. You got any more cheerful stories, Saddler?"

I said, "If you don't want to go to Australia, how about South America? Living is cheap, land is cheap. Buy yourself a nice ranch and raise cows."

Butch scowled, something he rarely did. It seemed like I had played a wrong note. "I know a lot about cows,

59

Saddler. Too much about cows. Anything you want to know about cows just ask me. I was punching too long to like cows. Around cows you get cowshit on your boots."

I said, "There must be something you'd like to do."

"Sure there is. Robbing banks and trains. It's not just the money, Saddler. It's knowing I can do it. The fat bastards that own them make millions. Me, I just want a few dollars, more or less."

I found it hard to fault him for his attitude. I don't like businessmen either. I don't hate them, but I can't like them. Everything about them gets my fur up. But since I don't have to drop my pants for them I don't get too excited about it.

"That's fine as far as it goes," I said to Cassidy, "but it can't last. They can't let you get away with it. You've been making them look like horses' asses. But worse than that, you've been hitting them hard in the wallet. You have any idea how much money they've been paying the Pinks? Already they're chasing you with the telephone. Now there's even talk of trying to find this place here with balloons."

This last part I'd made up. I wanted to surprise Butch and I did. I guess I surprised everybody at the table. Pearl, being so young, looked excited at the prospect at having Pinkertons flying over her head.

"Where in hell did you hear that?" Butch asked, outraged at the devious ways of the famous detective agency.

"Didn't hear it," I said. "Read it in some paper."

"What paper?"

"Some paper, Butch."

Sundance cut in. "Maybe it's true. They got balloons now they can kind of steer. Go high and low depending on the hot air."

Butch said, "You got plenty of hot air yourself, Harry. Now Saddler, what about these balloons?"

I wondered why the Pinkertons hadn't considered balloons as a way of finding the Hole. I guess I had read about balloons in some rag. Then I remembered what I'd read. I said, "Over in Sicily a lot of bandits have hideouts in the mountains. The soldiers and police have been using balloons to root them out. They sail over the mountains too high to get shot at and report what they see. Then the rest of the force moves in with mountain guns to batter down their defenses."

"This Sicily, where is it?" Butch asked.

"Part of Italy," I said.

"Saddler's talking about dagoes," Tom O'Day said, proud of his knowledge of the world.

Butch glared at the Irishman. "I know what Italy is, O'Day. A country where they sing all the time and make wine with their feet."

Pearl giggled. "I hope they wash them first."

Butch didn't hear her, so wrapped up was he in balloons and mountain guns. "Holy Christ!" he said. "Imagine being chased by balloons."

"It's the coming thing," I said.

Etta got mad. "Don't listen to him, Cassidy. Whole thing sounds like a storybook tale to me. Who's going to fly over these badlands in a fucking balloon? If they came down in the badlands they'd never get out alive. You know what I think? They can't get you out of here, all the ways they've tried, so they've sent this spy to talk sweet reason to you. You leave here, leave here now I mean, and they'll be waiting for you."

Butch said, "It's a thought."

"Sure it's a thought," Etta continued. "It's a thought and leaving here is a good thought, but not for right now. Some of what this so-called piano player has been saying is true, though not from the goodness of his heart. The Pinks have their whole reputation riding on you. If they don't catch or kill you, it'll be bad for their business. I can't see that we're going to last much longer. We've had the luck but no luck lasts forever. So it's time to make a fresh start someplace far from here. But it's not for this Saddler to tell you where. If you go where he says, then he'll know and so will the Pinks."

I didn't remind her that she had brought up the subject of leaving the Hole. It wouldn't have done any good to mention it.

Butch looked around the comfortable cabin. "Be a shame to leave this old place. To leave Wyoming."

Etta said a very dirty word. "Why don't you sing 'My Old Kentucky Home' while you're at it!"

"A good old song," Butch said.

Sundance looked up from his tattered almanac and grinned. "South American might not be so bad. All them señoritas and such."

Etta whirled on him with a cup of scalding coffee ready to throw. I wondered if she'd throw it and what Sundance would do if she did.

"Filthy, dirty greasers—spics!" Etta raged. "I'm good and mad at you, Harry."

Butch grinned at her fury. "She's mad all the time."

Sundance grinned too. "She wasn't too mad last night."

Etta threw the coffee at Sundance, but he was ready for it and dodged it easily, getting no more than a few stains on his shirt and pants. No longer grinning, Butch reached over and grabbed Etta. She squirmed but he held her fast.

I was beginning to feel uncomfortable.

"Be nice now, little lady," Butch warned, and for a moment I saw the killer in him again.

The rain beat down and I wondered again what I was doing there. Even with all the bickering and coffee-tossing the subject of leaving the Hole was being discussed, and even if Etta hated me I had found an ally in her. She wanted to get away from the badlands and to keep Cassidy alive while she was doing it. Sundance was just as important to her, I guessed, but Cassidy came first. Both men were her men. Probably she loved them in different ways and for different reasons: Butch the wild cowpuncher turned bandit; Sundance the New

Jersey kid with a price on his head. Sundance knew things Cassidy didn't know, not that he was an educated man by any means, but he carried himself like a man who had seen much and had done more before ending up in the Hole. Now he came to Etta's aid.

"Don't get mad," he said to Cassidy. "There's more coffee where that came from."

"Sure," Butch said. "But not for throwing at a man." He let Etta go.

Etta got up and collected the dirty dishes and put them in a basin of soapy water. I felt sorry for her. She was up against a game she couldn't beat; the deck was stacked against her. She was the smartest of the women—she knew that, and so did I.

You see, there was only one way Cassidy and Sundance could go, and that was to die with their boots on. It's hell if you have to hang around past your time and past your prime. For when all you know is the gun, then you have to live and die according to its rules. It wasn't such a bad way though. There are men who lust for freedom much more than they lust for women or money or whiskey. Some of them would have a hard time explaining that, but they know what they want even if they can't find the words to say it. A man like Tom O'Day would have done his time in jail for cattle rustling and other small potatoes, but I knew Butch and the Kid had never spent an hour behind bars. There was a friendship between them that I find hard to describe. It expressed itself in the easy give-and-take of their words. Etta was a big part of their lives, but she never could hope to be the main attraction in the center ring. Knowing that, I felt sorry for her.

Laura and Pearl went back to their cabin. O'Day left, too, after thanking Etta for the second breakfast. He said he was worried that one of his horses had worms.

"Don't believe a word of that," Butch said after the Irishman had gone. "Tommy's going to see if he can rustle up some more grub. That Irishman could eat his weight in feed if you put it in front of him."

Irritated, Etta said, "O'Day's all right, not like some in these parts."

"I don't know what you boys are going to do," Butch said. "I'm going to have a drink. How about you, Saddler?"

Well, it was a dull day, still raining, with the sky low and gray. "Sure," I said.

"I wouldn't say no to a drink," Sundance said, still perusing the *Farmer's Almanac*. That tattered old thing must have been his Bible. In the back of the book there were farm remedies and cures for whooping cough and snakebite, as well as a lot of general information, such as that Abe Lincoln grew a beard because some little girl had written and said he'd look better if he had one.

Butch got a quart and three glasses from a cedar chest. Nobody wanted water so he left that out. Butch did the honors and shoved whiskey at us. Sundance marked his place in the book with a match and snapped the drink against the back of his throat and wiped his yellow mustache.

"That Tommy O'Day is a caution," Butch said. He was still thinking about the walrus-faced Irishman, though he was long out of sight. "First time he robbed a bank he did it in a town called Winnemuca, and he did it by himself, only on the way into town he got waylaid by a skunk. But you have to know, Saddler, that old Tommy is a man of determination and wasn't about to be put off by a skunk. That Irishman cleaned hisself up best he could and went ahead with his plan. And, mind you—this is gospel— the son of a bitch didn't even have a horse, having just been released from the state pen for the stealing of a lone cow. I guess you have to be mighty hungry to steal just one cow. So into the bank he goes and there wasn't no need of caution after that 'cause everybody ran for the hills, the stink being so bad and all. I guess the bankers were only too glad to give him the money, if for no better reason than to get rid of him. Tommy got clean away because of the stink and the fact that he didn't have a horse. And so began O'Day's life in crime.''

We drank and Butch told other stories, all of them pretty good ones. The Kid had heard them before but he liked hearing them again. I still had to figure the Kid out. He was taller than Butch and had dark yellow hair. The hair of his mustache was lighter in color than the hair on his head, and in height he was pretty close to me, and that's tall enough. At the all-night party at the Jackson Hole whorehouse he was the only one of the Wild Bunch who looked at ease in his black suit, boiled shirt and black silk tie. He didn't exactly talk like a Westerner and yet he didn't sound like a dude strayed too far from home.

I guess he was very much a tough man, and later I was to discover how right I was. He had what certain lady newspaper writers call languid grace, and some of that was put on and some of it was real. Doing a pose is like that: when you do it long enough it becomes a part of you. I couldn't be sure how he took me, whether he was for me, was waiting for the right time to kill me, or just didn't give a damn. What he gave out to the world was that he didn't give a damn about anything, not even his life. And though I have known a few men like that, most of them are dead. The only people who didn't call him "Kid" or "Sundance" were Butch and Etta. To them he was Harry, his given name. It didn't suit him. To me he'll always be the Sundance Kid.

Etta didn't want to drink with us. Long after she washed the dishes and put them away she kept on bustling about the place, listening to what was being said but taking no part in it, angry at everybody, especially me.

Butch told the story about the killer he'd known who was deep in debt to a Mexican moneylender, an old man in Roswell, New Mexico. This killer did nothing but kill men for as much as he could get, and he got a lot because he never missed. He might have been rich, Butch said, except that he liked to gamble and wasn't good at it. Only in the killing of men was he lucky, and after 30 years there wasn't a bullet hole in him. Cards and dice were his downfall, Butch said, and to keep pace with his losings he'd had to borrow big from this wizened old Mex whose first business was a cantina. After a few years this killer got so deep in the hole that the old greaser said he'd have to have a reckoning—or else.

" 'So what should I do,' the killer asked this old rascal. 'I have no money, and no matter how many men I kill I'll never have enough.' 'Then do a robbery,' said the Mexican to the killer. 'Stagecoach or bank, it makes no matter to me, just get the money.' A funny thing, this killer was scared of the old man. I don't know why, but he was. So he went out to rob a bank and got killed."

At the end of that particular story, Sundance got up, yawned, stretched and said he was going to get more sleep. The door of the bedroom was open and Etta was sitting on the edge of the bed.

"Nothing else to do on a day like this," Sundance said.

I was wondering where I was going to bunk if Cassidy wanted me as a permanent guest. I was glad to visit Pearl and Laura, but I had to sleep part of the nights or I'd be no good. Besides I wanted some corner where I could sit and think without having to listen to a lot of talk all the time.

Butch looked surprised when I told him about the need for sleep, then he laughed. "I can see how them two ladies would wear a man down." He lowered his voice and winked. "Whenever Etta gets mad enough I just bed down with Pearl and Laura, and they're always glad to have me. You make yourself at home in the little cabin Frank Bisbee built for himself. You'll find it back of the girls' place. Got a horseshoe painted silver on the door. Some provisions are still in there, blankets and such. Anything else you need, come on back here and help yourself. Frank won't be coming back. Poor old Frank, he got shot."

Butch didn't offer to show me the way. I guess he wanted to get in there with Etta and the Kid. It was the best way to spend a rainy day in the badlands. Me, I just wanted to see what I could think up in the way of escaping.

I found the place without any trouble and Frank must have been shot fairly recently, because the cabin didn't have too much dust in it. It was built of stone and wood; the walls were well-chinked and the swayed roof was sound. They were a funny gang of outlaws all right, building cabins as if they expected to be in the stealing business forever. I got a fire going in the stove and that was all I did in the way of improvements. After that I stretched out on the rough bunk bed in the corner, pulled a blanket over me, and fell asleep.

SIX

I slept with my gun in my hand and I cocked it when the door opened with hardly a sound. There was Harry Tracy standing in the doorway. He looked at me with the same interest a starving man might have in a pork chop, and took no heed of my cocked pistol. Rain dripped from his hat and ran down his yellow slicker. His face creased in a wolfish grin as he stepped inside and closed the door.

"You won't need that iron," he said, meaning the gun. "It's best you and me be friends. Best for you, anyhow. No reason we can't get along, Saddler. I didn't want you here but now you are. I'm offering you friendship. You better take it."

Everybody in the Hole was offering me too much. "I don't want it," I said, pretty sure of what he had in mind. I guessed there were women around I hadn't seen yet, but no woman could give Harry Tracy what he wanted. He smiled again, and I had a vision of someone standing on my grave.

"That's too bad," he said. "Why do you want to make it hard on yourself? Like it or not, you're going to turn over for me so's I can spread the cheeks of your ass. You want to do it the hard way, I don't mind that neither." He edged a little closer and there was a crazy lust in his flat, killer's eyes, and I wondered how many men and boys he had cornholed in his time. You don't often run into men like that, but they are around. Get yourself tossed in jail and you find them quick enough. I've been in jail a few times and I know. But they aren't all in the pokey. Some are politicians, traveling salesmen, preachers, and prizefighters. I stay away from them whenever possible. As long as they don't bother me, I don't give a damn where they stick it.

I didn't want it stuck in me, though. "Get out, or I'll kill you," I warned. I meant what I said. You can't make threats if you aren't ready to carry them out. Tracy took another step and I squeezed the trigger. But Tracy didn't die, he laughed.

I dropped the hammer on another cartridge and Tracy laughed again. "Butch said to take out the powder and that's what we did. You were drunk and didn't know a thing. Hope you're not too disappointed, Saddler. You been all over, you know how it's done."

I knew damn well how it was done. There's nothing to it. All you do is pry out the lead, spill the powder, then crimp the load again. Cassidy, the son of a bitch! It was an old trick, but I hadn't thought of it, because it would have been simpler just to take my gun. Why in hell had he gone to so much trouble?

"I won't be too hard on you the first time," he said. "Could be you'll get to liking it after a while. You'd be surprised, the men that get to liking it. Could be it's something you always wanted to do but were too bashful. Now's your chance to find out."

Tracy's gun came out so fast, I hardly saw his hand move. He drew and cocked the pistol in one fast, slick motion. He reminded me of a rattler about to strike, and maybe he wanted me dead as much as he wanted me alive.

"You'll have to kill me," I said. "Where will that leave you with Cassidy?"

The warning was wasted on Tracy and he smiled again. Even at a distance of five feet the stink of whiskey and sweat gushed from him, and I knew the hulking killer wasn't going to back down.

"One thing at a time," he said. "You're first on the menu. I don't worry about Cassidy, I don't worry about a fucking thing." His left hand reached into his pocket and came out with a pair of shiny, nickeled handcuffs. He rattled them in his hand and the small sound they made wasn't too different from the rattle of a snake.

"You're going to put these on," he said. "The latest make there is—took them off a dead Pink. You don't need a key to put them on. All you do is put them around your wrists, then go click! Strongest cuffs in the world, is what they tell me."

I looked at the cocked pistol. "You'd better kill me," I said. I'm no hero, but I meant what I said.

"You'll put them on," Tracy said. "I've fucked tougher men than you, Saddler, and I'll break you. Usually all it takes is one hard fuck to break a man. He gets to feeling ashamed and so forth. The ladies won't like you so good after I get through with you. I'll just tell them it was your idea. Now I'm going to toss you the cuffs. Put them on and I'll roll you over."

I didn't know if I had any chance at all, but there was no way out of this. The only edge I had was that Tracy might want me alive more than he wanted me dead. If he hesitated about killing me, held back from killing for just an instant, then maybe I could take him. I didn't tense but I was ready when he took another step forward and tossed the cuffs my way. Tracy meant for the cuffs to fall on the bunk beside me, but I caught them in midair and threw them at his face with all the strength I could muster.

The cuffs hit him in the right eye. I dove off the bed as his gun went off. I felt the breeze of the bullet as I sprang toward him, tackling him around the middle, one hand grabbing for the gun. The gun fired again as we hit the door together, tearing it loose from its hinges. The door hit the porch with a flat crack and the gun flew from Tracy's hand and landed far out in the mud.

We rolled off the porch into the mud. First I was on top and then he was, trying to draw my face down into his snapping teeth. The stink that came from his mouth made me want to throw up on him. What I did was to go with his pull. I smashed my forehead into his nose and heard it crack. Blood mixed with mud until it was all over both of us. Tracy was heavier than I was, but he found it hard to get a firm hold on me. His hand fastened around my throat, then slipped away before he could start choking me. I knew I had to get up on my feet. If he could put his weight on me and pin me down, I wouldn't stand much of a chance.

We rolled again and before we stopped rolling I jerked my knee up into his crotch. I heard yelling but was too busy breaking Tracy's hold to tell who was doing it. My boots skittered wildly in the mud and I nearly fell again. Then I got my balance, sleeved the mud from my eyes, and waited for him to come at me again. With blood still streaming from his flattened nose, he shook his bullet head like a dog coming out of water. I kept trying to see where the gun was. The rain falling on us was cold and hard.

Then he came at me more like a savage animal than a man. Blood ran into his mouth and his teeth snapped. For most of a minute we circled about. I knew he was getting ready for a rush, a mad-bull onslaught that would hurl me back and throw me down. Then it came, powered by weight and savagery, but I dodged aside, tripped him and kicked him in the back of the knee as he went down. I kicked him in the side because I couldn't get at his head. He grabbed for my ankle, trying to turn it and bring me down where he could get at me. But he had to raise his head to do that, and I kicked him in the face and felt his teeth break.

Thus far he had been fighting silently. Now he reared back and let out a long animal howl. I stopped his howling with another kick and he crashed back in the mud and covered his face with both hands. No man of mercy, I kicked him in the stomach and kept on kicking. Then steadying myself for the last shot, I booted him in the side of the head and he went limp. I stood there sucking air into my lungs, grateful for the cold splash of the rain. Tracy lay on his back like a shot buffalo, and then I heard Butch Cassidy's voice and felt his hand on my arm.

I jerked my arm away. "Leave me alone, you sneaking bastard!" I didn't care whether he shot me. I started to walk away and he came after me.

"I didn't know this was going to happen," Cassidy said, taking no heed of the rain. He didn't have his hat on and when I looked down I saw he didn't even have his boots on. He went back and kicked Tracy savagely with his bare feet. Tracy didn't move.

"I had no way of knowing," Cassidy said. "I warned him away from you. Tracy never went against me before, so I thought it was settled."

I spun around on him. "All that's settled is that you gave me an empty gun. You know what I think, Butch? You're just as bad as Tracy. Why the hell didn't you just take the fucking gun? Then I'd have known to be careful."

Butch kicked at the mud and his mouth jerked before he spoke. "You wouldn't have liked me taking your iron," he said. "But I didn't know you and couldn't take a chance on getting killed."

I didn't buy too much of that. "How would a Pink-spy go about killing you in the middle of your own gang? Out here in the lands, how could he hope to stay alive if he shot you down?"

"Not a Pink-spy, Saddler. I wasn't thinking so much of that. I thought maybe you were some crazy man with a grudge against me. I've killed plenty of men and maybe one of them was your kin. You wouldn't care if you got killed as long as I was dead too."

I went on toward the cabin with Cassidy a few steps behind me. Rain was blowing into the cabin making puddles on the floor. I got the door up on its end and put it against the wall. I looked at Butch standing all wet on the porch. He looked dumb standing there in his bare feet.

"That's a bullshit story and you know it," I said. "The real answer is this. You're a horse's ass that likes to play dumb jokes."

Butch's face tightened. "Maybe you'd better use the soft pedal, Saddler. Nobody talks to me like that."

I straightened the door. "I just did, Cassidy. So what do you want to do about it? Shoot me yourself and turn me over to that queer out there? Answer me this if there's such a difference between you and him. Why do you let him hang on here? You got enough men to run him out. Kill him if he doesn't want to go."

Butch shook his head, almost admiring my gall. "You got as bad a temper as Etta. All right, it was a lousy joke I played on you. You don't have to keep bitching about it. You're alive, ain't you? What's more you just half-killed Harry Tracy, as mean a man as walks in leather. Hell, when word of that gets out men'll get out of your way like you're the Devil!"

"I don't want to be the Devil. Now I'll tell you one more thing. You have the guns and you can kill me anytime you like. And maybe that's what you've been planning to do all along. But keep that shitty-cocked bastard away from me. If he comes at me again I'll kill him sure. I'll kill him with a rock if I have to."

"Jesus Christ!" Butch marveled. "You're the bloodthirstiest man I've ever met. Come on now, Saddler, get a rein on that temper and we'll go get ourself a big drink. About Tracy, I know what has to be done about Tracy. But right now isn't the time. He's a useful man and he's been with me a long time."

"I think Tracy means to kill you and take over," I said. Some of my anger had drained away. "One of these days he's going to kill you."

"Well, yes," Butch said. "I know he means to try."

"Then I'll say it again so even you can understand. Kill the dirty pervert."

Butch didn't get mad at me for calling him thick. Maybe he thought he'd caused me enough trouble for one day. "Tracy's been with me a lot of years. Once he saved my life when I thought I was done for. Two new boys I shouldn't have trusted tried to murder me for the reward money. Shit! I wasn't wanted so bad at that time. The reward money wasn't even that good, but they were ready to back-shoot me for it. Etta and Harry had gone down to Jackson Hole and I was alone in the cabin. It was early in the morning and I was washing my face after shaving. Jesus! My eyes were full of soap and everything. These two traitors had been studying how I did things— and this looked like a right good chance to put ten or twelve bullets in my back. They didn't get to do it because Tracy had been studying their moves while they were studying mine. They were coming up soft-footed with their guns drawn when Tracy killed them with two shots in the back of their heads. That's how good Tracy is, Saddler."

"All the more reason to kill him."

"You didn't hear what I just told you, did you? Tracy may be a crazy queer, but he saved my life."

"Tracy just likes to kill people. Your two boys gave him the chance. Saving your life was just part of it."

"It got saved just the same."

"If you don't care about your own life, how about mine?"

"Nothing's going to happen to you, Saddler. Don't tell me you're afraid to get killed?"

"I'd like it to be for a better reason."

"Live and let live," Cassidy said. "If Tracy likes to do it the rear-end way, what's the difference?"

"No difference as long as he doesn't try to cornhole me."

Butch grinned. "You can't fault old Tracy for falling in love with you."

I bunched my fist and Butch stepped away from me, still grinning. "You got to be more tolerant of human failings, Saddler," he said. "But all right, I'll keep Tracy far away from you. Maybe I can get him interested in Tommy O'Day. Wouldn't that be something, though— Tracy and the Irishman. They could set up housekeeping and live happily ever after."

Yes, without a doubt, Butch Cassidy was a madman. No matter how serious—even dangerous—the conversation, he had a way of turning it into a joke. But there was cleverness, too. He made jokes because that way you could never be sure what he was thinking. You always had to guess.

"Cheer up, Saddler," Cassidy said. "We'll all be dead tomorrow."

That was what I was afraid of.

Butch went to get a bottle of whiskey while I fixed the door. It wasn't that hard. The hinges had been pulled cleanly from the wood and all I had to do was jam the holes with a splinter and nail them up again. I got the door in place and sat in my longjohns beside the stove. Not much later Butch came in with the whiskey and a towel to dry my head.

Watching me dry my head gave him cause for reflection. "You sort of set me back when you beat up Tracy so bad."

That called for a drink, and I had one.

I said, "I'm sorry I didn't kill the bastard. You mind telling me how I set you back by not doing that?"

Butch had another drink then gave me the bottle.

"Back there a while ago you asked me why I keep him around. A fair question, Saddler, 'cause Tracy is a rabid rat. They don't come any faster than he does, and he doesn't just pull fast—he's a dead shot."

"But you're not afraid of him?"

Butch got the bottle back and grinned. "Everybody not crazy is scared shitless of Harry Tracy. Everybody but me, that is. Tracy does what I tell him to do. Which is not to say he likes it, but he does it."

I was beginning to understand. "You think Harry Tracy is your trained ape?"

Butch said, "You ought to be kind to animals, Saddler. Tracy's an ape sure enough and I trained him just fine. If I can hand out orders to a man like Harry Tracy you think I'm going to get any back talk from the rest of the boys?"

"I don't know the boys," I said.

Butch said, "A man that can handle Harry Tracy would just naturally eat them for breakfast. A man who can do that is like the John L. or the Jim Corbett of the outlaw world. Why, he's the champion!"

Butch thought he had it all worked out. Pick out the meanest man alive and make him say uncle. It was crazy but it wasn't dumb. But now and then the smartest men get flattened. They get too confident and are killed. As long as he kept Tracy around, snarling at the end of his chain, Butch thought he had complete mastery of his gang. He was sure, but I wasn't.

"That's not the whole of it," I said. "What boys I've seen—the Irishman, Will Carver, Kilpatrick, Curry—all seem well-disposed toward you. So what's all this shit about keeping them in line?"

Butch thought my question was due to a lack of experience in the outlaw world. "You say that because you've never bossed an outfit. There's not a leader alive somebody don't want to knock over. That's human nature, Saddler. Men may set you up but there comes a time when they want to knock you over. May be against their best interest to do that. No matter. They still try to do it. But you're right. Some of the boys are all right and some ain't."

"Harry Tracy means to kill you and take over. Kill him now, Cassidy. Give me a gun and I'll do it for you. I don't say that out of love for you, not after what you did to my bullets. Something else you should ponder. Is all this talk about leaving the country going to do you any good? It's hardly your intention to take the boys along."

Butch took a swallow of whiskey. "Such is not my intention, sir. When we go it'll be just Sundance and Etta and me. You want to go along?"

"Like hell!"

Butch said, "Etta wants to take O'Day along, but whoever heard of an Irish butler?"

"But he thinks he's going?"

"Sort of," Butch said. "What you heard today wasn't the first talk about leaving the Hole. Only today there was more talk than before. It's come up because Etta keeps bringing it up. She's a one-note lady, that Etta. A week can go by and not a word about leaving, then out of the blue she gets back on that subject."

I studied the bottle in his hand. "Then why the hell don't you go? You know she's right."

Butch laughed at my ignorance of banditry. "Easy for you to talk that way, Saddler. You're one man, one gun, one horse. A loner, that's what you are. Come and go as you please. You hand yourself your hat and you're off. Well, it's different with me. I got responsibilities, son. I got ten or twelve other people in this place and without me they'd fall apart. Ben Kilpatrick has some ambition to be a leader, but I doubt he's got the brains or the balls to hold a gang together. Except for Tracy there's nobody else. And you know he'd get them all killed."

"You don't want the gang to fall apart?"

Butch found that funny. "Not till I'm long gone and they can't make a deal with the Pinks."

I was still mad at Cassidy. "You're all friends in the Hole," I said.

Butch wasn't offended. "Today's friends are tomorrow's enemies. A drunk in a saloon in Cheyenne told me that. The bartender said no to putting anymore of his drinks on the slate. He didn't have to tell me that. I knew it already."

"Why are you telling me all this shit?"

"'Cause I like you, Jim-boy. Anyway, why shouldn't I tell you things? What can you do with anything I tell you? Take sides with Tracy against me? No chance of that, I'd say. Trying to do that would be downright foolish. You hurt Tracy's feelings, not to mention his nose and most of his teeth. Tracy hated you before you did that. Now it's likely he hates you more."

"All this talk," I said. "What you're really saying is that there's going to be a showdown."

Butch smiled at me like a teacher with a bright pupil. "Not if I can get out of it. I been thinking about it, then thinking some more, 'cause for all the bad name the Pinks give me I'm a good-natured man. What I'd like to do is tell the boys it's been nice knowing you, but now it's time to bid you a fond farewell. For a long time I been working on my good-bye speech, but it don't seem to come out right. My point, sir, is I don't want the boys to think I'm running out on them."

"Bandits are touchy," I said.

"Well they are, Saddler. You think you're joking but you're not. Bandits are not like ordinary folk. You hit it just right when you said they're touchy. Proud people, they are. A ripe boil ain't any touchier than a bandit's pride."

My pants were dry and I pulled them on. "Just duck out," I said to Butch. "Forget the farewell address. You don't owe them one goddamned thing. Without you they couldn't button their flies."

Cassidy liked that and he laughed.

"Listen," I said. "You duck out fast and light and keep on going. You, Sundance, Etta and me. Cross over into Canada and take a boat from Vancouver. You can go anywhere from Vancouver."

Butch said, "They'd think it funny, just the four of us going."

I had a solution for that. "Take along a few of the boys and we'll kill them on the way."

Cassidy was shocked. "That's a hell of a thing to say. Kill my own boys! Which boys do you have in mind?"

"Kill one, kill all," I said. "I'll do it if you feel bad about it. Makes no difference to me which ones I kill. You can say you're going out to plan a new job. They'll like that."

"You're nothing but a murderer, Saddler."

"But only for a good cause. All right. You don't have to kill the ones we take along. Just tie them to a tree and leave them. With food and water, naturally. Come on, Butch, why are you hanging back on this? You keep saying you've got more money than God. That kind of money should take you far."

"How much money is much?" Butch looked embarrassed. "Tell you the truth, Saddler, I'm a bit low on funds."

I must have gaped at him.

Butch said, "A few thousand is all I have left. We never got as much money as the papers said. Well, sure, we got enough, but it sort of slipped through my fingers. I gave it away. I lost it. Poker and dice took a lot of it. I got trainmen and bank people on my payroll who have to be paid for information. Then there's the law. Greediest men in the world those crooked lawmen. Damn! I don't know where the money went, but most of it has flown from the nest."

"You can have the five hundred you gave me."

"Shit! That's just ham-and-bean money, Saddler. When I go I want to go in style."

That was just like him, the big-mouth showoff. "That'll get you caught, Butch. Go on a mule if you have to—but go!"

Butch said, "Etta wouldn't be caught dead on a mule. Etta's a lady. Would you believe it, she used to be a

79

schoolteacher! A schoolteacher like that is what every growing boy needs. I captured Etta one time when I was drunk. Fought like a wildcat she did. First she did, and then she got used to it."

I had been thinking about Etta. "Etta got her share of the robberies and, not having your loose fingers, she must have a lot left."

Once again, Butch was embarrassed. "She thinks she has plenty left. Etta is smart and always took her share in gold coin, USA and Mexican. She had it hid under a floorboard in back of the stove. I found it and borrowed it. I was in need, Saddler."

"What did you put in its place?"

"Washers. They make the same sound if you don't look inside the bag. I live in dread of the day she discovers the truth. But it's not like I stole it—I *borrowed* it."

The rain was starting to let up and I had a drink in honor of the occasion. "You stole it," I said, rubbing my eyes. "What about Sundance? How much money does he have?"

"Not a lot," Butch said. "A lot of Harry's money went to fix up Doxy Milligan's whorehouse in Jackson Hole. Harry's got a big interest in two other fuckshops. Most of Harry's money is tied up, as they say."

"Looks like you are, too."

Butch said, "Now you see why I got to hold the gang together. I need those boys to pull one last job."

Well, sure, that was it. I couldn't be sure that anything Cassidy told me was true. I don't know how much he lied, or if he meant to lie, and maybe he didn't either. What I did know was that he had taken the powder out of my bullets. And he had lied about the week of piano lessons. He had a big, open, friendly face and a lot of back-country guile. He was an open book and a puzzle at the same time.

I looked up from my empty glass. "It should be a very big job, this last one," I said, thinking of myself. "Big as you can find. If it isn't, then you'll have to go on to the next one."

Butch grunted. "You trying to tell me my business, Saddler?"

I said, "No matter how big it is, there won't be enough after you divvy up with the boys. So you have to double-cross the boys, then get the hell out of this country."

Butch grinned at the way the conversation was going. "Doublecross men I been friends with all this time?"

"Terrible to have to do that," I said. "But you've got your balls in the wringer and have to get them out. You got a special job in mind?" I asked.

Butch eyed me. "Maybe I do and maybe I don't," he said. "Don't tell me you have something lined up in this part of the country? You're not from around here, so you say."

"West Texas," I said. "That's where I'd like to be right now, but I'm not. A minute ago you said there was nothing I could do with anything you told me. What's happened to change that?"

Cassidy said, "Not a thing. I got a few jobs on the stove, but I can't be sure of my information. There's some money, only I don't know how much. I been hitting them so hard, everything's a big secret these days. They may be on to the people that have been giving me information. Etta's right. It's starting to get tight."

I said, "That's why this job has to be your last."

Butch sighed windily. "It has to be the last in this country. But I don't think I'll ever get the fever out of my blood."

I didn't give a damn what he did after he left the Hole. If he left, then so would I. "You mind telling me about these jobs?"

"Some I wouldn't bother with," Butch said. "There's a copper-mine payroll about three-day's ride from here. A few years ago that wouldn't have been so bad. These days they got payrolls guarded like the Denver Mint. Besides, this mine is in a tricky place, hard to get at, even harder to get away from.

"I do favor trains, but you never know what to expect. They got special trains out looking for me, fast locomotives with just a few cars. And where the baggage car used to be they got men and horses. The horses are kept saddled most of the time. These posses eat and sleep and live on the goddamned trains. There is one job that looks good, but maybe it's too good. I think my information-man is trying to set me up. There's just too much money involved, is all."

"If it's there, it can be stolen," I said.

SEVEN

"I heard what you said, but what does it mean?" Butch asked, full of whiskey but alert. "Don't talk in riddles, Saddler."

"You're the one who's beating about the bush. What I meant is, if they're planning to trap you, maybe we can turn it back on them. This job you keep hinting at, how good is your information?"

"My man has always been reliable in the past, but this time I get a bad feeling from him. I think they may be on to him, maybe threatening to send him up for twenty years if he doesn't play along. It's like he's too eager to set this job up. He keeps pushing for it, saying there's talk of the Pinks sending for Tom Horn. Tom used to be with the Pinks. Now they tell me he has a ranch somewhere. Saddler, I don't want to tangle with the likes of Tom Horn."

I knew something about Tom Horn. Everybody did. No two men could agree about Tom Horn. To some he was a cold-blooded killer and a thief to boot. Others saw him as the scourge of all the badmen in the West. I knew he had killed plenty of them. All that people could agree on was that he was the best tracker and mancatcher in the country.

"Why haven't they sent for him before now?" I asked. The Pinkertons always had the best of everything—men, weapons, horses.

"Tom and the Pinks didn't part as friends," Butch said. "There was talk that some of the stolen money he recovered stuck to his fingers. But nothing could be proved, then or now. Still, it was funny that the bandits who stole the most money Tom always brought back dead. And they all died broke, according to him. On the other hand, he often brought in smalltime outlaws who didn't mean shit. Now the Pinks don't mind if you bring them all in dead, but they do like to see a little stolen money along with the corpses. So they argued with Tom about that, and he quit. Tom's a greedy man. If he goes back to work for the Pinks, he won't do it cheap. I'd like to be long gone before he starts working again."

"What's this dread of Horn? You don't fret much about the rest of them."

"Tom's different," Butch said. "It's like having a ghost after you. He works alone and never gives up—*never!* He'll go for days without food, sleep out in the wet and cold, all so he can ambush a man. Ambushing is his stock in trade, and he'll be back."

I got back to the robbery Cassidy hadn't told me about. "Come on, Butch, why are you so sure it's a trap?"

"There's too much money. Of course, there may be no bait in the trap at all."

"No money at all isn't too likely," I said. "You haven't been pulling any jobs lately, so they know you're getting wary in your old age." Butch smiled at the idea that he would have an old age. "If I was setting a trap for you I'd set out a whole bale of money. If they don't expect you to get the money, why not use it to kill you?"

"You could be right," Butch agreed. "You want to know more about it so I'll tell you. The town of Mansfield's booming and they want to start a new moneystore. A lot of big English ranchers down that way. Cattle companies paying wages to hundreds of men. Got three or four packing plants so they can pack and ship their own beef without sending it to Chicago. West of the town they got some new copper mines. So this new bank wants to get in where all that money is and will be. My man on the railroad tells me they're going to bring in enough money to open their doors with a bang. Brass bands and speeches, a real celebration. Only the money will come in quiet, not guarded by a platoon of deputies like it usually is. That only attracts bandits, is their idea."

"Sure sounds like a trap," I said. "The express car may not be bulging with guards, but you can bet all the passengers on the train will be Pinkertons, posse-men, and railroad detectives, all dressed up to look like something else. And maybe a special nonstop train a few miles behind."

Butch shrugged. "Maybe anything."

"Of course your man knows just the place to rob this moneytrain?"

Butch grinned. "A real steep grade about fifty miles from Mansfield. There's a curve where the river bends, then the long grade begins. The engineer has to slow for the curve, then has to climb the grade. My man's thought is for us to tear up the inside rail and dig a hole where the rail ain't going to be. The locomotive, traveling slow, runs off the rail on the safe side so it won't lurch the other way and pull the whole train down into the river. The locomotive is stuck, can't go forward and can't back up. If the guards in the express won't give up, then we threaten to burn the train."

"No dynamite?"

"No dynamite. Back when I was starting out I had an unfortunate experience with dynamite and blew eighteen thousand dollars into confetti."

I said, "Your railroad man sounds like a real planner."

"Well, he's a smart man and has a pretty big job," Butch said. "Superintendent for the whole division. That's how he gets to know things other men don't. What you have to think about is this. He never steered me wrong before. I made money and so did he. It could be on the up and up. I'd like to believe it is."

"Do you?"

"No. It's too easy. The minute we got close to that train they'd cut loose from every window in every coach. They'd fill us with so much lead they wouldn't be able to lift us after we was dead. Just the same, if the money is there I'd hate to pass it up."

"How much money did he say?"

"About a hundred thousand."

"No need to pass it up," I said. "We'll skip the grade and do the job in town."

"In town!" Butch was startled. "Didn't I just tell you that's a busy town? It's got a marshal and I don't know how many deputies. You can bet they'll all be waiting at the depot when the train pulls in. If you can't add, that's a small army we'd have to take on."

"At the depot, sure it is, but not at the bank. You say this new bank isn't open yet?"

"My man says not. Just got it finished but can't open without money. They won't open till the day after they get the shipment of money."

"Then we'll wait inside the bank. Not the whole gang, just a select few of us. The bank is empty so they won't be thinking about that. If they plan to open the day after the money arrives they'll have tellers setting things up. We'll get in there long before the train gets to Mansfield, hold guns on the manager and the others. The Pinkertons, or the marshal, or both, will bring the money from the train, see that it's locked away safe, and then leave."

Butch gulped. "Jesus Christ!" he said. "What if they don't leave? We'd be trapped in there like rats."

Which was true, and I could expect to be killed or go to jail for the rest of my life. My kidnap story wouldn't earn me a day off when it came to sentencing, and knowing the Pinkertons, it might not get that far.

"Come up with a better plan if you don't like mine," I said. "My plan could work because it isn't your style to work quiet. Your style is to ride in like a dime-novel desperado and shoot up the place."

Butch didn't like his past exploits described in such a manner. "It worked well enough, Saddler."

"Not this time, it won't. You ever been in this town?"

"I know where it is, no more than that."

"So you can't be sure there is a new bank."

"Pretty sure."

"We have to make sure. Somebody's going to have to go in there, or it's all for nothing. You can't go because everybody knows what you look like. Same goes for the Kid and most of the others."

Butch eyed me suspiciously. "That sort of leaves you, Saddler. What's to stop you from selling me out?"

"I won't sell you out. Blood money isn't my style."

"Then you could just run out on me. I'd take that the same as selling me out. I'd be depending on you and you wouldn't be there."

"You're going to have to take a chance on me, Butch. You want to get out of the country, I want to get back to Texas."

Butch couldn't make up his mind about me. "I'd find you if you sold me out. I'd find you if it took ten years. I could spare ten years to find you. I like a joke and a laugh, but I can be mean. Texas ain't that far and big that I couldn't find you."

I had little doubt that Cassidy could find me if he set his mind to it. He was no worse than other men I've met and killed, but he was more single-minded about things like loyalty and friendship. Of course it was all warped in his fugitive's mind. I don't know why he thought I owed him a thing. He had kidnapped me while I was drunk, taken the powder from my bullets, and nearly got me killed. Yet he would take it as a personal affront if I went about my business, which was what I had been doing in the first place. Maybe the smartest thing I could do was to turn him over to the Pinkertons. The main problem with that was that they might not catch or kill him. He had dodged them before and was likely to do it again. Anyway, I didn't want to betray the son-of-a-bitch.

"I guess you could find me," I said. "But maybe you wouldn't like it when you found me. By that time you wouldn't have a gang to back you up."

Butch said, "I wouldn't need any gang. Maybe I do have to take a chance on you. You may be the gambler here, but I like to cover my bets. You've got to take somebody along when you go into that town."

That didn't suit me, but I thought about it. "Will Carver isn't known."

"Will Carver is too dumb, too slow with a gun," Butch smiled. "You're going to have to take Pearl. She's young, but she's smart as a whip and not known this far north. She's a regular Annie Oakley with a six-gun. Try anything sneaky and she'll shoot you sure. Don't say no, Saddler. It's Pearl, or nothing."

Well, I didn't want to take Pearl or anybody else, but I knew Cassidy was set on it. Pearl was easy on the eye, even better in bed, and if I had to take a watchdog to watch me, then it might as well be her. Fact is, it wasn't such a bad idea. We could pose as man and wife without arousing any suspicion. Of course, she'd have to doff her cowhand clothes and dress more like a woman.

"I don't mind Pearl," I said. "Just don't saddle me with Tom O'Day."

"Here's how we'll do it," Cassidy said. "We split up after we leave here. So many people riding together is bound to get noticed. You and Pearl go first, go ahead of the rest of us. Two days before you go into town we'll join up at a safe place I know. Then we'll talk some more. Then you and Pearl go on in a full day ahead of us. If there is no bank, or if it doesn't look right if there is, you come back and tell us. You'd better come back, Saddler."

"We've been over that," I said. "Now what about getting away after it's done. If it works it'll be the biggest robbery in years. They'll tear the country apart trying to find us. Shoot to kill, right down the line. And then there's Harry Tracy."

"And then there's Harry Tracy," Butch repeated.

"Why not kill him before we leave. Draw him into a showdown and we'll all kill him."

"Don't keep harping on that, for fuck's sake. If it comes to a running fight with the Pinks, Tracy is worth three men, maybe four. We're going to need that bastard."

The whole thing with Tracy was beyond me. "You're going to have to do it sooner or later."

Butch slammed his open hand on the table in brief anger. "You let me worry about Tracy. With all this planning of yours you seem to be forgetting this is my outfit."

"Nobody's forgetting a thing, Cassidy. I'm not even forgetting that I don't have real bullets in my gun. If Tracy comes at me again I'm not going to roll around in the mud."

Butch reached into his coat pocket and handed me a fistful of .44 caliber bullets. I kicked the duds out of my gun and reloaded. Butch watched me. I spun the chamber and fired a bullet into the wall.

In the small cabin the noise was deafening. Butch was offended though no longer mad. "Why in hell did you do that?"

I spun the chamber and fired again, putting the second hole right beside the other one. I didn't even take aim because I wanted Butch to see how good I could shoot. "You won't take my word, why should I take it on trust that these bullets are good?" I said. I kicked out the spent shells and reloaded two live ones in their place. "Now I know for sure."

The two shots brought them running from all over. Sundance came first with a gun in his hand. He got up on the porch with his back flat against the wall beside the door. "Who got shot in there?" The others hung back.

"Come on in, Harry," Butch called. "Nobody got shot. Saddler was just proving a point. Saddler talks loud."

"How's Tracy?" Butch asked when the Kid came in holstering his hair-trigger Colt .44.

The Kid helped himself to the last drink in the bottle. Then he sat down. "You can't kill Tracy by beating on him. You have to shoot him a few times in the right places. His nose has stopped leaking, but he's still spitting out broken teeth. I don't know what's happening to our happy family."

Butch told the Kid to send the others away. "Saddler and me's been talking. It's time you sat in on it."

The Kid came back inside. "You tell Saddler about the moneytrain?"

"I told him," Butch said. "You know how we been beating our brains how to do it and have come up with nothing?"

The Kid stared at me. "And Saddler has? If he has, I'd like to hear it."

Butch told some of it, and I told the rest. The Kid pulled at his yellow mustache. "Not bad. Better than that. If it has to be done, I don't see a better way to do it. Getting away will be harder than the job itself."

"That's what Saddler thinks."

"Saddler thinks like a bandit. You sure you never been a bandit, Saddler?"

I said no, never a real bandit. "As far as I know, I'm not wanted for anything."

"You'll be wanted when this is over," the Kid said.

"Not if I grow a beard and stoop a bit and wear farmer's clothes." I hadn't shaved for days and my beard comes up fast. I knew I could raise a bumper crop by the time I went into Mansfield. "Mostly they'll be looking for you and Butch. I plan to go back to Texas and mind my business. I'm not too worried about being wanted."

Butch said it plain then. "You think we can trust him, Harry?"

Now that it was out in the open, the Kid studied me hard. Finally he nodded. "Saddler knows what'll happen if he leads us into a trap. We may die, but so will he. I guess we can trust him. It's a way out, Butch, and I say we take it. How much you figure for your share, Saddler?"

"What's fair," I said, knowing it would sound fishy if I said I didn't want to be cut in. A week before I would have laughed at the idea of taking part in a bank robbery. But now my thinking had changed. I was putting my head in a noose, so why not make some money out of it? But getting clear of the Wild Bunch was more important to me than money. They were as doomed as men waiting to get hanged, and I didn't want to be part of a group photograph, with all of us standing upright in our coffins, which was the usual display they put on when a bunch of famous bandits got killed.

"How soon do we tell the others?" the Kid asked Cassidy. "You're right about them being restless, and I don't mean about being cooped up in here."

"That's Tracy's doing," Butch said. "We won't tell them till the minute we leave. That'll keep them from getting too organized. Then when we split up they'll have no way to talk."

Cassidy figured everything, and I've encountered that in other wild and crazy men. But it can have its drawbacks. Sometimes the straight way is the best way, though maybe not in his line of work. The Kid looked more straightforward than his partner, but looks can be deceiving. If Cassidy meant to doublecross his boys, the Kid had to know about it—that is, unless Cassidy meant to doublecross the Kid into the bargain. Butch's argument was that he had to doubleshuffle his men because they were plotting to do the same to him, by siding with Harry Tracy. He said they were, and probably they were, but old Butch was as crooked as a ram's horn, so there was no way to tell lies from truth.

"You sure Etta hasn't told any of the women?" I asked. To take the sting out of that, I added, "Women do talk."

Butch shook his head. "Not Etta. Etta is close to nobody but me"—Butch grinned—"and Harry." Butch stood up and so did the Kid. "It's settled then. Two days from now we'll be on our way. Make sure your door is fixed right, Saddler. Rain is fixing to come down again."

"We still haven't figured the getaway."

"Harry and me are going home to talk about that."

I asked if they wanted me to come along, then out of the corner of my eye I spotted the Kid shaking his head. Butch poked me in the ribs, and some of that was friendly and some of it was threat. He said, "We trust you like a brother, Saddler, but it ain't right to burden you with too many secrets at one time. You'll hear all about it when there's a need for it."

EIGHT

I got the hinges fixed and after that there was nothing to do for the rest of the day. A few squalls blew up but passed as quickly as they came. My horse was corralled with the rest of the mounts down at the other end, and I went there to have a look. When I got to the corral, an old man with a grizzled beard and a peg leg came out of the worst looking cabin I'd seen thus far and bid me good day. I hadn't seen him before. He was well into his sixties, or beyond, and wore a worn Colt .45 on a cracked leather belt.

"I'm Butch Cassidy," he said.

"Howdy, Butch," I said, thinking he was crazy.

He cackled and scratched his dirty white beard. "It's not what you're thinking, son. That's my real name. Young Butch took my name 'cause he liked the sound of it, 'cause I been knowing him since puppyhood. Butch never did like his own name, which was George Parker in them days. These days I tend to the horses for Butch and the boys. I look after the horses and I do it good. Been working on cow and horse ranches a good part of my life."

I asked him how he got his present job, which seemed to please him mightily.

"The law caught me making off with a few cows and sent me to jail for ten years. Guess I was lucky to get caught by the sheriff instead of the stockman. Had he caught me I'd of dangled. I got old in jail and wasn't good for nothing but odd-job work when I come out. I was swamping in a saloon when one night Butch come in and knowed me for an old friend. At that time Butch was just getting started in the bandit business and figured he ought to have a catchier name than George Parker. One that folks would remember. So he give me fifty dollars for the full use of my name. Not only that, he didn't make me call myself George Parker."

"You ask for this job or did Butch offer it?"

"Butch offered it," the old man said. "Was glad to take it. Easy work, the wages good, not a worry in the world. Naturally I'm too old to go out on any raids, and don't want to go."

"Doesn't sound like a bad life," I said. And for an old, half-crazy jailbird it wasn't.

The old coot liked my way of looking at things. "You're the first man ever said that to me, so I'll give you some free advice."

"What's that?"

The original Butch Cassidy stuck a short pipe with a cracked bowl in his toothless mouth. That made him spit. "From the cabin yonder I seen you looking at the valley walls. There's no way out, son. Butch, I would think, told you that already. Now I'm telling you in a friendly way, and I know this Wyoming country better than any man alive. There's nothing out there but badlands. Stick with Butch, son, and you'll be fine. You can have a lifetime job with Butch if he takes a liking to you."

After that the old rustler lost interest in me. He

peg-legged his way back to talk to the horses and I went to the dead outlaw's cabin to rustle up some grub. I fried a steak that was aged just right, opened a can of peaches, and made a pot of coffee. It looked like I would have to play out this hand to the end. On the way back to the cabin I saw Tom O'Day squelching through the mud from one cabin to another. The bad weather was keeping the rest of them indoors drinking and card playing.

Eating the steak and drinking coffee, I thought about this town of Mansfield, a place where my life might end. Butch said it was a lively place and that was better than some half-dead cowtown where I would get too much attention. A few days from now I'd know how lively or dead it was. Until then everything was guesswork. There might be no money at all, though it was likely there would be some.

I washed my plate and hardware and finished what was left of the coffee. I still needed sleep, dog tired after all the fighting and fucking and drinking, but this time if Harry Tracy came I would be ready for him. I tilted a chair against the door and piled tin plates on it. If he came he'd make a racket and I'd kill him. All my chores done, I stretched out, the gun in my hand, my finger resting outside the trigger guard. With the stove going good and new rain on the roof, I was asleep in no time.

I must have slept through the rest of the day. It was dark when I woke up, and the chair at the door was being moved. I got off the bed fast and edged my way along the wall to the door. Just when I got there the plates fell on the floor with a clatter. I waited with the gun cocked. Maybe 15 seconds passed before Etta's voice came in a whisper. "You in there, Saddler? It's Etta. Open the door if you're in there."

I couldn't be sure who was with her, so I kicked the chair away and jerked back from the line of fire.

"What's going on?" Etta said. "It's just me, nobody else. I'm coming in now."

The door creaked open and she was outlined against the light. Then she came in and closed the door behind her. I struck a match with my left hand and lit the lamp. Yellow light flooded the cabin as I put the chimney back in place and turned up the wick. Etta smelled as if she had just stepped out of a tin tub of soapy water. She smelled good and her hair, still damp, was combed back and tucked under her hat. In the lamplight she was very pretty and I wondered what the hell she was up to.

"Nice night," I said.

Just as politely she answered, "At least the rain has stopped. I hate rain. It makes me think of funerals."

That surprised me. Hard, cold rain and funerals were linked in my own mind, too, I'd always thought that was some quirk of my own.

"You got anything to drink?" Etta said before she saw the empty quart bottle Cassidy and I had finished earlier. "I see you don't. Here!" She took a flat pint bottle from her coat pocket and gave it to me.

I knew she wasn't there to drink or to pass the time. Of all the members of the Wild Bunch I expected to come calling, she was the last. While I poured drinks she put a brown cigarette in her mouth and said she didn't have a match. I struck one for her and had to get close to give her a light. I think she had a match—people who smoke that much always have matches—but she wanted to break the ice with me. I didn't know why.

Etta's own lines were like those of a thoroughbred mare, a young and pretty one, a fast trotter. She seemed to be doing her best to forget the hostility she had shown since I'd arrived in the Hole. But that wasn't easy for either of us, because she had been so obvious about it. "Why don't you sit down," I said.

Nothing was said about her reason for being there.

"Thanks," she said, but instead of a chair she used the edge of the bunk.

"Good luck," she said before she drank her drink.

"Same to you," I responded gallantly. The conversation was going nowhere, and to steer it a little I let her drink more than I did. I don't know if she noticed that or not. I was glad to let her drink more than her share. I had been lapping up too much whiskey lately, and if I didn't want to develop a shaky gunhand I'd have to go easy.

"Look, Saddler," Etta started off after the third man-sized drink. "I've been thinking and don't see any reason we can't be some kind of friends."

"Any kind is all right with me, Etta." I felt like smiling because Harry Tracy had used about the same words when he'd tried to bugger me. "I can't blame you for being suspicious at first."

Etta looked wise. "It's the life we lead, Saddler. Hunted from pillar to post. It frays the nerves and makes me jumpy. So I'm sorry I've sniped at you so much."

"What's past is past," I declared, not believing a word of it.

Etta reached over and rubbed my crotch when I said that. That broke the ice quicker than anything else and she lay back on the bunk when I pushed her down gently. My push was light as a feather, yet this tough gunwoman lay down for me. I kissed her with our clothes on, and then I started to take hers off. The gunbelt had to come first and she tensed slightly when I began to unbuckle it. Anybody who carries a gun all the time feels naked without it. But after I got the gun out of the way, getting the rest of her undressed was easy. I saw her small shapely feet after I got her socks and boots off. She was well-shaped all over, almost delicate, and I could well-believe that she had been a schoolteacher at one time.

Etta excited me more than the other women because she was much more dangerous. The threat of violence always lurked in her dark eyes, and I knew it didn't come from the wild life she led, but was a part of her nature. She could be as rough spoken as any man; some of that had become habit, and some was just plain put-on.

Lying back with her eyes half-closed, she watched me while I dropped my clothes on the floor. I poured the last of the whiskey into a cup, took a short drink to be sociable, and gave her the rest. Before I got in beside her she asked me to light a cigarette for her. She burned it down to the nub with a few deep drags.

Then, still unsmiling, she opened her arms and her legs for me. Her bush was thick and soft and I had to part it with my fingers to get my shaft in. She groaned and arched her back as I penetrated her to the hilt. She was so wet that I went in all the way with a single thrust. Maybe this whole business had started as a sham, some part of a plan cooked up by Cassidy, but all that changed as soon as I got my big cock in her.

Every thrust made her quiver like a strung wire, and her breath came fast and hot in my ear. All of her tongue was in my mouth, and though she smelled and tasted of strong tobacco, I didn't mind. Now and then, as she grew more excited, she made me raise up so she could look down and watch my cock pumping in and out of her. I got the feeling that, in watching herself being poked, she was watching someone else.

Whatever it was, soon she began to moan, almost crooning in her excitement, as she worked her way up to an orgasm, and when it came I could barely control her. Her doubled-up fists beat on my chest and her eyes closed tight, wanting to shut out all but the frenzied sensations inside her. Her first come brought me off in a volley of hot juice, and that got her going again, and she came and came until she cried out crazily, twisting and turning under me. I held her firmly and kept on moving until every drop I could shoot was inside her. And she kept moving too, quietly but in fierce concentration.

After a while I got hard again. Then, by gestures rather than by words, she let me know that she wanted to get on top of me. Obediently, I rolled over without taking my shaft out. With Etta on top of me, it was truly like I was being fucked by a woman. Many women like to get on top of the man because, as one woman told me, it gives them greater freedom of movement and is a change from the missionary position: woman on her back with legs spread, man on top with stiff cock. No fancy stuff, just straightforward fucking.

But when Etta climbed on top of me I knew she wanted more than freedom of movement. Pretty soon I realized she wanted to fuck me as much like a man as possible. That was all right with me. We all have our own ways of doing things, especially when it comes to fucking. But after a gentle enough beginning she started to get rough, jerking herself up and down on my shaft. She indicated by impatient gestures that she wanted me to clamp my legs around her back the way a woman does with a man. It was a new position for me, but I did it willingly enough.

She grunted—she didn't groan—as she pushed down hard on my shaft until it felt like she was driving into me instead of me into her. There was great anger in this lovely woman and she seemed to be punishing me for all the bad things men had done to her. Sweat coated her body and dripped from her face. Then she began to say "fuck" every time she drove my cock into her. Her body was rigid with lust and anger and when she finally came she kept on plunging like a man having a wild come. Gradually her plunging became slower, but she was still like a man trying to stretch out his come, not wanting to stop until his cock got soft.

Wet with sweat, she lay down on top of me, tired for the moment, just like a man. She didn't protest when I turned her over on her back with my cock still in her. Then I fucked her as hard as she had fucked me. I wasn't really rough, but there was no tenderness in that fuck. It was an honest fuck, nothing fancy about it. I made her spread her legs wide and I lay between them, driving myself in and out of her like a piston. She stared up at me with a strange look on her face. I didn't suck her breasts. I put my hands behind her head, lifting it slightly off the pillow. That gave me more control and she knew it.

I drove in and out of her until I was ready to come. I

raised her head even more so she could see my cock when I pulled everything out but the head. Then I squeezed the back of her neck and shoved myself in to the hilt and came hard, filling her hot cunt with my juice. That made her come, but this time she came like a woman. She arched her back, beat her ass on the bed and cried out in a frenzy of lust. Then, gradually, we both relaxed and I knew we could be friends again.

After a while she said softly, "I'm sorry, Saddler. You must think I'm an awful bitch."

"I don't," I said. "No need to talk about it."

"Then let's talk about you and me, what you're doing here."

Here it comes, I thought, the real reason she's here.

With her hand between my legs she said, "You know, Saddler, it wasn't right what Cassidy did to you. You'd be well on your way to Texas if he hadn't dragged you in here all roped and tied."

"I could have done without it," I admitted cautiously, wondering if Butch had his ear to the door. But I didn't think so because Butch had a heavy foot.

"Well, it wasn't right," she said.

"What the hell," I said. "These things happen in life. Anyway, we'll soon be out of here."

She was counting my ribs on one side, as if to make sure I wasn't missing a few. She said, "That's what I want to talk to you about. What happens after we get out of here."

"What happens?"

She took a deep breath, and looked like a troubled woman about to reveal some terrible and disturbing secret. "I don't think Cassidy is to be trusted anymore. He's changed a lot this last year. For sure he's not the man he was. Harry agrees we can't depend on him anymore."

I didn't believe a word of it. "The Kid said that?"

"He didn't say it first. I did. But he's been thinking about it and he says I'm right. This job is going to be

Cassidy's last, he swears. Harry and I think he's going to double-cross the two of us, not just the boys."

"You don't know that for sure."

Etta pressed on with her argument. "Cassidy talks in his sleep. First I thought it was just his usual rambling. Then later when I'd heard enough of it, I began to piece some of the words together. One night he said, 'I carried them long enough, but no more.' Another night he said, 'I got no real friends—nobody.'"

"Everybody feels like that at times," I said.

Etta had to work hard to hide her irritation. "There's more, Saddler. Harry owns half the interest in a private gentleman's club—all right, a whorehouse, but not Doxy's—and the madam there is a good friend of his and tells him things."

"Such as?"

"Well, there was this man who works for a riverboat company and he got roaring drunk and let a few things slip. The long and short of it is, Cassidy has been making plans of his own to get out of the country. Cassidy's plan—a smart one—is to go all the way to New Orleans as one of the boiler-room crew. Below decks all the time, he'll never have to show his face. If he shows it at all it'll be black as a nigger's. Who's going to look for Butch Cassidy in the boiler room of a riverboat?"

"Pretty smart," I agreed.

"This riverboat-man says he's arranged the whole escape for Cassidy. The day he gets to New Orleans he's to join the crew of a banana boat sailing for Honduras. Soon as he gets there, he can disappear."

"Maybe this steamboat-man was just drunk and lying," I said. "Some of them have got a mouth as big as a steam whistle."

"Harry's friend checked back on him through other friends. Seems one time this man tried to get Cassidy to rob a steamboat with gold bullion aboard."

"Hold up a steamboat!" That was a new one on me.

"Cassidy turned it down, but they did talk about it.

That's gospel. What more proof do you want that Cassidy plans a double cross?"

"I'm sorry to hear that, Etta, but it's up to you and Harry to deal with it. I'm just a stranger here. You know Butch better than I do. He's your friend, your partner."

"But you're part of it too, Saddler. A big part of it and we're going to need your help."

"To do what?"

"Help us turn Cassidy over to the Pinkertons. Here's what we think. Go into town with Pearl, get the drop on her and turn her over to the Pinks. She's wanted down south. They'll telegraph and find out you're telling the truth. They'll think you're a fine fellow. Then and only then do you tell them about Cassidy and what he did to you. Offer to make a deal for Harry and me. Sure we're wanted, but not as much as they want Cassidy. Tell the Pinks we'll turn Cassidy over to them. Say they can have Tracy and the others as a bonus. But you must make a deal for Harry and me. No jail time, not a day."

"You think they'd make a deal like that? They've been after you and the Kid for a long time."

"Sure they'll make a deal. Cassidy *is* the Wild Bunch. The rest of us just follow along. What do the Pinks want most? To break up the Wild Bunch, that's what. It's like when two men commit a murder and the only way they can hang one is to let the other go if he turns state's evidence."

"You'd give evidence against Butch?"

"No! No!" Etta said impatiently, burned at my Texas thick-headedness. "They don't even get to see Harry and me. You're the go-between, the dealmaker. They get Cassidy and we go free."

I looked around the cabin as if I might be overheard. Then I whispered, "But suppose they don't hang Butch. If all they do is send him to jail, he's sure to break out. You know what happens then?"

"They'll hang him," Etta said confidently. "How can they not hang him? They'll hang him so fast he'll get dizzy. But it has to be you that makes the deal. You collect the reward money on Cassidy and we'll split it three ways. Of course they're not supposed to know you have anything more to do with us. They won't care whether you do or not. Get it through your head, it's Cassidy they want. There's all kinds of money on Cassidy. Bank money, railroad money, Pinkerton money. Even the state legislature has a reward out on him."

"A lot of money?"

"More than twenty-five thousand."

"Not as much as we'd get from the robbery."

"But a lot safer. We could all get killed going in there. Cassidy plans to rob that bank and then us."

It was a hell of a story. "You sound bitter," I said with my hand between Etta's legs.

Etta squirmed but kept on talking. "Sure I'm bitter. I've got good reason to be. That son of a bitch stole every cent I had, all the money I was saving for a getaway. You know how many times I was shot at to get that money, and all the time thinking I could end up behind the walls for thirty years?"

I fingered her gently. "How do I know you and Harry won't double-cross me?"

There was a dew of sweat on Etta's upper lip. "Oh, we wouldn't do that, Saddler," she said, pretty sure she had me on the line. "Honest, we wouldn't. We're not like Cassidy. I won't say he wasn't all right once, but now he's turned rotten." To clinch her argument she began to stroke my cock.

"How would you go about delivering him to the Pinks?"

"The Kid and I will get the drop on him. He won't be expecting it, so it'll be easy. He'll be ready for delivery by the time you get back after making the deal. You take him back in and wait for the reward money."

"What about Tracy and the rest of the boys?"

"When you deliver Cassidy to the Pinks that'll be the only big news in Mansfield that day. Who's going to be thinking of the bank, with Cassidy in irons? We'll tell Tracy and the others to go in and rob the bank like we planned. And who do you think will be in the bank?"

"About fifty Pinks and possemen."

"You got it, Saddler," Etta said, stroking harder. "They'll be shot to bits. And so ends the Wild Bunch."

"It's neat," I said. "Except for one thing."

Etta looked eager. "What's that, Saddler?"

"In a minute," I said. "Just let me ease the tension a bit."

Etta was impatient, but she let me slip into her. I came quickly because this time she was helping. She wanted to hear my answer.

After I pulled out she said, "What were you going to say?"

"Just that you're a fucking liar. That whole thing is a bullshit story, and you know it. Go on back to Cassidy and tell him it didn't work. Tell the son of a bitch he can stop testing me. I'll keep my word as long as he does."

Dark-faced with anger, Etta kicked at me savagely and jumped out of bed. "You fucking bastard!" she raged.

I held my gun ready while she pulled on her clothes and boots. She started for the door and spun around when I called to her.

"Hey, Etta," I said. "What happens if it gets hard again?"

"Pull it," she said, and the way she banged the door nearly knocked it off the hinges again.

Cassidy was taking an awful lot of trouble with me. If I knew then what I was to know later, it wouldn't have puzzled me so much. I put my pants on in case there might be more visitors that night.

NINE

A bucket clattered at one end of the porch just after Etta left, and I knew it hadn't been blown over by the wind. I had seen it when I moved into the cabin. The rusting bucket was filled with clean, white sand, the kind used to keep floors clean in muddy weather. When the sand was strewn on floors it picked up the mud and could be swept out when it got too dirty.

I blew out the lamp and got out of there fast. The light was bad, but then I saw Tom O'Day picking himself up out of the mud. I yanked him to his feet and he stank of whiskey, but his eyes focused on me faster than the eyes of a drunken man ought to have. Then they glazed over. I guessed then that he was a lot less drunk than he pretended to be, but he made it appear that I had to hold him up.

"Out for a stroll, are you, Tom?" I remarked, still keeping a grip on his coat collar.

O'Day swayed on his feet and hiccupped. "Was coming to pay you a visit, Saddler. Got an attack of the cabin fever, decided to come on down here and say hello. Thought we'd swap a few yarns. Goddamn bucket!" O'Day kicked at the sandbucket and missed. He grabbed at me so I could give him support.

"Tripped over the bucket, did you?" I said.

"Hell of a place to leave a bucket!" O'Day complained. "A man could break his leg in the dark."

"Good thing you didn't, Tom." O'Day had tripped over the bucket all right, but he had fallen the wrong way. If he'd been coming instead of going, he would have fallen the other way. I knew I could be wrong, but I didn't think so. O'Day had been on the porch, listening. When Etta had left so abruptly, he tried to get away fast. Too fast. Hence the bucket and the stumble. I wondered how much he had heard.

"Goddamn bucket!" O'Day repeated. This time he kicked right and the bucket rang.

"Come on in and wipe off," I said, taking a hard grip on his arm.

O'Day was plastered with dripping mud. "I'll just muck up your house, Saddler me boy. I'll just get on home and sponge off."

Still holding his arm, I steered him toward the door. "Be glad to have your company, Tom. Was feeling kind of lonesome. Besides, you got a bottle and I'm all out. Been having a few nips, have you?"

A bottle stuck out of O'Day's pocket and he pulled it out to show me how much he'd been drinking. The bottle was about half gone, but it was no proof that the Irishman was drunk. Coming back from Jackson Hole I had seen him empty a full pint of whiskey in three swallows. And that pint was just to open his eyes. After he got it down he was able to sit his horse straight and talk in a sensible manner. Now, steering him toward the cabin, I figured he wasn't drunk at all.

When we got inside he flopped heavily in a chair and grinned at me. He held out the bottle to me and I filled two cups. "Sure there's food as well as drink in whiskey," he said. He drank off his cupful of whiskey. "On such a rainy day as this it's good for what ails you. Wards off chills and fevers and is good for snakebite." O'Day held out his cup for another one.

I was careful not to look at him as I filled the cup a second time. But I could feel him watching me carefully, and it wasn't just to make sure that he got a full measure of redeye. When I turned back to him his eyelids were drooping and his mouth was slack.

"Here's looking at you," I said, taking a pull on my own drink.

O'Day grinned. "To temperance!" He downed the whiskey and a smile spread across his ugly, whiskery face. "Did I ever tell you about the time I was courting this rich widow? Guess I didn't. Well, sir, I had her just where I wanted her till one night I showed up drunk. Mad as hell, this widow woman says to me: 'Lips that touch liquor shall never touch mine.' Quick as a wink I says back to her, 'That's all right, Mrs. Breckinridge, I don't drink nothing but beer.' How do you like that for a quick comeback?"

"It's a kneeslapper," I agreed, just as O'Day's eyes closed and he began to snore. He snored too hard and too loud, and I knew he was watching me through slitted eyes. I let O'Day pretend to sleep for a while.

I sat down and drank some whiskey, trying to decide what to do. Cassidy didn't know it yet, but he was in a mess of trouble. I was certain the sneaky Irishman had heard some, or maybe all of what had passed between Etta and me. I knew Etta's elaborate plan of a double double cross was just Cassidy's way of testing me. But O'Day, foxy but not given to hard thinking, could easily take it for what it seemed to be: a plot to do them all in. O'Day had hoped to tag along when Butch left the country, and he had been promised as much by Etta, who always had a smile and a meal for the ugly Irishman. O'Day, the most loyal of all Cassidy's men, would feel the most betrayed, and for my part I couldn't decide what to do about him.

I suppose I could have shot him dead where he sat

pretending to sleep. But I didn't think I could bring myself to do that. If I did kill him, how was I going to explain it? Butch might have believed my story, but what about the rest of them. O'Day was the mascot of the Wild Bunch, always good for a windy story and a laugh. I could hardly say I had killed him in self-defense. Nobody would have believed that. Tom O'Day was no killer. You can well believe that I roundly cursed Cassidy and all his stupid trickery. I would have to tell the stupid bastard about O'Day. That was all I could do, then the hell with the rest of it!

Tom O'Day woke up and grinned at me. "Must of dozed off. What you been doing?"

"Drinking your whiskey. There's a big drink left."

"One for the road then," O'Day said. "Then I'll be off to my bed. Good talking to you, Saddler. We'll have another visit real soon."

The sneaky Irishman gulped his whiskey and went out.

Maybe he was out there watching me when I went down the hill to Butch's cabin. The lights were out when I got there, but they came on quick when I rapped on the door. Butch came naked to open it with a gun in his hand. Pushing past the cocked pistol, I said roughly, "You're so smart you're stupid, Cassidy."

Cassidy led down the hammer on the pistol, but kept the gun in his hand. "What're you so mad about? Don't tell me Etta didn't make it worth your while."

The Kid had enough decency to pull on his pants before he came out of the bedroom. "What's going on here?" He saw me in the dim light and lowered his pistol.

"I didn't cook that up, Saddler." Butch said. "What did you do, think about it for an hour, then get madder and madder?"

"What I've been doing for the last hour is listening to Tom O'Day snoring. First he told a joke, then he snored."

Cassidy said, "In the morning, Saddler. We'll talk about it in the morning. You kind of interrupted something."

"This won't wait till morning, Cassidy. Get Etta out on the porch to stand guard. I caught O'Day snooping around just after she left. Fell over a bucket and I caught him. Pretended to be drunk. I pretended to believe him. He heard everything she said, every dumb thing you told her to say."

"Well, I'll be a dirty dog," the Kid said. "You sure he heard?"

"Positive."

Butch called Etta and she came out with a sullen face. "I'm going," she said. "You and your ideas, Cassidy."

We pulled chairs close to the table. I told about O'Day and kept it short. Butch didn't look so confident and carefree by the time I'd finished.

"You should have strangled him if you didn't want to use the gun," Butch said, chiding me for my lack of forethought. "We could have buried him in the dead of night."

I glared at him. "You don't know who else might have been watching. They could be watching right now."

The Kid swore softly. "What's the difference! They know by this time. Now they'll all go over to Tracy. I think we better get set for a showdown."

"Maybe not," I said. "Anyway, not right off. But you have to tell them about the robbery sooner than you planned. If they think there's all that money at stake, it's likely they'll hold off till we get it. I'd say tell them tonight, only that would look suspicious. First thing in the morning, is when you tell them."

Butch had painted himself into a corner and he knew it. "What if they decide to go after the money on their own? There's ten of them and four of us. I think we better get Pearl and Laura on our side."

The Kid knew what I was thinking. "O'Day may have warned the girls as well as Tracy. I'd better go and see if they're to bed."

A few minutes later the Kid came back shaking his head. "Bed's still warm but they're not in it. O'Day didn't waste any time getting to them."

I said, "Then that makes twelve against four. I still think they'll avoid a showdown right now. O'Day knows we're going to rob a bank in some town. That's all he knows. He heard Etta talking to me, but I knew what she was talking about and he didn't. There's a bank to be robbed and we have a plan for it. O'Day or Tracy can't know what that plan is. There's a double cross in the air, and maybe they know that already, but not when or where. Cassidy, I don't even know where."

The Kid gnawed on his mustache, his only sign of edginess. "So what's your thinking, Saddler?"

"First, I don't think O'Day knows I spotted him as a sneak. So he doesn't think we know. In the morning we all act like nothing's happened. I don't mean me, I mean you—you and Butch. Call them together and lay out the robbery for them. Tell the bastards everything, the information you got from this railroad man, the trap he's setting up, how we're going to rob the money when it gets to the bank. Tell it straight, Cassidy. For the love of Christ, this time no tricks."

Butch looked gloomy, and had no jokes or smiles. "That'll give them time to plan their own double cross." He brightened up a little. "Maybe we can get the girls back on our side."

I said not likely. "They'd be fools if they believed you. Face it, Cassidy, they've gone over to Tracy. I hate to say it, but you just gave Tracy every fucking thing he needs."

Butch tried to get tricky again. "I got an idea. You go to Tracy and beg pardon for beating up on him. Tell him everything Etta told you and how you said no dice to that. O'Day will bear that out. There's a chance they'll let you in on what they're planning to do. Then you get word back to us, and we're all set."

As a rule the Kid didn't go against Cassidy. Now he did. "You got to stop this horseshit. Sending Etta over to Saddler has fucked up everything. Quit your scheming and listen to hard facts. Tracy knows there is going to be a double cross. It's supposed to come after you're turned over to the Pinks by Etta and me. That won't happen, so he has to figure where the double cross is planned for next. Only one thing is certain: there can't be any double-crossing until we get that money."

"Where do you think?" Butch asked.

The Kid looked tired. "If I knew that, or could figure it out, believe me I'd tell you in a shot. All I know is yesterday we had twelve people on our side. Now we got nobody but Saddler."

Grim-faced, the Kid said to me, "You got any ideas?"

"Not right this minute. I'll think about it." I yawned and looked outside and was hungry in spite of everything. First light was brighter than usual and from the looks of the sky there would be a gaudy sunrise. Etta opened the door and said nothing was happening.

"They're not making a move," she said.

Sundance went to get the rest of his clothes on. "I'll take over," he said.

"Better not," I said. "The sight of you sitting out there at first light won't look so good. Let's just eat breakfast and see what happens. If they come with guns, we'll just have to make a fight of it."

Coming in to start breakfast, Etta glared at us. "A fine army we got here. Three generals and no troops."

We ate breakfast with our rifles lying across our knees, and as usual Etta smoked more than she ate. It wasn't a cheerful meal by any means. The gaudy sunrise came as promised, but did nothing to lift our spirits. Thanks to Cassidy's stupid trickery, what had once been a fairly good plan was wrecked. Getting the drop on Tracy wouldn't have been easy, but now it looked close to impossible. Twelve against four were lousy odds. At this point Cassidy couldn't even call off the robbery. If he called it off it would bring the showdown all that closer.

Etta went to the window and looked out. "They're up earlier than usual," she said. "Usually they lie in bed half the day."

I went to look and saw smoke from cookstoves rising

up straight into the early morning sky. The grass looked very green in the bright sunlight. The mud was beginning to dry.

Etta sat down and pushed a fried egg around her plate, not caring if she caught it or not. Suddenly her black eyes glowed with something that wasn't altogether anger. I think she saw the end drawing near and wanted to go out and meet it halfway. She yanked her beltgun and checked the loads in the cylinder. After she pushed the loading gate shut, she put the pistol on the table instead of dropping it back in its holster.

"What the hell!" she said. "It's finished, let's get it over with. Twelve of them, four of us. That means we have to kill three apiece."

Impending danger hadn't dulled Cassidy's appetite. He was surprised by her sudden burst of ferocity. "No way to ambush them in here."

"Who's talking about an ambush?" Etta placed her small hand on the heavy revolver. "I'm talking about this. Soon as you finish stuffing your gut we'll go out and meet them head on. Let Saddler ride out. He's got nothing to do with this."

Now it was my turn to be surprised, though I didn't say anything.

"Give him the password to get out of here," Etta said. "Then it's just the three of us. What's the difference how we die. Might as well be here as in front of a bank or along the right of way."

Butch told Etta to put the gun away. "We're not dead yet. It's like Saddler says. There won't be a showdown till after we get the money. Dying later is better than sooner."

"That's some consolation," Etta sneered. "You wouldn't be afraid of dying, would you, Cassidy?"

Butch shrugged. "I'd rather you didn't rush me into it."

The Kid ate everything he had piled on his plate, and that was plenty. "I can't figure what we're going to do after the robbery. It'll still be twelve against four. Not a hope they'll let us get out of their sight. Lady and gents, I don't see how we're going to get out of this."

"Well what are you looking at?" I asked. Cassidy had been staring at me.

Butch said, "I'm looking at you, my friend. For a man that's got so much to say, you been keeping mighty quiet. Ain't you got no ideas how to kill them off or whittle them down to better odds. You talk so straight, you have to be a bigger crook than I am. The crookedest man I ever knew, a merchant, had a big sign on his wall. You know what it said? Honesty Is the Best Policy."

I dropped my fork with a clatter and got some steak juice on my shirt. They all looked at me like I was about to have a fit.

"Jesus Christ!" I said. "That's how we'll whittle them down. Cassidy will tell them the truth. Shut up a minute and listen. They know you're planning some kind of double cross. They're hopping mad by this time, mad enough to kill, mad enough to nail you to the cross, or stake you out on an anthill."

"Is that the latest news?" Butch said.

Sundance cut in. "Let him talk."

I said, "You know what the preachers say? Let him who is without sin cast the first stone. It's like that with every man out there. Not a one of them hasn't thought of doublecrossing somebody sometime. Maybe some of them have done it already. They're robbers, aren't they? Not a one isn't a dirty, thieving robber like you, Cassidy."

"True," Butch said.

"So you were tempted. What man isn't tempted to double-cross his pals? With all that money it's only natural. For a hundred thousand dollars, I'd be tempted myself. You're greedy, you want it all for yourself, tell them. So would they. But now you find you can't do it. You've all been friends too long, have been through too much together. Now you're ashamed of your greedy

113

thoughts and want to share and share alike."

Butch protested. "We never shared like that. Me and Harry and Etta always took half and they had equal shares of the rest."

I said, "This time it'll be equal shares for all. You want to whittle them down, that's how to do it."

Sundance expressed his doubts. "The showdown will come when we divvy up the money in some safe place. Say there's a hundred thousand. In equal shares that's a little over six thousand and between the four of us that comes to twenty-four thousand dollars. If we go to a safe place to divvy up the money they'll be expecting a trick. The minute the moneysacks hit the ground they'll open up on us. We can't hope to win."

"That's not what Saddler means," Etta said.

"Your safe place isn't the same as mine," I went on. "What worries a bandit the most after a robbery? That he won't get his money. So he sticks close to the money until it's divided. He sticks to it like glue."

"Tell us something new," Butch growled.

I delivered my clincher. "This time we do it different —we divvy the money right there in the bank. That'll take time, I grant you that. But the bank isn't open so we have some time. We lay the money out and count it and give every man his share. Who's going to argue against that?"

The Kid said, "Harry Tracy is. Tracy will want to keep that money in one lump. So he can get it later and maybe not share it at all."

"The boys won't go for that though," I said. "Six thousand in a man's pocket weighs heavier than a lot of promises. Unless I'm wrong, the boys will take their six thousand and get the hell out of there. They can go one at a time. The gang is finished and they'll be looking to go where the Pinkertons aren't so thick."

The Kid drummed his fingers on the table. Butch frowned while he thought.

"They won't all go their own way, Pinks or no Pinks.

Some will stay with Tracy," the Kid said.

That was true. I said, "If half of them take their money and run, that leaves only six we have to face when they come after us. They'll come all right. Six thousand won't satisfy Tracy. He'll be looking to add our twenty-four thousand to his take. But he'll want more than that. He'll want us dead, all of us for different reasons."

Butch said, "Tracy would like to form a new Wild Bunch, with him as the leader. Hell! I can't let him do that. A man like him would drag the name through the mud."

I waited until Cassidy got through expressing his indignation. "He'll do worse than that if he takes us alive." I told them about Harry Tracy and his new-style handcuffs and what he used them for. "If he takes us alive we'll get a taste of that. Tracy has to die no matter what. The others with him aren't that important."

Butch stood up and checked his gun. "I'd best whistle them down here and see how they take it. If they don't buy my wares, I'll take Tracy. The rest of you kill anybody you can."

"No," I said. "Not now. We'll all kill Tracy when the time comes. If we have to die it won't be so bad, knowing he's dead."

Sundance nodded agreement. "Same thing goes for me."

Etta turned away from the window and her face was hard and tight, but not afraid. I knew then that Cassidy wouldn't have to do any hog calling to assemble his gang.

"They're coming," Etta said.

TEN

If killing had to come, it was a nice day for it. A bright, sunny day with white, fleecy clouds high in the sky. It was the kind of day when you can hear the flowers grow, if you listen hard enough. But instead of flowers we heard a lot of boots getting closer to the cabin. We moved apart and took up our positions and waited.

The door was open and the porch creaked under their weight as they all stepped up together. Harry Tracy was in the lead and along with the gun in his holster he had another pistol stuck in the waistband of his pants. His face looked like a cavalry troop had run over it. Blood caked his fleshy mouth and his nose was flat and no longer centered in the middle of his face. Pearl, pretty but tense, stood beside him. Beauty and the beast, I thought. Every man and woman in the Wild Bunch was there, and the only one missing was the original Butch Cassidy.

"You look like a committee," Cassidy said. "Come on in. Sorry there ain't enough chairs for everybody."

They trooped in with wary eyes, Harry Tracy in the

lead, Pearl right behind him. I think Pearl saw herself as the new Etta Place, the new queen of the Wild Bunch. The others followed, but there was no chorus of howdies and good mornings, as there might have been a day earlier. Tom O'Day brought up the rear like the brave feller he was. But he was resolute enough, in a shaky way.

We faced off, twelve against four. I knew Kilpatrick, Big Nose Curry, Will Carver, Billy Reeves, and Stitch Fallon. The rest of the men I didn't know at all, but they looked mean enough. Two looked like brothers, though one was a good ten years older than the other. The door was open, but the big room smelled of sweat and whiskey.

Butch stepped away from the wall to give his gunhand free play. The rest of us stayed where we were. Butch was smiling, but the smile didn't get as far as his eyes. We'll know in a minute, I thought. Tracy's eyes flicked to me, then back to Cassidy.

Butch said quickly, "Ain't this a coincidence though. I was about to call a meeting of the clan and here you folks are without me saying a word. Now, why don't you loosen up and listen to what I have to say. You want to or not?"

Harry Tracy had his feet planted wide and his hand wasn't far from his gun. "It could be past time for talking, Cassidy. Me and the boys have been deciding a few things."

"Sure you have," Butch said easily. "Let me guess what you been talking about. We ain't pulled any jobs lately, and the money ain't coming in like it used to. You're sick of the Hole and the rain and the long days with nothing to do. Well, boys, so am I. That's what I want to talk to you about. What would you say if I told you we're about to pull the biggest job ever pulled in these parts?"

Tracy sneered. "I'd say you was just talking."

Cassidy's eyes narrowed but his gunhand didn't move. "Walk soft," he warned. "I'll say it again, boys. I'm talking about more money than you ever saw before. I didn't tell you before 'cause I wasn't sure we could do it. Hell! I been craving some real action bad as the rest of you. Only there was nothing worth the trouble. What did you want me to do? Lead you out of here to stick up a dry goods store? Maybe get some of us killed for a few hundred dollars? You know as well as I do that the Pinks and the railroad shooters are all over the country."

"Anything is better than doing nothing," Pearl said. "You been talking a big job a long time, Butch. One day it's this, the next day it's something else."

Butch said, "This job is the real McCoy. I had to keep it under my hat till I figured out how to do it. Now I have. It won't be a snap, but it can be done. Now you want to hear about it, or did you come here to bitch about hard times?"

Ben Kilpatrick, lanky and slow talking, pushed his way to the front. "You better not be bullshitting, Cassidy. I been with you a long time, but there comes a time when a man has to look out for himself. It's like you been forgetting who your friends are."

Butch did his best to look contrite. "Maybe I have, Ben, and I beg pardon for it. Things change, a man changes. It was different when we could range this country like free men, taking what we wanted, nobody daring to stand up to us. You're a smart man, Ben. How long do you think we can go on?"

Ben Kilpatrick shrugged his bony shoulders and kicked at the floor like it was dirt. "The way they been chasing us, not much longer. We damn near got killed that last job over in Bear Paw."

Harry Tracy scowled as only he could. "Talk for yourself, Kilpatrick. The Wild Bunch has been going a long time and can last till kingdom come. All it takes is sand and guts."

Butch took another step forward though it was hardly the smartest thing to do. "You're welcome to stay in these mountains as long as you like, Tracy. You can throw your guts at the Pinks and blind them with your sand. Now does anybody in this gang want to hear about the robbery?"

Ben Kilpatrick nodded slowly. "Tell it, Butch. We'll hear you out."

Everybody shut up while Cassidy told about the shipment of money, how his man on the railroad thought it should be taken, the river curve, the long grade, the pried-up rail, the string of passenger cars jampacked with Pinkertons and possemen.

"We might as well ride into a rapid-fire gun," Butch said.

Butch should have been a politician. Hell! He was a politician. Except that this bunch of voters would mark their ballots with bullets. He was damn good, playing on their fear and their greed at the same time.

Then he got onto the new bank in Mansfield. No credit was given to me, and I didn't want it. The whole thing was Cassidy's idea. They weren't sure they could believe him, but they liked the sound of the plan. I was proud of it myself.

"Nobody's going to be guarding an empty bank," Butch said. "So all we got to do is get in there, stay out of sight and wait for the money to be delivered. The first ones to go in get the banker to unlock the back door. He's got to unlock that back door 'cause it'll be made·of iron, barred and double locked. The rest of you come in that way. We divvy up the money in the bank. That way every man has his rightful share before he lights out."

Ben Kilpatrick said with some astonishment, "You plan to split the money right there in the bank. I never heard of that being done. We never did that before."

"How much money?" Pearl wanted to know.

"About a hundred thousand." Butch made that sound as casual as he could.

Now there was real excitement. Harry Tracy's eyes flickered uneasily. I guess he felt his new authority slipping away from him.

"It's easy to talk big money," he said.

"It's there," Butch went on. "All we got to do is take it. Now I'm going to tell you something else that ought to please you. This time it's going to be equal shares all the way. That means I don't get more than any other man. Same goes for Harry and Etta."

Tracy looked around. "Butch has turned into Santy Claus."

Big Nose Curry hadn't said anything up till now. "What's this about equal shares, Butch? That don't sound like you."

Butch put on a sorrowful face. "I don't know how you're going to take it, Curry. How you and the others are going to take it. Boys, I hate to tell you this is going to be my last job. I'm getting out and advise you to do the same. I'm telling you straight, man to man, so no man can say old Butch Cassidy run out on his boys. I'm telling you in time. Maybe Tracy is right about the Bunch not being finished. That's for you and Tracy to decide. I'm sick and tired of it and want to quit. I just been at it too goddamned long. Can you fault me for wanting to quit the business?"

"We can if we like," Tracy said. No one else said anything.

"I think you're talking for yourself, Tracy." Butch took another step until he was no more than a few feet from Tracy. "You think you'd like to stop me?"

"First we talk about the money," Tracy said. "This equal shares bullshit. How'd that get started?"

Butch looked like a kid caught stealing a cherry pie from the pantry. "Might as well tell you the whole of it," he said, taking in a deep breath. "I'm ashamed of myself, boys. Ladies too. I was fixing to double-cross the lot of you. That's right. Grab the whole hundred thousand and take off for parts unknown."

There was a sudden shifting in the gang of outlaws though they didn't really move. Butch's confession had caught them completely off-guard. Now they stared at him, not knowing what to make of him.

Tracy sneered. "Maybe you still plan to do just that."

Butch said, "You tell me how I'm going to manage that. We divvy up the money right there in the bank. That's about six thousand a man. Or woman. Like I said, after the job we split up and go our own way. You tell me how I'd go about rounding up the hundred thousand. Follow one man south, another west. That leaves north and east and points in between. Anybody here ever know me to work that hard for six thousand dollars? That won't wash, Tracy, and you know it."

Ben Kilpatrick looked uncertain. "You sure about the divvy in the bank, Butch? There won't be no going back at the last minute. That's kind of important."

"Ben, after what I just told you I know it is. I tell you, I was sorely tempted to steal all that money for myself. I admit to that now and I'm sorry for it. But there's more. I made a name for myself and don't want folks to remember me as a man who would steal money from his old friends. I'm not asking you to trust me, if you don't want to. There's enough guns here to blast me all the way to hell. But you folks has got to decide how it's going to be."

Butch turned his attention back to Tracy. "You so rich you can pass up six thousand? How much did we get from that last train job? Case you forget, a measly sixteen thousand. How far did that go? It didn't do shit! But a man with six thousand in his pants can go a hell of a long way. Go a long way or stay here in Wyoming and keep on doing what he's been doing. Only you got to decide what you want to do. If we're going to do this job we got to leave today."

Tracy said, "We're going outside and talk. About you quitting, the job, a lot of things." Tracy looked around. "We'll let you know. You ain't going no place."

They went out, stepped down off the porch, and clustered too far away for us to hear what they were saying. Butch grinned. "Tracy's arguing for them to do the robbery without me. He's saying with us dead it'll mean four extra shares to be divvied. Look at old Ben Kilpatrick shaking his head. Ben has some good sense.

Little Pearl is talking a blue streak. That sneak O'Day is so scared he's ready to shit his pants."

Butch sounded like somebody calling off a horse race for a blind man. "They're coming back in."

"Jesus Christ!" Etta snapped. "Will you shut your big mouth. We've got eyes and ears."

I knew there wasn't going to be any gunplay when they trooped in again. The hundred thousand dollars had worked its magic. Once again, Harry Tracy was in the lead and he seemed to have regained some of his lost authority. The others stood waiting, but you could have cut the tension with a knife.

"We'll do it," Tracy said. "Me, I don't hold with quitters and if I had my way—"

Ben Kilpatrick interrupted quietly, "If Butch wants to get out, that's his business. He told us, he didn't just sneak off. We had good times here, but so be it. You ain't told us all of it, though." Kilpatrick grinned in spite of himself. "You never do. Who's going to look over that town?"

"Saddler, that's who. Saddler will do it right. He knows I'll find him and kill him if he don't do it right."

Tracy liked the idea of killing me for any reason. "If you don't kill him I will."

Butch shrugged. "What you boys do after the job ain't none of my concern." Butch stabbed a finger at Pearl. "You, little lady, will go into town with Saddler to see he don't get any wayward ideas."

Pearl hadn't expected that and her eyes shone with excitement. That girl had a quick mind and there was something else in her eyes besides excitement. Her eyes jumped to me, taking my measure all over again, and I don't mean my cock. Lord, I thought, won't it be good to get back where everybody isn't trying to double-cross everybody else? Or no more than usual, that is.

"I'll watch him good," she said.

After that some of the tension drained away. Butch talked on. That man should have been a sideshow barker. The magic words were "a hundred thousand dollars," and he kept repeating them, beating on the words like a drum.

And then, finally, it was all set, and they drifted off to get ready for Butch Cassidy's last job. It was getting on toward noon when the boys left and Butch said he was hungry. Etta prepared the meal in utter silence while we sat around waiting for it. Butch grinned at the Kid, who didn't grin back.

Uncorking a bottle, Butch banged it down on the table and told us to throw our lip over some good whiskey. I needed that first drink, and the second one didn't hurt either.

"Well, that wasn't too hard," Cassidy said, pleased with himself. "You see the look in Tracy's eyes?"

"We'll be seeing that look for a long time," the Kid said. "How many you figure we'll have to kill after the job? The ones that'll join up with Tracy?"

Butch used his cup of whiskey as a crystal ball. After he got through staring into it, he said, "Fallon and Reeves for sure—they're bone-born bastards. The Gundersen brothers—them fucking Swedes never did like me. Pearl, pretty Pearl, wants to take Etta's place in the gang. And then there's that broth of a boy, Tommy O'Day."

Etta turned from the stove with a fork in her hand. "That's crazy, Cassidy. Tommy's no killer."

Butch said she was right about that. "O'Day will join Tracy 'cause he's no good by himself. O'Day's fine as long as he has somebody to tell him what to do. You might say the Wild Bunch is the only home he ever had. But that man is a dirty sneaking rat."

"You don't think Kilpatrick will try to double-cross you, Butch?" the Kid asked.

"Ben's a man of honor," Butch said, hitting the bottle again. "Ben knows he can join any good gang in the country. Ben's got a good name and a fast gun. No, sir, Ben will take his six thousand and be on his way. Could be Curry and Will Carver will go with him. They was together before they joined with me. Laura I'm sure won't have anything to do with Tracy. Chicago is where that young lady wants to go."

"Then that makes seven," I said.

"It's better than twelve," Butch said. "I'd be a lot more worried if Tracy had Kilpatrick and Big Nose. Look, I'm telling you it won't be so bad. We kill the seven of them and that puts an extra forty-two thousand dollars in our kick."

Etta asked the question I was forming in my mind. "What if by some chance Tracy doesn't come after us? You aren't fixing to go after him? Him and the forty-two thousand?"

"Lordy no!" Butch answered, though I knew the thought had crossed his tricky mind. "A deal is a deal, even when you make it with a dirty fighter like Tracy."

Etta pulled the skillet off the fire. "You better honor the deal, Cassidy. This has to be the end of it, I mean it. You try to pull a switch, even with Tracy, and that's the last you'll see of me."

"You mean that, Etta?"

"Damn right I mean it. If six thousand apiece is all we get, it'll just have to do."

Butch turned to the Kid. "How about you, Harry?"

"Etta's right," the Kid said. "This has to be the end of it."

"There's no chance that Tracy will let us go," I said. "Another thing, you could be wrong about some of the others. There may be more than seven. You still haven't said how we're going to kill them."

At this point Butch played his trump card. "My namesake is going to show us how. That's right. The original Butch Cassidy. He's old and don't look like much. No matter. That old man knows every inch of Wyoming. He'll show us a place where Tracy and his boys will be like a snowball in the hottest part of hell."

Butch took his steak off the plate and went out, eating

it from his hand. "I'll go and visit the old boy right now."
At the door he turned and looked back at Etta. "Don't
bother washing the dirty dishes, my love. You ain't never
going to see them again."

A few minutes after Butch left, the Kid said he was
going to look at his horse. Etta cleared off the table and I
put my Winchester and Colt on it. Etta sat and smoked
and watched me while I worked on my weapons. I
cleaned and oiled the carbine and the pistol, then
reloaded them. Etta got a box of cartridges from the
cupboard and I filled my pockets.

"You got some kind of a farmer-looking hat?" I asked
her.

"Ought to be one in the slop chest," she said.

After digging into a mess of stuff she came up with a
black hat with a round crown that looked Mormon. I
banged it into shape and put it on. Etta got a mirror from
the bedroom and held it up so I could look at myself.
With that fool hat on, and my beard coming up good, I
guess I had a farmer look.

Etta looked doubtful. "That shirt you have on isn't
right for a farmer. Take it off and I'll find you something
else."

The baggy shirt she dug up smelled musty, but it was
homespun. I struggled into it and tucked it into my
pants. She stood back and inspected me. "I guess you'll
pass if they don't look at you too hard."

"How's about if I smoke a corncob pipe?"

Etta got mad. "Don't be like Cassidy, Saddler. This is
no time for jokes."

"No corncob pipe," I agreed. And for a while we sat
without talking.

Etta broke the silence. "You think there's a chance
we'll get away with it?"

"I don't know," I said. "It depends what I find in that
town."

I was surprised when she reached across the table and
took both my hands in hers. "Forget the threats. Forget

everything Cassidy said. I know you could sell us out if you wanted to. You could sell us out and get away with it. Cassidy thinks you're afraid of him. I know you're not. I'm begging you not to betray us. I never begged for anything in my life, but I'm begging now. These two men—don't ask me to explain it—are all I have in the world. I'll get down on my knees if I have to, Saddler. Give me this last final chance."

I squeezed her hands and let them go. "I won't sell you out," I said.

I went back to my cabin to think. I was up to my neck in trouble. When you set out to rob a bank you have to be ready to get killed. You can plan a bank robbery every which way, until it seems it's just a matter of putting the money in sacks and strolling out the door with it. It can work that way, but all too often it doesn't. All the dead bank robbers rotting in markerless graves are proof of that. I felt like a man standing on a gallows and hoping the trap would fail to open at the last moment. I racked my whiskey-sodden brain to find a way to get out of it. Not a right thought came to me. Not one goddamned thought, so finally I gave up on it.

It wasn't that I was so much against robbing banks, and it wasn't that I didn't have the nerve. That part didn't come into it. What it boiled down to is that I like an easier kind of life. I like to come and go as I please, enjoy a woman, a card game, and a full bottle of Jack Daniels. Being hunted all the time isn't much fun. I have had sheriffs after me for small transgressions of the law, and even that wasn't very entertaining. What a man has to do is find the kind of life that suits him, then stick to it. The life Butch Cassidy led didn't suit me at all.

There was a knock on the door and the Sundance Kid came in.

"You can put up the gun," he said, cool as ever. "Mind if we talk a while? We haven't had a chance to talk while you been here."

"There's a chair," I said. "What's on your mind?

Things have been kind of hectic for talking."

"You mean Harry Tracy?"

"Tracy and other things," I said, smiling.

The Kid was quicker than Cassidy. "Aren't those women something though," he said. "You can hate them at times, but they're what makes life worth living."

"Never a truer word was spoken," I said. If the Kid wanted something, he sure as hell was taking his time to get to it. But he was the best-mannered of the Wild Bunch and I hadn't noticed him making any hard eyes at me. In that place, that was something to be grateful for.

After putting fire to a cigar, the Kid looked at me through the smoke. Suddenly he didn't seem so cool after all. There was a hint of embarrassment in his voice when he spoke next.

"Butch and Etta are all the family I have, Saddler. Back in New Jersey, my folks died when I was just a kid. Had to start work at eleven. Worked as a coachman for a minister, a man of God and a real son-of-a-bitch. That old sky pilot gave me some book learning and a lot of whipping. There wasn't a day he didn't threaten me with the wrath of God."

"I know what they're like," I said.

The Kid blew a series of smoke rings. "I doubt you do. Be glad you don't. It's hell on a kid to be told all the time he's nothing but an orphan headed straight for the fiery pit, as the old man called it. Every fucking thing was a sin, according to him. I couldn't go to the outhouse without him coming around to see if I was pulling my prick."

"What kid doesn't?" I said.

"It's a way to get started," the Kid said with a smile. "One time he snuck up and caught me at it, not in the out-house, in the cellar. He gave me such a flogging, he drew blood. How I hated that man of God. For years it's been on my mind to go back and kill him. Only I can't do that because he's dead. From the age of eleven till I was fifteen I didn't have one happy day."

"You took off when you were fifteen?"

"Like a bat out of hell. The old man had a single-shot pistol he kept in the house for fear of robbers. On the day I was fifteen, I stole that old pistol and robbed the ticket seller at the railroad depot. Didn't get more than thirty dollars. With that money I bought a better gun, a real six-shooter, and worked my way West. I felt free and wild and, by Christ, nobody was going to give me a bad time ever again. I did my share of robbing. It takes money to pay for women and whiskey. I couldn't get enough of both once I got started. It was like the whole world was opening up for me. The old man used to tell me I'd get my reward in the next world. Bullshit!"

I smiled at the lanky outlaw. "Then I take it you're not religious?"

"Damn right," the Kid said. "This world is all there is, and you got to make the most of it. Once I got a taste for the wild life, I threw off all moral restraint, as that bastard minister would say. I was ready for Butch and Etta when I finally met up with them. I guess you've been wondering about Butch and Etta and me?"

"No," I said.

"Our arrangement must look peculiar to most people. It's just right for us. Don't ask me why, but it is. I don't know why people are so against two men and a woman. For that matter, two women and one man. It's about the closest family you can have. You had a taste of two women and one man the other night. How did you like it?"

"I liked it fine. I've done it before. Never had three women at one time, though. Four in a bed is too many."

The Kid nodded his agreement. "Three is exactly the right number. The times we've had, the three of us. Having that third person makes all the difference. When two of the parties involved start getting on one another's nerve, that's when the third party steps in and cools things down."

"Sounds right workable."

"It is for sure," the Kid went on. "Which brings me back to the first point. Like I told you, Butch and Etta are all the family I have. Without them I don't know what I'd be doing. Could be I'd still be a small-time gun artist."

The Kid paused and leaned forward in his chair. "I lost my first family, Saddler. I don't want to lose the second."

"I hope you won't."

"I'm glad you said that," the Kid said. "'Cause if you do anything to make me lose my family, I'd just have to kill you. I'm not like Butch. I don't talk a lot, but I get things done. You follow my meaning?"

I said I did. The Kid offered me his hand and we shook. Then he said good night and went out.

ELEVEN

It was getting dark when we went out through the ravine. Except for the girls, I had no fond memories of the Hole in the Wall, and I was glad to see the last of it. In the narrow places brush whipped at our faces and the going was slow. For a long time nobody had anything to say, not even Cassidy. Once we were through the ravine, we began the long descent to the flat country below.

We rode all night and rested up for a few hours after the sun came up. After that we split up. Pearl and I went on ahead. Pearl had shucked her range clothes in favor of a faded gingham dress and a sun bonnet. Dressed like that she looked very young, but that didn't matter. In farming communities a girl who isn't married by 18 is considered an old maid. Before we left, Cassidy told us where we would join forces again—at the base of a big rock called Old Man's Dome. We couldn't miss it, Cassidy said. It was 15 miles from Mansfield, and about a mile off the road.

All through the day Pearl and I kept up a steady pace, but we didn't do any hard riding because that would have looked suspicious. Pearl was excited at the thought of going into a real town for a change.

"Can we stop in a real hotel?" she asked. "One with real bathtubs and plenty of hot water? And maybe there's a real theater in that town. Singing and dancing or even a play."

"We're going in there to look over the bank," I said.

Pearl made a face. "The bank robbing won't happen till tomorrow. Let's have a good time tonight. Tomorrow we could be dead."

That was a sobering thought and it was perfectly true. There was no knowing how it would turn out. Anything could go wrong. Pearl knew that as well as I did, but it didn't seem to bother her. Danger affected her like whiskey. She talked a blue streak, and more than once I had to keep her from kicking her horse into a gallop.

Later in the afternoon we came to a Dutch farmer's place on the Mansfield road. He was more civil than friendly, but he did tell us to drink as much of his good spring water as we liked.

"Won't charge you a cent for it," the Dutchman said.

"You happen to have a buckboard we can buy or hire? We're both tired of sitting a saddle and would like to ride in comfort for a change."

"I might have a buckboard for hire," he said. A buckboard stood in plain sight under a lean-to at the end of the house. "I'd kind of like to get it back. That means you'll have to leave some money."

"Whatever is right," I said. "Only don't make it too steep. We sold out our place and it is our intention to settle some place around Mansfield. They say she's a comer, that town."

"You heard right," the Dutchman said. "You look like honest folk, but you're going to have to leave fifty dollars. You can see that buckboard is practically new."

It wasn't, but it wasn't falling apart either. I gave him the money and he hitched it up for us. I tied our horses to the back of the buckboard and we started off for the meeting place. We spotted the big rock from a long way off, standing up above the trees. Then, making sure we weren't seen, we turned off the road, reached the rock, and waited for the rest of them to get there.

By nightfall they were all there, but you could hardly describe the atmosphere as friendly. Cassidy said the train with the money was due in Mansfield at one p.m. the following day, which meant that Pearl and I had to be up bright and early to check the bank and to look around for signs of an ambush. I wasn't wanted for anything, but there was always a chance that some sharp-eyed Pinkerton-man might remember Pearl for her banditry in the Southwest.

The town was going good as we drove in on our rented buckboard. Mansfield had the look of a place with strong law. Nobody was shooting out lights or riding horses into saloons. The town was too far north to get many Texans, and that was just as well because Texans have a way of joining into gunfights that are none of their business. If the Pinkertons were in town, they would be as much, or more, than we could handle.

Pearl loved the bustle of the town, the saloons going full blast, the crowd of miners and cowhands on the sidewalks. Mansfield was one of those towns that happen in a hurry. Practically everything in it was new. A few stern-looking deputy marshals walked around keeping an eye on things. Looking the way we did, we didn't rate more than a second glance.

Instead of looking for the bank, we put up our horses at one of the three livery stables. The bank, a new brick building, was easily visible on Main Street. It could wait till morning, though.

"Well, will you look at that hotel!" Pearl said.

I thought it looked a little too fancy for a farm couple. However, my shy lady said she'd be damned to fucking hell if we stayed anywhere else. It was a great big barn of a place, and so new that the painters hadn't finished doing all of it. Pearl was like a kid with a jar of rock candy.

"This is what I call living," she whispered while I was signing the register.

Taking us for hayseeds, the dumpy little clerk behind the desk smirked and bowed. He turned the register on its swivel so he could read our names.

"Mr. and Mrs. Rufus Ambrister," he said.

I winked at the little bastard. "Just got married," I said.

Pearl blushed modestly and we went upstairs. Up there she pulled off her dumb looking sunbonnet and threw it against the wall. Then she grinned at me.

"It was funny to hear that man calling me Missus." She kicked off her elastic-sided shoes and waltzed around the room. "You ever think of getting married, Saddler? You don't take good care of yourself, you know that?"

I got a bottle of whiskey out of the carpetbag. "I do all right," I said.

"No you don't," Pearl said. "You look all neglected. Come on now, let's see a big smile on that battered face of yours. This may be the last night of our lives, and I want to have fun. I want to have a bath and then we'll go dancing. Don't tell me you can't dance?"

She was crazy, that girl, but I liked her. Not being able to trust her didn't mean I couldn't like her. "I like to do my dancing lying down," I said. "I don't get as tired."

Happier than I'd ever seen her, Pearl dropped her clothes on the floor and came into my arms. "I'll never get tired of that kind of dancing," she said.

"Would you like it better if we had Laura here?" I asked her. "That was a good night we had, the three of us. You girls sure wore me out."

I didn't expect that to offend her, but it did. She snapped, "I'm not enough for you, is that it. In bed I'm the equal of two women. I'll show you!"

And show me she did. Once I got her clothes off and stretched her out on the bed, she went wild. She spread her legs as wide as she could until her cunt-lips showed pink. She was very young and had the energy to go with it. I got between her legs and was about to guide my cock into her when she grabbed it and did it herself. She was very wet and it went in all the way as smooth as melted butter.

We kissed while we fucked and she sucked on my tongue at the same time. Her girlish mouth was soft and sweet. Suddenly she tightened her cunt muscles, squeezing my cock. She tightened and let go, tightened and relaxed, catching me off guard every time she did it. It looked like she was trying to prove that she alone was enough to satisfy me. She closed her eyes as I went in and out of her. Her legs were locked around me, but they were high on my back, almost around my neck. Her ass was off the bed and I supported it with both hands. She was athletic, that girl. I was as excited as she was, the way we were doing it.

She lifted herself and she gave a little scream when she came. The come flowed out of her and wet my hands. To keep her ass from slipping off my hands I had to squeeze it tight. That made her come again and I came myself. There was no use trying to hold it back. This wild, horny young girl excited me so much I couldn't hold it back. My balls tightened up and I creamed with my cock pushed far into her. Then I let her ass down on the bed and she pulled my cock out of her and began to suck it. She didn't wipe it off first.

"I want to taste myself," she whispered. "I want to taste your come and my come." She smacked her lips as she sucked me. "It tastes so good. Sort of salty, but good."

She sucked me for a very long time, as if she couldn't get enough of it. It's easy to get hard all over again when you're sucked like that. I didn't mind if she sucked me till morning. The bed was soft and there was nobody to disturb us. Then she began to move her head back and forth and it was like I was fucking her in the mouth. She held her head steady and I began to do just that. Then she lay on her back with her head on the mattress and I moved up and really fucked her in the mouth. I came, and though I hadn't touched her cunt, she came too. For a farm couple we were pretty fancy fuckers. Finally we dropped off to sleep.

First thing in the morning, Pearl and I ate breakfast in a restaurant run by a fat woman with a mustache. Pearl looked pretty with her face shiny from soap and water, and I don't think anybody noticed the way her purse sagged from the weight of the stubby revolver in it.

After we got through eating we started for the bank. We got there at nine and it was a bank all right and not something the Pinkertons had thrown up as part of a trap. It was raw, red brick with the mortar showing white between the spaces. The big-lettered sign over the door proclaimed it to be the First Bank of Mansfield. There were green blinds and thick bars on the windows, and it was so new that there were brick chips and a dusting of wood shavings on the sidewalk out in front.

I tried the doorknob and found it locked. Then, to make it look good, I took out my silver watch, thumbed open the cover, and looked at it. Then I rattled the doorknob and called out in my farmer voice, "You folks open for business or not?" I rattled the doorknob again, louder this time. We stood and waited and after a minute or two a cranky-looking man with a bald head and a brocaded vest unlocked the door and glared at us. He glared at us before he saw how pretty Pearl was.

I beat him to the punch. "You open for business, mister? I was of a mind to start an account in your bank. My name's Rufus Ambrister and this is my lady, Edwina."

Edwina got a short bow from the banker. I guessed he was the manager. I knew he couldn't be a teller, not with that fine gray suit. "Sorry, folks, but we're not open for business yet. We're new, as you can see. Yes, sir, this is going to be the leading bank in town. Why don't you come back tomorrow and you'll be treated with every courtesy. Ask for me if you like. My name is Mr. Philpot."

"Getting set up, are you, Mr. Philpot?"

The banker sighed, a busy man carrying a heavy load. "There's so much to be done. Now, if you'll excuse me."

The door closed and the key turned in the lock. I had to dig my fingers into Pearl's arm to keep her from giggling as we walked away.

"I'll surely enjoy robbing that old fool," Pearl said.

I got the buckboard from the livery stable and we started out of town at a walk. Nobody took the slightest interest in us. Why should they? When you've seen one farm couple, you've seen them all. I didn't whip up the horses until we were out of sight of the town, and then I put them through their paces. After a few miles I slowed them to a walk after I decided that it wasn't seemly for a respectable looking couple to be traveling at such a pace.

Pearl hadn't said anything for a long time. Another half mile passed in silence. Then she turned on the box and laid her hand on my arm. "We could rob that bank all by ourselves. That banker knows what we look like and he'd let us in if we went back. At least he'd open the door. We could hold guns on him and everybody in there. We could gag and tie the tellers and make the manager do the talking. Why, I could even get behind one of the windows and look busy when they came in with the money. You could hold a gun on the manager from a crack in the door. That old fool would do exactly as you told him to. The minute the money is in the safe and the guards are gone, we just tie the manager and walk out of there. What do you think?"

"No dice," I said.

"Why couldn't it work? Who's going to be looking for a farmer and his wife?"

"We do it as planned. You're a bad girl, Pearl, and I want you to shut up before I get too tempted."

Pearl sulked prettily. "You're a fool, Saddler. You want

to know something else? You'll never get rich because you're a fool."

I grinned at her. "Then I'm a fool. Now will you shut up."

Pearl didn't give up so easily. "You could have me and the money. I'd be faithful to you, Saddler. I'd spread my legs for no man but you. No matter how tempted I was, I'd keep my legs together."

"Don't be so romantic," I said.

For a moment Pearl looked scared. "You won't tell the others what I said?"

"I never even heard you. You'll get your fair share like all the others."

But Pearl didn't trust anybody. "If you say a word, I'll say you brought up the idea. I'll say you tried to talk me into ditching the others. That'll get you shot, Saddler. Oh, why don't you go to hell!"

Crazy bitch or not, she was a pretty girl, and I find it hard to get mad at pretty girls. "Hell is where we're all headed, little sister. You and me and all the others!"

She stayed quiet for the rest of the journey. It was a good road and we made good time. Another ten miles and we turned off and headed into a stretch of low, bare hills. I caught the flash of field glasses when we left the road. In a few minutes we were there.

"Hot damn!" Cassidy whooped when I told him about the bank.

"It's the genuine article," I said. "Even talked to the manager and he said they were opening in the morning. Come on now, we better get going if we're going to beat that train to town."

It took no time to get saddled up. I watered the horses and we headed back toward town. Cassidy and the others gave us a good start and before long we were back on the outskirts of Mansfield. We went to the livery stable to put the buckboard away, and then we headed for the bank again. My watch said it was ten minutes to one.

The same cranky man opened the door when I banged

on the glass panel. At first he just pulled back the lace curtains and shook his head. I kept pointing at the ground, at a place he couldn't see from inside. He kept shaking his head and I kept pointing. His face got red with exasperation, but finally he yanked the door open.

Pearl smiled her sweetest smile, but this time it didn't work.

"Folks," the banker said. "Didn't I tell you this morning the bank isn't open yet. Now what is it you want? I'm a very busy man. I have a bank to open, or have you forgotten?"

Crowding in close, I dug my gun in his fat gut. "You just opened," I said. "Now walk in ahead of us like nothing's happening. My lady here will see to the door. Walk on now and be talking and laughing while you do it. Say something businesslike."

Behind the brass cages three tellers were stacking papers and doing other bank work. They looked up in surprise when the manager came in with us behind him. I pushed the banker away from me and covered them with my gun. Pearl got her own gun out after she locked the door.

"Go around and see if they have any guns," I told her.

Pearl, holding the stubby revolver, went from cage to cage. "No guns," she called out. Then to make sure, she made them take off their coats. "No guns," she repeated.

The manager tried a bluff. "This is crazy! There's no money here, not a cent."

I pointed to the door of the manager's office and told Pearl to take the three tellers in there. Taking rawhide thongs from her bag, she herded them inside. I walked the manager over to the door so I could be sure she was tying them tight.

Pearl finished with the rawhide, and then she gagged them and put them on the floor. In the distance we heard the blast of a steam whistle; the train would be pulling into the depot in a few minutes.

Pearl came out and took off her sunbonnet and dusted

off her clothes. "Do I look like a bank teller?" she asked me.

"I'd give you money anytime," I said. Then I turned to the manager, who looked about to collapse from fright. "Mister," I said. "I'll kill you if I have to. I don't want to, but I will. I know the money shipment will be here soon and how much. Now, it's not your money, so why die for it?"

"Why indeed!" he said, sweating like a pig.

"Good," I said. "I like a man with sense. So here's what we do. I'll be in your office with the door open a crack. I can see you and the vault from there. Do anything—anything at all—and I'll kill you with a bullet through the head. Dive for the floor and you'll be dead before you get there. No matter who dies, you die first."

"I don't want to die, first or last. Just take the money and let me live."

"You'll live if you're smart. When they knock you let them in. They'll come in with the money, you open the safe, sign a receipt for the money. If they want to hang around and talk a while, then let them talk. Don't rush them out and, for Christ's sake, stop shaking. You'll be all right. Think of all the years ahead of you."

The banker mopped his face and took a deep breath. "You won't get any trouble from me. You mind if I sit down?"

"Sit and wait," I said.

I stuck the gun in my waistband and covered it with my coat. Then I went to the windows to make sure nobody could see in. I checked the door, too. Down at the other end of town the train was clanging its way into the depot. I looked at my watch: the train was right on time, and I figured they'd be there with the money in about ten minutes.

When five minutes had passed since the train pulled in, I said, "Time to open the rear door."

"Anything you want," he said. He was the most cooperative banker I'd ever met in my life.

I marched him down a hallway with storerooms on both sides. At the end of it was a heavy oak door banded with hoop iron. It had a drop bar and a lock. I lifted up the drop bar and he unlocked the door with a big key. I pulled the door open and there was Cassidy grinning like mad.

"Nice to see you, Saddler," he said, ever the clown. Harry Tracy was behind him. So were Kilpatrick, Curry, Etta, and all of the others. I let them in and closed the door, turned the key in the lock and left it there.

"Where are the horses, Butch?"

"In a cottonwood grove right outside town. Old Butch is looking after them."

"Get in the office and keep quiet," I said. "Pearl and I will handle it. Don't come out till I make sure the law is gone. I'll tell you when."

Tracy looked at me, but didn't say anything. He and the others followed Butch into the manager's office. The banker sat behind one of the tellers' cages, but didn't look too bad. I guess he was thinking of home and family.

Pearl turned, "I think I hear them coming." I shook my fist at her and she turned back to her ledgers. But she was right: they were coming. I watched the manager through two inches of open door. I felt Cassidy's breath on my neck and elbowed him away. Knuckles rapped on the glass panel of the door and the manager jumped with fright. But then he took a deep breath, straightened his cravat, and called out, "I'm coming!"

Before he opened the door he lifted the shade and looked out. "All right! All right!" he called out in a brisk voice. I liked that manager for being so sensible. He unlocked the door and four hard-looking men with stars on their chests came in. Two of them carried big canvas moneysacks. The other deputies, carrying sawed-off shotguns, backed in after them.

I pegged the toughest-looking badge toter to be the marshal. He carried a rifle. "Here it is," he said, pointing the men with the moneysacks in the direction of the huge vault built into the wall in back of the tellers' cages. "Nothing happened on the train, nothing happened at all. I don't know, but they must have been warned. Maybe they were too scared. The moneybags are still sealed, as you can see. Thought for a minute they'd try to get at us on the way here. Nothing!"

"Thank God!" the banker said. He turned and went to the vault with the marshal behind him. The banker spun the dials quickly, then yanked down on the handle, and the massive steel door opened silently on oiled hinges. The banker turned. "Just set the bags down in there. On the floor is all right. I'll get to it later."

The two deputies came out of the vault and stood waiting. The banker shut the door with a soft thud and spun the dials. Then he tried the handle. It didn't budge.

"That's a corker, ain't it," the marshal remarked. "To blow a thing like that you'd need an awful lot of dynamite."

"Dynamite wouldn't work," the manager said, playing out his role. "All that dynamite would do is jam the lock, then no one would get it open."

The banker took out his handkerchief and dabbed at his face. The marshal laughed. "Makes you nervous, hey, Mr. Philpot? Don't blame you one bit. Just getting it here from the train made me nervous. But I guess it's safe enough where it is. If that's all you need, I'll be getting home to eat. I guess I can eat now that it's over."

"Thanks, Marshal," the banker said fervently.

At the door the marshal turned. "If Cassidy tries to rob a bank in this town we'll be ready for him. My deputies are the best there is."

The banker nodded and nodded. "Everything's all right," he said, and locked the door behind them. I left the office door half-closed when I came out to check the street. The marshal and his five deputies were walking away.

"It's all right to come out," I told Cassidy.

I steered the banker toward the vault. Cassidy and the others watched as he spun the dials and opened the vault again. Pearl had cleared everything off the long counter that ran behind the tellers' cages. Butch broke the seal on the first sack and dumped the money out on the counter. Some of it fell on the floor. God! You never saw so much money in your life. Sundance lifted the other bag and emptied it. I stood behind Harry Tracy while they were doing it. Butch started to count and Tracy objected to that.

"Let somebody else count it," he growled.

"He's right," I said. "Let Pearl and Etta count it. Kilpatrick and Curry can band it when it's ready."

"Suits me," Tracy said.

I watched Tracy instead of the money because with a madman like that there was no telling what he might do. All it would take was one gunshot to bring the whole town down on us, and I was not of a mind to face those shotgun deputies. A trickle of sweat ran down the back of Tracy's thick neck. He sensed me watching him and turned. I traded hard looks with him before he gave his attention back to the stacks of bills.

The counting went on and on, and no matter how fast they worked it still took time, for there is no quick way to parcel out $100,000 in bills no larger than fifties. Etta and Pearl pushed the stacks of bills along to Curry and Kilpatrick, who slipped rubber bands around them. Everybody was sweating, including me. The door handle rattled and everybody froze. They stayed that way while I went to the door with my gun in my hand and looked out by the edge of the blind. An old man in a rusty black suit stood there chewing his lip. After a while, muttering to himself, he went away.

"It's nothing," I said. "Keep going."

Each time one of the women slid a stack of bills along the counter I knew it was getting closer to the end—the end of everything. I could sense the killing lust as it built up in Tracy. The hulking son-of-a-bitch was so close to getting everything he ever wanted: leadership of the Wild Bunch, and more money than he knew existed. The horses were waiting down in the cottonwood grove, but that didn't mean much. The real trouble would start once the money was shared out. Butch was sure about Curry and Kilpatrick. I wasn't sure of anything. I'd said it all along—Tracy was the one to get—but Cassidy wouldn't listen to me. The crazy bastard still thought he could walk hand in hand with death, then just walk away before it got a firm grip on him.

The tension fairly crackled as the two women started on the last batch of money. Etta had been making notes on a sheet of paper. "One hundred thousand dollars to the penny," she said. "That's it."

"Pass it out, ladies," Cassidy said. "One bundle to a customer. Step right up, folks, and get what's rightfully yours."

And that's what they did. One after another they took their bundles of $6,000 and stuffed them in their pockets or inside their shirts. Some grinned, some didn't. Ben Kilpatrick nodded at Cassidy. "You played it straight, Butch, and I'm obliged to you."

Harry Tracy was stepping forward to get his bundle when I pulled my gun and slammed him across the back of the neck. Cassidy's gun came out like a flash, and so did the Kid's. I had to hit Tracy three times before he went down. I let him fall on his face. Cassidy and the Kid had the rest of them covered. Etta yanked her gun and covered Pearl.

"What're you pointing that thing at me for?" Pearl complained. "I wasn't going to side with Tracy. He's lost, hasn't he?"

For an instant there was silence as we moved apart. Ben Kilpatrick was dark-faced with anger, and I knew he was going to draw even if it got him killed. Curry was just as mad.

"You lousy bastard," Kilpatrick rasped at Cassidy, his hand swinging close to his holster. "You planned it this way all along. They said you were a son-of-a-bitch, but I didn't want to believe them. They were right all the time."

I had given Cassidy the chance to get the drop on Tracy. But that didn't mean I was going to let him rob the straight-shooters who had been with him for a long time. I knew Cassidy was tempted to do just that. I moved over beside Kilpatrick and Curry.

I said, "Tracy's out cold so that gives you a start on him. I say let the rest of the boys take their share and go their own way. If Tracy wants to follow along when he wakes up, then you'll have to deal with him."

Cassidy stared at me as if I'd gone mad. "Saddler, we could split the hundred thousand four ways. Me, Etta, you and Harry."

"I didn't hit Tracy for the money. Put the gun away or start shooting."

Butch scratched his head with his left hand. "Aw, shit! It's only money." Butch put his gun away and grinned at Kilpatrick. He got a grin in exchange. Butch held out his hand and Kilpatrick took it.

"Of all the fools!" Etta said.

"You said it right," Pearl agreed.

"Get on with the sharing," Cassidy said.

One by one, the men got their money and went out the back door. Finally there were only five of us left; six, if you counted Harry Tracy, lying on the floor.

Cassidy went over and kicked Tracy in the ribs. "I think I'll be sorry if I don't kill him. I could knife him. It'd be quiet. But I just can't do it, Saddler. No matter what you hear, I never killed a man in cold blood."

"Then kill him in hot blood when he comes after us. If the Pinkertons don't get him, that's what he'll do," I said.

TWELVE

When we got back to the cottonwood grove we met the original Butch Cassidy, bearded and peg-legged, not knowing what was going to happen next.

"I stayed, Butch," he quavered. "All the rest of them took off, but I stayed. You're going to take me with you, ain't you? You'll always need somebody to look after the horses."

Cassidy patted the old man on the shoulder. "You're going to get us out of this country, oldtimer. Some of our own boys will be coming after us. Our own boys and the Pinks will be chasing us to hell and gone."

"I'll get you out," the old man said. "You can depend on me, Butch."

Butch shoved Harry Tracy's six thousand dollars at the old man. "Here! Buy yourself a cigar."

The old man's eyes popped at the sight of all that money. "Holy Christ! I'm a rich man. Let's be going now before they start throwing lead at us."

We mounted up and rode out wide and circled the

town. It looked like we still had a jump on them. The old man pointed toward the mountains to the west. "That's how we'll do it. Go clear across the mountains and down into Nevada. After that it's California and you can get into Mexico from there."

"You mean to cross those mountains?" Cassidy said. "That's worse country than where the Hole is."

"No other way to do it," the old man said. "But I'll get you across, and after I do I'm going back to the Hole in the Wall. Yes, sir."

"You plan to go back in there?"

"You just made me rich," the old man said. "I'm going back to the Hole with every damn thing I need for the rest of my life, which ain't going to be long, but I mean to enjoy it. I'm going to pack in a whole mule train of supplies. Grub, guns, a saloonful of whiskey. Two saloons. Then I'm going to blow that dynamite so no living man can disturb my peace."

We rode all that day and far into the night. Before us the foothills lay jagged and broken. I couldn't see if we were following any particular trail, but the old man seemed to know exactly where he was going. A few hours earlier we had heard something like a cannon going off. It sounded more like a cannon than dynamite. Then a little later we heard it again.

We made cold camp on the lower mountain. As high up as we were the glow of even a small fire would have been seen from a long way off. A cold moon sailed across the sky and the peaks seemed to climb right up to the top of the world.

We took turns standing watch, then moved on again before first light. The country got wilder and at one bad place we had to lead our horses along a ledge that dropped down hundreds of feet. The mountains seemed to go on forever, one long range following another. The old man was up ahead of us, stopping now and then to shade his eyes with his hat.

"You sure he knows where he's going?" I asked Cassidy.

"He ought to," Cassidy said. "In the old days he prospected all through these mountains."

I shrugged. What I didn't say was that men get old and their memories go bad. But we were there and had to make the best of it. By now we were two days out from Mansfield, and there wasn't a sign of pursuit. But these mountains were so rugged that they might have been no more than a mile 'or two behind us; with the wind blowing so hard, no dust would be seen.

Now we were rounding the highest of the peaks, cutting through ravines that seemed to have no end. The old man turned in his saddle and pointed. "About forty more miles will take us down from here. That's when we start hitting the desert. Soon as we get to the top of that next high ridge we'll stop a while."

I looked back and saw nothing. Not a thing moved out there in that rocky wilderness. We got to the top of the ridge and took our horses down to the safe side of it. Then, flat on our bellies, we scanned the country behind us. An hour passed and nothing happened, but the old man said we'd best wait a while longer.

We had been there for more than two hours when I saw the first of them coming up out of the deep ravine we had come through earlier. The distance was too great for any accurate shooting, but I was able to make out the great bulk of Harry Tracy astride his horse. I counted six other men and I could just make them out. Tracy had recruited Fallon and Reeves, the Gundersen brothers and Tom O'Day. Tracy rode in the lead, looking at the sign we had left.

"What do you think?" Cassidy said to me.

"We can hold them here for a time," I said. "But if Tracy can pick up our sign the Pinkertons can do the same with him. The Pinkertons will have a lot more men than Tracy."

"Saddler's right," the old man said. "We'll still be trading lead with them when the Pinks show up. We can't beat a whole big posse of Pinks. It looks like we'll have to find the right place to finish Tracy for good."

"It better be before the desert," I said. "You got any ideas?"

The old man pulled at his beard. "There's a place that might do. Two ravines run along a distance from each other. It's kind of hard to see the first one because of all the brush. If they come riding at us full tilt they'll drop like stones. Course if they don't we'll be in for a real fight."

"Then it's off we go," Cassidy said, running down the slope and vaulting into the saddle.

Everybody got down the slope at a fast clip, then Pearl's horse stumbled and broke a leg. Pearl jumped to her feet cursing like a mule skinner. Without thinking she yanked her gun to shoot the horse. I rode right down on top of her and kicked the gun from her hand. Then I reached down and grabbed her by the back of the belt and threw her across my saddle.

She kicked and screamed so hard I felt like dumping her off. In a minute it wouldn't have mattered if she had shot the pony because Tracy's men heard the commotion on the far side of the ridge. They hadn't opened up yet because there was nothing to shoot at. That would come in a minute. I could hear them yelling from a long way back.

We still had cover when we crossed the next low ridge, but they were coming fast. Butch and the others had a good start on me, with the old man leading the way. From the second ridge there was a long downhill run for about a quarter of a mile. I turned to look back, but I couldn't see them. Below me I saw the old man leading the others to a narrow place in the first ravine. They jumped their horses across. I followed on down hoping I could get across before Tracy got close. If they caught on about the brush-screened ravine the ambush wouldn't work.

"Hold still, you damned fool," I snapped at Pearl. "You're going to get us killed."

I aimed my horse at the narrow place in the ravine. My

horse was carrying double, but at least Pearl was light. I had to risk a fairly wide jump with a double load. I urged my horse to do his damnedest. That deep, narrow ravine came at me like Judgment Day. Then up and over we went, the brush whipping at my horse's legs. His forefeet touched earth and we were safely across. Up ahead Butch was yelling at me to get a move on. Then he skidded his horse down into the second ravine. I made it there and if my horse hadn't been so sure-footed we might have been killed or crushed as we went sliding down in a shower of sand and shale.

Once the noise stopped we heard them coming, hard, desperate men with blood in their eyes, thinking of all the money that was getting away. Yelling, they came down the slope at a reckless pace. We lay along the lip of the ravine with our rifles ready. It was all pure gamble. If they spotted the trap we'd be in for a hell of a fight, and that would finish us if the Pinkertons showed up in the middle of it. There was no hard evidence that the Pinkertons were on our trail, but we figured they would be. Those boys knew how to narrow things down because that was their business. If we hadn't gone out the other ways, then we just had to be heading west.

Butch yelled his excitement when Tracy tried to turn his hard-running horse before it plunged over the edge of the first ravine. But he was riding too hard and the horse went over screaming in panic. We opened fire as he did. Some of the others dropped and some went over with their horses. Fallon managed to skid his horse to a stop. I shot him. Butch shot Reeves, who managed to throw himself from the saddle.

Everybody was dead except Tracy and O'Day. There was no sign of O'Day. I wondered where Tracy was when suddenly I saw him come charging up from the side of the ravine. The son-of-a-bitch came charging at us like a maddened grizzly. We all fired at him at the same time, but he was running fast and I don't think he was hit. I've seen that happen—a whole lot of lead thrown at one man and none of it doing any harm. I followed Tracy's run and fired. He threw up his hands and fell. He didn't get up. I turned my rifle away from Tracy and fired at a man who stuck his head up from the ravine. I was squeezing the trigger when I recognized the walrus face of Tom O'Day. The bullet from my rifle blew away a chunk of his head.

Cassidy whipped off his hat and used it to shade his eyes. I had better eyes than Cassidy and didn't need any hat. Far back I saw a bunch of riders coming hell for leather.

"Pinks!" Butch yelled, and like the rest of us he scrambled to get out of there. Once again I had to put Pearl up in front. This time she didn't fight it.

We ran, heading downhill, straight down into the desert shimmering blue-gray in the heat miles away. Already the sun was hotter, but that was just the beginning. There sure were a lot of Pinkertons. I didn't stop to count how many. There were enough of them to do for the lot of us. These were the slate-eyed men who hunted and killed other men for a living. They killed men the way undertakers build coffins. Mercy had no meaning for them, and they would kill a wild sixteen-year-old rustler as readily as a bloody-handed murderer.

We were scrambling into a scatter of rocks and mountain juniper when the Pinkertons opened fire. It sounded like a small army had opened up with rifles and handguns. Unless we got awful lucky my criminal career wasn't going to last much longer, I thought. I was part of Cassidy's gang, like it or not. I gave no thought that the Pinkertons were in the right, and we in the wrong. I would kill Pinkertons to keep from going to jail for 30 years. After all, I was the feller who fronted the robbery for Cassidy. I had talked my way into that bank. I could just about hear the bank manager and the tellers testifying at my trial, if I lived that long. Jesus! I'd be lucky if I didn't get hanged.

Thinking of the rope, I urged my horse to greater

speed. There wasn't much shooting now, but they were following fast. We had a start, but I wasn't sure it would do us much good. We had run a good two miles from the place of ambush and were dropping down fast to the desert. So far we had a small edge on the Pinkertons, the only consolation being that they had been traveling just as hard as we had.

Along about now they would know they hadn't killed Cassidy or Sundance, always the main targets of their hate. We could scatter the stolen money around, every dollar of it, and that wouldn't slow their pursuit or cool their fierce determination. From what I knew of the Pinkertons they wouldn't hesitate to leave all that money behind if it meant getting Cassidy, who was the one badman they hadn't been able to catch or kill. Bringing him in dead or alive would be invaluable advertising. If they could catch Butch Cassidy they could catch anybody.

This was their best chance, the best they'd ever had; now they had him far away from his natural haunts. Butch had always relied on his knowledge of the wild country north of Jackson Hole and on his impregnable hideout. Near the Hole in the Wall he could outfox and outrun them. But here in the desert he was just another hunted man.

"What now?" Butch asked the old man. He didn't sound mad at anybody, but for a change he wasn't grinning. I think Butch saw the end drawing near for the first time in his reckless life.

The old man pointed out toward the gray wasteland in front of us. I guess he thought Butch's question was a dumb one. So did I.

"What nothing!" the old man answered. "Out there is where we have to go. It'll be as hard on them as it will be on us."

"That's a great help," Butch said. "What about water? It's running low."

The old man said, "There's—there used to be—a

waterhole about twenty miles from here. Maybe it's still there."

"Be hell if it ain't," Butch said. "If it is there we'll fill up, let the horses drink as much as they can, then choke it with sand."

Pearl asked, "And after that?"

Butch shrugged. "First we find the hole. Come on now, they'll be able to see us pretty soon."

Cassidy was right. A rifleshot rang out before we had gone more than three miles. I looked back and could see them bunched up on top of a bare brown hill in the distance. It was still too far to count and I didn't try. Half their number would have been enough to put an end to us. I wondered how well the women would stand up to the desert. I'm never one to downgrade the toughness or determination of women, but if the women caved in on us, our force would number three men and one peg-legged old man who might know the country all right, but was no kind of hard case. So, in the end, that left three men against a whole mess of Pinkertons. I hoped I'd be wrong about the women.

I had to have mercy on my horse, so I got down and kept up with the rest of them as best I could. That wasn't so hard because you can't push a horse, any horse, in desert country. If you do, you end up with a dead horse. Butch and Sundance just looked at me. Both were big men and they couldn't add Pearl's weight to their own. Etta was light and could have shared her mount, but she didn't.

After another hour it didn't matter much. The horses, bred in Wyoming, weren't used to the desert heat and it was beginning to show. Come to think of it, apart from me, none of the other humans there had had much truck with the desert. Once upon a time the original Butch Cassidy might have been something of a desert rat. A long time before, that is.

"You better all climb down or you'll walk all the way to California. If you get there at all," I said.

Butch, the ex-cowpuncher, didn't like the idea of walking. "This is a good strong horse, Saddler."

I said, "Not for this country. Right now the horse looks all right, but you're using up strength maybe you'll need later. The old man should get down while we're in stony desert where he can manage with the peg leg. Do what I tell you, Butch. This is more my kind of country than yours."

They climbed down when they saw the sense of it. The old man clumped along as best he could, now and then getting into difficulties when he ran into a patch of sand. I let Pearl lead my horse and walked with the old man. He glared sideways at me, mad because he thought he was the one who should have told them about the horses.

"What's beyond the waterhole?" I asked him.

"What do you think? More desert is what there is."

I told him to answer the question straight. "If the waterhole is there and we fill it in, how far is the next one?"

The old man said, "If the waterhole is there it won't take much filling in. It never was much of a hole, in the best of times. How far is the next one? Maybe another thirty miles. Saddler, if the first one ain't there, we ain't going to make it to the second."

The old man quickened his pace to get away from me and I began to figure things. A waterhole in the desert, when it existed at all, took a long time to fill. Of course there were the exceptions, but this didn't sound like one of them. A bad hole, or a weak hole as the oldtimers called it, might take days to fill up with a few inches of water. I was betting that if we could dry up the first hole, the Pinkertons would have to turn back toward the mountains. There wouldn't be a whole lot to gain by that. Still, there might be some water in the mountains if they looked hard enough. For us, we didn't even have that much choice. If the first hole proved dry or sanded over, then we were dead.

THIRTEEN

I dropped back to tell Cassidy what I was thinking and he scoffed at the idea that the hated Pinkertons would give up the chase. Maybe his pride was injured.

"You don't know them bastards. They're this close to killing me," he said, measuring off a space between his thumb and forefinger. "You think they're going to quit now? The fuckers always have everything they need— latest guns, special trains, private telegraph lines. How do you know they don't have all the water they need? If they filled enough canteens, they'll have all the water they can drink."

"Water is weight," I said. "They couldn't have been sure you were in the mountains. And maybe they didn't think it would get this far."

Butch scowled. "They won't turn back," he said. "I'm the one they want. You said that yourself, Saddler."

"They're just men," I said. "They work for wages. There's a difference between doing a job and dying for it."

Butch turned to scan the desert behind us. "I can't see

154

them, but I know they're coming. They must be a long way back."

I shook my head. "Not so far back. The heat shimmers are hiding them right now. You may see them close enough when the day begins to cool."

Butch looked away from me. "They won't quit," he repeated, and after that I couldn't get any more talk out of him.

We moved on through the worst heat of the day. There wasn't enough distance between us and the Pinkertons to allow us to rest. I knew Butch was wrong about the Pinkertons having all that extra water. I had been in desert country half my life and never knew anyone to carry enough water. You can't load a horse with canteens. Hang enough canteens on a horse and you have the weight of a small man or a large boy.

Toward mid-afternoon we had to cross a stretch of sandy desert and the old man had to mount up because his peg leg kept bogging down with every step he took. After that the worst part came when we had to climb high gypsum dunes that rolled away like breakers on the sea. It took some doing to get over to the other side, and when we got there rocky desert started again. The heat was bad, but not nearly as bad as it had been. There was a hot stillness in the air as the sun began to go down. The desert wind stopped blowing as it always does at that time of day. After the sun went down it would blow up again, and as darkness settled in it would start to get cold.

Now and then, as the day cooled, I looked back. There was still no sign of our pursuers. I was looking back for the third time when I saw them. The image was that of a lot of men and horses bobbing in a cracked mirror. Maybe they were five miles back. Guesses don't count for much in the desert, where nothing you see is for sure until it's right on top of you. But they looked like they were mounted up, pushing their horses now that the worst of the day's heat was over.

"How far to the waterhole?" I asked the old man.

"Maybe three miles, give or take," he said.

"Everybody get mounted," I said. "We're going to make a run for it. They're coming right up on us."

Everybody's head jerked around but mine. I vaulted up behind Pearl and set my tired horse to running as best he could. Not riding the horses had paid off and we struck out across the rocky desert at a fair clip. We had given most of the remaining water to the horses an hour before. Even so, I didn't think we could get much more than three miles out of them. After a while it seemed as if we had gone more than three miles. I was wondering if the old man's memory had failed him, or if the hole was sanded over. What had once been a waterhole might now be a hill of sand. I yelled at the old man and he said to look for a red rock sticking up out of the ground. I tell you my heart jumped in my chest when I saw it off to the right. It looked like a monument somebody had placed there.

I jumped down and ran for the red rock, the others behind me. The old man stayed with the horses. And then, by Christ, there it was—a shallow pool of dark-colored water. I lay beside it panting and scooped up a handful and tasted it. It was warm and brackish, but it was safe. In a minute we all lay beside it drinking and filling canteens. Pearl was guzzling and I pulled her away. "That's enough. Everybody has had enough. Let the horses drain the rest."

Good with horses, even mine, the old man led them to the hole and let them drink. After days of short supply they greedily sucked it up. I stared into the gathering darkness trying to see our pursuers. I couldn't be sure if I saw a shape or not. The horses were down to licking wet mud when the old man pulled them away and we started kicking sand into the hole. Suddenly I heard them coming, horse hoofs tearing across hardpan.

When the hole was covered, completely sanded over, Butch was jubilant. "Come ahead, you bastards. If you can get a drink out of that I'll kiss your shitty asses."

"Get moving and keep moving," I yelled, throwing Pearl up in front of me as gunfire ripped the evening quiet. Cassidy began to return their fire and I yelled at him to quit. He fired off two more shots before he holstered his pistol and took off after the rest of us. Bullets chased us, but it was too dark for proper aim. Refreshed by water, the horses responded well, and gradually we drew away from the Pinkertons. The shooting stopped as we put distance between us. The night was getting cool as the wind blew up after sunset.

The horses were starting to labor again, and I yelled at Cassidy to go easy. We all reined in and listened. The only sound was the wind.

"The bastards! The dirty bastards!" Cassidy yelled. "You were right, Saddler! They don't have water or they'd be right after us!"

Nudging my horse again, I said, "They may have some water, more than we had. They may follow us for a while. We'll keep on going and see what happens. Go easy on the water. Save it for the daytime. Come morning we'll know what kind of a chance we have."

It turned out to be a brilliant, starry night. The light of the stars seemed to become more brilliant as we traveled on across the desert. In that cold light you could see for miles. Nothing moved out there. The wind blew colder and Pearl shivered in front of me. It got past midnight and we kept moving. Nothing happened. I wasn't sure whether the Pinkertons turned back when they found the waterhole dry. They might have been hanging back just far enough so we couldn't see them.

By the time red painted the sky we were ready to drop. We spilled water in our hats and watered the horses. Now that the sun was coming up I could see a line of jagged mountains in the distance. We were still in desert country, but its nature had changed. Behind us had been nothing but rock and sand. Now there was some vegetation: yucca, barrel cactus, creosote. The desert flowers were bright in the morning light. There was no sign of the

Pinkertons. To make sure, I climbed a tall rock and lay on top of it, watching. I came back to where the others lay in the shade of a barrel cactus, taking careful sips of water from their canteens. Even though the horses had been watered, they drooped with fatigue.

"How's it look?" Cassidy asked.

"So far nothing," I said. "They may still come, but they have to rest and so do we. We'd best stay here until the sun is past the noon mark." Pearl had fallen asleep with her hat over her face. Etta had the bright-eyed look that often disguises exhaustion. The Sundance Kid asked me if I wanted him to take the first watch. I said I'd take it; he should get some sleep.

It was beginning to get hot. The barrel cactus provided some shade, but in an hour the desert would be boiling again. A few minutes later everybody was asleep, their faces and clothes coated with alkali dust. The horses twitched in the shadow cast by the cactus.

Maybe it was going to be all right, I thought. If the Pinkertons had quit the chase all we would have to face, at least for now, was the hardship of the long journey to California. That didn't mean we might not have to face other agency men when we got there. But this was the here and now and California was later. As soon as we got out of the Nevada desert—if we did—I was going to cut loose from Cassidy and head south to Texas. I might even drift on down to Mexico and lay low until the stolen bank money was gone. In a few months there wouldn't be much to connect me to the Wild Bunch.

I sat in the shade of the big rock and watched the desert behind and thought of cold beer and hot women. It was hot enough, so I thought mostly of beer—good, dark Mexican beer in bottles right off the ice. You could get ice-cold beer even in Mexico if you went to the right places. Hell! I thought. The beer didn't even have to be cold just as long as it was wet. You get such thoughts in the desert. It would be good to walk into a dark, cool cantina, then watch while the bartender uncorked the first bottle. Then when it was ready you could hold it in your hand for a while. The foam would begin to settle, but you always blew a little off because it was something you always did.

Suddenly I was jerked out of my daydream. Something was moving a long way out. Something black moved against the white of the sand and then it was gone. I blinked and waited for it to move again, but nothing happened. It had to be a man because nothing but men moved in the heat of the day. I watched for signs of dust and saw none. I saw nothing, yet it had been there a moment before. One thing was sure. It was no posse.

I gave it a few more minutes before I slid out from the shadow of the rock and woke Cassidy. The Kid woke up when he heard us talking.

"What is it?" the Kid asked.

Butch rubbed at his dusty eyelids. "Saddler thinks he saw something."

"I saw it," I said. "Not the whole posse, more like one man. It was like he stepped out from behind a big cactus, then hid himself again."

"Makes no sense," Butch complained. "If the rest quit, why would one man keep coming?"

I had no quick answer for that. "I'm just telling you what I saw. You've had an hour's rest, so we'd better move on."

Butch said all right, but first he climbed up on the rock and lay on its baking surface, studying our back trail. He came down.

"The heat's getting to you," he said. "There's nothing in the world to be seen."

I walked toward my horse, spilled water into my hat and let my horse drink. I drank a little myself. "You say there's nothing there. Fine! You stay and go back to sleep. I'll be moving on."

Butch looked doubtful. "You been right a lot lately, so maybe you're right about this. You think the main party has sent one man ahead to scout us?"

I didn't know what to think. "It could be that, but I don't think so. Why would such a large force hang back? If they have water it would make more sense for them to surround us, wait us out. Then we could choose surrender or suicide."

"Suicide is all they'll ever get from me, besides a bullet in their heads," Butch said.

I woke the others and we headed out, right at the time of day we should have been resting in the shade. Etta looked sullen but said nothing. We led the horses and went as fast as the worn-down condition of the animals allowed. That wasn't a lot. We weren't in as bad a shape as the animals. Just the same, we were getting there. Pearl started to look more like a kid than at anytime since I'd seen her—a pretty kid who had strayed into bad company and was wondering what she was going to do next.

I dropped back for a while but saw nothing. The sidewinders were smarter than we were. They were under rocks. So was everything else. I caught up to the others and told them my findings.

"See! I told you," Butch said, trying to grin in spite of his blackened lips. "All you done is ruin our rest, Saddler." He held up his hand. "All right, for Christ's sake! We'll do it your way for now, but I tell you they ain't coming."

"Somebody is," I answered.

"You're pretty sure of that?"

"Pretty sure."

Butch didn't like what he couldn't explain, or couldn't see. Men of reckless courage are often like that. So long as it's something they can kill they aren't the least bit afraid of it.

"You think some old desert rat is waiting for us to die so he can steal our guns and saddles?" Butch asked.

"White men don't live in this kind of desert. What you call desert rats don't wander that far from water."

Butch frowned in bewilderment. "Some crazy Injun cast out by his tribe?"

"The same answer as before," I told him. "Nobody lives in country like this."

Butch exploded into anger. "Goddamn it, Saddler! You're the one said the Pinks have turned back."

By then my own temper was just as edgy. I had a bad feeling about what I had seen. I couldn't explain it either. As I had told Cassidy, the Pinkertons were just detective agency operatives who worked for wages. They wanted Cassidy, but they wouldn't die to get him—or the reward money. It was a strict agency rule that none of them could accept or claim rewards of any kind. They got bonus money when they did a good job—that was all they got.

"Go to hell, Cassidy," I said. "If you want to find out so bad, why don't you start back the way we came? Do that and I guarantee you'll find out for sure. You're the big, tough desperado who's afraid of nothing. Why don't you start back?"

The Kid eased his way into the argument before we could trade any blows, not that either one of us was in shape for fisticuffs. I'll say this for the Kid, he always stayed cool.

"Best thing to do is find a place with a clear field of fire behind it," he said. "A bunch of rocks to give us elevation. Then if whoever he is shows up, we'll nail him with our long guns."

I nodded agreement: I had been thinking the same thing before Cassidy started running off at the mouth. We still had water, not a lot of it, but we weren't dying yet. We would lie in wait and see what we could see. But even as I thought about it the bad feeling came to me again. When you have faced danger for most of your life you develop a sense of it. And in my experience, that sense of danger was wrong only when it wasn't strong enough. Right then it was very strong. So strong it was close to being a smell. It's not crazy to say that. Danger, real danger, has a smell.

"We'll do it when we find the right place," I said. A few miles ahead a pile of great rocks stood up from the floor of the desert. Between where we were and the rocks there was nothing except low creosote bushes. "Even if he crawls we'll be able to see him from there."

Etta spoke for the first time. She stared at me with dark eyes. "Unless he comes in the night," she said.

That had been another of my thoughts, one I didn't like. We could move on through the night, but so could the man who was tracking us. We could move on until we were too tired to walk another step.

We made our way to the line of rocks and went past them, and when we were out of sight we turned the horses back into what shade we could find. The women and the old man stayed with the horses while we eased our way up into the rocks, which were blistering hot to the touch. I could feel the water draining out of me in blobs of sweat. The rocks gave us good cover because we were as gray as they were. We took up our positions, rifles ready, and waited. The sun beat down on us and still we waited.

"You see anything?" Butch asked.

I'd never met a man who found it so hard to be quiet. Instead of speaking, I shook my head. Butch was counting on our rifles to get the job done. I wasn't. A man ready to face the desert alone wasn't likely to be foolish. More than a little crazy, yes, but not foolish.

I felt like hell because I hadn't had any sleep at all, not that the others had had very much either. Fine sand blew in the hot wind. I hate everything in the desert, but I hated that stinging sand most of all. You can be all muffled up and still feel it gritting against your skin. It clogs your nose and burns your eyes. You wonder what you're doing in such a godblasted place.

Far out in front of the rocks a clump of barrel cactus provided the closest cover. The man following us could be in there by now. We all had Winchesters, long guns that wouldn't shoot that far. He would have to get closer if we had any chance of killing him.

Then we all saw the black shape and our rifles jerked to

our shoulders. I think he wanted us to see him. Just the shape of a single man beyond rifle range. He didn't have a horse. He stood for an instant, then disappeared behind the cactus.

"He's coming," Butch whispered. A split second later a heavy caliber bullet splintered rock close to his head. Butch cursed as the rock slivers cut his face. Blood ran down his face.

"No, he's not," I said. The man tracking us was carrying a long-range rifle. Suddenly I knew who he was, or thought I did. "He'll be along, but not right now."

Sundance nodded. "You're right," he said. "That's Tom Horn out there."

Butch just gaped. "That's crazy," he said. "You're both crazy. That's just some Pinkerton with a big rifle. A lot of them carry big rifles. Mickey Dwyer from Denver always brought along a Buffalo Sharps on his big jobs. I ought to know. He shot at me with it one time. Damn near killed me with that cannon. I was hiding behind a barn door. You'd think a door that thick would stop any bullet. Like hell! Mickey knew I was in there and let fly with the Buffalo Sharps. Those big bullets tore right on through and came close to cutting me in two."

"Mickey Dwyer's been dead for two years," the Kid said quietly. "The Banner boys killed him in Leadville, Colorado."

"All right, Mickey Dwyer's dead. What about Mendoza, that foreigner with the waxed mustache? He's been known to carry a big English rifle. They use them for shooting elephants or something of that nature. Why couldn't it be Mendoza?"

"You don't keep up with things," the Kid said. "Mendoza keeps to the Chicago office these days."

"Then who the fuck is it?" Butch didn't seem to want to come up with the obvious answer. He knew who it was, but he didn't want to face it.

For that matter, neither did I.

FOURTEEN

"It has to be Tom Horn," I said, keeping my head well down. "You told me the Pinkertons were trying to hire him back. There he is in the flesh. They must have rushed him to Mansfield by special train right after the robbery. Or maybe he was already on his way."

Cassidy's face took on a strange look. The thing he feared most—maybe the only thing—had finally happened. The most feared tracker in the West was after him. The man who never gave up was on his trail. I didn't feel any better about it. Tom Horn was a merciless killer, but he was a lot more than that. He was about the best scout and hunter the army ever had. His reputation as a Pinkerton agent was known to every outlaw in the West. Far from being a regular Pinkerton operative, he worked by none of the rules set down by the agency. He broke all the rules and they let him break them because he was the best. Tom Horn was the best at everything— and now the Pinkertons had him back. So the bad feeling in my gut hadn't been wrong.

We were in a standoff, but the standoff was all to Horn's advantage. Over the years he had trained himself to endure hardships that would kill the toughest Apache. They said he could go for days without food or water. Well, of course the going for days without water was just dumb talk. Every man has to have water, if only a little. I guessed Horn needed very little. It was said that he didn't drink or smoke, and that figured. We had done nothing lately but lie around in the Hole in the Wall soaking up whiskey and eating a lot of heavy, greasy food.

The Kid said quietly, "Horn must have been the one who figured we'd go across the mountains. That's how the posse got on us so fast."

I nodded. "He led the posse in, but he didn't need them. All the time he was fixing to work alone."

"The way he always does," the Kid said. "He thinks we won't get out of the desert. That's why he left his horse behind with the others. You think we're going to get out of this desert, Saddler?"

"Maybe," I said. "It's time to move on." I turned on my back on the safe side of the rock and pointed to the country ahead. The desert out that way wasn't flat anymore. As it ran toward the mountains it was broken and rocky. There would be some cover there for us—and for Horn.

Butch said, "If he gets here before we make the next cover he can pick us off with the long-range rifle. If he has a scope on that rifle he can fix us like a pin. What do you want to do?"

"I'm for moving on," I said. "If we go now maybe he'll hang back just long enough. He's got a lot of ground to cover between there and here. Three Winchesters could get him quick if he gets close enough. I'm betting he'll wait awhile."

"Let's go then," Cassidy said. "But if he moves out sooner he'll have us cold."

What was there to say? It was possible that Horn could

165

head for the rocks at a dead run. If he got there fast enough, we'd be fish in a barrel.

We slid down from the rocks and got the others started away from there. Pearl quivered with excitement when she heard Horn's name. Etta's eyes got that death look again. Etta was beginning to spook me with that look. I got the feeling that she was ready to welcome death with open arms.

"Walk the horses fast as you can," I said. "If he sees dust I'm still betting he'll hang back. We could be leaving one or two behind to cover our back trail."

We moved out with all the energy of people going to be hanged. We were tired people with tired horses, and with a relentless killer not more than a mile behind us. Not far from where we started, the old man fell and snapped his peg leg in two. He lay in the blistering sand and kicked at Cassidy with his good leg as Cassidy tried to lift him. He kicked with the stump, too.

"Leave me be," the old man groaned. "I can't go on now, no matter what you do."

"Come on now!" Butch tried again and got a kick that sent him staggering.

The old man gave a cry that was more a sob than a shout. He closed his eyes and reached out his hands, the fingers trembling. "Kill me, Butch. Horn uses the knife on men when he takes them alive."

I didn't know about that. Maybe Horn used a knife when he needed to get information. Eyes still shut tight, the old man reached out again.

"A last good turn for an old friend, Butch. Kill me now!"

Cassidy's face twitched. His hand reached for his beltgun, then dropped away. I got between Cassidy and the old man. Valuable time was being used up. I drew my gun and cocked it. Pearl looked away, but Etta didn't. The old man's body stiffened at the sound of the pistol being cocked.

"God bless you, Butch!" he moaned.

I shot him in the head. One bullet was all it took.

We moved on, expecting to get one of Horn's bullets in the back at any moment, and when one finally came we were just about out of range. Horn fired just once. The bullet missed me by a foot. Horn didn't fire again. He was testing the range.

Just before we made it to the next cover I looked back and Horn was standing up high in plain sight on top of the rocks we had left. He was a real showman, that feller. I guess he was crazy, but like I said, he wasn't foolish. Among the lot of us we didn't have a gun that could reach him.

Throughout the long day we moved like that, always finding cover just in time. My guess was that Horn wasn't trying all that hard. I guess for him there was no special hurry. We were like a boxer in a losing fight. Still game but still losing. Every time we showed fight he knocked us off balance one more time. Maybe he was even enjoying himself. For the natural-born hunter the chase can be more important than the kill. Of course it was that goddamned big rifle that gave him the edge. That long range made all the difference. It could reach out and kill at 500 yards in the hands of a man who knew how to use it. I couldn't tell what kind of rifle he was using. It could be the biggest caliber Sharps they made, or a Remington hunter. Or even one of the new Schuyztens. It didn't matter much, so long as he had it.

I looked up at the sky. It was beginning to darken and the wind was rising. The sand blew harder in our faces. All the signs were there—we were in for a sandstorm, a big blow. It started before we reached the next cover, but it would be a while before it gusted up to full force.

Staggering against the force of the wind, I yelled at Cassidy. "Head for cover and dig in best you can." I grabbed my saddle blanket and shook it out. It flapped in the rising wind.

Ducking his head, Cassidy yelled back at me. "What the hell are you going to do?"

I fought to get the blanket under control. "Dig in here. Go on now."

"But you're only halfway to cover," Butch yelled through the bandanna that covered his mouth.

"Halfway to Horn's rifle," I yelled back. "If he doesn't spot me, this will get me close enough. Get out of here, Butch. Get the hell out of here."

"You're crazy," Cassidy yelled, but he did what he was told. The wind blew him about as he followed the others. Soon he was lost in the blowing sand.

The sun darkened over as the fury of the sandstorm increased. It glowed dull red through the sand-filled sky. Then there was no longer any light. Bracing myself against the gale, I wrapped myself and my rifle in the blanket and lay down in the sand. The wind blew harder, howling like a demon, and I could feel the sand piling on top of me. I sucked in sand and air until black spots danced in front of my closed eyes. The storm howled on for I don't know how long. In a sandstorm all sense of time is lost. At times you think you're dead.

Maybe the storm lasted for an hour. All I knew was that I was encased in sand. The wind began to lose its force, and it was time to get set before the storm blew away completely. I was taking one hell of a chance, but I didn't know what else to do. If I didn't stop Horn, he was going to stop us.

I had to be careful not to disturb too much of the sand that covered me. I moved the blanket carefully so I could get at my rifle. It was loaded, the muzzle plugged with a rag. I wasn't sure it would shoot. I guessed that I'd know pretty soon.

Keeping the muzzle plugged, I scooped sand from the pile in front of me. I hoped I looked like just another hump of wind-shifted sand. As the storm blew itself out, I was able to see the last cover we had left, a bunch of cactus and rock. In a few minutes the wind died and the sun came out in all its rage.

Nothing happened for a while, and I felt like a man in

an oven. If Horn didn't kill me, the heat would finish me before another hour had passed. I don't think I was sweating anymore, and that's the worst thing that can happen in the desert. My strength was going fast and if I didn't get water soon I wouldn't have the energy to pull the trigger. I had to force myself to keep watching our last cover.

Tom Horn came out in the open. I was close enough to make out a fairly slight man, not even tall, holding a big rifle. I was close enough to see him pretty well. He was close enough to kill me at will if he spotted me. For a moment I thought he was looking my way. Maybe his wary eyes were just moving about. Then I realized he was looking past me, staring at the place where he knew the others had to be holed up.

I unplugged the muzzle of my rifle as Horn began to do the same thing. My fingers quivered as I cleared the muzzle. A shell was in the chamber ready to be fired if the mechanism wasn't fouled. The sunglare burned my eyes and I was lightheaded. I sighted along the barrel, but Horn seemed to dance up and down. I just couldn't hold my aim steady. I tried again and then I fired.

Tom Horn dropped under the impact of the bullet. I think I hit him in the thigh. I raised my head, but couldn't see him. I jacked a shell and waited. Five minutes passed and I crawled out from under the weight of sand. If he wasn't finished, now was the time to do it.

I was raising up with the rifle when a bullet touched the lobe of my left ear. I fired back at nothing and dropped to the sand. Another bullet sang at me, spattering sand in my eyes. I waited, but there was no firing after that. I thought I'd hit him, but maybe I hadn't. A man like Horn would throw himself flat at the sound of a bullet. It could be he had done that, yet there was something in the way he had dropped—the suddenness of it—that convinced me that he'd been hit.

I lay there expecting to get a bullet. Staying still was my only chance of survival. Minutes dragged by and he fired again, but the shot was way off. I knew then that he had to be wounded, to shoot like that. But wounded or not, he had cover and I had none. There was no way I could crawl up on him. If I crawled close enough, he could brace the rifle and blow me apart.

Staring at the place where Horn was, I thought my eyes were dimming out when I realized that it was getting dark. The sand in front of me was turning a red color. I waited for more bullets. None came as dark descended on the desert. When it got dark enough I started to crawl the other way.

I don't know how I made it to where Cassidy and the others were. I was fairly close when a loading lever clacked. Other gun noises came after the first one. I raised my head from the sand and told them not to kill me. What I said came out as a croak.

"Jesus Christ, it's Saddler," Cassidy said, only a burly shape in the darkness to me. Just as I lost consciousness, I felt myself being dragged and I think I heard Pearl's girlish voice.

A wet bandanna on my face woke me up. Water trickled into my mouth and I coughed. First light was showing in the eastern sky and the desert was peaceful and cold. It was so cold I shivered though I was covered by blankets. Butch and the others were huddled around me, silent in their misery. The Kid was up on the rock with his hat pulled low over his eyes. He didn't take his eyes away from where he was watching.

Pearl trickled more water in my mouth, then Butch lifted my head and Pearl let me drink my fill. "We thought you were going to die," she said.

"What in hell happened?" Butch asked. "We was going to go back and get you."

I was able to talk better then. I must have sounded like a rusty hinge, but the words came out all right. "I'm sure I hit him in the thigh. I don't think he's faking. Any sign of him?" Butch shook his head. "Harry's been up on the rock since it got light. No sign."

Butch helped me to sit up. Pearl gave me more water until I told her to stopper the canteen. There couldn't have been much water left.

"Then maybe he thinks we're gone," I said. "Wounded he may be. Just don't count on him being dead. I didn't shoot so good."

Butch dusted sand off me until I told him to stop it. "We've got to get to the next waterhole," I said. Butch and Pearl got me to my feet. "If he's wounded there's a chance he'll die there."

"Amen to that," Cassidy said. He squeezed my arm. "Goddamn it's good to see you, Saddler. Holy Christ! I'm looking at the man that shot Tom Horn!"

"Maybe the man that shot at Tom Horn. A lot of men have shot at Tom Horn. Let's be off."

The Kid said he'd stay behind and give us cover in case Horn hadn't been hit. Nobody argued because Horn had more tricks than a carnival magician. Besides, I wasn't able to travel very fast and Butch had to support me a good part of the way. We were resting in the shade of a barrel cactus when the Kid caught up to us. We all waited for the bad news.

Instead, the Kid grinned. "Not a sign of him," he said, unstoppering his canteen and allowing himself a small drink. "Whatever else he's doing, Tom Horn isn't walking around today. I watched good and he didn't show an inch of himself. I'm beginning to cheer up, ladies and gentlemen."

"Don't get too cheerful," I said.

Butch glared at me. "There you go again, Saddler. Always looking on the dark side of things. What the hell, what am I saying! You did it, you Texas son of a bitch. You stopped Tom Horn dead in his tracks. Anyway— wounded him if he's not dead."

Butch dragged himself to his feet. Some of his old cockiness had returned. "On to California," he said, yanking me to my feet. "We still got the money and we still got our health."

It was only about five miles to the next waterhole. The old man had described it as "a good un." It was only five miles away, but in the condition I was in it might have been fifty. More than rest I needed water, an awful lot of water, because the hours under the blanket in the sun had just about drained the life out of me.

It took us half the day to travel those five miles. By early afternoon we could see the rocks that sheltered the waterhole from the ever-blowing sand. There was so much shade at the hole that the water was close to cool. The hole was deep and the water clear. Butch lay beside the hole and reached down with his hand.

"I can feel it coming in," he yelled. "You know what that means?"

Pearl filled a canteen and brought it to where I sat with my back against a rock. I drank until I couldn't drink any more. Then Pearl poured the rest of the water over my head. The horses drank until their bellies were swollen, then lay down in the shade. Now all the canteens were filled and stoppered and the hole was filling up again. Butch was standing guard and, without turning his head, he called out, "Not a sign of our friend, Mr. Horn."

I slept and when I woke up Etta was watching for Horn. I called up to her and she shook her head without turning it. Full of life-giving water, Pearl was beginning to swagger again, to regain her bad-kid jauntiness. There was so much water that she had washed her face and poured water over her short-cropped hair. I lay there wondering if this would be the last place I'd see on earth. Butch and I had talked about Horn, and we decided that it was best to take a chance and stay at the waterhole until people and horses were strong enough to travel again. There was some dried beef, so there was no danger of starvation.

We stayed at the waterhole for two days and Horn didn't show up. On the second morning Butch was in a cheerful, bloodthirsty mood and was all for going back to see if he could cut off Tom Horn's head. Pearl giggled but Etta looked disgusted.

"It's only five miles," Butch yelled in great good humor. "Nobody else has to go. I'll go myself. I want to express that head to the Pinks, from the first town we come to. I have a yearning to express that bastard's head—salt it first, of course—all the way to Chicago. 'Dear Mr. Pinkerton: I think you lost something so I'm sending it back. I know we can't never be friends, but here's hoping you will think more kindly of me in the future. Yours truly, Butch Cassidy.' What do you think of that, ladies and gents?"

Etta glared at him. "I think you're losing your mind. What mind you have left. You're turning into a savage, Cassidy. That's the most disgusting thing I ever heard of in my life."

Pearl just giggled.

It was pretty disgusting, but I wasn't as high-toned as Etta, the ex-schoolmarm. So I grinned. Damn! It was good to be alive.

"That's a dumb idea," I said, grinning. "Besides, it wouldn't look like Horn by the time the head reached Chicago. Maybe we got lucky with Horn. That remains to be seen. But I don't think he'll be coming after us."

The Sundance Kid called down from the guard position. "I vote no on that head business too."

I had finished filling my canteens and was ready to go. "You're out-voted, Butch. Now everybody drink till you leak and we'll be on our way." I pointed toward the mountains in the distance. "California starts on the other side."

Butch looked disappointed at not being able to express Tom Horn's head to Chicago, but he accepted the majority decision. "Horn may be just wounded. But if he's wounded he'll die. Out here he will."

"There's a good chance of it," I said. "But we can't get careless and we can't slow down too much."

We moved out toward the mountains. All the next day

we led the horses to save their strength. In time the desert gave way to arid country, still hard and dry but nothing like the blistering hell we had come through. In the clear, dry air you could see the mountains from a long way off. On the far side of those mountains lay northern California, good, green country full of lakes and well-watered valleys. The plan at present was for Cassidy, Sundance and Etta to make their way to San Francisco, and from there to go by ship to Central or South America.

Pearl decided she was coming with me. That part had been agreed on long since, though it hadn't been put into words. I knew taking her with me might be a mistake. What the hell! I'd made mistakes before. Anyway, she had no place with Butch and the others. Etta was a two-man woman and Pearl wouldn't fit in.

In slow stages, Pearl and I drifted down to Texas, and from there to Mexico, to lay low for a bit. I wasn't too worried about the Pinkertons. I never did see any wanted posters on us, not that far south. We lived high for as long as the money lasted, which wasn't all that long. After a few months we found ourselves back in Texas, and with the money gone it was back to gambling for me. Pearl kept at me to teach her how to play poker, and I did my best to show her how. I tried hard, but it didn't pan out. Poker is like no other card game, and it takes a certain temperament to be good at it. Pearl didn't have it. She giggled when she was winning and pouted when she wasn't. And as we all know, that is no way for a gambler to be. It got so that the other players could read her like a book, and she lost more than I won. I always made enough for us to get by on, no matter how much she lost. That wasn't the problem. The problem was Pearl. The wildness in her could never be quenched.

Toward the end—we were in El Paso—she got restless and spoke of going back into the bandit business. Pearl had a lot of ideas. One of them was to go East and rob banks that hadn't been robbed before. She urged me to go along, but I had to say no. I had robbed one bank and gotten away with it. I wasn't about to press my luck. Besides, I prefer poker.

I knew she wanted to take off for parts unknown, and I didn't try to stop her. One night I came back to the hotel after a two-day poker game and she was gone. She didn't even leave a note. Maybe by this time she's married, with kids, and lives in a rose-covered cottage. But I wouldn't bet a dime on it.

Tom Horn, limping badly, got hanged up north for murdering a twelve-year-old boy. Some kind of bush-whacking job for a few dollars. Old Tom said he thought he was back-shooting the boy's father. He kept saying that until he dangled.

All this happened to me a long time ago in Wyoming and other places. And don't ever ask me how I like piano music or you're likely to get shot.

YUKON RIDE

ONE

The knocking on the door grew louder, more insistent, and I got out of bed in a hurry.

"I thought you said your husband was in Alaska," I said to the naked woman who had been under me for most of the night. She was beautiful as well as naked, and I hated to leave that bed, so sweet and smelling of perfume and clean sweat.

"He *is* in Alaska," she whispered. "Perhaps they'll just go away." Cynthia used to say "maybe" when I knew her in the Colorado mining camps. Now it was "perhaps." Why not? She was the lady of the manor.

"Doesn't sound like it," I said, grabbing my shirt and pants.

"Mrs. Slocum," a voice called. It was followed by more knocking. "Mrs. Slocum, I have a telegraph message for you. The Western Union boy said it was most urgent."

I took refuge in the bathroom while Cynthia Slocum

5

slipped on a quilted robe. An empty whiskey bottle and two glasses stood on a bedside table, and she put them in a drawer before she unlocked the door.

The butler's name was Travers and he was a real Englishman. Nothing but the best for good old Cynthia, who had parlayed her beauty and bed knowledge into one of the finest mansions on Nob Hill. But for my money she was a lot more of a lady that most of the old society biddies who tore into her behind her back.

Travers sniffed the bedroom air with that long beak of his, and there was no way he couldn't have known there was a man in there. I guess Cynthia entertained a lot and all her gentlemen callers came up the back stairs after dark. I had done just that the night before.

For a girl who was dragged up in a Colorado mining town Cynthia can be haughty when she wants to be. Like I said, she was a real true-blue lady no matter how many times she spread her legs.

"Yes, Travers, what is it?" she demanded, gathering the robe around her.

Servants are worse snobs than the people they work for, and I could see that old Travers dearly longed to make some snotty remark. But he had a good job and he knew it.

The old bastard had a Western Union envelope on a silver tray and he held it out to her. His eyes flicked toward the bathroom and he knew I was watching him through a crack in the door.

"Will there be anything else, madam?" he asked, deadpan as an Indian.

"Judge Slocum is dead," Cynthia said. "I'll ring for you if I need you."

"May I tender my deepest regrets?" Travers said.

Cynthia nodded him out of the room and locked the door. I came out of the bathroom tucking in my shirt. Rain pattered on the windows—it rains a lot in San

Francisco in the fall—as Cynthia sat on the edge of the rumpled bed holding the message from Western Union.

"Phineas died a month ago on the Alaska-Yukon border," she said. "I told him, other people told him he was too old for that hard country. But you know Phineas."

I didn't know Phineas Slocum and didn't want to. What I knew most about him was that he was known as the harshest federal judge in the West before he retired from the bench. In some ways he was like Hanging Judge Isaac Parker of Fort Smith, Arkansas; and if he wasn't quite as bloodthirsty as Parker, he came a close second. He bullied juries into guilty verdicts, and handed out death sentences and life terms like free beer at a picnic. In recent years he had become enormously rich speculating in mines, lumber, and cattle.

"You feel bad about it?" I asked.

"Not bad enough to cry," she said. "I know people hated him, but he always treated me alright. The whole Slocum family cried bloody murder when he said he was going to marry me. After we got married, never once did he mention what I'd been. That meant a lot to me. But I guess I never changed. You know how many men have been in this bed?"

"Your business," I said. "There's no use feeling guilty about it, if that's what you're thinking. You're a young woman, he was an old man."

"Thanks for telling me, Saddler. The funny thing, I think Phineas knew about my men, but never brought it up. We had an arrangement we never talked about. I needed what he couldn't give me and he accepted that. I was a good wife in my way. At least I tried to be discreet."

"Sure," I said.

"Don't say 'sure' like that. You know, the only reason he stopped being a judge was me. He said he was tired of

7

it. I knew better. After all, how would it look, a federal judge married to a fallen woman?"

"Drop it," I said. "What else does the telegraph say?"

"They want to know what to do with the body. Phineas died at a mining camp called Dulcimer, but the message was sent from Dawson. Now Western Union says the wires are down between Dawson and Skagway. Listen, Saddler, I have to get his body back so he can be buried with the rest of the family. I owe him that much. Will you do it?"

I guess my mouth hung open for a minute. "You want me to go all the way to the Alaska-Yukon border? You have any idea how far that is? It's fall here but it's nearly winter there. The rivers'll be frozen solid, the passes blocked with snow. Not much moves up there in winter."

"But you've been up there, haven't you?"

"I was there in the army and didn't like it. There must be men willing to sled the body to the coast. After that it's just a boat ride."

"Western Union says nobody wants to take the job. There may be other reasons besides winter. Phineas was far from popular. A lot of men hated him."

I looked at her sitting there with the robe half open. There was a lot to see when you looked at Cynthia.

"I didn't hate him. I didn't know him," I said. "I just don't want to go to the Far North."

Her gray eyes turned a trifle hard. Cynthia might be a lady now, but she hadn't forgotten the lessons of the mining camps. She could be tough.

"You owe me a few things," she said. "Like the time I staked you to that big poker game in Leadville. You were busted, flat broke, down in your luck. I hate to say that."

"You're saying it," I said.

She looked away from me. "I know I am. All right. Forget about old times and all that bullshit. Name your

8

price and I'll pay it. What do you say to five thousand?"

I shrugged. "That's a lot of money."

"Double that, make it ten," she said angrily. "I told you to forget the old days. We're talking money here."

"I wasn't trying to up the price," I said.

"I don't care what you were trying to do. I want my husband's body back. So don't act like a shit-kicker. Will you do it, or not?"

"Why me? For ten thousand you should be able to find men here in Frisco."

"I can find men but can I trust them? What's to stop them from taking the money and heading for the hills? What's to stop them from going to Alaska, then changing their minds? Or saying the job just can't be done?"

"Maybe it can't," I said, but at the same time I was thinking about the ten thousand. By trade I'm a gambler and lately the cards had been running kind of cold. They have a way of doing that no matter how good you are at the gaming tables. When that happens all you can do is wait out your streak of bad luck. Still and all, hauling dead bodies down frozen rivers and over icy mountain passes wasn't quite my line of work.

"You can do it, Saddler," Cynthia urged. "You'll do it if you say you'll do it. You'll do your best, and that's all that matters to me. Don't tell me you can't use the money. Hell! The wild way you live, you're broke half the time. Be a friend, Saddler. Do it for me."

Well, I couldn't say she hadn't been good to me in the past. In bed and out of it. Of course, our paths didn't cross all that often—the West is a big place—but when we did meet we were always glad of it. Now we were in Frisco, arguing about a corpse.

"How soon do you want me to start?" I asked her.

"Not right this minute," she said, letting the robe fall from her shoulders and holding out her arms. "Poor Phineas won't get any deader than he is, and you'll be gone a long time. I'll be good to you now and when you come back."

I knew she wasn't thinking about money, and neither was I. Getting back between her legs for the rest of the morning was my only interest, and if you think that wasn't altogether respectful to the dead judge, you may be right. On the other hand, the judge was dead—left out to freeze solid, I figured—and we were very much alive. And if Cynthia felt any lingering grief for the dear departed, it didn't show in her face when I drove into her and she wrapped her legs around the small of my back.

What Cynthia doesn't know about wild sex you could fit into a thimble and still have room to spare. Her cunt was sweet and hot, and I thought with gut-wrenching regret how much I was going to miss it on the miserable, dangerous journey I faced in the wilds of Alaska. Getting in there at the start of winter was going to be bad enough. How I planned to get the judge's body was a thought I hadn't even rolled around in my mind. In the years since I left my hometown, Jonesboro, West Texas, I had taken part in many foolhardy enterprises, but this one beat all. The more I thought about it, the more inclined I was to finish my fuck, kiss Cynthia goodbye and head back south where it's warm. Up north it's a nice day when it warms up to freezing; it's country fit only for gold-crazed madmen, and while I could understand some of their craziness, I've always preferred to make my money indoors, with a bottle and a cigarillo and maybe a thick steak close at hand.

Yet I knew I wasn't going to run out on Cynthia. I had given my word and I was going to keep it. Most men of honor are a pain in the ass, and although I am somewhat less than honorable at times, especially in my dealings with women, there are things that have to be done, no matter how dumb they seem. Under me Cynthia was bucking like a wild thing, and I had to do everything I could to hold her down. You would need a chalk and blackboard to check off all the men she had been in bed with, but the nice thing about her was that she never got tired of it, never got enough. Or if she got enough, it didn't last very long.

"Oh Saddler, I'm going to miss you so much," Cynthia cried out, climbing up to her orgasm. "I'll be thinking of you out there on the trail. I won't know what to do."

"You'll figure something," I said.

There were beads of sweat along her hairline and she gripped me hard. "That's a lousy thing to say. I swear I'll miss you like crazy." Her nails raked my back.

I grinned into her face. "You're going to miss me so much, why don't you come along? We could bundle up on the snowy nights. It's not like you haven't camped out before this."

Cynthia didn't answer until she had shuddered herself to satisfaction. Then she sighed and said, "Not lately I haven't. I wouldn't be any good on the trail, Saddler. I'd just slow you down. Anyway, it wouldn't be right: you and me snuggled up warm and the judge cold in his coffin."

Once again common sense warned me to get the hell out of there. Cynthia must have read my thoughts, because she ground her crotch into me, arguing with the best part of her. As usual, that's the one argument I have no defense against, and I held her steady while I shot my load deep inside her. She came again when she felt me coming—I like women who respond so generously—and after that we lay side by side, not saying anything.

From the grille in the floor came the soft, whooshing sound of forced hot air. It was warm as toast in the big comfortable room, and I could have stayed there for a dog's age, or at least until I got tired of Cynthia, or she tired of me. Fog from the bay drifted against the windows; the rain had stopped. It can get cold in San

11

Francisco in the fall, but it's nothing compared to Alaska.

"I'm going to have a lot of money," Cynthia said. "Think of all the things we can do when you come back."

"It's going to be a long time," I said. "Months."

Cynthia kissed my ear. "I'll be right here waiting, Saddler. It'll be winter then and we can go some place where the sun shines all the time. Down south there's a new resort called Palm Springs where rich people go. There's a big new hotel and it's hot by day and cool at night."

I made one last try to get out of going to Alaska in winter. "How about this for an idea," I said, putting my hand between her legs. "We'll go to Palm Springs now and I'll go fetch the judge in the spring. The rivers will be thawed by then, and I can take the judge back by steamboat. In the spring the judge can have a real nice funeral. Flowers and everything. What do you think?"

Cynthia stroked my stubbly chin. "I think we should have a bath and you a shave. We've been at this since yesterday and we're starting to smell a little gamey."

I couldn't deny that, and a nice hot soapy bath with a good looking woman is always a pleasure, but there was something about her determination to recover the judge's body that bothered me. The old man was dead, and in the bitter Alaska cold the corpse would keep forever, so why not wait for spring? It made sense. Or at least it made sense to me.

I asked her why not.

The huge bathtub was filling with water and she was sprinkling bath salts into it. In the bathroom the steam from the tub condensed on the frosted window and trickled down. The faucets that filled the tub looked like solid gold; none of that plated junk. Everything in Cynthia's house spelled money, the bathroom no less than any of the other rooms.

"Why the big hurry?" I said again.

"Because I want my husband's body back now. Why are you going on with this, Saddler?"

"Because I think you want to get the judge's body back for some other reason. Not just to bury him with his family. I don't care what your reasons are. Just tell me what I'm getting into."

Cynthia tested the water with her toe before she got in, and before she answered she soaped a gold-backed brush and gave her shoulders a few strokes. There was plenty of gold in the Slocum mansion, plenty more in the bank. I was thinking that the return of the dead man's body had everything to do with gold.

"The reason, some of the reason is money. I want him to have a proper funeral, but the money *is* important." Cynthia said at last. "My husband is dead in Alaska, I don't know how many thousands of miles from here. It's possible that if I don't get him back—to bury him—the family will say he isn't dead at all. I know his will leaves everything to me. They don't like that. There was no love lost between Phineas and his brothers, Bart and George. They'd like to contest the will, break it if they could. If Phineas's body stays up there all winter, God knows what will happen to it. No body, no final reading of the will—not for a long time. It could drag on for years."

I got into the tub with her and she gave me the brush so that I could scrub her back. "They'd have to make a settlement with you," I said. "What's wrong with that?"

Cynthia gave me a cold-eyed stare that I'd only seen a few times before. "I want it all, Saddler. Those bastard brothers hate my guts and would like to do me out of what's mine. You want to let them do that?"

I shook my head. I didn't know how mean, how greedy Phineas Slocum's brothers were, but I was thinking about it. Men will do anything for money—some men—and I was considering the idea that the only trouble I faced wasn't going to be ice and snow.

"Be honest," I said. "You've said that I owe you. All right, I do. Now you be straight with me. You think the Slocums will try to stop me? What are they like? Tell me that."

Cynthia turned on the hot water again and turned so I could get at the rest of her back. She groaned with pleasure as the soft bristles tickled her skin.

"Come on," I said.

"They're bad enough," Cynthia said. "Bart failed in business and George gambles and drinks. They keep big houses and can't afford them. Bart is the mean one, though. There's always been talk that he shipped escaped convicts from Australia. That was in the old days when his shipping line was going bust."

"Did this Bart ever run coast steamers to Alaska?" I was beginning to get interested in Bart Slocum. Any man who did business with Australian convicts, as bad a breed as there was, would know where to find gunmen. After the Gold Rush the Sydney Ducks, as the Australian thugs were called, had been the terror of San Francisco, and it took a lot of lynchings by the Vigilance Committee to chase them out.

Cynthia told me to face the other way so she could do my back. "Bart ran coast boats," she said. "But not any more. From here to Seattle, then on to Skagway. I don't think you have to worry about Bart. Not the way you mean. He's a year older than Phineas was. That makes him an old man."

"A little lower," I told her. "About Bart, a man doesn't get good just because he gets old. Nothing meaner than an old man. Nothing meaner than a poor old man. How does Bart get on with the other brother?"

"Not too good. Better than he got on with Phineas, I guess. You've got all these doubts, Saddler. Make up your mind. You going to Alaska or not?"

I got out of the tub although I hated to. But the longer I stayed, the more doubts I would have. Somehow Cynthia wasn't the same careless, good-hearted woman I had known back in Colorado. I wasn't sure how she had changed, but there was a foxiness about her that I didn't like. It had taken too many questions to pry the truth out of her, when all the time she could have just laid it on the line. I don't ever expect to get the whole truth from anyone—a woman least of all—but Cynthia and I went back a long way, and she could have made a stab at it.

"Well, are you going?" she said again.

"When I get ten thousand dollars—cash—and a picture of the judge, I'm going. I'd hate to travel all that way and come back with the body of some poor drunk that died behind a saloon. If your brother-in-law is as tricky as you think he is, he might try just that. Another thing. The ten thousand you give me is for bringing out the judge's body. Everything else is extra. The fare on the boat. Supplies. A dog sled and dogs. Whatever else. Agreed?"

"Agreed, you stingy son of a bitch." Cynthia began to towel herself dry. "I get the feeling that you don't like me any more, Saddler. Is that true?"

I grinned at her. We were getting it straight now. It wasn't true that I didn't like Cynthia. Not altogether true anyway. It would be hard not to like Cynthia. But I'd come close to losing my life because I liked and trusted people too much. That was in the past; it hadn't happened lately. You have to look out for yourself.

Seeing my grin, she flared into quick anger. "I'm better than you are, Saddler."

"Maybe so, but that isn't saying much. Now why don't you give me the money and the judge's picture and I'll be on my way."

"You don't have to like me to fuck me," Cynthia said, coming up close to me. "You know that's true, no matter what bad feeling has turned up between us. If you say no, there will come a time when you wish you said yes."

"I always say yes to a beautiful woman," I said. And we climbed back into bed for some friendly fucking.

TWO

That last session with Cynthia was so good I thought I would start for Alaska on my hands and knees. But as it turned out, I was in pretty good shape when I left the Slocum mansion with $12,000 and the judge's photograph in my pocket. We had agreed that I wouldn't see her again before I took a coast boat for Alaska. I went down the back stairs and was walking away from the bottom when something—I don't know what—made me look back at the house and I saw Travers staring at me from a third-floor window. He jerked his head back when he saw me looking, and when I looked again there was no sign of him.

I knew nothing about the departure times of the boats to Alaska. Neither did Cynthia. All I knew was they sailed from San Francisco, pulled in at Seattle, then went on to Skagway from there. I didn't know how long it would take me to book passage. It could be a day, it could be a week. The big gold rush of some years later hadn't started yet, but all of California and other parts of the country were getting all heated up about the recent gold strikes along the frozen creeks. The mines and creeks in northern California were all played out; the Far North was the coming thing, everybody said. It seemed that otherwise sensible men were selling all their worldly goods in a wild rush to get to the land of forty below. San Francisco, always a bustling town, bustled more than ever in that year. In the streets there was more excitement than there had been during the California gold rush of nearly forty years before. Everywhere there were posters tacked up by steamship companies, promising luxurious accomodations to the stupid or the unwary. All these companies guaranteed the same thing: a lot for a little. None of the steamship posters stated there were gold nuggets to be found in the streets. But all suggested that the gold-seeking pilgrim had only to dig a little.

There was a drift of mankind toward the docks. Some women too. And I went along with it. There were dumb farmers with all the money they possessed sewn in the lining of their coats; discharged soldiers jostling with deserters; there were the runaway apprentices, whores, gamblers and shifty-eyed thieves. All hoping to get to Alaska, where all a man had to do was buy a shovel to get rich.

The first place I tried to buy a ticket north was the Columbia Inland Passage Company, and when I elbowed my way to the ticket window a sallow man with a waxed mustache laughed at me for my foolishness, saying I must be new in town to think I could get to Alaska just like that. I pushed a hundred-dollar bill across the counter and told him that wasn't part of the fare. It took another hundred on top of the fare, before he said he could get something for me, and he smiled so nicely when he said it that I wanted to break his jaw.

"Steamer sails noon tomorrow," the ticket-seller said.

"Name is the *Falmouth*. What's the name . . . sir?"

I gave him my right name. Why not? I wasn't going to Alaska to rob a bank.

After I got my ticket, I went to look for a place to stay the night. It wasn't that hard because everybody was pulling out of town. I got a fairly clean room in a hotel down by the Embarcadero, and after I paid the room clerk in advance on my way upstairs, a dish-faced youngster came into the lobby, hawking the evening edition of the *Chronicle*.

The kid was yelling the news about the death of Judge Slocum, and after I bought a copy there was my own name right under the judge's. At least the newspaper didn't have a picture of me, and for that I was thankful, but there was more about me than I wished to see, and more than I wished other people to see. At first I thought of that sneaky butler Travers when I saw the story. But then I decided that the story might have come from someone else. According to the newspaper, the judge was a very important man in San Francisco. The paper said he had been a stern but eminently fair jurist, and would be mourned by all. I had my doubts about the last part, but I read on, and what I read I didn't like one bit. The story in the *Chronicle* said too much about me: it said what I looked like, how old I was. It said I was going to Alaska to bring the judge's body back. So it looked like it was Travers, after all.

I had sold my horse, but I still had my single-action Colt .44 and Winchester. Upstairs, I lay on the bed and, with the Colt close to my right hand, I read what there was left to say about Phineas Slocum. There was some information, a lot of it, about Phineas Slocum's career as a judge of military tribunals during the Civil War and after it. I smiled at the rubbish about Cynthia—the beautiful bitch. The newspaper said she was the only daughter of a mine-owner in Colorado. I liked that part best of all: the closest Cynthia had come to mining was fleecing miners of their pokes. I didn't like what was written about me. I was too well described. Maybe the whole thing was just newspaper guff, and I would have liked to believe that, but I didn't. My outermost thought was to pick up the judge's frozen corpse and deliver it to San Francisco, and yet there remained the suspicion that I'd been had.

I kept the Colt handy during the night, but not one thing happened, except there was a lot of noise from drunks coming in late. A whole bunch of them must have clung together and fallen down the stairs. When it happened—whatever it was—it sounded like a wagon falling to the bottom of a cliff.

After that it was quiet.

During the night I didn't sleep so well, but by morning there had been no attempt to murder me, and so when I got up at first light I didn't feel too bad and was hungry. It was foggy and I heard boats hooting in the harbor.

Downstairs a grim-faced Chinaman who ran a restaurant complained in Chinese as he fried a steak for me with two eggs on top. I ate the steak and eggs and thought of Cynthia sleeping in her warm bed, which is where I should have been. Or maybe not asleep but just thinking of money. Or fucking some other man—maybe.

After I finished a second cup of the Chinaman's bad coffee, I walked down to the docks to make sure the steamer hadn't sailed without me, for it was well known that now and then the shipping companies sold more tickets than they had room for passengers. But the *Falmouth* was still there, and so was a burly man with a Winchester lever-action shotgun who waved me off when I tried to come on board.

"You got to wait till the purser gets back from the whorehouse," the watchman growled, then went back to scratching under his armpit.

Well, I wasn't about to argue with a 10-gauge repeating shotgun. A few blasts of that thing and there wouldn't be enough left of me to make a sandwich.

All along the dock there were people gawking at the ships; the *Falmouth* got the most attention because it was the biggest and because it had brought half a ton of gold from up north. I guess a lot of people there didn't have the price of a ticket, or anything else, but the *Falmouth* was a link to the promised land.

Early though it was, all the dockside stores were open, and there were signs warning one and all to get their goldfield supplies while they lasted. Fur coats, sheep-lined boots, trousers with fur seats were selling as fast as the clerks could take in the money. So were sleeping bags, miners' tools, rifles, compasses and canned goods. I bought a fur coat, fur boots, a sleeping bag, a compass, and a pair of mittens.

I went to a saloon to drink beer until the boat sailed. Earlier it had been raining and the muddy-floored saloon had the musty smell of men in damp clothes. The air was full of tobacco smoke and talk of gold. Everybody in San Francisco talked of gold. One old man with a white beard and no teeth claimed to have been to Alaska and was bumming drinks on the strength of his experiences. His tales grew wilder as he knocked back beer and whiskey; after a while the faces of his listeners took on a doubtful look, but nobody went so far as to call the old gent a liar—they wanted to believe. A sailor from one of the Alaska ships came in and took all the attention away from the old man.

I was still at the bar when a man in a sack suit and a derby hat came in and stood next to me. He had quick eyes and a watch chain that probably had a good watch at the end of it. After he got a mug of beer, he turned and gave me a friendly nod.

"Going north, are you?" he said casually, one early

drinker to another. "Looks like the whole country is going up north."

"That's where I'm going," I said.

"Well, good luck to you," he said and went out without finishing his beer. That was all the conversation we had, but I got the feeling that he had been sizing me up, and maybe identifying me for somebody else. I knew who it was when I spotted a hard-faced man looking at me in the mirror, and when he saw me watching him he pretended to be checking if he needed a shave. He was dressed for the north, in a fur coat and a beaver hat, but he didn't look like a working man to me. Hardass was written all over him, but he had a capable look that said he wasn't just any gunman or skullbuster. His hands gave him away when he looked in the mirror and rubbed his chin. Real professional gunmen always take good care of their hands; some go so far as to rub them with corn oil to keep them supple. A good leather valise stood at his feet.

He opened his coat and picked up the bag with his left hand before he started to leave. I kept my back to the bar and waited for him to make his play, whatever it was. He stopped when he got to me. The way he pretended to recognize me wasn't very good, but he gave it a try.

"You're Jim Saddler, am I right?" he said, doing his best to smile, and that wasn't very good either. Whoever he was, he didn't have the face for it. He had the dead eyes of a man who killed for money.

"Do I know you?" I said. I knew I didn't.

"Guess you don't remember. Why should you? We weren't introduced." he said. "Ben Trask is my name and we sort of met down in El Paso. When I say 'met,' I mean you were in a big poker game and I was at the bar. You sure cleaned them out that night."

"Best way to play cards," I said.

"Never was that good at it myself," Trask said. "Buy

you a drink? I'm surprised the newspaper boys haven't been following you about. Saw a mention of you in yesterday's *Chronicle*."

The bartender gave us beers. "That damn thing," I said.

Trask said, "You really going to Alaska to bring back Judge Slocum's body? I thought maybe that was just something the *Chronicle* dreamed up."

I was inclined to tell him to go to hell, but you don't learn if you don't listen. "Mrs. Slocum hired me to bring it back."

"One Texas man to another, you may be in for more than you can handle."

"Don't doubt it. That's hard country up that way."

"I wasn't talking about the country."

I knew he wasn't. "What were you talking about, Trask?"

"The old judge was one of the most hated men in the country. Sent too many men to the gallows. Men that should have got jail got hung. Men that should have got five years got twenty-five. I wonder that old man wasn't shot long ago. Lord knows there were plenty of men wanted to do it."

I said, "Too late for that. They can't kill him twice."

Trask sipped his beer. Maybe he didn't drink at all, and I find it hard to like men like that.

"It's going to stick in a lot of craws if you bring the judge back to Frisco. I used to be a detective here and still hear a lot of things."

"Such as?"

"The judge wasn't just hard on small men. Here in Frisco some big politicians still hate his insides. Nine years ago there was a big graft scandal and he sent some big men to jail for a long time. A few of them are still behind the walls. What I hear is these big men don't want to see the judge honored. Too many old hates will get stirred up if you bring back that old man's body. Big men—small men too—want the judge left where he is. Gone and forgotten, is what they want."

It was ten o'clock and I was getting sick of Trask. "Sorry I'm going to have to disappoint them," I said. "They'll get used to the idea after they think about it."

"Might as well tell you the rest of it," Trask said. "The word I get is it could be dangerous for you to try. That's how determined these men are. I just don't like seeing another Texas man get shot for nothing."

"Not for nothing," I said. "I wouldn't do it for nothing. I'm obliged for you telling me all this business about the judge. Really appreciate it, one Texas man to another. What part of the state you from?"

"All over." Trask's eyes were completely dead.

"It's a big state," I said. "It's been nice talking to you, and maybe we'll meet up again."

"If you're sailing on the *Falmouth* we'll meet up all the time. I decided to try my luck in the goldfields. You might do worse, Saddler. That's good advice."

"Thanks again, but I already got a job. See you on board."

"Sure," Trask said, going out. He turned at the door. "There's not many places to hide on a boat."

Well, I could have provoked a fight, and probably killed him, but they don't like that kind of gun-work in Frisco. It was different in the old days when the gangs were running wild. All that came to an end when the Vigilance Committee started stringing up gunmen from balconies, telegraph posts and hay-hoists. That's gone too, but mindful of their bloodstained past, the citizens are very strong for law and order. And what the citizens want, the police and the courts provide.

Anyway, there was nothing to be gained by killing Trask; if they were out to stop me, there would be other Trasks. He had been fairly direct in the warning he gave me. Now the question was, who was behind it? The Slocum brothers might be pulling the strings, or indeed it might be possible that there were men who hated the dead man so much, that they wanted to deny him the honor of burial in his adopted city. That part of it I found hard to believe, not being a determined hater myself, and yet I'd heard of crazier things.

Men were hurrying down to the *Falmouth* dock when I left the saloon. Frisco might be a law and order town, but it was no guarantee that I wouldn't get a rifle bullet in the back before I reached the gangplank. A man in a window could get me with one shot. There was so much noise it might not even be heard. But nobody shot at me, and I got aboard without having to bribe anybody else.

The *Falmouth* was the damnedest ship you ever saw; a flat-bottomed stern-wheeler about ninety feet long. There was a one-story deckhouse with three-tiered bunks. Everybody except the captain and crew slept in that one big bunkhouse. It didn't take long to see that the ship was grossly overcrowded. The dining saloon and ship's galley were also enclosed by the deckhouse. I looked for Trask and didn't find him. I wondered how long it would take to reach Skagway, or if we'd make it at all. There were two life-boats for about sixty men.

In the bunkhouse the noise was deafening and the stink was bad enough to make you blind. The boat hadn't sailed yet and already men were fighting over nothing. Those not fighting eyed each other suspiciously; men without enough equipment were looking for what they could steal. I could see that few of them knew a damned thing about gold mining, though there were some oldtime prospectors among them, men who had searched for gold all over the world and were on the prowl again.

The *Falmouth* was truly a coastal boat. If it didn't hug the coast, it would sink like a stone in the open sea. After we left Frisco there were great banks of fog, but the sea was calm enough. I saw Trask a few times, and that was all. The *Falmouth* followed every nook and bay, took advantage of every sheltering point of land. The engines were old and didn't push the ship at more than ten miles an hour, and when there was any kind of strong sea running, the stern wheel raced powerlessly in the air.

I stayed out of the bunkhouse as much as I could, but as we made our painful way up the coast of British Columbia, the wind began to get a knife edge. One day, with a fair wind behind us, we made nearly a hundred miles before dark, when the ship had to lay over along the unlighted coast. Even so, considering the layovers and stops for wood, it was said that the *Falmouth* was making good time. There were no women on board, but it wouldn't have mattered if there had been. These weren't tropic seas where you could screw a woman on deck in the moonlight.

The food was rotten, the coffee thin and bitter-tasting, as if they were using the same grounds over and over. But nobody complained too hard, because getting to Alaska was all that mattered. At one wood stop a party of hardy souls went ashore to shoot rabbits. I took no part in the rabbit shoot, and neither did Trask.

I noticed that Trask spoke to no one. If someone spoke to him, he might answer, and no more. He made no attempt to strike up another conversation with me. He slept at the far end of the bunkhouse, and with men always moving around in that overcrowded space, it wasn't always possible to see him. But I was careful not to go on deck at night. The thunder of the engines would hide the sound of a shot all too well. A few times Trask went on deck after dark, as if trying to draw me up after him. I stayed in my dirty canvas bunk.

Everybody was beginning to smell bad. On the *Falmouth* there was no place to wash or shave, and the few men who tried to stay clean, soon got as dirty as the others. Everybody was bone-weary of the wallowing old tub. The food got worse and the cook was fortifying the rotten coffee with roasted corn meal. A man got stabbed for trying to steal a can of peaches from a man with a whole sack of them. There was talk of throwing the wounded man overboard; finally the friends of the injured party decided that stabbing was punishment enough.

The wounded man died anyway, sometime after we left Queen Charlotte Strait and were beating north toward Calvert Island, and there was much grumbling from the thief's friends, who were inclined to avenge his death. But the trouble died down after the captain and most of the crew broke out rifles and the troublemakers were warned that they'd be put ashore at some Canadian port and turned over to the redcoats. That cooled their ardor because the Mounties don't take kindly to men getting killed over a can of peaches.

Nothing else happened until the *Falmouth* was back in American waters and out of reach of any good law. By now the bunkhouse smelled like a boar's nest, the floor smeared with tobacco ash, scraps of food and spit. There was a movement by some hardy souls to let in some very cold fresh air; it was voted down. We were less than a day from Skagway, the jumping off place for the Alaska and Yukon goldfields when the captain appeared one morning and said the bunkhouse was going to be cleaned with a steam hose.

"We're going to clean out one part at a time," the captain shouted, trying to make himself heard above the din of complaints. "Stow your gear at one end while we work on the other. Get a move on, boys. I'm not going into port looking like this. New batch of passengers will complain like hell. I said move it now."

To back his play, the captain drew a big Remington

revolver from his belt and let it dangle from his forefinger. At the same time a crewman came in dragging a reinforced hose with a brass handle for turning it on and off. The captain went out and the crewman scalded the floor with a blast of steam that immediately clouded up the bunkhouse and made it almost impossible to see. The crewman worked his way down to the other door, using the powerful hose like a broom, sweeping the rubbish in front of him. Crowded in with the other men, I felt a bump but didn't think anything about it. Everybody was bumping into everybody else.

The crewman finished steam cleaning half the bunkhouse, then waved us to come down to the wet part. A man with steamed-up glasses walked into the wall and cursed like a bastard. After the crewman finished the whole place he turned off the hose and put it down. I was making my way back to my bunk when something made me look behind me and I saw four tough-looking men coming at me. Three had pistols, and one had a blackjack, about the biggest I'd ever seen. The biggest thug, who looked like a prizefighter turned saloon bouncer, pointed his left hand at me.

"You just stole my watch, you fucking bastard. Let's have it back, then you go over the side. Maybe you'll make it to shore."

They were still coming forward through the clouds of steam when I grabbed up the hose and dropped the latch on the nozzle. A blast of steam across the legs cut them down, and when they fell I put another blast right over their heads. They rolled on the wet deck screaming in agony. All the other men were scrambling for the doors or huddled against the wall. I looked for Trask and didn't see him.

I gave the big man another blast in the legs. By raising or lowering the latch on the nozzle you could aim the steam jet like a gun. I shut off the steam and pointed the nozzle at the big man's face. He knew I could turn his face to dripping jelly with a single blast.

"Don't do it!" he yelled. "It wasn't my idea."

While he was yelling one of the others made a grab for his fallen pistol. I blew his face away with steam. It cooked his face and blinded him instantly. I turned the hose back to the big man.

"Who put you up to it?" I said, knowing damn well it was Trask. The theft of the peaches must have given him the idea.

"Don't know his name," the big man howled, staring at the hose in mortal terror. "Man in a beaver hat."

Just then Trask stepped out from behind a mass of frightened men and fired a pistol at me. I couldn't use the hose because it would mean disfiguring innocent men. Instead, I dropped the hose and had my pistol out before it hit the deck. He fired again and clipped a patch of fur from my coat. Then I fired and got him squarely between the eyes. I heard the captain yelling outside and put my gun in my holster. In a minute I found myself looking at the captain's cocked Remington. Behind him were six crewmen with rifles. All those guns were ready to kill me. This was a tough ship in tough country.

Backed by his riflemen, the captain came forward to look at the man without a face. Then, covered by seven guns, I told my side of it. It took some prompting to get the scalded thugs to tell the truth, but they changed their minds when the captain, a bitter-faced Scotchman, picked up the hose and pointed the nozzle. After that the other passengers had their say, and I was a free man.

"Just don't run too fast," the captain said after I gave him the watch the man who bumped me had planted on me. "They may want to talk to you in Skagway, but *I* guess you're in the clear."

I wasn't one bit sure about that.

THREE

Only one man wanted to see me in Skagway, and that man was Soapy Smith. Jefferson Randolph Smith was his real name, and he came from a good Virginia family, but he didn't object if you called him Soapy to his face. Although he had a smooth, oily voice, the nickname didn't come from that. Old Soapy got his start in life selling cheap soap at high prices; the name stuck to him like a soap ring in a bathtub. Some years later he worked as a confidence man—all Colorado knew him as the King of Bunco—in various parts of the Southwest, before he fled north by way of a jail term and a jailbreak in California. There, in Skagway, he had made himself undisputed ruler of the wildest, most lawless town in Alaska.

Of course I didn't know Soapy was boss of Skagway when I arrived there. But I was to find out before many hours had passed. Operating from the back room of Jeff's Place, Soapy controlled a gang estimated to number between three and four hundred. This collection of badmen included card sharps, confidence men, buncosteerers, pickpocket whores, highway robbers and murderers. Early in his Skagway career the good people of the town tried to run him out by forming a Committee of One Hundred and One. Soapy countered by forming his own Committee of Three Hundred and Three. There was an election a few weeks off and he rigged it and filled every political office with his own men. In Skagway, so remote from the rest of the world, if you didn't get along with Soapy you stood a good chance of getting killed.

Like I said, I learned all this fast. On the face of it, it looked like my kind of town. By that I mean no law of any kind, territorial or federal. There must have been a hundred saloons, gaming houses and whorehouses in the place. The main street was called Broadway and it was hard-packed with snow and bright with yellow light when I came up from the docks looking for a room. After weeks on the steamer I wanted a bath and a long drink of whisky and especially a woman. The judge would have to wait.

Money had little value in Skagway unless you had a lot of it. The bottle of whiskey cost me $20, and it was a doubtful-looking brand at that. I found a rickety hotel and for one night they didn't charge me more than a working cowhand made in two months. And that was just for a night. But at least I didn't have to bunk in with three or four other fellas. The man behind the desk was some kind of foreigner, and when I asked about the bath, he said sure—and how about a "nize gurl?"

I said I wanted a "nize gurl" that wouldn't make me piss funny for a month and the clerk got huffy about it.

"Ve haf de cleanest gurls in the woild," the clerk said.

Well, I sure hoped so because I didn't want to start out on the trail with a dose. But you have to take chances, and I was horny as a bastard. I got the room key from the clerk and he told me I could find the bath-house at the end of the hall. He said I could tell the wash-house attendant about the girl when I got through with the bath.

I took my guns, clothes, a bottle of whiskey, everything to the bath-house. In a wild town like Skagway you can wind up naked and broke if you're careless about bathing. The hotel was new but smelled old, all but the wash-house: a strong soapy smell came through the half-open door. When I opened it I found a strong-looking girl who looked like a farmer's daughter strayed far from the south forty. There were three tin tubs and the floor was wet and she was mopping it. A big copper tank bubbled on a kerosene burner.

The girl was young and blond and dressed in a clean canvas miner's suit and wooden shoes. I guess the clogs kept her feet out of the water. She was sweating from her exertions and she brushed her hair out of her eyes with a sigh.

"You want a bath?" she asked.

"A bath and then a girl," I said.

"The girl isn't me, mister."

"That's too bad. I think I'd like you better than the other girls."

I didn't mean anything, but she got mad just the same. "Don't include me with the other girls. I'm no whore."

"Whores are just women. No need to get preachy about it. How about drawing some hot water for me? I can argue just as well from the tub."

"There's a time limit," she said. "If you're real dirty and want a second bath you have to pay double. If you want me to scrub your back that'll be extra."

I thought back to having my back scrubbed in Cynthia's gold-fitted bathtub on Nob Hill. This farm girl probably didn't have Cynthia's know-how. Even so, she wasn't bad. Not by any means.

"I'll take ten dollars worth of back scrubbing," I said. "And while you're at it, why don't you lock the door and I'll pay for all three tubs."

I was sitting in hot water drinking whisky and she gave me a whack with the back of the brush. "Behave yourself, mister. This house is strictly business—I rent it from the hotel—so no more dirty talk."

"It wasn't so dirty," I said. "You mean you run this place?"

She scrubbed hard at my sweaty back. "That's what I said. I am going to work hard in Alaska, then go home and get married. But not to some man who thinks he owns me because he feeds me. Maybe I will be the one to feed him."

"Lucky man," I said. "How are you doing with the money?"

She sighed. "Not so good. Men are so dirty in Alaska. It's so hard to keep clean, they don't even bother."

"That's hard to believe, with your back scrubs, I mean."

"They know that's all they'll get, so they'd rather keep the money."

"Men must offer you money for other things?"

"Very few offer enough. I am very expensive."

"How expensive?"

"Two hundred and fifty dollars."

"Why that figure?"

"I like the sound of it. And I must like the man before I agree. I do not like men with bad teeth, fat bellies, skinny legs. You think two hundred and fifty dollars is too much?"

"If you want it bad enough. I do."

Well sir, it turned out that she was a sweet fuck; what the colored people call a honey-fuck. For all her dealings with naked men, she was sort of shy. It was plain that she

33

didn't have that much experience, but she made up for it in energy and willingness to please. She had a well-cushioned body and her waist was far from waspish, yet I liked all of it. Her muscled legs gripped me like a vise. I had been tired when I got into bed with her—that steamer was hell on sleep—but I soon revived after a little more whiskey. She gave me a good fuck and a good massage, kneading my back and neck muscles with her strong farm-girl hands. Something she did to my neck made it snap, and after that I felt ten times better. She was tight for such a large girl, and the muscles of her hot, sopping cunt worked like a mouth on my fiercely thrusting cock. Jesus Christ! It was good to be on top of a soft, pretty girl in a big bed with clean sheets. And she wasn't one of those women who grab you and stare into your face while you're fucking them. This girl kept her eyes closed all the time. She hadn't spread her legs for so many men that she had become mechanical about it. After I'd been in her for just a few minutes she came with a great sigh of contentment that was pleasant to hear, and after I had my own come she held me tight, moving easy but saying nothing until I got hard again.

One thing was for sure: this girl who wanted to make enough money to go home and get married to a respectable man was going to bring a lot of experience to the marriage bed. I felt like telling her not to show too much experience; her respectable husband might—probably would—enjoy it, but it would be taken as a bad sign. But maybe she knew all that and would act the blushing bride.

But there was nothing bashful about the things she did to me. I had given her the two hundred and fifty dollars and no doubt she was looking forward to later sessions at the same price. Who could blame her? Four long fucks and she'd be a thousand dollars richer. But money or no money, she fucked like a woman who really loved having a big cock inside her. She was still tight because she hadn't fucked a lot, not at that price. And she was strong all over, especially her hands, what with all that massaging and back-scrubbing.

After I came again my balls dropped down, as they do after a fuck, and she kneaded them gently. An inexperienced woman who rubs your balls can hurt you. This young blond girl did anything but. After working on my balls she worked on my cock so expertly that it began to stand up straight and when it was ready for her mouth she sucked it. I wasn't sure I could come again so soon, but there was no one banging on the door demanding a bath. She sucked me until my eyes were popping out of my head.

My cock was rigid, my whole body was rigid as she sucked faster and faster. Finally when I could stand it no more I came in a gush and she swallowed it. I was covered with sweat and she insisted on giving me another bath and she didn't even charge me extra. Feeling her hands all over me, especially when she washed between my legs, got me hard again and I fucked her again and had to get another bath.

After moving to my room, the fun just got better.

I had two more drinks and, she turned me over, sat on my ass and worked on my back a second time. Sweet fucking Christ! but it felt good. Before I drifted off to sleep I heard her say, "You're a nice man, mister. Whoever you are."

I must have slept for about two hours, and then I heard the door opening. "You came back, little sister," I said, flipping back the blankets so she could get in with me.

"That's what I done, little sister," a rough voice said. "Don't reach for a weapon or I'll have to use you up. Me here, two more in the hall. I'll just light the light and you put on your pants. Nobody's about to rob you, all right?"

Gun talk always clears my head, no matter how much whiskey I take aboard.

"Then what?" I asked, smelling the lemon drops on his breath.

A match flared and light from the lamp flooded the room and then I saw a fat man, with a mustache and a quilted coat, holding a stubby pocket revolver on me.

"Then what?" he repeated, grinding the hard candy between his store teeth. "The what is Soapy Smith wants to talk to you." He put the short gun in a side pocket. "Sorry to point a gun at you, Saddler. Just a precaution, you understand. Better you than me is my motto. Soapy said you were smart in the ways of not getting shot."

"Good for Soapy," I said, getting off the bed to drag on my pants. "Didn't know the old boy was in this neck of the woods."

The fat man laughed until his jowls shook. "Then you must be awful new in these parts—which of course you are. My name is Jerry Sullivan, by the way. You want to shake hands?"

I got my pants buttoned and my shirt stuffed in. "I always shake hands with a man with two friends in the hall."

We shook hands cautiously and Sullivan said, "Soapy said you were a card. Years ago in Denver we met if you recall the place that Soapy was working at the time. No blame if you don't recall. That time, in them days, I was a lot thinner than I am now. Make a joke on that if you like. These days I'm rich as well as fat. These days I'm Soapy's righthand man."

Well, he said I could make a joke. "There's enough of you to make three right hands, Jerry."

Sullivan laughed with the evil good nature of his doublecrossing kind. "Soapy said you were a card," he repeated. "You don't recall me, do you, cowboy?"

One thing I hate to be called is cowboy. It's like calling

a farmer a farmer, or reminding some other man that he has a birthmark or jug ears.

I said, "Sure I remember you, Jerry. You were beating up sick whores back then. I heard you killed a few that couldn't work."

Sullivan stuck another handful of lemon candy in his mouth while I was pulling on my boots. His fat man's smile wasn't working as well as it had been.

"I don't think you're such a card, Saddler. Let me ask you something. How come you ain't afraid of me? Your guns are over there on the dresser. Mine is close to hand. So how come you ain't a-scared?"

I got my coat on. "Because Soapy gives the orders in any outfit he runs."

Sullivan spat a piece of candy on the floor. "Fucking goddamned right he does. In this whole *town* he does."

And so he did.

I went out ahead of Sullivan and we went down the street where the hotel was, Seward Street. When we were crunching along the icy boardwalks of Broadway I saw Jeff's Place, and by the size of it I knew how well Soapy was doing. It was so big that it took up most of a block, and there was so much light and noise that it looked like four circuses going full blast. It was a three-story building with saloons and gambling halls on the first and second floors. In Skagway, on the coast, it doesn't get half as cold as in the interior, and some of the windows were open. The so-called music of racket made by mechanical pianos was deafening. A bottle broke a window and there was a shot and then the noise was no worse than before.

Walking with me—the two gunmen behind—Sullivan said through his lemon drops, "How you like it, Saddler?"

"A garden of Eden," I said.

The ex-pimp had no more smiles now. So close to

home, he felt safe. "What the fuck does that shit mean?"

I said Holy Bible shit.

Sullivan said walk on in.

Once we got inside it was clear that Sullivan was of some minor importance in the helltown of Skagway, for the loudmouth boozers and gamblers made way for us as we cut through the crowded saloon to the door of the back room. In front of this stood not one, but two shotgun guards with unfriendly faces. Sullivan gave them a nod and they opened the door—and there was Soapy Smith, fifteen years older—and I had never known him to be young—sitting at a polished table with a great smoking steak, a long cigar and a tall drink in front of him. Across the table a young woman, no more than eighteen, was pushing her tits back into her blue silk dress. There was no steak on her side of the table, but there were spots of meat gravy on the front of her dress.

Well, I thought, Soapy is getting old and has to do something different with his women. Like maybe smearing their breasts with steak gravy.

"How do, Soapy?" I asked him.

"Right good, Saddler," he answered. "Better than good. Been a long time I haven't seen you. You hungry for steak, or you want the other kind of meat?" Soapy Smith gestured toward the girl.

"Just had some of that, Soapy. Maybe later."

Soapy snapped his fingers at the girl and pointed to the door. "Scat, honey," the great man said.

Soapy poured a drink for me. I knew it wasn't poisoned because he had a drink from the same bottle. It was real Jack Daniels, my favorite sourmash, and it went down as smooth as spring water after the slop I'd been drinking.

After he got a good cigar going, Soapy puffed clouds of contentment at the ceiling. He seemed in no hurry to talk, but that was always Soapy's way. The fine broad-cloth suit he was wearing said he'd come a long way from peddling soap. If he ever dug for gold, it was in other people's pockets.

"Sullivan says you run this town," I said by way of a compliment. I didn't want to tangle with Soapy if I didn't have to. Looking at Soapy, thinking of the power he had, suddenly I felt a long way from home.

"I always wanted my own town," Soapy said. "Back in the States that's a hard thing to do. In the States even a powerful man has to play ball with other powerful men. Then there's always some reform movement raising its ugly head. No such thing in Skagway. This is my last stop, Saddler, and I'm going to make it a good one. I could retire now on my takings, but don't want to. The only thing that bothers me about this country is the cold. But I get around that by staying indoors all I can. I'm like a general safe and snug in his tent. I let other men go out in the cold and do the fighting."

"You always were smart," I said.

"Well yes," Soapy agreed with a slight smile. "But I never got organized till now. And to think I owe it all to the judge."

A copy of the San Francisco *Chronicle* lay folded on the table. I guessed it was the one with my name on it. My name and Judge Phineas Slocum's.

"The judge sent you to prison," I said.

"Twenty years hard labor in federal prison," Soapy said. "But I broke out after two years and made my way here. A lucky thing I picked Alaska to run to. Now I'm a rich man, a free man with the finest pardon money could buy. I owe all that to the judge. You think I'm as rich as the judge was?"

I helped myself to another Jack Daniels. "Probably not," I said. "The judge came from a rich family and got richer along the way."

Soapy studied the back of his hands, admiring the shine of his nails. Still viewing his gambler's hands, he said in his guarded way, "They say the Slocums are worth millions. I don't mean the judge's two brothers. The rest of the Slocums. I mean the widow and the others in Los Angeles. But I mean the widow in particular." Soapy tapped the newspaper with a skinny finger. "Here it says the widow will come into ten million, maybe more when it's all counted up."

"That's what the paper says. Why all the interest? You got yours."

"I only got about a million, Saddler. How much are you getting for bringing back the body?"

I told him because I figured he knew.

"I hear you did some dirty work on the boat," Soapy said. "Scalded a gang of skullbusters and killed a man named Ben Trask."

"No way out of it," I said. "Before I left Frisco Trask warned me off."

I explained what Trask had said. About how old enemies of the judge wanted him to rot in the ice and snow. Naturally, I said nothing about the Slocum brothers, Bart and George.

"You ever hear of this Ben Trask?" I asked.

Soapy said no. "Of course I wasn't in Frisco that long before I got nabbed in the swindle. Sullivan went to look at the body, and he didn't know him either. You believe Trask's story about the bad boys hating the judge so much?"

"I don't know. Trask said he was a city detective at one time. There was a big graft ring the judge broke up. The ringleaders and a lot of others were sent to prison."

"The judge sent plenty of good men to prison."

"He sent you to prison."

"Sure he did, I'm glad he did."

"Then you don't hate him like the others?"

"For two years I hated him. After I broke out I put it down to the fortunes of war. A man shouldn't break the law if he can't take his punishment. That's the way it works, or ought to. I tell you the judge gave me everything I have."

I wasn't sure I believed him. Professional crooks like to pretend they have a business arrangement with the law. Maybe some of them don't hate the judges that send them away, but I found Soapy's story hard to swallow, especially when I considered that the old bastard got twenty years for a fairly small swindle and had never been convicted of anything else.

At last I asked the main question because it had to be asked. I'd known the elderly crook for fifteen years, and we weren't enemies of any kind. On the other hand, Soapy didn't make much distinction between enemies and friends.

"Level with me, Soapy. Do you have anything to do with the men Trask was talking about?"

Soapy pulled the point of his well-trimmed beard. "Me?" he said in surprise, or in what might have been one of his con man's acts. "My friend, if I wanted you dead, you wouldn't be here talking to me, drinking my whiskey. Sullivan and the boys would have killed you and nobody would blink an eye. I could have sent twenty men to kill you. Didn't I tell you I run this town? Absolutely run it. Is that good enough for you? On my word as a gentleman, I had nothing to do with Trask. You're forgetting it takes a long time to get from here to Frisco. I didn't know a thing about you till I got the *Chronicle* a few hours ago."

That part of it made sense, but I wasn't ready to trust Soapy or anything about him. The man had been a double-dealer since the moment a doctor slapped his backside and brought him to life.

"Your word's good enough for me," I said.

Soapy poured us a drink. "That's the spirit," he said. "How do you plan to get to the camp where the judge is? It's four or five hundred miles from here. You even know where the camp called Dulcimer is?"

"I know where it's supposed to be. Somewhere west of Dawson. I figure to go over White Pass, across Lake Bennett, then down the Yukon to Dawson, then stay with the river until it crosses back into American territory. You know if the steamers are still running this time of year?"

Soapy smiled at me. "There's only one steamer, Saddler. It's on a run to Dawson right now. If the river doesn't freeze up too fast it may make it back before winter. If not, it'll stay there till spring."

"There must be other boats on the river," I said.

"Some boats, plenty of rafts. It's a bad, wild river and freezes up without warning. If it's frozen now you'll have to walk in or sled in. You'll have to wait till spring to bring the body out. Then you can take the steamer."

"The widow doesn't want to wait till spring."

"Impatient woman, this widow. How does she want you to bring the body out in the dead of winter. By balloon?"

"By dog sled."

"You're crazy. I don't know that it can be done. You'll have a coffin as well as a body."

"The widow wants the body soon as possible. I'll come back the same way I go in. Across the ice, then back over White Pass."

Soapy shivered at the thought of all that hard travel. "This widow, would I know the lady? Newspaper says her name is Cynthia."

"Cynthia Diamond that worked in the Bella Union in Denver, as well as other places."

"Ah yes," Soapy said, sucking on his cigar. "A juicy

lady. You been dipping your wick around there, have you?"

I grinned to show good fellowship. "Around there," I said.

"No wonder you want to get back so fast. I always thought Cindy was too good to be selling it for the prices she got. Think of it now, Cindy Diamond married to a federal judge. I still think you're crazy."

"Maybe I can get help."

"Not likely. Men crazy for gold won't throw down their tools to sled out a corpse. You're forgetting what a superstitious bunch gold miners are. All they believe in is luck. They won't want to have anything to do with a stiff. Mark my words, Saddler. You'll be all by your lonesome. But who am I to stop a man that wants to get back to Cindy Diamond's sweet bush? Not to mention ten million dollars. By the living Jesus, that's a nice pile of money. You got all the things you need?"

"Everything except supplies," I said.

"I can help you there," Soapy said. "Prices are a bitch in this town." He smiled. "I help keep them that way. You'll be needing plenty of fatty bacon, among other things. Nothing like fat to keep out the cold. Of course I wouldn't know about that."

"Thanks, Soapy," I said, wondering why he was being so good to me. But his boys hadn't killed me, which was a plus.

There was a knock on the door and Sullivan, still grinding lemon drops, came in and whispered in Soapy's ear. Soapy made a face at the candy smell and waved the ex-pimp back outside.

Soapy said mildly, "You're full of surprises, Saddler. I guess you forgot to say you'd been in Alaska before?"

"Somebody say I was?"

"One of the bartenders recognized you as a man he'd

been in the army with. Not in Skagway, he said. No army ever here. Way up north. Fort Yukon. Bartender's name is Dave Durkin."

"Good old Dave," I said.

"How'd you get in the army, Saddler?"

"I shot a man had a rich daddy and figured the army was a good place to hide out. I hoped for Arizona or New Mexico, got sent to Alaska instead. I was there a year before I got transferred."

"Then you know the country pretty good?" There was some hardness in Soapy's voice that hadn't been there before. "You won't be just another pilgrim, is what I mean."

"I hope not," I said. "I wouldn't take this job if I was."

"That's good to hear," Soapy said, smiling again, as if he had made up his mind about something. "I always say there's nothing like a man that knows his way around. Otherwise he might get lost or take a wrong turn on the trail."

I smiled too. "Not me, Soapy. Over White Pass, down the Yukon River, back the same way." I didn't know what the old con man's game was, but I didn't like it. If there was any other way back to the coast, I was going to take it. What I didn't understand was, if Soapy didn't want me to fetch the judge's body, then why wasn't I dead? But for now all I could do was play the hand I'd been dealt and see what happened.

"If anyone can do it, you can do it," Soapy said. "You've got a reputation for seeing things through. Now I'll call Sullivan and you can tell him what you want. See you back here in a few months. The best of luck to you."

Soapy shook hands without getting up from the table. We smiled at one another. Then he called the ex-pimp.

Like it or not, I was on my way.

* * *

White Pass looked like the entrance to hell. A frozen hell. Snow was blowing and Skagway was twenty miles behind. Men laden with equipment—some with too much equipment—were toiling their way up to the windblasted summit of the pass. There were a few men that didn't make it to the top of the pass, but that was only the start. Somewhere on the other side of the pass was Lake Bennett, twenty miles away on the downgrade. There the wayfarers built boats and rafts that would take them downriver to Dawson, biggest of the boom towns in the Yukon. Well over half of them sank or were ripped to pieces in the rapids of the Yukon, and unless I could pay my way on a sturdy craft I might have more to worry about than Soapy Smith or the others.

Near the top of the pass, which was the start of Canadian territory, there was a Mounted Police post manned by tough-looking lawmen in their bright red uniform jackets. They were turning back men without enough supplies for the journey ahead. One redcoat had a thick sheaf of wanted posters from the States and was checking every man seeking to enter Canadian territory. There was no wanted notice on me, at least not lately, and after they looked at my supplies, my sleeping bag and other gear, they let me through.

It was all downgrade after that. I had enough grub to last me six days. More than that would have been too hard to carry. The snow stopped and the great gray mountain peaks came into view. I had started early from Skagway and there wasn't much light left. There was no way to reach Lake Bennett by nightfall, and I didn't want to try. Travel in that country is dangerous at any time; at night it's a sure way to get killed unless there is a bright moon. After the snow there was rain and fog that lasted for well over an hour. I was glad to see the lights of a relay station.

It was operated by a man who was packing in supplies for the Mounted Police. He let me sleep on the floor but didn't ask any money for it. In the morning he gave me a mug of black tea and a bacon sandwich. I never did get his name, but he was a gloomy-looking man with almost nothing to say.

I was on my way again as soon as the sky was a dull gray. Sometime that morning I caught sight of Lake Bennett far in the distance, a long gray sprawl of water trapped between the mountain peaks. This was the beginning of the waterway that led to the goldfields of the Yukon and finally emptied into the Bering Sea, nearly two thousand miles away. This was the end of the land trail from the outside world; the place where boats were built, for the 600-mile journey down the Yukon to Dawson. It was the last place in the world I wanted to be.

It took me hours to reach the big lake. All along its shores a shack-and-tent city had sprung up, but there was none of the whiskey-fired foolishness of Skagway. This was a place of hard work and firm determination. Long before I got there I could hear the sounds of rafts and boats being built. The sounds of saws, hammers and axes echoed across the icy waters of the lake. Smoke curled up from dozens of fires, the only cheery sight in all that wasteland.

As I came into camp men stared at me with that flat suspicion you find in all bleak places where men live by their guns and their fists. A few men nodded stiffly, but no one spoke. A few looked at my fur coat and sleeping bag, my rifle and sheep-lined boots, and I could see the greed in their eyes. This country was better policed than the American side of the line, but the redcoats were few and far between. Here, any man who didn't watch himself all the time was a goddamned fool.

After looking around for a bit I found a group of men who had stopped to eat. They had a fire going in an old bucket with holes in it. Coffee was on and it smelled good. They looked like Americans, not that being a fellow American would mean anything if they decided to be unfriendly.

"How's the work going?" I asked one of them, a rangy man with a scarf wrapped around a battered leather cap.

"All right," he said curtly. "You're welcome to use the fire, but there's no grub for you. Hardly enough for us. Thought we could buy enough in Skagway, but were told wrong about the prices. Sons of bitches there are robbing the people blind. Now we're short as you can see."

A handful of fried potatoes sizzled on a greased skillet.

"And that's the last of the coffee," the man said. There were grim lines in his unshaven face.

"I got coffee and bacon and beans. You're welcome to some of my grub." I said. "I plan to shoot game along the way. Used to be a hunter, and was in this country for a whole year."

"Well now, is that a fact," the man said, nodding me closer to the fire. "Maybe we ought to have a talk."

FOUR

The big man held out his hand to me. "I'm Rollins and these men are Kelso, Irwin, and Leonard."

I told them who I was and we shook hands on the introduction. My bacon was frying on the fire and I unsacked some of my canned goods. The boat they were trying to build was a sorry-looking thing and Rollins saw me looking at it.

"What do you think?" he asked. "You say you were a year in this country."

"In the army. Up north, Fort Yukon. That boat of yours won't stand up to the river. Take my advice and start over. Want me to come in with you?"

It was plain that Rollins was bossing this outfit, though he was as hungry-looking as the rest of them. But there are men who always take charge. Rollins was one of them.

"What can you do?" he asked me.

"Show you how to build a strong boat," I said. "I can

shoot meat—deer, bear, birds—when the grub runs out. It's not full winter yet. There will be enough to eat."

The one called Kelso eyed me suspiciously. "We don't know a thing about you, mister." He was a stocky man who might have been a teamster at one time.

"I'm not here to rob you," I said. "What have you got worth robbing?"

Rollins laughed. "He's got you there, Kelso. I don't see that we have anything to lose. If we don't get downriver before it freezes we'll have to walk."

"You want me to go away while you talk this over?" I asked. I guessed these men had come from the same part of the country. They sounded like Kansas.

"It's all right with me," Rollins said. "How about the rest of you?"

Kelso was the last to nod. I couldn't see that I'd done anything to get his back up. Maybe he was just naturally suspicious, which wasn't a bad thing to be along the Yukon.

It turned out that I was right about Kansas; they had left their families behind while they came north to hunt for gold. They might come back rich men, or as starving paupers, or not at all. None of us might get to Dawson. The Yukon is one of the wildest rivers in the world; over the years it has claimed the lives of countless men. Then there is disease and frostbite and the loneliness that drives men crazy. They would have been better off back in Kansas, but I wasn't about to say so.

"Boat's got to be as sturdy as we can make it," I said. "The rapids will do us in if it's not. How's the lumber holding out?"

"Everything close by has been cut down," Rollins said, pointing at the snow-covered hillsides that sloped up from the lake. "There's still a fair stand of spruce that can be got at."

"Then we better get at it," I said.

After we ate the bacon there were a few hours of light left. The wind whipped up the water on the lake and the mountain peaks loomed over us like implacable enemies. Irwin, a small, hardy man, stayed behind to guard the supplies while the rest of us started out to cut the first timber for the boat.

The spruce was ten-inch and had to be cut and peeled before it was dragged a quarter–mile back to the edge of the lake. There it was hoisted on a trestle where it was ripped into one-and-a-half-inch boards. Kelso and Irwin did the ripping, one in a pit under the trestle, the other above. To keep the saw cut straight, the log was marked with charcoal blackened string.

By the time darkness closed in we had a small pile of rough boards, but that was just the start of it. For supper we ate bacon and beans, huddled close to the fire, trying to ignore the bite of the wind. Everybody was too tired to talk and as soon as we built up the fire we dropped off to sleep.

We started work again as soon as it was light, stopping only to eat. It snowed during the day, but there was nothing to do but keep on working. The days passed like that: work, eat, sleep. Gradually the boat took shape: thirty feet long with an eight-foot beam, a square stern and a pointed bow. It had two-by-four ribs to brace the sides against the force of the rapids. I showed them how to caulk it with flower sacks boiled in spruce pitch and then, finally, after a lot of blisters and bad temper, the damn thing was ready for launching.

We loaded on what supplies we had, and that wasn't a hell of a lot: flour, bacon, dried apples, canned beans and tomatoes. I managed to buy a whole ham from a wild-eyed man—he had three of them—who said he was going to turn back, and maybe he was the smartest man on the shores of that godforsaken lake.

We started out at daybreak. There was a dust of snow, and the ice on the lake was a quarter of an inch thick. Dawson was still about six hundred miles ahead and there was no guarantee that we'd make it out of the mountain lakes and into the river before the ice closed in solid. With the square sail we made fair time for a couple of hours, then the wind died and we had to use the oars. This was the hardest work of all because of the ice, but then the wind picked up again and we got down the twenty-five mile length of Lake Bennett without too much hardship.

By nightfall we were well into the next lake. This was Lake Tagish, and it was a lot more treacherous than the one before. There was a moon and we kept going until the wind blew too hard, and I knew we were getting close to the worst part of the lake. This was the place where there was a split in the mountains that sucked down all the wind from the high mountain valleys. There was nothing to do but put in to shore and wait out the windy hours of darkness.

At the foot of Lake Tagish there was a Mounted Police post and beyond it was Lake Marsh, out of which the waters tumbled into Miles Canyon, the beginning of the Yukon River. The first run of bad water lasted for about three miles, where the water, jammed up between two sheer cliffs, tore along at forty miles an hour. Half a mile beyond the entrance there was a sharp bend that formed a whirlpool, turbulent and white.

"Jesus! You mean we have to go through that?" Rollins said, and I knew that he had never seen anything like it in Kansas.

"That's Squaw Rapids down there," I said. "We can portage the supplies around it. No way to portage the boat. The boat will have to go through. It's that or leave it behind. Look, these rapids have been run before and can be again. We can do it."

Kelso scowled at me. "Then why are these other boats tied up?"

"They're scared," I said.

"Goddamn right they are," Kelso said.

I shrugged. "I'll take the boat through by myself if it makes you feel better."

"You saying I'm scared too?" Kelso asked.

"I'm saying you can walk around the rapids. The water is going to stay as rough as it is."

"The hell with it," Rollins said. "I didn't come all the way from Kansas to stop now. I'll go with you. The rest of you go around and we'll pick you up on the other side."

"Your funeral," Kelso said.

While the others watched we headed into the gorge where the water ripped through rock walls not more than thirty feet apart. Icy spray whipped our faces as the bow rose and fell with the force of the current. At one point we were heading straight for a jagged rock, then I yelled at Rollins to shift his oar. The boat scraped the side of the rock but the heavy timbers were strong enough to take it. Then we were out past the worst of it and the gorge was behind. We steered the boat into calm water and waited for the others.

That night we camped at White Horse and had a feast of lake trout we bought from some Indians. Everybody cheered up except Kelso, who ate in silence. We slept on the boat and started out early the next morning.

The next day put us at the head of Lake LaBarge, a big lake thirty miles across. There was a fair breeze dead astern and we made good time. On the lake ice was forming fast, but the wind held and we made it across without getting iced in. Now we were into the river and should be making as much as a hundred miles a day. The only bad stretch after that was filled with sand bars and hidden rocks, but our luck held as before. It was getting colder all the time.

I shot a moose that was standing on a sand bar and that night we tied up near an abandoned Hudson's Bay trading post. I figured we had come more than two hundred miles from Lake Bennett. Past that point freezing temperatures held throughout the day and there was ice even on the fast-flowing river. At one point we had to chop through two hundred yards of pancake ice before we could get the boat back in the current.

Three days later we rounded a bend in the river and there was Dawson, a cluster of tents and shacks half hidden by a light fall of snow. Above the town a well-timbered mountain dominated everything. It looked like the last place to build a town, even a ragtag town like this one. Even so, there it was—ugly, dirty, and gold crazed.

And I still had a long way to go.

The steamer, with its reinforced bow, was pulling out from the dock as we tied up. Men stood looking after it, wanting to go back to civilization and yet wanting to stay, held there by the lure of gold. Dawson looked like the most miserable place on earth, but I was goddamned glad to see it. There would be whiskey and hot food, maybe even a few women.

After coming down the river with Rollins I couldn't just walk away from him, so I helped him get the boat out of the water so he could take it apart and build a cabin with the boards. That was how it worked in Dawson; if you didn't build your own cabin you froze.

"What are you fixing to do?" Rollins asked me while he worked out nails with a clawhammer. The snow was getting heavier and his face was red with cold.

"Go on downriver," I said. "I got business in a camp called Dulcimer."

"You don't mean gold-mining business?"

"That's right."

"I figured you didn't."

I liked Rollins, a straightforward man in his slow Kansas way. The others didn't mean anything to me, especially Kelso, who hadn't let up in his dislike of me. It seemed to me that Kelso was one of those men who never make a go of anything and hate the world because of it. He had a dumb, resentful face and little piggy eyes without much going on behind them. As he worked he glanced at me now and then. I'd be glad to see the last of him.

"You need some money?" I asked Rollins.

"Could use it," he said. "But don't know when I could pay you back. Or where."

"Don't worry about paying it back. If you get the money send it care of Jim Saddler, post office, El Paso, Texas. They'll hold it for me. How much do you need? A hundred be all right?"

"It sure would help us to get started. The other men are as broke as I am."

I dug into my coat and peeled off one of Cynthia's hundred dollar bills. Kelso's eyes narrowed when he saw the money, then he turned away and began to stack the boards from the boat. The wind was blowing hard and the snow was starting to drift.

Rollins rubbed his face. "Damn! It looks like this could turn into a blizzard. You're not going to start out before it clears?"

"No, my business in Dulcimer isn't that urgent. First I have to buy a sled and some dogs. Then I'll follow the river the rest of the way. I'd better get to it if you don't need any more help."

"We're all right now," Rollins said. "Good luck to you, Saddler. One way or another you'll get the money back. That's a promise."

I went up into the town to get a drink and found it in a ramshackle saloon jammed with gold-seekers making a lot of noise. Like in Skagway, nobody talked of anything but gold, but here the fever burned hotter. There were men there who shouldn't have been there at all; men who didn't know what the hell they were doing. More than a few of them would be buried there. Some might have friends; the others would die because this was country without any mercy.

As usual there were desperate men looking for grub-stakes, and before I had been there for five minutes I was approached with any number of deals. The more desperate the man, the wilder the deal. They all knew where the gold was; all they needed was money to get it out. There was some money to be made in the diggings, working for other men, but that was the last thing anybody wanted to do. To have to work for someone else was a sure sign of failure.

I got talking to a man who didn't try to bum any money off me and he said dogs were going to be hard to find anywhere in the gold fields.

"Any kind of good dog'll cost you two or three hundred dollars," he said. "And the cost of feeding them will set you back about a dollar a pound for meat. They'll eat most anything, but most anything is scarce in these parts."

Well that didn't sound so good. I knew I was going to need six dogs, so that meant I was going to have to shell out more than two thousand dollars for a sled and team. I asked the man where I could find some of these high-priced dogs, and he said to look for Duncan McClure over in Lousetown on the other side of the river.

"McClure's your best bet," the man said. "He's got the best dogs and won't rob you more than's fair. But you won't find him there today. He's up on one of the creeks hauling supplies. Be back tomorrow or the day after. Ask anybody over there and they'll tell you where to find him. You know anything about handling dogs?"

"Some," I said.

"What you need most of all is a good lead dog. Without a strong lead you'll be in for a hell of a time. Keep them well fed, mister, or they'll turn on you. Men in this country have been eaten up by their own team."

I had heard such stories but wasn't sure they weren't just tall tales of the frozen North. Yet windy stories sometimes turn out to be true, at least a few of them. Sled dogs can be vicious bastards, and it's no wonder, the hellish things they're put through. I had done some sledding in the army, and that wasn't any time lately, but I figured I'd get back in the routine fast enough. When you're new to sledding or haven't been at it for a long time, the first days are always the worst. Handling a sled isn't just letting the dogs whip it along. A lot of the time you have to manhandle the damn thing. If you're traveling on ice you have to watch out for holes and do your best to avoid them, because once you're in water there's no way to get out and you freeze in minutes. Then, too, you have to keep up with the dogs; when they're well fed they can set up a lively pace. That means you have to run a good deal of the time. In the end, though, the worst strain is on the arms.

After I got through drinking at the bar I bought a bottle of whiskey and went to look for food and a place to sleep. The food was caribou steak and black coffee and I got it in an eating place that was half tent and half shack. Snow blew in through openings, but with the stove going full blast in back it was warm enough. There were two long trestle tables with men wolfing down grub anyplace there was room to sit. Heavy food is the only thing that keeps you going in that cold and they were laying in all they could afford. I put away two steaks at $15 apiece and three cups of bitter coffee at a dollar a cup.

I asked the cook-proprietor if there was a hotel where I could put up. He looked at all my new gear, especially the fur coat, and frowned.

"We got a few places they call hotels," he said in a Yankee twang. "But they'll rob you for a bed and maybe they'll rob you in the bed. Men have been murdered for less than you got. Mounties do their best, but they can't be everywhere. You want to rent a snug little shack, maybe I can fix you up. Place has got a good stove and a real window. I don't mean a window made of empty bottles. A genuine glass window. Door is strong, has a drop bar on the inside, so they can't rob you in your sleep."

I got another dollar cup of coffee. "You mind if I look at a hotel first?"

The cook shrugged. "Suit yourself, mister. Only don't wait too long. I'm offering you my rent shack because you look like a man won't wreck the place or burn it down if you get drunk. Last month I rented my first extra shack to a man that brought in ten others. They broke everything in sight, even the stove. That's what set the place afire. Since then I watch who I rent out to. You want to leave some money to bind the deal. Got to ask you for twenty dollars to hold it for you. You think that's too much?"

"Not in this town," I said, and gave him the money. "I'll probably be back."

"Can't refund the money if you change your mind," the Yankee said. "Go look at the hotels and you'll see what I mean."

I thought I knew what he meant all right. Dawson was a hard-drinking town full of wild men from all over. I guess the Mounties tried to keep the lid on the cutting and shooting, but I knew there would be plenty of noise all night long. My thoughts turned back to the Slocum

57

brothers and Soapy Smith. I knew the Slocum brothers' interest in the judge's body; what Soapy had in mind I had no idea, but knowing him it had to be sneaky. He might have sent men ahead of me, or right after me. And who knows? Ben Trask might not have been the only hired killer on the boat.

The snow was still whirling in the wind when I went to check the first so-called hotel. It was a two-story place and some of the windows were broken and boarded over. There was a small saloon on the first floor, and like every other saloon in Dawson, it was jammed with boisterous drinkers fortifying themselves against the blizzard. As I came in one of several bouncers picked up a raging drunk and tossed him out into the snow.

I went to the desk and got a laugh from the clerk when I asked for a room. "You must be dreaming, mister," he said. "Here they sleep three to a bed and they sleep in shifts. You get your eight hours, then you pay for another eight, or you get out. You want to sleep on the floor, the rate is half."

I got much the same story at the next place I tried. By now the Yankee's rented shack was looking better and better. With men sleeping in shifts all the rooms in the hotel had to be louse ridden. I could just about smell the piss-and-puke-soaked blankets; the bed-bugs would be out in force.

On my way back to the cook tent the snow was so thick I could barely see. Suddenly I felt a blow on the back of my head that might have killed me if not for the fur hat. Even so I went down on my knees. There were white lights in my head and it wasn't the snow. The second blow caught me on the shoulder without doing much damage and I managed to roll away from the third. But I lost the rifle in the roll and when I grabbed for it all I came up with was snow. Now I could see there were two of them, bulky shapes in the half light. Both had clubs and they were swinging them at my head. I kept fumbling to get my coat open, but I had mittens on and knew I wasn't going to make it. I guess I had seconds to live when a third shape, very tall, grabbed one of the club swingers from behind and tossed him against the side of a building. The tall figure picked up the dropped club and slammed the second man across the side of the head. A slap in the ear is as bad as a kick in the balls. He screamed and tried to run. Another crack across the back of the neck dropped him like a stone. I felt myself lifted by powerful arms and propped against a wall.

"You all right?" a husky voice said. A woman's voice: there was no mistaking it. Well, I was so surprised you could have knocked me down again with a lot less than a club. I must have mumbled because she shook me and slapped me lightly in the face. She had to be six feet tall, not an inch less, and even through the blinding snow I was able to make out an angular, determined face. Her accent was Swedish, some kind of Scandinavian.

"How do you feel?" she asked, and shook me again, and even through the fur coat I could feel the strength of her fingers. "Listen to what I am saying."

I straightened up against the wall. "My head hurts, that's all."

The first man was beginning to groan and she kicked him twice in the thigh muscle to keep him from getting up. "Stay down or I will cripple you," she warned in a voice that was suddenly dangerous.

Then she bent over the two men and took revolvers from their pockets. "You know these men? They tried to rob you, yes?"

I bent down to look at the man she had kicked. All I could make out was the outline of his face, but I knew I hadn't seen him before.

"Not this one," I said. It was a day for surprises all right, because when I turned over the second club-swinger it was my old pal Kelso. I told her his name and how I'd come downriver with him. "Maybe they were out to rob me. Maybe it was something else. You mind telling me who you are?"

"Hella Kekkonen," she said. "You have heard of me, yes. I am famous all over the Yukon and Alaska."

I told her my name. "Famous for what?"

She sounded disappointed, a little resentful. "Then you have not heard of me. I am famous for mushing."

I didn't get it at first. Maybe it was the blow on the head. "You mean for driving dog sleds?"

"That is what it means, Mr. Saddler. Anywhere there is mushing to be done, I do it. I have a contract to haul the mails. I go wherever supplies are needed. I make a lot of money at what I do. Now you will guard these men while I go for the redcoats."

After she came back with two Mounties we all went to the police barracks, a squat log building with bars on the windows. A sergeant with red hair sat behind a desk in front of a fire. Rifles were chained to a rack on the wall and the whole place was neat and smelled of scrubbing soap. There were cells in the back and in one of them a drunk was yelling for water. The sergeant looked weary from long hours and lack of sleep. He was an irritable man, like so many men with red hair.

But he listened patiently enough while I told my story, keeping it as short as I could. "Is that what happened, Hella?" he asked when I finished.

Her hair, peeping out from under her fur hat was so blond it was almost white. She had the slanted eyes and high cheekbones you find in some Scandinavians. I guessed she was a Finn.

"That is how it happened, yes," she agreed.

The sergeant made Kelso and the other man empty their pockets out on his desk. Between them they only had six dollars and change. Neither had a watch or any other valuables.

"Robbery with violence, attempted," the sergeant said, writing down the charge in a book. "Mr. Saddler, you'll have to remain in Dawson until the judge gets back from the other camps."

That didn't suit me much. "How long will that be?"

"About two weeks. The weather is turning bad. You'll be here. Case'll be dismissed if you don't show up in court."

"Can't you just ship them back to the States?" I said. "I'm on my way downriver to the Alaska side."

The sergeant let out an exasperated sigh that showed how tired he was. "I'd like to ship a lot of Americans back to the States. These two thugs I'd prefer to ship off to prison. What about you, Hella?"

Hella shook her head. "I too have urgent business."

The sergeant closed his book with a bang that made Kelso jump. "Very well then," he said angrily. "If that's what you want, so be it." He pointed at Kelso and the other man who said his name was Al Rebstock. "You're going back to White Pass under guard. We know what you look like now, so don't come back. If you do I'll find a charge that will put you away for a long time. Until a supply party is ready to go back you will remain in the lockup."

The prisoners were locked up, but there was no kicking or pushing as there might have been in an American hoosegow. Mounties are the politest lawmen in the world. "Wait a moment, Mr. Saddler," the sergeant said. "I'd like to know your business downriver. I want you to tell the truth. There is such a charge as obstructing justice."

Leaving out the parts about Soapy Smith and the Slocum brothers, I told him about bringing out the judge's body. "That's the general intention," I said.

"Mr. Saddler, you're crazy," the sergeant said. "In the dead of winter, you have to be crazy."

I grinned at him. "Everybody keeps telling me that, Sergeant."

"Everybody is right," the sergeant said.

Outside, Hella said she was going to take a look at my head. "Do not argue about it, Mr. Saddler. It is my custom to have my own way. If there is concussion you could die on the trail. You have a place to stay? My own house is far from town. I do not like the noise and stink of the town."

"I think I have a shack," I said. "No, there's nothing wrong with my head. I just have to pay the rest of the money."

And I explained about the old Yankee in the cook tent.

"Old Percy," she said. "We will go there, make a fire, drink whiskey, and look at your head."

The Yankee took the money and told me where to find the shack. "If you want to stay on after tomorrow, come back and pay for it. You'll like it down there by the river. Got a nice view. Here's the key and go easy on the stovewood."

The snow was easing off by the time we found the shack. It was smaller than I expected, but it was clean enough for a ratsass town like Dawson. There was wood in the stove and the oil lamp was full. The cabin was built of chinked logs, with a packed dirt floor covered with river sand. As the Yankee promised, the window was real store glass and could be shuttered from the outside. There was a table, a chair and a good-sized bunk covered with Hudson Bay blankets.

"Take off your hat," Hella ordered.

"Yes, ma'am," I said obediently, hoping that I was going to take off more than that before the night was over.

FIVE

The stove burned bright in minutes and I got tin cups from a box by the stove and poured us drinks. I held the lamp while Hella felt around the top of my head with expert fingers. After she looked at my eyes she decided it was just a knock on the head and nothing more.

"You will have a lump there for a few days," she said. "Now you will lie down and I will put some ice on it."

"Well, there's plenty of ice around here," I said. "Look, I can do without the ice."

"Do not say foolish things," she said.

I handed her the drink, a big one, and she drank it off in two swallows.

"I like to drink whiskey, Mr. Saddler."

"Make that Jim or just Saddler, will you. You make me sound like an old man."

"How old are you . . . Jim?"

She had a way of making everything seem simple and honest. "Thirty-three," I said. "You think that's old?"

"Not so old. I am twenty-seven."

Warmed by the whiskey, she told me about herself. She was a Finn like I thought, but from the far north of her country. It was much like Alaska, she said. Long bitter winters and brief summers.

"This country was no surprise to me when I got here," she said. "Ten years I have been in Alaska and the Yukon. My poor father came to look for gold, but died after one year. In that year we were in many wild places. Since then I have been in many more wild places than few people have ever seen. At first men laughed at me when I became a musher, but they were wrong, yes. I am very strong and healthy and the cold has no terror for me. My father said I should have been an Eskimo. He made foolish jokes like that, poor man."

"Why didn't you go back to Finland?"

"There is nothing there for me. All dead. I am the last of them. If I went back there I would be nothing in that old country. Here I am famous and my name has been in the newspapers many times. I have broken records with my team and I will break more."

"I don't doubt it for a minute. But don't you ever get tired of it? All those weeks on the trail with no one else around."

Hella poured more drinks for us. The cabin was warm enough for us to take off our coats, and I saw that she had a fine supple body and firm breasts that jutted against the heavy wool shirt she was wearing. Her white-blond hair was short and cut carelessly. But it was her slanted green eyes that held my attention. They were clear and direct and very beautiful.

"On the trail, with the snow blowing from the drifts, that is the best time." Hella brushed snow from her coat. "I love this wild country. When we came here we crossed America by train and passed through many cities and towns. Noise and dirt and too many people. This town has too many people, but only a few miles away nothing has changed. You do not like this country?"

"I'd be a liar if I said I did."

"Then why are you doing this?"

"For a lady, the judge's widow."

"Ah," Hella said. "But not just any lady. I can tell from the sound of your voice. Is she a beautiful lady? Is she as beautiful as me?"

I said in a different way. "We've known each other for a long time. If she doesn't get the judge's body back she may lose all her money. She'd hate that."

Hella smiled. "Poor lady. Do you love her?"

"Not exactly. We're more like loving friends."

Hella nodded in her grave, wise way. "I think that is possible. It will be a long time before you get back to her. And there will be no loving friends on the trail."

I had just enough whiskey in me to say it. "You could come along with me. Or I could come along with you. Then the trail wouldn't be so lonely. Besides, I'll split the money with you. I'm not doing this for the money, if that's what you're thinking."

The lump of ice she was holding to my head was melting fast and she got up to throw it out the door. She slammed the door before too much snowy air could rush in.

"I am not thinking anything," she said. "We all do things for our own reasons. You think my life is strange—I know that—but it is right for me. When my father died I was very poor and had nothing. Now I am independent and will remain that way. Tomorrow I must start on a long journey to Cooper's Creek with mail and supplies. If I don't go I will lose my contract."

"Is that the only reason?"

"No. What you are going to try will make you famous if you succeed. If I came with you I would have only a share of your success. I have been alone so long, I do not like to share. It is not meant to be selfish. It is something I can't explain. But now you are going on a dangerous journey and I will share something with you. Because I like you."

"What do you want to share?"

"At this moment, your bed."

I didn't think she wanted me to undress her, so I didn't try. But the way she did it was as good as if I'd done it myself. It was warm in the cabin and she didn't just peel off and jump under the blankets. I was grateful to Old Percy and his little box of a cabin. My cock was standing up like a rod before I got my pants off and Hella took it and put it between her legs while we were still on our feet. We were almost the same height and I was able to slide it into her without having to bend down like you do with short women. She gave a gasp when it went in all the way. We stood like that for a while, tall and strong together. Then I lifted her, with my cock still in her, and she wrapped her legs around me, gasping with pleasure. She was so wet I could feel her hot juice running down my leg. Slowly, still driving in and out of her, I eased her onto the soft blankets. I don't know what made it so good. Most of it was her wonderful body; part of it was the wind howling outside, the feeling of being inside a warm, beautiful woman. It was good and it got better. They say that Scandinavian women are freer about sex than any women in the world. This one certainly was. She pushed her tongue into my mouth and her breath was sweet and fresh except for the pleasant, lingering taste of whiskey. Her whole body seemed to respond to every thrust of my cock. Her heels drummed on the blankets and she reached down from behind and stroked my balls, causing me to get bigger and harder. Then she came with a scream of delight that was louder than the shrieking of the wind. One orgasm followed another until her body quivered like a taut wire.

"Oh Jim, come deep inside me!" she cried out. "As far as you can go. Push it in hard as you can. I want to feel myself all around you when you come." Just as I was about to come, she swung her legs up over my shoulder, so I could get in as far as possible. I went in until my bush was hot and wet against hers. My balls were tight with longing for her. I volleyed into her, sucking her breasts as I shot my load.

"Oh Jim, that was wonderful," she said, running her fingers over my face. "It has been so long I forgot what it was like. I am so grateful to you."

Of course that was the craziest thing I ever heard in my life. Any man in his right mind would have been glad to get down on his knees and beg for a chance to make love to this beautiful woman. We lay together exploring each other's bodies, and I knew that I would remember her for a very long time. There were women and there were women. This one was the second kind. Smiling, she took a mouthful of whiskey, but didn't swallow it. Still holding the whiskey in her mouth, she took in the head of my prick and for an instant the whiskey burned, but then it grew hot with sudden pleasure as the liquor took its effect on the nerves. She hummed until my cock vibrated with a feeling that was almost unbearable. When I exploded in her mouth she swallowed the whiskey and my jisum.

Later, wanting to repay the pleasure she had given me, I separated her legs and put my mouth between them, searching for her with my tongue. We lay together there panting.

It was well into the evening when we rolled apart, pleasantly jaded with lovemaking. The stove threw out its cheerful glow and I hated her to leave. We were going in different directions, and there was no telling that I'd ever see her again. I don't say I wanted to marry her—I'll never marry any woman—but I wanted it to last for a while. Everything comes to an end naturally, but this was over too fast. I wanted more of her. I wanted all I could get.

Hella's fucking was athletic; she could bend and use her body in ways that seemed incredible to me. She was nothing less than a sex contortionist. At one point she hooked her ankles over my shoulder and I fucked her that way. That changed the angle of my shaft; I had seldom felt anything so good. Then she got down on her hands and knees and we fucked dog-style, with me sticking it between her legs from behind. Her ass was like a firm but resilient cushion.

"Slowly, Jim, do it slowly. It feels so good this way. It is one of the favorite ways in my country. I think it is a favorite because it feels so different."

I had to agree it was different, and I was getting as much pleasure as she was. She crooned softly every time I thrust deep into her. She spoke soft words in Finnish. I didn't know a word of Finnish, but I didn't have to—I knew what she was saying.

We continued to fuck dog-style, then her entire body began to quiver and she came with a loud gasp. I continued to pump in and out of her, not wanting this favorite Finnish fuck to end. Her hands gripped the blankets when I thrust my shaft in all the way and held it there while I came. She moaned, tightening her cunt muscles, then relaxing them. My cock was getting limp, but I kept pumping as long as there was some stiffness left in it. Finally I had to stop and I lay on top of her, with my soft cock still in her. The softness and smell of her body were wonderful.

"I like having your weight on top of me," she whispered. "Often in bed at night I long to have a big man's weight on top of me. The weight and the warmth, that is what I miss. Now I have it and I am happy."

"Me too," I said.

"I have had a few men here," she whispered. "Very few. Men here, most of them, are so dirty. And all they do is talk of gold. One crazy man who had struck it rich wanted to buy me. Not marry me, buy me. I knew he was crazy because he told me all his life he wanted to buy a beautiful woman if he got rich enough. He wanted me to be his slave girl, he told me in bed. He was a nice enough man, but he was a lunatic and not so good in bed. I got rid of him as quickly as I could. I wonder if he succeeded in his search for a sex slave."

"He'll find someone," I said.

"I pity the girl," Hella said. "How ugly to be a sex slave! I find it hard to believe there are such men."

"You'll never be a slave, sex or otherwise."

"Never. I like my life. I like what I am."

"So do I. And I like your favorite Finnish way."

Hella laughed. "We will do it again if we meet. It's possible. I would like us to get together again."

"There's nothing like hope," I said.

"I will think of your big cock when you are far away. I will cherish the memory of your big cock. Take care of it, Jim."

"You bet I will. And out on the trail I'll think of you. Your sweet pussy, the rest of you."

We fucked again when I got hard enough. One great thing about being a woman is you don't have to wait. That's why really horny women fuck twenty times a day. I knew we would have to part soon—this would be our last fuck—so we put our hearts into it. This time Hella's fucking was almost frantic. I knew I was going to miss this woman, as much for herself as for her wonderful fucking.

"I must go, Jim," she said quietly. "I have many things to do before I start tomorrow. So have you. Now you must sleep and get your strength back. Tonight you have given all of it to me."

I could see that it was no use trying to persuade her to come with me. She had chosen a strange, lonely life. It wasn't for me to say she was wrong.

"I'm sorry to see you go," I said.

"Don't be sorry. There is nothing to be sorry about. And don't say you will escort me home, like a boy in a story. My cabin is only a few miles and there is no danger. Everybody knows me here. They would hang the man who tried to harm me."

"You have a pistol in that big coat?"

"I carry a rifle on my journeys, that is all. Goodbye, Jim. I hope nothing happens to you." She kissed me and was ready to go.

"Stay safe," I said.

I barred the door behind her and heaped more wood in the stove. Then I lay on the bunk and drank the rest of the whiskey until I was ready to sleep. Tired or not, it was a long time before I closed my eyes.

The next day I went across the river to Lousetown to look for McClure. Folks in Dawson looked down on the neighboring settlement, though I couldn't see much difference between the two towns except that Dawson was somewhat bigger. Otherwise they had the same miserable appearance; in Lousetown tents and shacks drifted up the hills from the river, now frozen over and covered with snow. The sky was as clear as it ever gets there in winter, meaning that it was a dull gray and whipped by artic winds. Gold-seekers were still heading out to the creeks that emptied into the Yukon, but most of the citizens seemed to be settling in, like bears, for the long, hard winter. A man flattening tin cans to make a facing for his shack pointed up the hill and told me I could find McClure in a big cabin with a horseshoe nailed above the door.

"Mac came back during the night," the man said. "I heard him yelling at his dogs."

McClure was still asleep when I banged on his door. It took more banging to get him to open up, and when he did he was in right bad humor. Like half the men in that part of the country he was Scotch, and he eyed me with the natural wariness of his people. He had hard, blue eyes and the kind of red skin that never tans no matter how much it's exposed to sun and wind. He lived with his dogs and they came snarling at me when he opened the door.

"Well come in, for Christ's sake," he growled. "Pay no mind to the dogs. They won't attack you unless I tell them to. Then they'll tear you to bits."

That's how they are in the Yukon: always full of good cheer. "Thanks for telling me," I said. "You Duncan McClure?"

"The same," he agreed. "You mind telling me what you want so I can get back in my bunk?" He yawned and scratched himself, pushing through the pack of dogs that filled the cabin.

The cabin had two rooms and there were dogs in both of them. I don't know how many dogs he had in there. At least three teams. There were even dogs under his two-tiered bunk. The whole place stank of dogs and fish and tobacco and dirty clothes. A pot of coffee simmered on a red-hot stove and the walls were hung with everything that could be hung on them. Snowshoes, dog whips, boots, rifles, a sled harness, other things I couldn't even place.

McClure sat on the edge of his bunk and put a match to his pipe. "There's a chair," he said, pointing. "Just knock that gear to floor and say what it is you want."

"Dogs," I said. "And a sound sled."

"Thought you might," he said. "Well, sir, one thing I got is dogs. You think you want to go into the freighting

71

business? It's all spoken for, if that's what you have in mind. Between me and that Hella woman it's tied up tight."

"She said you had good dogs," I said. "You want to sell me a team? I'll give you fifteen hundred for a team and a sled."

The Scotchman had a short laugh at that. "You'll give me twenty-five hundred. Couldn't take less than that. Dogs are worth more than money up here. You don't believe me, ask around."

After some dickering we settled on two thousand for the whole shebang, and McClure even gave me a cup of coffee to seal the bargain. Now that he had my money in his pocket he was ready to be friendly in a watchful way.

"You heading for the creeks?" he said. "Tell me to mind my own business if you like."

"You know a camp called Dulcimer on the Alaska side of the line?" The air in the cabin was thick enough to make soup, and every time I spoke to McClure the dogs growled.

"I've been there," McClure said. "The other side of Fort Yukon. If that's where you're going you're in for one hell of a journey. And if I do say so, you picked one hell of a time to be making it."

"I figure to follow the river most of the way. I know where the fort is. How close to that is Dulcimer?"

McClure scratched his beard with the stem of his pipe. "About thirty miles, I'd say. But miles don't mean that much in winter. If you want my advice, which you don't, Dulcimer is a good place to stay out of. It's got no law at all and there's more shooting there in a week than we get here in a year. All the trash the redcoats keep out on this side end up there. And for all the soldiers the fort is near as bad."

I was surprised. "You mean there's a town there now?" In my time Fort Yukon was nothing but a log fort and a trading post. It had the name of being the worst duty in the whole U.S. Army.

"What passes for a town," McClure said. "Stores, saloons, even something that calls itself a hotel. Man that used to run the trading post got murdered. Now it's run by a Canuck halfbreed name of Du Sang. A right bad egg, that fella. But they got plenty of bad eggs besides him. The fort's got no say in how the town is run, so they keep out of it except when one of the men gets in some kind of trouble. I made a few runs down that way till I decided I'd end up gut-shot or throat-cut. When you get down that way, lad, you'd better sleep with one eye open or maybe you'll never open them again. Now if you're all done with that coffee I'll feed the dogs some fish and crawl back in bed."

Well, there I was with my sled and my six huskies. Their names, according to McClure, were Siwash, Horse, Haggis, Blackie, Watson, and Fox. Fox was the lead dog because he was the smartest and the biggest. A man may boss the whole outfit, but the lead dog is his second in command. He keeps the other dogs in line and without him there is no discipline at all. Fox was about a hundred and twenty-five pounds; the other dogs averaged a hundred or so. McClure had no dogmeat or fish to sell, so I would have to buy that in Dawson. I was to talk to a man named Phipps, the Scotchman said.

Crossing the river with the team, I felt the pull of muscles I hadn't used for a long time. Every kind of work from punching cows to chopping wood uses a different combination of muscles, but I'll be damned if mushing a dog team doesn't use every muscle in the body. McClure said the dogs he sold me hadn't been worked lately and therefore were kind of soft. That was all to the good, according to him, because they wouldn't set me too hard a pace for the first few days. I knew the dogs would be a bit skittish at first, even with a strong lead dog like Fox, but they were well fed and eager to get out on the trail. Thinking of my snug cabin with its glowing stove I wasn't half as eager, but there was work to be done and I had come a long way to do it.

I found the man named Phipps and he charged me fifty cents a pound for dried fish and caribou meat for the dogs. It was about twenty below zero, mild weather for Dawson, and the sky was like lead. This would be my last chance to load up on supplies, so once again I went over what I had. I had food and bullets and whiskey and there wasn't anything else I could think of.

It was time to move out.

SIX

The river was to be my road to the American side of the border, and though it wasn't frozen solid to the bottom, I figured the ice was thick enough to travel on. Dawson and all its glories fell away behind me and it was good to get away from the stink of unwashed men and all the babble about gold. Yet in some ways I was sorry to leave it behind, because I am a man who likes company and the sounds of a saloon, the clink of whiskey glasses and the slap of cards. I guessed Hella had started out by now and I smiled when I thought of her mushing behind the dog team, all bundled up in furs with that determined look in her eyes. At first there was a lonely feeling when I thought of her, but that was soon forgotten when Fox, my lead dog, barked furiously and started the team to one side of a weak place in the ice. After that I kept my mind on the business at hand, which was staying alive in a land where anything could kill you. Anything at all.

The sun came out, if you can call it that, in the middle

of the day. It looked like runny egg yolk against the leaden sky. I was sorry to see it weaken and vanish, because in the days to come it would not appear at all. In time to come there would be nights that were brighter than the days. On such nights, if the sky wasn't overcast, the moon, stars and Northern Lights would shine with a brilliance that could almost hurt the eyes. There was no one else on the river, not that day anyway, and though my arms ached, I was beginning to get the feel of a dog sled again. In my army days I had done a considerable amount of it, and whenever I got leave I explored the Canadian side of the line. It wasn't that I liked it so much but it gave me a chance to get away from the fort. I learned a lot about the country and unbeknownst to the post commander, or any of the men, I built a shack under the lee of a cliff in a deep draw. There I would spend time with an Indian girl and a bottle from the trading post at the fort. . . .

I decided that McClure was an honest man after all, for Fox was all the dog the Scotchman said he was. The big bastard had intelligence that went far beyond anything I've ever seen in an animal; that takes in a lot of men too. I've never been one for dogs, not having the need of one, but I was beginning to like that barrel-chested husky.

The miles passed in swift silence on the river and soon daylight was gone. I fed the dogs dried meat and we all rested, me most of all. Then we traveled on in that strange light that comes in the early hours of night in the Northland. Day changes to night in a way that is hard to explain; one shade of gray replaces another. Just when it should be getting dark it gets bright again, if the clouds aren't heavy, and if it gets bright enough, you can travel far into the night, or all night if you feel like it.

I didn't feel like it. That night I made camp in a stand of trees, and got a fire started with the kindling I'd brought along. There was plenty of dry deadwood under the snow and I fed the dogs before I ate. I had several hundred pounds of dog meat on the sled and they were putting it away at the rate of two pounds a day per dog. I cooked up a supper of fat bacon and beans and made a pot of coffee. The night was cold and clear, but I didn't feel too bad sitting by the fire all wrapped up to the eyebrows. Of course this was the easy part of the trip; I didn't have an old man in a coffin to worry about. It was not my intention to return by way of Dawson and Skagway. There was something about Soapy Smith that still made me uneasy. There was another port, a little place called Valdez, higher up the coast. The only trouble was it was on the other side of the Alaska Range. If the mountains had been crossed by any white man I hadn't heard about it. Maybe Indians had done it, but I hadn't heard about that either. But I couldn't see that there was any other way to go if I wanted to avoid Soapy and his gunmen. If I did make it to Valdez, it would be clear sailing after that.

The huskies had made burrows in the snow and were curled up for the night. Contrary to what you might think, a hole in frozen snow makes a warm place to sleep. I built up the fire, then dragged a dead log to top it off. The log would burn all night and I wouldn't have to fuss with the fire in the morning. Except for the wind and an occasional whimper from the dogs, it was as quiet as the first day of Creation. I hurt all over, especially in the upper arms and shoulders. I'd be stiff in the morning, but a few hours on the trail would take care of that. In a way it was a good feeling to test myself against the wilds. For months I hadn't done much of anything but buck the poker tables; there had been too many all-night sessions with too few dollars at the end of them. I hadn't suddenly got religion, nothing as drastic as that. What I mean is, I was breathing clear air and I was bone-tired from hard work. I think I fell asleep before you could count to ten.

I was up and off at first light, holding steady to a five-mile trot for the first hour. Then I slowed down to four and held steady at that pace. Along the banks of the great river the woods were still dark, sort of blue-colored as the morning light faded from one shade of gray to another. The sun was weak when it came, yet it did take some edge off the cold. I traveled all day without seeing another human being. Nothing broke the stillness—not a wisp of smoke, not a sound. But I was getting used to that by now. In a way, traveling in the frozen North is like traveling in the desert. Both are places of great danger, but the sense of desolation is the same.

I made about thirty miles by nightfall, if that's the right word to describe the changing of the light. Once again it was a bright clear night and I could have journeyed on. In time to come I would travel at night; right then my tortured muscles were begging for mercy. I cleared a campsite using a snowshoe for a shovel, then I built a fire to cook food for the dogs. The dogs always come first even if you have to go hungry yourself. The dogs do the real work and without them you're in a real bad fix. So far my dogs were working well, thanks to Fox, and I figured I wouldn't have any serious trouble with them. Yet you can't ever be completely sure how it's going to be. Sometimes a team starts out fine, then one or two dogs start acting up. Or a well-behaved dog will turn vicious without warning. Huskies are half wild after all, and only a fool will try to treat them as anything else.

My muscles were so sore I found it hard to cut wood for the fire. After the dogs were fed they dug their burrows and slept. I was falling into the routine of the trail, doing exactly the same things day after day. Cooking supper was the best part of all; the day's work over, with nothing ahead but a big hot meal and grateful hours of sleep. The routine never changed. First the slab of bacon was put on to fry, then the flapjack was cooked in the bacon grease. The beans came last. As soon as the coffee boiled supper was ready.

It snowed during the night, but I didn't know it until I woke up. The new snow was deep and soft and I knew there was going to be trouble with it. I had to mush ahead of the dogs, breaking trail with my snowshoes. This cut down our speed by about half. It snowed again in the afternoon and there was nothing to do but make camp and wait for it to clear. I was clearing a campsite when I saw a big lynx watching me from atop a snow-covered boulder. The dogs howled when they smelled the cat, but that was the only excitement.

One day followed another. Early on the morning of the fifth day the dogs set up a howling that woke me from a sound sleep. I knew it could be the lynx still following us in a search for food. I rolled out and grabbed my rifle, thinking I might as well put an end to the pest, if that's what it was. If it hung around too long the dogs would be nervous and maybe taken a notion to chase after it. I eased my way into the trees holding a chunk of raw meat in my hand. I was about to throw it when far off I saw a tall figure moving along fast on snowshoes. Snow was blowing from the top of the drifts and at first I couldn't make out much. Then the snow cleared for a moment and there was Hella. She had a rifle and a pack and that was all. I yelled when I saw her and before the echo had gone she unlimbered the rifle. There was something wild and desperate in the way she did it that I knew something was wrong. I yelled again, this time calling her name, and then she recognized me and came ahead as fast as she could move. She would have fallen if I hadn't caught her.

"Easy, don't talk yet," I said, helping her to my camp. There was a bruise on her cheek, another on her forehead, and her eyes had lost their calm look. I got a bottle

79

of whiskey from the supplies and made her drink half a cup before I filled up the rest with black coffee.

"I thought you were so far ahead of me I would never catch up," she said. "I traveled all last night to find you."

"Drink the rest of it," I said. "Then tell me what happened. Who marked your face?"

"Men came to my cabin looking for you," she said. "They thought you had hired me to work for you. To bring out the body. I said I did not know you, but they had been talking to people in Dawson. They knew about the two men who tried to rob you. They took me by surprise. They grabbed my rifle before I could get at it. I had no chance against them. There were five of them. One, the leader, chewed lemon candy all the time."

"Lemon drops," I said. "That's Sullivan. They all work for a man named Soapy Smith in Skagway."

"The criminal?"

"That's the one. Tell me the rest of it, Hella. They beat you. What else did they do?"

"They raped me, all but the leader. Then they killed my dogs so I could not follow you. They said if I tried to follow you they would kill me. What does it all mean, Jim?"

Quickly, I told her what I knew. "Smith must have changed his mind after I left Skagway. Smith may be working on his own or the Slocum brothers sent a man to talk to him. You see any sign of Sullivan and his men on the way here?"

"I saw them on the river. They were not making such bad time. I passed their camp in the night. We must move on and keep on moving. I am all right."

Hella stared at the embers of the fire. "What happened to me, will that make a difference to you?"

I kissed the bruise on her cheek. "What do you think?" I said. "Before this is over I'm going to make them pay for it."

"Good," she said. "And I will help you."

She ate while I harnessed the dogs. "You will sleep in my bag on the sled," I said. "Don't argue about it. You've been traveling night and day with no sleep and hardly anything to eat. Get in my sleeping bag and sleep. Sleep all day and we'll keep going through the night."

"Yes, Jim," was all she said.

In minutes she was asleep and her face lost most of its tension. Her weight hardly slowed down the dogs; anyway, they had eaten her weight in food since we left Dawson. The dogs were toughening up fast, their pace increasing all the time. I wondered how far Sullivan's party was behind us. The more I thought about Soapy Smith, the more I was convinced that he was working for the Slocum brothers. Or they thought he was. Soapy trusted no one and couldn't be trusted himself. He might sit in on the Slocum brothers' game, but he'd find a way to cheat them if it meant more money.

What we had to do was find a good place to ambush Sullivan and his men. There were five of them, so the odds weren't too bad. I didn't know how good Hella was with a rifle. I guessed pretty good. It was too bad she was mixed up in this, but there was no going back on it now. The bastards had killed her dogs, and I could make up for that with money, but I couldn't make up for the rest of it. And I couldn't buy back her life.

Hella woke up in late afternoon and smiled up at me. "I feel so much better now. Soon we will be coming to a place where there are ice jams and sometimes open water. The current keeps the water there from freezing. We will have to go around it. There! You see that big rock. There used to be a danger flag there but it blew away or someone stole it."

We got around the bad stretch of river and the rest of the day passed quickly. Hella got off the sled and we stepped up the pace. She took over the sled and urged the dogs on with strange yipping sounds that she must have learned in Finland. I thought I'd been handling the dogs pretty well but, Hella had me beat all to hell. The dogs seemed to know a real professional musher was in command and they broke out into a six-mile pace that ate up distance.

Hella saw me scanning the riverbank. "You are looking for a place to kill them, yes?"

I nodded. "We have to get them with the first shots. If not they'll circle us. It could go on for hours. How good are you with the rifle?"

"Very good," Hella said without false modesty. "I have killed many kinds of game."

"You ever kill a man?"

"I have never had a reason."

"Will it bother you? You can't hesitate at the last moment. That could get us killed."

"I will not hesitate, not with these men. I would like to torture them."

"All we want to do is kill them. We'll wait another day until they're good and tired. Maybe some of them are hardened to this country, but Sullivan isn't. We'll catch them right at the tag-end of the day when they're worn out and hungry."

"If we kill them there will be no more trouble, yes?"

"I don't know," I said. "I'm beginning to think you should get out of this. You can get a sled and a team in Fort Yukon and head back to Dawson."

"I will not do that," Hella said. "I will go with you to the sea. We will cross the Alaska Range together. Then when you leave on the ship I will decide what I am going to do. It will be good to do what never has been done. Will they put our names in the newspapers?"

I grinned at her. "Most likely. They're always looking for something new. We'll be famous, at least for a few weeks. If you come to San Francisco you'll be famous there too and part of the biggest funeral for years."

"But what about this woman, this loving friend? I would not want to be the cause of fighting."

"Don't worry about her. We get together now and then. I never lasts long. That's how we are."

"I will have to think about all this," Hella said.

Hella might have been thinking as far ahead as Frisco. My own thoughts were concerned with the telegraph line that went by relays to Fort Yukon. The line went all the way downriver to the sea. I had thought of going out by that route; it was just too far. Going over the mountains to Valdez would be a tougher journey, but it was hundreds of miles closer. Besides, I could be sure of getting a ship at Valdez; ore ships from the States made regular calls there.

I thought about the telegraph line and wondered if trouble was ahead of us as well as behind. McClure said Fort Yukon and Dulcimer were crawling with badmen from all over, so it would be easy for Soapy to hire on a few. The best we could hope to do was get in and out fast. If somebody hadn't stolen the judge's body by now, we would load it in the dead of night and head for the coast. Along the way we would have to depend on our rifles for food. I wondered how much the judge weighed. I hoped his corpse wasn't as heavy as President Taft's. I smiled at the grisly thought. I had forgotten to ask.

That night it was bitter cold, worse than anything I'd come across so far. It would be just as cold the next day, Hella said. I had no reason to doubt her; she knew the country a lot better than I did. We didn't make camp until about midnight, and by then the dogs' muzzles were covered with ice and my own fast growing beard was as stiff as a thorn bush. The air was full of frost crystals and it was painful to breathe. The dogs dug in as always and we ate our supper in weary silence. Neither of us felt like talking.

"It's going to be a tight squeeze in that sleeping bag," I said. "You want to try it?"

Hella smiled and nodded. "I have never been in a sleeping bag with a man. Or with anyone. It will be warm."

In that temperature, at least fifty below, it would have been madness to take off any clothes except the outer ones. Luckily, the bag was a roomy one and we were able to take off our bulky lined coats and boots. We wrapped the boots in the coats and put them a safe distance from the fire. I built up the fire until it was shooting sparks high into the air.

Below us on the river an ice-jam made cracking sounds like rifle fire. The noise kept on for a while. It was good to lie in the sleeping bag with the firelight in our faces. Then, cramped or not, our hands began to move around. I unbuttoned Hella's trousers and she unbuttoned mine. It's amazing what you can do if you really want to do it. I knew Hella was thinking about the men who had raped her. I thought about it too, and wanted her to know that it made no difference to me. But I did it slowly. Women who have been raped sometimes panic and I didn't want that to happen. I was gentle with her as I've never been with a woman before and the slight rigidity of her body softened as my hands moved over it. She shifted her position so I could get between her legs and after that she made love as naturally as she had in the cabin. The dogs heard us moving around and growled at this unusual activity. Hella laughed and I knew she was going to be all right.

"Let us sleep now," she said. "Those men are still far behind. Tomorrow we will kill them and the world will be a better place when they are dead."

The ice-jams grew worse after that; they were higher and closer together. Stretches of open water were more dangerous; it was all bad. A dozen times Hella, with her quick eye, spotted danger where I did not. Most dangerous of all were the places where a thin sheet of ice was covered with snow. If the heavily loaded sled started to go into the water there would be no holding it back, not unless you wanted to go along with it.

At times we had to portage for miles and in places this was hell because the banks of the river were high and covered with ice. If Hella hadn't been there I'm not sure I could have managed. Or if I did manage, it would have cost me many hours of valuable time. Without Hella the sled would have to be unloaded over and over. I asked Hella why we didn't leave the river altogether; she said the river was still the fastest way to go. No matter how tough the river was, it ran right to Fort Yukon.

During the early part of the day there were great banks of fog on the frozen river. Then howling, icy wind blew the fog away and kept on blowing after the fog was gone. The gale stung our eyes. Still, I was toughening up all the time. The hard pace Hella set for the dogs didn't bother me now. Hella herself was a wonder, running tirelessly behind the sled, never out of breath, never faltering for a moment.

With only a few hours of light left I saw the place where we were going to kill them. There was an ice-jam that could only be crossed with a lot of effort; beyond it, fifty yards away, was another jam of almost the same size.

I pointed. "We'll cross with the team, then take the team out of the river so they won't start barking when they hear Sullivan's dogs. We'll be behind the second jam. As soon as they come over and are heading down for the flat we start shooting. No mercy, you understand. If they put up their hands, kill them anyway. It has to be done if we're to have a chance."

Hella said quietly, "I am glad to do it. We may have a long wait."

"This is a good place. We'll do it here. Come on now. Let's get the dogs across."

We manhandled the sled across the two ice-jams. The wind was still blowing hard. I hoped to hell it wasn't going to snow again. In that country the weather can change ten times a day and all of it is rotten except for a few weeks in summer.

"You watch the river, I'll take the team ahead," I told Hella. "If you see them coming, fire one shot, then pull out. There won't be time to get set up if they're that close."

Hella nodded. "One shot."

"Don't waste time trying to kill somebody," I said. "Just fire a shot and get the hell out of there. I don't want to get you killed. You're too good in a sleeping bag."

"Thank you, Jim," Hella said and lay down behind the ice-jam.

I looked back at the river and it was wide and empty. The wind was blowing away our tracks in the snow, but they would be sure to see the cuts left by the sled runners on the ice. I wondered what kind of men were with Sullivan; a few of them had to be old Alaska hands; the ex-pimp would never dare tackle the Yukon River with inexperienced men. By himself, Sullivan wasn't much of a threat, not unless he got right behind your back with a knife or a gun. But the others might be able to smell out an ambush; there are men who can do that.

"Nothing," Hella said when I came back after leaving the team and sled in a stand of pines away from the river. I tied the dogs and gave them plenty of meat to keep them quiet.

"We will hear the dogs first," Hella said. "Do we kill the dogs too? I hate to kill the dogs, but I will do it if you say so."

I sighted my Winchester along the desolate river. "We'll take their sled and dogs if we can."

"What about the Mounties?"

"I guess the bodies will be found sooner or later. But we'll be in American territory in a few more days. Anyway, it has to be done."

"Listen," Hella said, cutting me off. "Did you hear it?"

I hadn't heard anything, so I shook my head. "You still hear it?"

"Not now," she said. "It came on the wind, but now it's gone. I heard something."

We lay together behind the wall of ice. Hella had a new Marlin lever-action, a fine weapon and just as good as the Winchester.

"I heard it again," Hella said. "The barking of the dogs. They are coming."

I still hadn't heard it. "How far back?"

"A few miles. The sound carries a long way across the ice. You would hear it clearly if not for the wind. They will be here in about thirty minutes. Will you fire first?"

"When they are coming over the top we'll fire together. But wait until they're all over. I don't want a stand-off. Sullivan is the one to kill because he's bossing this outfit. Sullivan is the one with the lemon drops."

Hella's jaw was hard as she sighted along the rifle. "I know who he is. He watched while the others raped me. He sucked on that filthy candy all the time they were raping me. He spat some pieces on the floor close to my head."

"Don't get too mad or you'll miss," I warned her. "Think of them as targets and you'll be all right."

"No," Hella said. "I will not think of them as targets. But I will not miss."

While we waited I heard the dogs for the first time. It sounded like they were coming pretty fast. I wondered how the fat-gutted Sullivan was holding up. The expimp had spent most of his dirty life indoors, beating up on girls; this couldn't be to his liking at all. But you didn't talk back to Soapy Smith when he wanted something done.

Hella pointed far down the river. There was a bend and they came around it, a single sled and dog team. Three men ran beside the sled in snowshoes; one man was mushing. I grinned when I made out Sullivan riding the sled, all bundled up against the cold. The vicious bastard didn't know it, but he was really riding a hearse.

I slid lower on the ice and pulled Hella after me. "We'll hear them coming across," I said. Sullivan will have to get off the sled to cross the ice. The others all have rifles. Sullivan will try to use a pistol."

"Try, yes. That is what he will do."

There was something in the way she said it that convinced me she was going to be all right. I hadn't doubted her courage for a moment, yet courage and a willingness to kill are not always found in the same person. It's easy enough after the first time, but there has to be a first time. Most people never get that far.

Now they were close enough for us to hear their voices. It was impossible to hear what they were saying because of the dogs, still making a hellish racket. I guessed they had spotted our sled tracks on the first icejam. I glanced at Hella and she had her gloved finger outside the trigger guard of her rifle. There was more loud talking and then the scrape of sled runners on ice. They were coming over.

I didn't dare take a look at the man who came first. I guessed he was staring right over our heads. There was a lull in the barking and I heard him say clearly, "Their tracks go on from here. Bring the team across."

I chanced a look when they were all pulling on the sled. Then there was a sound of the sled being let down to the bottom. The dogs started barking again and maybe they smelled us. They were at the bottom now and about to start for our position.

I nodded to Hella and we both raised up and fired. My first bullet got Sullivan in the face and he fell across the sled with a scream that drove the dogs crazy. Suddenly all the dogs were fighting, snarling like demons. I fired twice and killed two men. Hella killed another man who tried to scramble back over the ice jam. Only one man was left and he ran toward the riverbank. We raised our rifles and killed him together. It was over in seconds and the dogs were still fighting. There was nothing to do but let them fight.

We came down from the ice jam to look at the bodies. There were no wounded, so there was no more killing to be done. Sullivan lay on his side on the ice. A lemon sourball had fallen out of his mouth.

"How do you feel?" I asked Hella.

"Just fine," she answered. "They are dead and now I can start to forget what they did to me."

We left them where they lay. Soon the bodies would freeze as hard as stone. If there were wolves around there wouldn't be much for the Red Coats to find. We took some canned goods and the fine fur robe Sullivan had been covered with on the sled. But we left their weapons. On the trail every extra pound can be the one that kills you. Sullivan was the only one with any real money on him. I took that—five thousand dollars—and gave it to Hella.

"You can buy a lot of new dogs with that," I said. "Start your own freighting company if you like."

"Maybe I will," she said.

The wind dropped and after that it was just biting cold. But cold is a fact of life in that country. If you can't stand it you have no business being there. The night turned out to be clear and we put many miles between us and the scene of the ambush. We made camp in a grove of trees. Hella had come through the ambush just fine, but now the strain was beginning to tell on her. Her face was drawn and there were tiny lines at the corners of her eyes. I fixed her a big drink of whiskey and black coffee and insisted that she drink another before she crawled into the sleeping bag. I crawled in after her, but she was already asleep. I didn't mind that because we'd been having a fine time on the snowy trail and there were other good nights ahead of us.

"You should not have let me sleep so long," she murmured when she woke up hours later. It was about an hour to sun-up. Her hands moved over me in the half-darkness. In their snow burrows the Huskies whimpered in their sleep.

"You needed the sleep," I said. "We'll have other times, don't you know that?"

"I don't know anything," she said. "I just know we shouldn't waste any of the time we have. The other night you were asleep and I woke up and looked at you and wondered how long we would be together. And when I thought of that I was afraid. I do not get afraid so easily so that made me all the more afraid. Do you know what I am talking about?"

"Maybe I do, but what's the use of dwelling on it." I kissed her. "Could be the worst part of this is over. If Smith thinks Sullivan is still alive—why shouldn't he?— we may be able to get the judge's body out of Dulcimer without too much trouble. Once we get into the mountains they'll never find us."

Hella nodded vigorously. "Yes, they will not find us in the mountains. They may not even dare to follow. I wish we were there now. But I wish we did not have to bring along a dead old man. How can a dead old man cause so much trouble? How many deaths has he caused so far?"

"Six," I said, wondering how many more men would die before the judge was shoveled into his grave.

Three days later we crossed into Alaska.

SEVEN

Now I was beginning to know the country because when I was in the army we patrolled to the Canadian border and back to the fort. Many's the day I cursed the ill luck that brought me to such a place, but I was younger then and given to cursing a lot of things. It was strange to see landmarks I thought I'd never see again. A peculiar looking rock high on a hillside, a dead twisted tree that looked like a bent old man. It was like coming home. I just hoped I wouldn't be buried there.

We were resting ourselves and the dogs, and Hella was boiling up coffee. It was the middle of the day and the sun was warming up the air just a mite. We had just lugged the sled around a bad ice jam. We were good and tired.

"There used to be a way-station about ten miles from here," I said. "Man named Ginnis used to feed travelers on the river. If the place is still there we can get real food and a place to sleep."

"I like the sleeping bag," Hella said, smiling.

"At least the food," I said. "You ever eat bear meat? Ginnis used to have bear and moose and caribou. Sometimes small deer."

"No bear meat for me. This man Ginnis may be dead by now."

"Then it's back to bacon and beans till we get to the fort."

It was on toward nightfall when I saw the lights of the old way-station perched up on a hill, well out of the way of flood water. It looked like the original log building had been added to; anyway there were more lights.

A track had been cleared from the river to the way-station and we got up there with no trouble at all. The name Ginnis was still above the main door and it was lit by a shielded lantern. Along one side of the building was a penned-in shed for dogs and sleds. There were three sleds and three dog teams, but whether they were coming to, or leaving Alaska, there was no way to tell.

When the dogs started barking Ginnis came out to see what was disturbing them. Ginnis had put on a few years; otherwise he looked much the same. The shed for the dogs was divided into sections to keep them from fighting; he showed us where to put ours. He kept glancing at me. Finally he said, "Don't I know you, mister?"

I grinned at him. "Sure you do, Ginnis. Jim Saddler. Used to be a soldier at the fort."

"I'll be damned to hell," Ginnis said. "I guess you are at that. I recall how you used to bitch about being there. You came back and you brought a pretty lady."

I told him who Hella was.

"I've heard of you, ma'am," Ginnis said. "In a nice way, you understand. Come on in and we'll have a chin wag about old times. Got moose steak and fried beans on the stove. Two kinds of pie, apple and blueberry. Canned fruit naturally, but I got a way of fixing it up."

Four men were eating at two tables and they looked up when we came in. They all had beards, fur hats and lined boots. Their parkas hung on pegs on the wall. After they got through gawking at Hella they went back to the food.

Ginnis pointed to a table in a far corner. "Make yourself to home and I'll go get your supper. How you like my new place, Saddler?"

"Looks like you're doing good," I said, grinning at him. "You always did make plenty of money. How much do you charge for a meal these days?"

"Used to charge five," Ginnis said, dropping cut wood in a huge stove. "Now I charge ten, fifteen. Depends what and how much you eat. You folks I'll go easy on. A lot of coffee first, am I right?"

"You couldn't be righter," I said.

Ginnis brought in the biggest coffee pot you ever saw, then went back to the kitchen for the steak and beans. "I'll sit with you, you don't mind," he said.

Ginnis was a Southerner, from what part I didn't know and never asked, and he had been in Alaska for well over twenty years. I always had the feeling that he was hiding from the law because of something pretty bad. Murder? Bank robbery? A vengeful, hated wife? Something like that. Maybe Ginnis wasn't even his right name, which was nothing new in Alaska, where half the citizens were trying to live down something in their past. But he'd always treated me right, even to making loans to tide me over till payday. There was an enlisted man moneylender at the fort—every fort has one—but I hated the greedy bastard and wouldn't do business with him. I wondered if Ginnis knew anything about the judge.

I asked him, keeping my voice low.

Ginnis wasn't the kind to show surprise. "A traveler

told me about him dying up in Dulcimer. You got something to do with him? Guess you do at that. Didn't think you'd come to root for gold. Hard work's not in your line. You want to know what I know. What I know is the judge is dead and plenty of hardcases are glad of that. Too many men from California up here. Men the judge put in the pokey for too long. Me, I keep away from judges, so it's no matter to me."

"But the judge is all right," I said.

"He's not all right, Saddler. He's dead."

Hella laughed and some of the men looked up, some with subdued lust, some with sentimental longing. Women are scarce in Alaska, and Hella was the kind of woman for a lonely man to dream about.

I laughed too. "I mean the body, Ginnis."

"Body's in its coffin in Dulcimer, all froze solid and standing up agin the wall of an open woodshed. Saw it myself 'cause I had dealings with a man in that miserable town. Men come from all over to take a look at it. And do other things, from what I hear. Don't like to say what, with the lady present."

"That's pretty bad," I said, thinking of hardcases pissing on the old coot's coffin. Still, they hadn't burned it or put it through an ice-hole in the river.

"I'm going to bring the body out. The two of us." I nodded toward Hella, who was eating moose steak like the big woman she was. "You think they'll try to stop me, the hardcases?"

"Why not just burn a hole in the ground and bury it?" Ginnis asked reasonably enough. "Ground will freeze over it like stone. The badmen wouldn't take the time to dig it up again."

"They want the judge back in Frisco," I said. "He was a very important man."

"He's not important now. I'll go get the pie."

He came back with a steaming apple pie and a hunk of

hard cheese. I was beginning to feel good in spite of it all.

I said, "You think we can make it over the mountains to Valdez? You been in this country about as long as any man."

"I guess anything can be done," Ginnis said. "I'd just hate to be the one to try it. You want a suggestion, Saddler? One that'd make it easier and save you much hardship and grief?"

"I'm ready to listen."

"Go on back to Frisco, find a dead tramp someplace, put him in a cheap pine coffin, batter it a bit, say here's the judge. He's been dead a long time, will be dead a lot longer by the time you get him back. They'd never open the coffin after all that time."

I said, grinning, "He's frozen solid. The idea is to keep him frozen in a block of ice all the way back so his widow can have him unfrozen so she can prove who he is."

"Doesn't she know what he looks like?"

Hella laughed into her coffee cup. "It's a legal matter, Ginnis."

"I get it," Ginnis said. "A money thing. Then why not just cut off the head and freeze that? Then they can compare it to a photograph."

Ginnis was pleased with all his ideas.

"They can't let a head lie in state," I said. "They want the whole corpse for a big funeral."

"This is a depressing conversation, Mr. Ginnis," Hella said, attacking a big wedge of pie.

Ginnis nodded. "I agree, missy. I'll go get us a drink."

After Ginnis got a bottle of rye from the kitchen he and Hella had a drink but I held off until the four men paid and left. Then I heard the sound of their teams moving out and I went out to see if they really were going away. The night was clear and I could see them moving upriver toward Dawson. I stood and watched them until they disappeared before I went in and joined the others.

"What's eating on you?" Ginnis asked, already bright-eyed and merry with whiskey. "Nobody fools around my place, never have."

"Just being careful," I said.

"What kind of trouble you in?"

I had my first drink, a big one. "You know most everything that goes on in Alaska, anyway this end of it. You know if any of Soapy Smith's boys operate around Dulcimer?"

"Course they do," Ginnis said. "Soapy's more than the King of Skagway. He's the King of Crime all over the territory. If the governor was elected instead of appointed, Soapy'd rig the election certain sure. As it is, the governor, such as he is, hasn't done one thing about Soapy. What you got to do with him?"

"I think he's got ideas about the judge's body."

"What kind of ideas?"

"Steal it maybe."

Ginnis said, "You only had two drinks this far, Saddler, so it can't be that. Now why would Soapy want to steal a corpse?"

I told him about the judge's brothers, his widow, the money. "Soapy's the kind to do anything."

"Truly said. I don't know what to think, though. Mark my words now. You'll have a bad enemy—the worst—if you go against Soapy Smith. It's been tried and the men who tried it are all dead. On the Yukon side of the line you might get some protection from the Mounties. On this side . . ."

Ginnis shook his head, then drew his finger across his throat. "Forget this dead man and go into the sledding business with your friend here. Or hunt for gold. Or open a saloon—that's where the real gold is. Failing that, go back to the States and stay there. The old soap merchant can't bother you there."

I had another drink and it made me braver than I was.

"We're going ahead with it."

"Well, we all have to die sometime," Ginnis said cheerfully. "I've had my say and you've had yours. One last word: watch out for a halfbreed calls himself Du Sang when you get to the town of Fort Yukon. That feller's a Soapy Smith man and it's rumored he murdered the owner of the biggest trading post in the place. The body wasn't found so nobody could dispute Du Sang's signed bill of sale for the post. Not that anybody would want to dispute it. Like as not, the halfbreed's boys stripped the poor man and left him for the wolves. Those gray bastards even grind up the bones so there's nothing left."

I looked at Hella, who wasn't one bit put off by Ginnis's grisly theory. In fact, she was smiling. But even so I wondered if I shouldn't force her to stay behind. With all her trail experience, getting back to Dawson would be like a stroll down a country road.

"Don't even think it," she said, reading my thoughts. "Few wolves are left around here. Most of the wolves are in the mountains."

"That's where we're going," I said.

"We have rifles," Hella said. "The wolves will be more interested in the dogs than us. We will build big fires."

Ginnis hiccuped. "I know what I'm going to do. Go to bed. You going to stay the night?

"We'd like to," I said. "Sleeping in the snow can be wearisome."

Ginnis said, "I got four for-rent rooms in the build-on. They're all vacant right now. You can take your pick. Not much of a pick though. They're all the same. "Finish the whiskey. There's more in the kitchen. The rooms are through that door."

"How much for the meal?" I asked him.

"Nothing." Ginnis turned away with a strange look on his face.

"Why not?"

"I'd as soon not say," Ginnis answered. Then he barred the door and went to his room in the back.

After his door closed Hella said quietly, "He is sure we are going to die."

I nodded. "He could be right. You're not afraid?"

"I am just sleepy and want to go to bed. Come on, Jim. We will drink the rest of the whiskey under the blankets."

That night was the best one we'd had so far because of the awareness of death, of its possibility. It had taken someone else to say it, to make it plain. I don't know why that was so, for we had just ambushed the gang of killers on our trail, yet there it was. In bed there was a real wildness in Hella; it wasn't just the whiskey but the knowledge that we might not have long together. I felt it too so I handled her like a precious object, which she was. Outside the wind howled and the penned dogs barked, but after a while we forgot about danger and death and concentrated on what we were doing.

We were both tired when we started to fuck, but as soon as I thrust into her she revived and so did I. But we fucked slowly—we had a long night ahead of us and we didn't want to wear ourselves. Our slow fucking gave us as much pleasure as if we had gone at it fast and furious. I took my time as I slid it in and out of her. At times we rested and I lay on top of her, smelling her blond hair. Her hair was whiter than the white of the pillow. We hadn't had a bath lately, but it didn't matter.

"I love fucking slowly," Hella whispered. "Your big cock seems to get bigger when we do it slowly. Doing it the slow way makes me so wet I am afraid Mr. Ginnis's sheets will be badly stained. Do you think he will be mad at us because of me?"

"Don't worry about Ginnis," I said. "He rents rooms on the river and gets all sorts of people. He expects to get his sheets stained. Anyway I'll leave some money over there on the dresser. He doesn't want to charge us, but we'll be gone before he finds it."

We both came together and when it was over we were as weary as we had been when we arrived. We both longed for sleep; in a few minutes we slept. Hella murmurered in her sleep; the words were Finnish. I was only half aware of her voice. Sometimes you are half-aware that you're asleep and how enjoyable it is. That was it with me that night. Even while I slept I knew there was a warm, beautiful woman beside me in the bed. Once Hella threw her leg over mine and I stroked it. Later I was conscious that I was stroking her pussy. She crooned a little when I did that. A few times she giggled like a young girl.

The night passed that way.

In the morning Ginnis gave us a big breakfast and some supplies and we started out for Fort Yukon, thirty miles away. A gray dawn brought snow flurries and a wind that grew stronger with every mile we traveled. The dogs began to falter and the only thing was to rig up shoulder harnesses, standard equipment on all Northern sleds, and give them a hand with the heavy sleds. We faced into the wind with bent heads, encouraging the dogs with shouts. We went on like this for an hour, then the wind began to die. By then the dogs were exhausted and so were we. The snow kept up but it was light and feathery now, and we were that many miles closer to Fort Yukon.

It took us the rest of the day to reach this new town everybody said was so tough. The old fort was right on the bank of the river; the sprawling raw town was about a mile back from it. Hella was surprised when I said we were going into the fort.

"But why?" she said.

"I want to talk to the officer in charge. The judge was federal. Maybe that'll make a difference. If there's going to be trouble in Dulcimer I'd like a few troopers along."

The gates of the fort were open: no Indian trouble in Alaska at any time. But the sentry yelled at us to halt when we started in. There was a small glowing brazier in the sentry hut where he was trying to keep himself warm. He was young and looked miserable.

"You want the town not the fort," he said peevishly. "Town's up on the hill. That's where I'd like to be."

"We want the officer in charge," I said. "Federal business."

"What kind of federal business?" I knew he didn't want to be rooted out of his hut.

"Just show us where we can find him."

"Captain Riggs won't like this," the soldier said, but he came out in the cold and pointed. "Over there, that new building all lit up."

"It's a lot fancier than the old commandant's quarters," I told Hella when he passed us through. "In my day the commandant lived in a log hut. This officer's had the men working hard."

A sour-faced man in his late fifties, with an unbuttoned tunic and a glass in his hand, came to the door when I knocked on it. He stared at us with unfriendly eyes and took a gulp of whiskey. "What the blazes do you want?" he said in a rasping voice that was as bitter as his face. I could see he was slightly drunk.

"All right if we come in?" I said. "I'd like to talk to you. We're cold and it won't take long."

Reluctantly, he moved out of the doorway to let us in. "Imagine being cold in Alaska," he said. "Be brief, mister, whoever you are. I haven't had my supper yet."

There was a big room with rough but comfortable furniture. A log fire blazed in a stone fireplace. Other rooms branched off the main room and cooking smells came from one of them. Over the fireplace was the tinted photograph of a pleasant-looking woman in her thirties; no other feminine touches brightened up the big room. Beside the fire there was a leather-covered armchair with a table pulled close. On the table was a bottle of whiskey, mostly empty.

"You're Captain Riggs?" I said.

"I'm the officer in command," he said as if I'd called him a dirty name. He sat down by the fire and put more whiskey in his glass. Here was a man with a heavy chip on his shoulder. He didn't even ask us to sit down.

Hella went to the fire to warm her hands. I said, "It's about the body of Judge Slocum in Dulcimer. I've come to take it back to San Francisco."

The ill-mannered captain put away more whiskey. "What's stopping you?"

I told him what he must have known, that there was hard feeling against the judge. I said there were men there who might try to stop me from recovering the body.

"Rubbish," he said. "But if you have trouble, what's it got to do with me? The whole thing is a civilian matter. It's got nothing to do with the United States Army."

I wanted to slap his drunkard's puffy face, but that wouldn't get us any further along the road. Besides, he was too old. So I held my temper and said, "He was a United States Judge. A federal judge. You don't think his body should be treated with respect, get a decent funeral?"

"What's this about respect, mister?"

"They've been pissing on his coffin, that's what," I said.

"Who the hell told you that?"

"A man who was here, a man who doesn't lie."

He glanced at Hella but was drunk enough not to care what he said. Which was, "A little piss won't hurt him."

"Then you won't help me, give any protection if there's trouble with these hardcases? All I'm asking for is an escort out of town. Then we'll be on our own."

The captain made an impatient gesture with his glass, slopping some of the liquor. "You're on your own now." He drank what was left in the glass. "You think you could report me for my attitude, is that it?"

I managed to keep my voice calm. "I could do that, Captain."

Suddenly he broke into harsh laughter that spoiled the comfortable atmosphere of the big room. Hella stared into the fire, not liking any of it.

"Report all you like," the captain said. "I have only a few weeks to go to retirement, so you can go to hell. Twelve years I've been in this hellhole. Twelve years. A jail sentence. A lifetime. I applied for a transfer ten times in twelve years. Always the same answer: request denied. My wife died here two years after we arrived. Pneumonia. You'd think they'd transfer me after that. The bastards posted me here because I drank a little. What man doesn't drink? I could have straightened out. They wouldn't give me a chance. How'd you like to be still a goddamned captain at fifty-five? Got nothing to say to that, do you?"

I hoped he might talk out his anger, then change his mind. "I wouldn't know how I'd feel, sir."

"Damn right you wouldn't," he went on. "Well, now I'm through with the army, the army is through with me. And if you want to know all the truth, here it is. I don't want any trouble with the miners in Dulcimer because I own two claims there. I've got four men working for me. In a year I'll be a rich man, a very rich man. I don't need their stinking pension, but by God I'm going to get it. I've earned every miserable cent of it. That plain enough for you?"

I made one last try. "Send one of the junior officers,

sir." Lord, how I hated to 'sir' that mean-spirited bastard.

He gave out with that laugh again. "I'm in command here. They'd know where the order came from."

An enlisted man, a fat soldier with an apron tied around him, stuck his head in the door. "Supper's all ready, sir." He ducked back and I could see how afraid he was of the overbearing captain.

The captain lurched to his feet and said with his back turned, "Make sure you shut the door good and tight." Then he roared, "Dobson, come out of that kitchen and see to the door. Then call the sergeant of the guard and tell him I said to escort these people off the post. They are not to be allowed to enter again for any reason."

An enlisted man came running, still wearing an apron, and went outside with us. On the porch he yelled for the sergeant of the guard and he came running, too. He was a tall man with a Southern accent.

"What's up, Fatty?" he wanted to know.

The fat enlisted man told him and he looked us over. "All right, folks, you heard what the captain said. Move along now and don't come back." He lowered his voice. "You got business here, come back in a few weeks. The son-of-a-bitching drunk bastard will be gone by then. I never said that, understand?"

We were at the gate. "Thanks, Sarge," I said. Then we were heading up toward the town. The wind was rising again and there was sleet in it. For once Hella looked dispirited and I didn't feel so great myself.

"That awful man," she said, shouting to be heard above the wind. "Why do they let him stay in the army?"

"Must have friends," I yelled back. "They let him stay, but they shipped him up here to get rid of him. It's no use talking about it. We're not going to get any help. But we can't go on tonight, not with the weather like it is. You tired?"

"I am very tired," Hella shouted, running behind her sled.

It was evening now and the town was going full blast. We passed the original Fort Yukon trading post, the sturdiest building in town, the one the halfbreed DuSang had murdered to get. There were lights and people in it. A few men on the porch stared at us as we went by. In the short main street there were six saloons, three eating places, two hotels, if you could call them that. The sleet whipped our faces and all the dogs except my lead dog, Fox, were starting to falter. Fox, game old brute that he was, turned in the traces and snapped at the others in the team. Soon there would be a fight. Hella's team was just as rebellious, and I knew we had to rest, humans and dogs, even if the weather improved.

"We'll try one of the hotels," I yelled. "If we can't get a room we'll find shelter and bundle up for the night."

We got lucky on the first place we tried. Hella waited with the teams while I went inside looking for the clerk or the owner and was surprised to see a determined-looking woman reading a newspaper behind the desk. She was middle-aged, Irish, I decided. Irish was what she was, but this was no sweet, gentle colleen.

"You got a room for two?" I asked her. "My woman and myself."

The Irishwoman laughed and put down the paper. "At least you didn't say she was your wife. Not that it'd matter in this neck of the woods. It happens I do have a few rooms. Clean too, mister. Those yahoos dirty up my rooms they don't get back no matter what they pay. You wonder why I have empty rooms. Well, sir, the fellas that had them left in the middle of the night. That means they got news of a strike. My name's Bella Tanzey, what's yours?"

I said Jim Saddler. She saw me hesitating and laughed again, a loud hearty laugh. "You're thinking every hotelkeeper says their rooms are clean. Mine are and you can depend on it. My colored boy cleaned the rooms this morning, clean sheets on the beds, clean water in the jug and basin. I'll be offended if you ask to look at them."

"I wouldn't want to do that," I said quickly. "What's the tariff?" I asked, not caring what it was. If the room was only half clean, it would do fine.

"One hundred dollars a night for the two of you," old Bella said. "There's a place for your dogs. That don't cost nothing extra."

I wanted to whistle but didn't. A hundred bucks a night! No wonder she was laughing all the time. It's always like that in a gold rush: the people who provide the lodgings, liquor, women, and supplies make the most money. I once knew a man who made a fortune running a string of boardinghouses in the Colorado mining camps, and his beds were crawling with lice, fleas and bedbugs.

"That'll be fine," I said.

She took the money, saying, "Ah yes, sure Fort Yukon's a fine little settlement."

We got the dogs put away for the night, then fed the brutes. They ate like the half-wolves they were, and growled themselves to sleep. It took us a while to do our dog chores, and when we went back into the hotel there was a man waiting by the desk. I thought Bella's face was kind of grim, but she wasn't giving this gent any arguments. She wasn't talking to him either. He was a halfbreed with a face like a glazed ham, as if he'd come through a bad fire at some point in his life. The reddish skin with the shiny white burn patches gave him a sinister look. Rightaway I knew he was DuSang.

He was wearing a fur hat and he tipped his finger to it when he saw Hella. "My name is DuSang. Frank DuSang, and I'm a friend of a friend of yours. Mr. Smith. You want to talk a minute?"

"Sure," I said, giving Hella the room key. "I'll be up in a minute."

Hella took the key without a word, but her face was drawn with worry. The landlady picked up her paper and buried herself behind it. She was a determined old tub; it was just as clear that she was frightened of Frank DuSang.

I nodded toward some chairs against the far wall. "These will do." I spoke quietly. "You heard from Soapy?"

We sat down and DuSang said, "Had to telegraph me about some business the other day. Said to keep an eye out for you. Give a hand if it was needed."

DuSang opened his parka and there was a bullet-studded gunbelt under it. He was short but broad shouldered, a strong, hard man, and from what I'd been told, a vicious one. His English, except for a slight French accent, was the same as anyone else's. The hair that stuck out from under his hat was lank and oily.

"That was neighborly of Soapy," I said. "You know what I'm here for?"

DuSang nodded without smiling. I don't think he could smile, not with that face. Or maybe the memory of how he got the face made it impossible for him to smile.

"Then you don't need any help?" he said. "Soapy says you're a friend from way back and would like to see you back in Skagway in one piece."

"Old friends are the best," I said. "The next time you talk on the wire, tell Soapy thanks for me. I'll see him in Skagway soon as I can."

DuSang didn't say anything for a moment. Instead, he studied me with black, expressionless eyes, as if trying to make up his mind about me. At last he said, "I'll do that, Saddler."

Then, without another word, he got up and left.

I felt as if I'd had a visit from the Angel of Death.

EIGHT

The sleet storm passed in the middle of the night, and we headed out for Dulcimer at five o'clock. There was no one in the street as we took the sleds over the crackling ice and followed the trail west. It was a well-traveled trail and the going was easy; there was no one following us that I could see. For once there was no wind, and if it hadn't been for the rasp of the sled runners there would have been absolute silence. For Alaska, at the start of winter, it was a lovely morning.

The dogs were rested and fed and soon we were moving at a five-mile pace. We stayed with the Yukon River for ten miles, then swung onto Campbell's Creek, the last stage of the long road to Dulcimer. On the creek there were no ice jams; it was flat as a floor. All moisture had disappeared from the windless air and the temperature kept dropping all the time.

I kept trying to puzzle out what was going on. Why had Sullivan and his men come after us if Soapy Smith expected me to come back through Skagway? DuSang turned my stomach, but I decided he was telling the truth when he said he'd talked on the wire to the King of Crime. If Soapy wanted me dead, why hadn't DuSang made a try in Fort Yukon? DuSang had the men to back him up, not that he needed anybody but himself. The halfbreed might be a vicious bastard, but he looked like a man who wasn't afraid of anything. I got no answers to any of my own questions, so I gave up. The answers would come soon enough—in Dulcimer.

With still three hours to go, we rested the dogs. It was colder than it had been, but without a wind it was bearable. I made a fire and Hella made coffee and we talked about what was to come. The woman at the hotel said there was a telegraph line in Dulcimer, strung there from Fort Yukon, and I was thinking about that. Nothing definite, just an idea, and I wasn't sure I was going to do it.

"You think they'll try to stop us?" Hella said.

"It depends," I said. "A few soreheads won't mean much. But if there is one man, some hardcase jailbird with a real hate for the judge, there could be trouble. DuSang didn't say. I guess he had his reasons."

Hella said, "I think DuSang is worse than any of them. I only saw him for a moment, but I could tell."

"All it takes is one look to know that," I said. "He'd be a good man in a fight. I just wouldn't want him behind my back. I wouldn't want him anywhere around, back or front. We don't have to worry about DuSang right now. He had his chance last night and didn't take it."

Hella looked at me with clear, direct eyes with no fear in them. "Are you sorry you got into this, Jim?"

It was a simple and sensible question, honestly put, and I'd be a liar if I said I was pleased about the situation we were in. When I started out I figured all I'd have to deal with was the Slocum brothers—maybe. They could hire their thugs, but ordinary thugs don't bother me much. But then Soapy Smith invited himself to the party for reasons I still didn't understand.

"I'll ask you a question before I answer," I said. "Are you sorry you joined up with me?"

Hella wasn't like me: she didn't hesitate for a moment. "Oh no, Jim. Not sorry at all. Before I met you I lived in my own world, having nothing to do with anyone. I wasn't afraid of anything or anybody. Now I'm afraid, a little bit afraid, and I'm glad of it. I feel more human. You understand me, yes?"

"In a way," I said. You understand, yes?" She smiled when I said that "yes" with a question mark after it. "But I'm not scared and I'm not sorry I got into this. It started out as a favor for a friend. Now I'm doing it for myself. Who the hell do they think they are, Smith and the Slocums, the rest of them?"

Hella laughed. Her laugh had a tinkling sound in the dead silence along the frozen creek. "The hell with them, Jim—we can do it."

"Then let's be on our way," I said. "There's just one more question I'd like to ask you before we start. You mind?"

Hella's face took on a mildly concerned look. "Of course not, Jim."

"How come you never say 'mush' to the dogs? All the other mushers say 'mush.'"

"Mush is what you eat for breakfast, you fool," Hella said, smiling.

We saw the smoke of Dulcimer in another two hours, and as we got close it looked worse than Dawson, worse than Fort Yukon, worse than anything I'd seen before, and that's saying a lot. The whine of a steam sawmill greeted us: loud, screaming, hard on the ears. But it was the right kind of music for Dulcimer. The name itself was a joke. Now I don't know what dulcimer music sounds like, never having heard it, but I'd always imagined it to be soft, soothing, sweet. The town of Dulcimer was just the opposite: hard, nervous, ugly. It straggled away on both sides of Campbell's Creek, a disgrace to man, an insult to nature. Dawson, in its way, made some feeble pretense at being a town—Fort Yukon was the crippled stepchild of Dawson—but Dulcimer didn't even try. There might have been uglier settlements in the world, but I doubt it.

We went up from the creek past piles of rusting tin cans and things I couldn't put a name to. Hella wrinkled her nose. Dulcimer stank in the still, cold air. It would have smelled bad in a wind storm. And here the judge—a man with a beautiful wife and millions in the bank—had come to the end of his life.

I figured the judge's body, if it still existed, would be at the carpenter shop that made the coffin. The shop was about two hundred yards from the beginning of the town, beyond a saloon sign. What surprised me was the high wooden fence that shut it off from the street, because carpenter shops in frontier settlements are just padlocked at night. Then I saw the crudely lettered sign over the gate that went into the place:

SEE THE BODY
OF THE FAMOUS HANGING JUDGE
PHINEAS SLOCUM
ONLY 50¢

Jesus Christ! The sons of bitches had put the old man's corpse on display. Judge Phineas Slocum was part of a sideshow.

"Incredible!" Hella said, shaking her head in wonder. "They would do such a thing?"

"They've done it," I said. "Let's pay our fifty cents and take a look-see."

We tied the dogs and went to the gate to be faced by a happy man with a button nose and a granite jaw. It was easy to see why he was so happy; a fair-sized nail barrel was nearly filled with money.

I gave him a dollar and he smiled with what teeth he had left. "Best show in town, folks. Yes siree, you'll never see another like it. Over there in the shed where the other folks are standing."

Well, I've seen things and I've seen things, but nothing like this layout. I saw it so I can say it. There was the judge, out of his coffin and frozen solid, standing—I guess they couldn't bend him—behind a rough copy of a judge's bench. He was propped up by a board behind him, so he leaned slightly backward; a sort of gavel had been forced into his dead hand. Behind him the wall had been covered with board and painted brown to give a paneled effect. Somewhere in this place God forgot they had found an American flag and nailed it to the fake courtroom paneling. They must have thawed the judge's eyes and propped them open with toothpicks until they froze that way. They hadn't made him smile; a hanging judge is supposed to look stern. All in all, he looked pretty good, Judge Phineas Slocum of the federal bench, retired.

The man with the button nose and the happy face hadn't left out a thing. Instead of being just plain cheap pine, the judge's coffin now shone with a thick coat of black varnish, and a tin plate giving the Judge's name and his birth and death dates—no brass in Dulcimer—had been nailed to the lid. The son of a bitch had gone to a lot of trouble to make his sideshow look good. In a minute I was going to ruin his business for him. But that's the way of the world. There's always some spoil-sport out there ready to put a crimp in your plans.

"Don't dawdle, folks," the sideshow man called out good naturedly to the people already there. "Give the rest of the people a chance to see the judge. Judge Phineas Slocum, folks, the man that sent more men to their deaths than any judge in the history of the world. Come on now, folks, you can always come back another day. Come back, bring your friends. In years to come, when you're back in the States, rich and happy, you'll be able to tell your grandchildren you saw Judge Phineas Slocum hold court. Move along now, friends, so's I can let the others in and make some money in the doing of it."

The yard, now filled with gawkers, began to empty out. Hella and I were last to go to the gate. The proprietor smiled at us. Two more satisfied customers, he thought.

"Get your money's worth, did you?" he wanted to know.

"Close it down," I said. "You've made your last dollar off the dead man."

His smiled faded. "What the hell are you saying? Who the hell are you?"

"A friend of the family," I said. "The judge's widow sent me to bring him home and that's what I'm going to do. Don't look so sour. You've made a pile."

"You're just trying to start your own show." I guess the man was thinking of all the work that had gone into this ghoulish exhibition.

Holding the rifle with my right hand, I dug inside my coat until I found the letter from Cynthia. It was wrapped in waterproof paper. I shoved it at the man without opening it.

"Read it if you can read," I said. "It's got the Slocum name—Mrs. Phineas Slocum printed at the top. Try to tear it up and I'll tear you up, understand?"

He could read all right. He knew it was real because where in hell would I get embossed stationery in the wilds of Alaska? Still, he hated to give up that money-making corpse. He looked over at the judge in his courtroom. I guess the judge looked as stiff-necked and solemn as he had in life.

"You mean you're taking him back in the spring?" he said. "Of course you are. What else can you do? Tell you what. I'll split fifty-fifty till spring. That's a good deal, mister."

"Put him back in his coffin," I said. "Do it now or the Slocums will have the law on you."

He looked surprised. "What law? There's no law here."

I didn't want to start trouble, not in Dulcimer. "You think the Slocums can't send some law after you? The Slocums could find you at the North Pole. I'd hate to have all those millions after me. Back in the coffin, all right?"

"Who's going to pay me for all the work?"

"Nobody. You've been paid enough. You made the coffin?"

"Damn right I did. You going to pay me for that?"

"I'll pay for the coffin," I said. "How much?" I knew the cheap pine coffin was going to cost as much as a bronze casket.

"A hundred dollars," he said. "A hundred for the coffin. A hundred for storage. I think that's fair."

"It isn't fair. You'll get fifty for everything. I could charge you instead of the other way around. Take fifty or take nothing."

Outside the gate another crowd of fools were waiting to get in. "What's the hold-up, Smiley?" one man called out. "You in business or ain't you?"

"Close the gate. Tell them it's over," I ordered. "Talk nice or they could get mad enough to burn the place."

The crowd went away grumbling, but they went away. "All right," I said. "Now that it's quiet, you want to make a deal about storing the judge the rest of his stay in Dulcimer?"

"Not for no fifty dollars," he said sourly. "You want him, he's yours."

"Course he is," I said. "I don't just want you to store him, I want you to guard him."

"From what? Termites?" The son of a bitch thought that was funny.

"From anything. Pay is a hundred dollars. You can't say no to that."

"I can but I won't." The talk of money had restored some of his good humor. "Money in advance."

"Half in advance. I want you to keep that gate locked until I knock on it. You got a weapon?"

"In this country? What do you think? Sawed-off, 10-gauge. I don't figure to get shot for no hundred. You'll be close to hand?"

I said that's where I'd be. "Anybody tries to take the judge, fire off a cartridge then get out of harm's way."

"Count on that," the man said. "You want to give me a hand getting the old boy back in his box?"

It took very little doing to put Phineas Slocum in his shipping crate. The body was stiff as a board and not much heavier, for which I was glad. I had forgotten to ask Cynthia how much the judge weighed, and I was happy to see he wasn't one of those jowly, swag-bellied old men you often see up on the bench.

Staples, that's the name he gave, was nailing down the lid of the coffin when Hella and I went away from there.

"It is all craziness," Hella said.

I had to agree. "So it is and we're in the middle of it. You want a drink so we can test the waters of this muddy creek? I think I'll have to send a message to the governor after all."

"What message?"

"A message that won't bring any help but might do some good: 'Dear Governor: I'm trying to bring out the body of a federal judge and they're making it tough for me. Send troops.' How does that sound?"

Hella laughed on the way to the nearest saloon. "Crazy, like the rest of this. Alaska is not even a territory yet and he is not really a governor."

"Then what is Alaska?"

"A possession of the United States."

"That'll do," I said, and we both laughed.

Some of the men who had been turned away from Staples's side show were in the saloon and they scowled at us, figuring that we had something to do with lowering the curtain. The saloon was a dirty, noisy pesthole with mud inches deep on the rough plank floor. With the door closed and the stove going full blast, it smelled as if a herd of goats lived there. Goats would have probably smelled better. Again, Hella was the center of interest; if she had been fat, warty and ugly she would have attracted attention. But . . . well . . . she wasn't.

The man behind the bar looked like an ape with clothes on. Coarse hair grew low on his forehead; the backs of his hands were thick with the same kind of hair. He grunted at us.

"Whiskey," I said. "Two big ones. Where's the telegraph office?"

"How would I know?" he said. But when he came back with the whiskey his curiosity had gotten the better of him.

"It got something to do with the judge?" he asked in a voice that was very like his apish appearance. The ears of the men closest to us seemed to grow bigger. Some went so far as to stop staring at Hella.

"Could be that," I said. "You still don't know where I can find the telegraph office?"

"That was just a joke, mister."

The bartender looked like the last man on earth to

make a joke. He didn't even look mean, just dumb. The eavesdroppers were all but cupping their hands to their ears.

"Then maybe you can tell me?" I said.

"Oh sure," he said. "Down the street past a store that says Naylor's Supplies. There's a flag."

I expected half the saloon to follow along when we went out. As it was, about a dozen men came out and stared after us. Hella laughed in her reckless way. "You are going to send that message the way you said it to me?"

"Not exactly," I said. "The message will be the same but in different words. It'll be all over town inside of an hour. Least I hope it will. I wish to hell the judge had the decency to die on the Canadian side of the line. Nobody is crazy enough to fool with the Mounties."

We took the two teams down the telegraph office and found the telegrapher dozing over his hand-set. I guess the telegraph line had been strung to Dulcimer so agents for the big mining companies could report on how the gold strike was going. Farfetched though it seemed, a man in this cesspool of a town could talk to another man in Chicago or New York or anywhere. I just wanted to send a message to Fairbanks.

The sleepy telegrapher gave me a message form and a pencil. I didn't ask the governor to send troops; all I asked for was an escort to see me to Skagway with the judge's body. I said I was acting on orders from the Secretary of the Interior who had empowered me to seek any and all help I needed from federal officials in Alaska. It was all bullshit, naturally, but you should have seen that telegrapher's eyebrows go up when he read it over.

He read the last part aloud; the last line was: WILL WAIT HERE FOR ESCORT.

"You'll have a long wait," the telegrapher said. "You

know how far Fairbanks is from here?"

"Makes no difference, I'll wait," I said.

"What are you doing?" Hella asked when we got outside. "You are so full of tricks I cannot keep up with you. What do you mean—'Will wait?'"

I said, "It means we'll leave long before first light in the morning. It may work, it may not—it's a try. Real badmen aren't much afraid of federal law. Most other men are because it's the one kind of law that'll keep after you. Maybe this so-called governor, whatever he is, will send an escort, only we won't take that chance. Let's go see how our friend is doing, then we'll start making plans for the morning."

Staples was working in his carpenter shop when we got there, but there was a ten-gauge close by. He had removed the courtroom bench and the rest of the junk. All that remained now was the judge's shiny black coffin with the name plate cut from a flattened tin can.

"I ain't going to sit up all night with that thing," Staples said, waving a chisel at the coffin outside in the cold. "My charge is for guarding during the hours of daylight. You want to guard him at night, you come here and do it yourself."

"I'll be here," I said, glad I didn't have to bring up the subject myself.

Staples wanted to get back at me in some way, so he said, "And no smoking around the lumber. Burn me out and there's not enough money to pay for it."

"Anybody been around asking about me or the judge?" I asked.

"Nobody. You be here eight o'clock or I'll just walk off and the hell with it. I wish to hell I'd never seen that dead man. You're probably thinking I stole his wallet. No such thing, mister. Old boy dropped dead out on the creeks and whoever stole his poke wasn't me."

"Makes no matter," I said. "I'll be here eight o'clock on the button. Go easy with that ten-gauge when I bang on the gate.

"We'll have to make do with the supplies we bought from Ginnis," I told Hella. "If we start loading up now they'll know we mean to pull out rightaway. We'll have to shoot what we can't trap."

"There is enough to last us for a while," Hella said. "It will not look suspicious if we buy a lot for the dogs."

That made sense because the usual thing was to buy hundreds of pounds of dog meat at one time. Hella said not to buy any more fish for the dogs. It didn't give them the strength that came from meat, and naturally they didn't like it as much.

What we did buy was a good tent that we set up not far from Staples's place. After the dog meat was loaded on the sleds we cooked a meal and fixed up the tent with a wood floor as if we planned a long stay in Dulcimer. Men drifted by to look at Hella, but no one spoke to us. There was no sign of DuSang. Some of the men who stared at us might be working for DuSang; there was no way to tell.

"We'll head out when it's time and keep on going through the night." Hella nodded her agreement. "If we can get a good start they may not be ready to follow us into the mountains."

"It would not be too hard to follow us for a while," Hella said. "Bad weather will be better than good if they do follow us. But DuSang looks like a man who has endured many hardships. I can tell he was not always a storekeeper. You think he will pursue us?"

I nodded. "He will when he finds out we're not going back by way of the river. Smith thinks we are, so does DuSang. For now he does. I hope that's what he thinks. My guess is Smith wants me to do all the work, get the body back to Skagway, then he figures he'll take it away from me."

"But what about Sullivan? The other men we killed?"

"Sullivan may have decided to go into business for himself. Or Smith sent him as insurance. Or he was working for the Slocum brothers behind Smith's back."

Hella laughed. "Or what else, Jim?"

"Or nothing. I just don't know. If we can get over the mountains to Valdez it won't matter who's working for who. Once we're on an ore ship bound for the States, there isn't a damn thing they can do. You'll like Frisco. I know you don't like cities. Neither do I, but you can have a good time in a city if you don't stay too long. How long is it since you wore a dress and a pair of shoes?"

"Two hundred years," Hella said. "I cannot remember, Jim. I think I would look funny in a dress and ladies' shoes."

I couldn't see much of her, bundled-up as she was. But then I'd seen her without clothes of any kind. "Like hell you would. You were made to wear fine dresses, silk bloomers, everything."

"Bloomers!" Hella blushed. "Do not make fun of me, Jim."

"Just speaking the truth," I said. "I want you to wear silk bloomers so I can take them off. I want to run my hand under your silk bloomers and see what I find underneath."

"That would be nice," Hella agreed. "I want to feel your hand under my bloomers." Suddenly she looked fierce. "There will be so little time once we start to run. Oh, I hate those men for that. I think we should go into our tent now. Eight o'clock is still hours away. You think so too, yes?"

I thought so too, yes.

Dulcimer was a busy little place, but we were just as busy once we were in the tent with the flap laced and the blankets unrolled. There, right in the middle of town, with boots clumping past in the frozen street, we took off just enough clothes to make it work. But any way we did it was all right with me: in a four-poster bed with silk sheets or in a wind-shaken tent beside a dirty street. We didn't talk at all because there was no need.

When I went outside at fifteen minutes to it was snowing hard.

NINE

Wind-driven snow stung my eyes as I headed for Staples's carpenter shop, and there was light in the saloons but no one in the street. The hush that comes with heavy snow was everywhere; there wasn't a sound on the creek or in the town. There was some light—thick and white.

The hairs on the back of my neck stood up when I got to the gate and found it open. It creaked a little in the wind. With my back to the fence I eased around the side of the gate and then I heard the voices. The voices were muffled by the snow and wind. Underfoot the snow was soft; it hadn't frozen yet. I rubbed snow from my eyes and stepped inside and after that I could see. Two men were moving around the upended coffin. One was splashing the coffin and the side of the building with kerosene. Even with the wind and snow I caught the pungent smell as he emptied the rest of the can and set it down without a sound. I came forward and their backs were still turned to me. They grunted and stepped away from the coffin. I was right behind them when a match flared. I smashed the one with the match in the back of the head and he went down, dropping the match. The match hissed out in the snow. The other one turned, fumbling for a gun, and his hand was inside his bulky coat when I smashed him in the face with the butt of the rifle. The force of the blow slammed him back against the coffin. The coffin crashed to the ground and the man went after it. He tried to get up and this time I smashed him in the throat. He tried to scream and nothing came out of his mouth but a rush of blood. I kicked him in the face and ground my foot into his throat until he stopped breathing. I turned the other man on his back and killed him the same way. I was sweating in the cold by the time I got through.

Inside the carpenter shop Staples lay beside the stove with his throat cut. I jacked a shell when I heard somebody coming. Then I heard Hella calling my name and I went outside and found her staring at the men I had killed.

"Close the gate," I told her. "They were going to burn everything. We're going to have to move out now."

She closed and barred the gate and came back to me. Her voice was steady. "I knew something was wrong. You think they were sent by DuSang?"

I was using handfuls of snow to wash the kerosene off the coffin. Everything stank of kerosene. "Not likely," I said. "DuSang could have burned the body any time. These men came on their own—or the Slocums sent them. Makes no difference. We have to move. You see anybody else in the street?"

"No one," Hella said.

Hella waited with the teams in the snow-swirling street while I got the judge's coffin up on my back and out through the gate. Down the street the saloon lights winked through the snow. I was roping the coffin to my own sled—all the supplies, sleeping bag, the rest of it—were on Hella's, when I heard a sled coming into town. It passed us and though our dogs barked furiously the sled went on without stopping. We didn't move until the sound of the runners died away.

"You ready?" I asked.

"Ready, Jim," Hella said.

"In a minute," I said. Then I went back and dragged the two dead men inside and threw them beside Staples's body. The outside wall of the shop was still wet with kerosene. I touched a match to it and flame licked up fast. I ran to the sleds.

We had hardly reached the end of the street when the carpenter shop, with its cans of turpentine and pitch, exploded with a sound like thunder. I looked back and flames thirty feet high were shooting skyward. No matter how hard the snow fell the shop would burn to ashes. The dogs plunged wildly when they heard the explosion, but they settled down when there was no more loud noise.

Fighting the snow, we headed away from the creek, out toward the long valley that led, by stages, to the foothills of the Alaska Range. At least we were on our way to—*what*? In front of me the judge rode the sled, snowflakes melting on the lid of his coffin. The temperature had risen fast and would stay that way as long as the snow lasted. It might snow all night and all the next day and the day after that. For now the snow and the fire were giving us the cover we needed to get a jump on the first leg of the journey. It was what Alaska people call "good snow," meaning that it was dry and powdery; snow that would pack fast and hold the weight of the sleds. But even with good snow it wasn't possible to set more than a three-mile pace; after the snow stopped and froze we could step up the pace by at least two miles.

In two hours Dulcimer was six miles behind us and it was time to rest the dogs. Then we moved on, bearing always to the left, following a course that would take us into the Frazer Valley, still thirty miles away. Frazer Valley was nearly a hundred miles long; after it ended there were other valleys without names. Or if they had names, those names had been cooked up by mapmakers who had never been there. As far as I knew—had heard—no one had ever been there. Long before we even reached the foothills we'd be crossing completely unknown country.

With two more stops we traveled on for nine hours until the dogs began to voice their complaint with a high-pitched barking that was different from their usual trail sounds. I wanted to drive them ahead, but Hella shouted that we had to stop.

It must have been close to morning when we got a fire going and fed the dogs. The poor brutes dug their burrows in the snow and fell asleep. The snow eased off and the branches of trees took shape in the half light. Hella, dropping coffee in the pot, said she thought we had come about thirty miles from Dulcimer.

Well, that was a fair start, yet I wasn't counting on anything. Even without sufficient food for ourselves, we were carrying fair loads on both sleds. The dogs would lighten the load by eating their way through the meat; there was nothing to be done about the judge. Sitting by the fire drinking coffee while Hella fried bacon and beans, I got a sudden mental picture of DuSang and his men starting out with hardly any supplies at all. Light sleds that would skim over the snow crust with the speed of a toboggan on a slope. They could do that, they could shoot their meat, even meat for the dogs.

"What are you thinking about?" Hella asked.

"You in silk bloomers," I answered.

"You are thinking about DuSang."

"I was thinking I'll have to kill DuSang somewhere along the way. If he comes he'll have to be killed. His men won't be worth a damn after that. But he hasn't come yet. We better get some sleep."

We slept for four hours and could have managed with less, given the circumstances, but we had to be patient because of the dogs. As it was we had to fight hard to get them out of their snow burrows. The snow had stopped altogether and the temperature began to drop, freezing the snow in minutes, giving us a good surface to travel on. Once the dogs knew there was no hope of going back to sleep they worked well. Hella pointed: up ahead was the entrance to the Frazer Valley, the funnel that would take us into the mountains. Once into the long valley there would be no easy way out. There could be no backtracking or change of plan. In that frozen valley we'd be caught between the mountains and DuSang—if DuSang came. One part of mind argued that DuSang, the prosperous storekeeper, would give up on the whole thing; would get on the wire to Smith and tell him we'd gotten away. But my mind was no match for the gut feeling that the halfbreed would follow us like the half-savage he was.

Traveling was easy on the packed, frozen snow and we stepped up the pace to a six-miler. We moved into the long, narrow valley, all the time urging the dogs to greater speed. It was very cold and the wind made it colder. The valley seemed to run all the way to eternity; no matter how hard we worked the dogs we wouldn't come to the end of it for at least three days.

Day turned to dusk and then to night. The next day began the same as the day before, but then, about noon, the valley grew narrower, with the timber growing in close, almost blocking our way. We lost time getting the teams through the timber; it was dusk again when we got back to open country. Two hours later we hit a long stretch of land that would have been swamp in summer. Now it was frozen over, but there were treacherous places where the ice was thin, barely covering deep pools and channels.

There was nothing left to do but make camp for the night and move out again as soon as the light could be trusted. "Take it easy, Jim," Hella said while she busied herself with the inevitable bacon and beans. "They may come, but not tonight. We are too far ahead of them. Now eat your supper and pretend you are eating—what do you like best?"

I said steak and onions. "If not that, fried chicken, Texas style."

"Texas style? Is that a special style?"

"No, it means the chicken has to be born in Texas. Chickens born in any other state or territory won't do. And even in Texas there are different kinds of chickens. East Texas chickens are fatter, but Panhandle chickens are tastier."

"All this is ridiculous," Hella said. "I think it would be good for us to have a drink. There is half a bottle left. After tonight I think we will have to stand guard, so we will drink the whiskey now."

After the cooking things had been put away she matched me drink for drink until the bottle was empty. We sat by the blazing fire; DuSang might have been ten thousand miles away. The burning spruce smelled good and the whiskey had driven away the feeling of danger.

Hella said sleepily, "You can leave me in Valdez if you like. With two sleds, two teams, I can start my business again. And I have the five thousand dollars you gave me. I will be set up for life. I would like to come with you to San Francisco, but there is no need to take me."

"Don't talk so much," I said.

Hella stared into the fire. "I am just being practical,

Jim. All my life I have been practical. I have been forced to be practical."

"Then what are you doing here?"

"I want to be here."

"Which isn't one bit practical."

"I meant practical in the future."

"Don't be too practical. We'll go to San Francisco, have a good time, then you can decide what you want to do. If you get too lonesome for the Yukon you can always go back. I'll see you get ten times the money you need to start your business again. You can have a real big outfit."

Hella looked angry. "From this widow? This woman? Your loving friend? You would get the money from her, yes?"

"That's the one," I said. "Look. She'll be so glad to get the judge back she won't be Scotch about the money. I know the judge wasn't—isn't—much to look at, but he's worth millions of dollars to her. Five, ten, fifteen thousand dollars is just a drop in the bucket. We'll go to San Francisco and we'll all be friends. You'll like her fine."

Hella's voice rose in anger. "I will not get in bed with you and this woman."

I laughed so hard that some of the dogs jerked awake and began to growl. "You're crazier than I am. Nobody said we're going to make it a three-handed game, not that it wouldn't be a bad idea at that."

Still mad, Hella reached for the coffee pot. "I will scald you with coffee, Saddler."

"Not unless you make a fresh batch."

The empty pot came flying at me and I had to duck. A dog jumped up and barked furiously.

I dug the coffee pot out of the snow and put it back by the fire. "Peace," I said. "For Christ's sake let there be peace before you run off the dogs."

Hella remained sullen for a while. Then she said, "I

hate this woman, this widow. I do not want to meet her."

"All right. Then we'll leave the judge on her doorstep, yank on the bell and go to Texas. If you don't want her money we'll go to Texas and get jobs after the money is gone. I'll clerk in a store, you can be a waitress."

Hella smiled as only she could smile. "But that would not be practical, Mr. Saddler."

"That it wouldn't, Miss Rasmussen," I said.

After that there was peace in the camp we called home. We'd had our first fight, a coffee pot had been thrown, and now all was forgiven. Christ! I thought, it's just like being married. At any other time such a thought would have chilled my bones, but I guess being with Hella was different.

In the morning we edged our way through the frozen swamp. Here Hella was a lot more useful than I was: she had an eye for the weak places in the ice, now covered with frozen snow. She marked a path with twigs and kept on going until she reached the other side. Then she came back and we took the teams across. The whole thing took two hours—hours we couldn't spare.

After that we made good time. The dogs were rested and so were we. The miles fell away behind us and we were in good spirits for a change. That's how it is in snow country: your mood keeps changing. There are dull gray days when you feel so helpless, so powerless against the climate, that you don't want to take another step. Then there are other days, clear and cold, when the sun sparkles on everything and you couldn't feel better. This was one of those days.

But you have to watch yourself when you get to feeling too good, because that hard country is always ready to betray you. At the end of the day Hella said we were more than halfway into the valley. The night held clear and we kept moving until common sense—and the dogs—warned us to stop. That night, as planned, we stood watches for the first time. We built a fire but after the cooking was done we slept away from it, for nothing makes a better target than someone outlined against a fire at night.

Nothing happened during the night. It snowed a little, and that was all. Starting out early, we made the end of the valley just after dusk the following day. They might still be following us. If so, they hadn't caught up yet. Yet there were times when I felt like dumping the judge and high-tailing it for Valdez. The hell with Cynthia and her money! Judge or no judge, she wasn't going to starve. Far from it, the house—the mansion—she lived in was worth a fortune by itself. And yet I knew I was going to see it through.

The walls of the valley gave way to open country for a while, and here the wind blew harder, knifing through our furs, trying to kill us. It was noon when we saw the river. More a creek than a river, it was wide enough just the same. Hella said we'd have to be careful because some of the rivers closer to the sea didn't freeze completely like those in the interior. Again she went ahead while I stayed behind and kept the dog teams under control.

Hella took her team across without any trouble. I was more than halfway to the other side when the ice cracked with a sound like breaking glass. The crack ran right under the feet of the dogs and they barked, recognizing the danger. I tried to turn the dogs away from the widening crack, but they kept on a straight course in their panic to reach the opposite bank. We would have gone into the water in another minute if Hella hadn't run out onto the ice and dragged and kicked the snarling huskies away from the danger. We had just reached solid ground when the whole surface of the creek broke up. The ice I had just crossed now bobbed and floated loose.

I looked back at the wide creek and said to Hella, "You

think that thing has a name?"

Hella shook her head. "I hardly think so."

"Then we'll call it after you," I said. "Hella Creek."

There was no more excitement during the rest of the day. We entered the next valley at nightfall and kept on going far into the night. Well-fed so far, the dogs didn't give any trouble. There didn't seem to be much game, and that bothered me some, but Hella said there was sure to be more game in the mountains.

We woke up to face a wall of fog that stretched across the valley. It came right down to ground level, thick and clinging, but rather than give up any more time we started into it, holding the dogs to a walk. The fog was so thick I could barely see Hella, only five yards away. As the temperature rose the surface snow became mushy and there were places where the sleds bogged down and had to be lifted out with the gee poles we carried with the other gear. So far this was the worst part of the journey.

One miserable mile followed another. By noon, after five hours of this, we were ready to drop, and the fog was as thick as ever. We could have been anywhere. Everything was shrouded in fog, we were breathing fog, and with no sense of direction the dogs whimpered their bewilderment. Finally we decided to call a halt when we found ourselves climbing the wall of the valley.

It could have been any time of day or night. We fed the dogs without unharnessing them; without a fire to hold them they would wander off and God knows if we'd ever find them again.

The fog lifted during the night; there was even a moon that grew brighter as the hours passed. It was close to morning, with the moon still bright, when Hella called out to me and pointed.

"The mountains!" she said. "Look, Jim—the mountains!"

And there they were, dim in the far distance, but I

could see them. Ghostly shapes in the moonlight, and now that I could see them I began to think we were going to make it after all. What we had to do when we reached the mountains was to find a pass, a way through to the other side. There might be many false starts; if so, we would have to backtrack and keep on looking. And if we didn't find a way through, we were as good as dead.

The mountains faded with the moon and there was more of that goddamned snow. But it wasn't so heavy that we couldn't travel, and then suddenly it was night again. By this time I didn't even know what day it was, not that it mattered a helluva lot. I asked Hella and she said she thought it was Thursday.

"Or Friday."

"Or Tuesday," I said.

It snowed for a full day and part of another, but when it cleared and the feeble sun struggled forth the mountains were no longer dim shapes in the distance. Now they were solid; they had depth. By the middle of the next day we were traveling on an upslope, gradual at first, so gradual that we hardly noticed. But when I looked back after an hour I was able to see far back into the valley. The long climb had begun.

The snow wasn't as deep as it had been in the valley, but so far the surface was crisp; deeper into the mountains there wouldn't be as much ice as snow. We were still in the foothills and a search for a pass wouldn't come until much later. Here the sun was stronger and it burned for a longer time each day. I was so glad to see that sun, for it reminded me—and I needed to be reminded—that there was another world that didn't freeze over for ten months of the year. I checked our back trail again, but by now fog covered the valley and there was nothing to see. Up where we were the air was clear and very cold, and the sun was shining bright. That was all that mattered. We were still well below the tree line;

another day would take us to where there was no firewood.

So we rested the dogs and collected as much dry wood as we could find. After this fires would have to be small, used for little more than cooking. The drier the wood, the lighter the load. With that in mind we picked carefully, passing up anything that wasn't old and well seasoned. We used our trail hatchets to cut the longer pieces into more manageable lengths, and by the time we finished there was enough firewood to take us over the mountains, if we used it sparingly.

That night we heard wolves for the first time. It started with one long, drawn-out howl that seemed to drift all the way to the moon. I don't know if it's true that wolves howl at the moon. This one seemed to, and I tell you it was the most lonesome sound I ever heard in my life. People who don't know what they're talking about like to say that wolves and coyotes sound much the same. No such thing. The howl of a wolf is like nothing on this earth. Compared to it the coyote's howl is like the caterwauling of a horny old tomcat on a backyard fence.

The first howl was answered by others until there was a whole chorus of howls echoing through the foothills. One by one, the huskies woke in their snow burrows, snarling with their muzzles raised to sniff the night wind.

Hella woke too and crawled out of the sleeping bag. "They are not close, the wolves," she said. "But they know the dogs are here. If they get hungry enough they will come closer. They will come closer every night. They are afraid of humans except when they are starving. Then they will attack even a man with a rifle. But mostly what they try to do is to entice the wilder dogs away from camp so they can kill and eat them."

Something in her manner puzzled me. "There's something you're not saying. Out with it."

"All right." She gestured toward the coffin on the sled.

"I think the wolves are interested in *that*."

"But how can they be? The judge is frozen solid. How can they know?"

"I don't know," Hella said. "But I have seen it in Finland—and here. They know there is something, and so they will keep following us. They will become bolder as our fires grow smaller. But if we can keep the dogs under control the wolves cannot do us any harm."

"Unless they're crazed with hunger?" I said.

"You wanted the truth," Hella said. "Now go to sleep, it is time for my watch."

I slept but I didn't sleep well, at least not for the first few hours. You know how it is. You wear yourself out sleeping badly, then not long before it's time to get up you sleep like a drunkard. That's how I was when Hella shook me awake and handed me a cup of coffee. Bacon was frying on the fire. It was daylight and the wolves were silent. During the night Hella had harnessed the dogs and they still slept in the traces. More and more I realized how valuable she was. In the desert I could have given her lessons; here she was the one with the knowhow.

"Still no sign of DuSang," I said.

"Don't even talk about him," Hella said.

TEN

We were making our way up a long slope when a rifle boomed and Hella dropped with a bullet in her back. She cried out and fell on top of the sled and the frightened dogs were dragging her away before my brain took in what was happening. Hella lay on top of the sled with her feet dragging the ground behind. Other rifles opened up, but I wasn't hit, not even scratched. The runaway sled with Hella on it went over the top of the slope. The first rifle boomed again—a heavy caliber, by the sound of it. The bullet clipped a piece of fur from my coat, but I was over the top of the slope before the big rifle fired again.

Hella lay in the snow beside the overturned sled. The runners of the sled were dug in deep and the dogs, pulled up short, were snarling and barking. I ran to Hella. Her eyes were open and her breath was coming light and shallow. She tried to smile.

"I can't move my legs, Jim," Hella whispered. "Get my rifle and put me where I can see them. You go on.

Please get my rifle and go on."

"Like hell! We're in this together."

I tried to stop her when she began to crawl toward the upended sled. "The rifle. Get me the rifle," she kept saying. I could hear them shouting from the bottom of the slope.

I carried Hella to the shelter of some rocks and gave her the rifle. "There's no pain, I can shoot," she whispered, and to prove that she jacked the loading lever of the Marlin.

Two men came running and I shot one of them. Hella shot the other. When the bullets hit them they rolled all the way to the bottom. The big rifle boomed again and the bullet shattered on a rock close to my head. Two other rifles joined in, firing from the bottom of the slope. Then it got quiet and I heard DuSang's voice yelling at me.

"Send the coffin down the slope, Saddler. Your only chance to live. The woman's shot and you're on your own. Send the coffin down and we'll clear out."

"Like hell!" I yelled back. "You want the coffin, come and take it!"

I looked at Hella and she was dead. Just dead. There had been no death struggle. She just died.

Her head lay on the stock of the Marlin. Her fur hat had fallen off and her white-blond hair was bright in the mountain sun. Her face was turned sideways, toward me. Her face wasn't peaceful. It had no expression at all.

I don't know how I felt. I guess I didn't feel anything at all. The bastards opened up again and I jumped up like a crazy man to return their fire. Bullets tore at me and still I wasn't hit. But then I threw myself flat when I saw I was giving DuSang a chance to kill me. I wanted to live, not because I was afraid to die, but because I wanted to kill DuSang. But this wasn't the place to do it. I wanted to pick the place, to make sure the killing got done, because if I didn't kill DuSang, all that Hella and I had been through together would have no meaning.

I looked at Hella stiffening in the snow. "I have to leave you," I said. "You understand, yes?"

All I took was Hella's rifle and the sled with the Judge's coffin on it. I still couldn't take it in. Hella had died for a dead man.

They opened up again and I returned their fire without giving them much opportunity to kill me. They couldn't have seen me when I took my team and moved out. There was a long gulch on the far side of the slope and I headed into that, not knowing if there was a way out at the far end. DuSang had lost two men, had two men left, so maybe he wouldn't be so brave about coming up that slope. That would buy me some time.

In the gulch there were deep drifts and I had to use the gee pole to get over them. My luck held and there was an opening at the far end that led to another slope. I looked back and there was nobody coming after me. So DuSang wasn't so brave after all, or maybe he was just smart.

Beyond the next slope there was a wide canyon strewn with big rocks. Finding a way through was hell; if they came at me now I wouldn't stand a chance. But nobody shot at me and I made it through. Hella's death had left me numb. It might have been different if there had been some warning. That's how it is with sudden death; no matter how many times you've seen it, it always comes as a shock. I wondered why DuSang had shot her instead of me before I realized there was no way to tell us apart at that distance. Two tall figures bundled up in furs. DuSang picked one and fired his big-caliber rifle, maybe a bolt-action English sporting rifle fitted with a scope. Whatever it was, it had broken her spine. Mercifully she had died, a lifetime in a wheelchair would have killed her great spirit.

I began to move up a wide slope, a great gash in the

earth that must have been made in ancient times by a glacier. It cut deep into the side of the mountain. It might end at a blank rock wall, but I was gambling that it was the start of a pass. The day was bright and clear, but the wind-whipped powdery snow blew from the top of drifts, making it hard to see far ahead. Laboring under the weight of the coffin, the dogs were forced to slow down, yet I never even considered dumping the judge. If I hadn't been a little crazy, I would have dumped the coffin, turned the dogs loose and gone over the mountains on foot. I had a rifle and plenty of ammunition, the weather was good now, and I could make it a lot faster. DuSang would have no more interest in me, once he got the judge's body. But crazy as I was then—and I was to get crazier—I just couldn't give up. The judge meant nothing to me, not a thing, and like as not he'd been the miserable old bastard everybody said he was. On the other hand, in my half-crazed state of mind, I felt somehow that he belonged to me. The judge and I were partners now. Come hell or high water, I was going to bring him home.

As I urged the dogs to move faster, I kept looking for a place to ambush DuSang. Doing that wasn't going to be easy; DuSang had the look of a man who had hunted many men in his time. But I had to kill him before he killed me. Before he caught me in the sights of that big rifle. He was traveling light and I was burdened by the coffin.

At first I didn't understand why he wasn't making better time, then I knew he was playing the hunter's game of letting me wear myself out. After all, where the hell could I go? If I ran the dogs too long and too hard, they would drop with exhaustion, and so would I. When that happened all he had to do was creep up close and kill me.

The pass ran straight into the mountain; now there

was no way out. If I could climb up high I might be able to get a shot at him, but so far the walls of the pass went up without a break. The few places that looked halfway possible were sheeted with ice; even mountain-climbing irons wouldn't have helped much. All I could do was move on and keep looking.

Going deeper into the pass I expected to get a bullet in the back at any time. I was braced for it, but it didn't come. I knew DuSang wouldn't try for a head shot. What he would do was take aim at my spine; try to kill me the way he'd killed Hella. It's hell waiting to die; when it's so close you almost want to get it over with.

It started to get dark and that evened the odds a little. Once it got dark DuSang's big rifle wouldn't have that much superiority over my Winchester. I had no idea what the men with DuSang were like. Killers certainly. Anybody accompanying DuSang on this expedition had to be a killer. Maybe they were halfbreeds like DuSang. That would make them meaner than usual, because halfbreeds get it from both sides on the frontier, so they might decide to kill me in their own special way.

I moved on into the darkness, stopping now and then to listen for sounds of pursuit. Nothing was close behind, or else DuSang was coming after me without the sled. After going on for another hour, there was nothing to do but hole up for the night as best I could. I gave the dogs far less than their usual ration of meat; they were still snarling with hunger after they gulped it down. I sat behind a rock chewing on a chunk of raw meat I had saved for myself. It was frozen when I put it in my mouth and I had to chew hard before the rank dog meat was fit to swallow. All I had to drink was melted snow.

The dogs dug into their holes and slept. Huskies have it all over humans when it comes to cold. I wrapped my face, breathing through my scarf, trying to keep the mountain air from freezing my lungs. I slept in fits and starts, all the time getting colder. The sleeping bag was on the sled, but I didn't get into it, because I wanted to be ready to move fast if DuSang came in the night.

Move fast! That was a laugh. By the time I roused the dogs before first light I was so stiff I could hardly move. The bitter cold had seeped into my bones, making every movement painful. It took a long time before my muscles were working again, and even then I hurt all over. In that country the moment you stop eating hot food the cold starts to take over your body. No matter what you're wearing, your body starts to freeze. The dogs weren't as sluggish as I was, but they weren't working well. A husky is more a machine than a dog, but these dogs needed fuel to keep going and there was going to be less and less of it as long as DuSang continued the hunt.

Night faded to gray dawn. The pass continued as before; it seemed endless, as if the mountains went on to the end of the world. Looking up at the jagged peaks I couldn't understand why I was still alive. Just barely alive was all I was, but I struggled on, driven by anger, vowing not to give up until a bullet ended my life. At times I thought about burying the coffin in the snow and coming back to get it at some later date. That's it, I thought. I'll hide the coffin, push onto Valdez, then return in the spring, well fed and well supplied.

But all I did, in the end, was keep moving. Other ideas came to me, not one of them worth a damn. Killing DuSang was the only thing that would get me out of this fix. If I didn't kill him he would probably kill me. There was no way around that. The long-range rifle gave him a great advantage. My death, if I didn't do something, was as inevitable as death itself.

The sun came up bright and cold over the mountains. Now with darkness gone, I was a target again, a moving target outlined against the glare of the snow. Nothing stirred in the pass behind me; the world was white and empty as far as I could see. There were bad places that had to be crossed, where the snow had melted and frozen again, to form great sheets of ice. The dogs' feet skittered on the ice and I fell more than once, hanging on to the sled to keep from sliding back down the slope. I was beginning to feel that awful sense of despair that comes over a man, no matter how tough, when he has been hunted too long, when the hunter seems to hold all the cards and all he has to do to win is wait. My mood grew worse because I knew I was doing Smith's work for him. After DuSang got the body—I was more or less resigned to dying—he could get to Valdez without much trouble. From there he could find a boat to take him down the coast to Skagway.

"Got something for you, boss," I could hear him saying to Soapy. And then they would have a good laugh at Saddler, the fool, who'd done most of the work for them.

Thoughts like this drove me on while my body begged me to lie down and die. They say death by freezing isn't painful at all. You just give up and let it happen. Even so, I wasn't ready to die like that. If it came to the point where I couldn't go on, I would use my handgun to put a bullet through my head. I hoped I'd have the strength and the resolve to do it.

The pass flattened out for a while and the going wasn't too bad until it began to climb again. The pace I was setting myself and the dogs was killing me, yet there was nothing else I could do. But if I didn't find a place of ambush soon, it wouldn't make much difference what I did.

I managed to beat on until it was close to noon and I saw a broken place in the wall of the pass. There had been a rock slide and it looked like I might be able to climb up high and shoot from cover. Ice covered the rocks and getting up there would be hell, but I saw it as my only chance. The cold sun glared in my eyes as I looked up, and I felt dizzy. The dogs were startled when I let go the steering handles and yelled at them to go on. The sled lurched ahead and the dogs kept on going. I knew they would eventually slow down and just stand there growling. I hoped they'd be out of sight by then. I looked at the track left by the runners and hoped that would be enough to fool DuSang if he glassed the slope from a distance. If it didn't, I'd be high in the rocks with no place to go. DuSang and his men wouldn't even have to attack—I'd freeze as solid as the judge.

There was a twist in the pass and the dogs went out of sight. I knew they wouldn't go far before they lay down in the snow. When the shooting started, they'd be likely to move on, but that wouldn't last long either. I could catch up . . . if there was any catching up to be done.

I stuck the Winchester inside my belt and buttoned up my coat again. Then I heaved myself up onto the slick, icy surface of the first rock. I lay there, breathing hard, and when some of my strength returned, I clawed my way up to the next foothold. I went up like that, inch by inch, nearly falling in places but somehow managing to hang on. Halfway up, I rested again, not sure I was going to make it. I came to a narrow slit in the rocks where it was hard to get through because of the bulky coat, and I had to shift the position of the rifle before I was able to climb again.

It must have taken me thirty minutes before I was even close to the top. To get all the way up used up another ten minutes, but when I got there and lay on my belly on the ice, I was able to see down the pass for more than a mile. They hadn't showed yet, so all I could do was wait and hope they wouldn't take too long.

Minutes passed—just minutes—but it seemed like hours, and then I saw them coming a long way off. My face was numb with cold and I had to blink hard to get my eyes in focus. There they were all right, moving up the pass at an easy pace. One sled and three men, confident that they had me exactly where they wanted me to be. I saw the flash of binoculars and I jerked my head down and waited. They were getting closer all the time.

I stayed low and let them come to me. The distance was still too great to tell one from another, but I knew DuSang wouldn't be driving the sled. The sled stopped when they were under half a mile away, and the binoculars flashed again. That would be DuSang using the glasses, following the tracks up into the pass until they disappeared at the bend. The sled moved on at the same easy pace, and in my rage to kill, I cursed them for not coming faster.

My gloved hands tightened on the rifle when the sled stopped again and one man went ahead of the others, holding his rifle at the ready. He came on up into the pass, stopping now and then to shield his eyes from the sun. In minutes he was passing right under me; I could hear his feet crunching in the snow. I dared a look and saw him looking at the tracks of the dog team and the sled. Still wary, he went up the pass a little ways, but stopped short of the bend. If the dogs started barking now, I was done for.

But he came down again and waved the others to come ahead. DuSang was in plain sight now, a squat figure dressed in black furs. It would have to be done fast. First, DuSang, then the others. I couldn't let any of them get ahead of me. If they did that, they'd be able to shoot at me from two sides. Come on, you bastards, I swore silently.

There was a patch of ice about fifteen yards below my hiding place. A gust of wind sent snow flying in the air. It cleared just as quickly and I steadied the rifle and fired at

DuSang, but instead of hitting him in the chest I got him in the leg and he fell on the ice and slid down from where he was shot. I fired at the man behind the sled and he went down without even a yell. The other man got off one shot before I killed him, too. I turned the rifle to look for DuSang and fired at his legs as he crawled behind a rock. The bullet tore up a chunk of ice and ricocheted off the rock wall of the pass. DuSang raised up to fire the big rifle and the bullet spattered rock splinters in my face. I heard the snap of the bolt right after the shot and knew I was going to have a hard time killing the halfbreed.

Up in the pass all the dogs were barking: my own team and DuSang's. DuSang's team had run away. Now we were in a standoff. I was freezing on the icy cliff; DuSang was wounded in the leg. We traded shots, each of us trying to figure out the next move. My Winchester fired faster, but DuSang's bolt action was a more formidable weapon. It had terrific velocity and even when its bullets smacked into the rocks close to me, there was always the danger of being blinded by the lead fragments. Most of an hour passed and we were still at it. I had DuSang pinned down, but as long as I remained where I was there was no way to get at him.

High up, in the wind, I really began to freeze. My hands were numb and I wasn't shooting so good; it could only get worse as time dragged by. DuSang was wounded, but if it bothered him, it didn't show in his shooting. There must have been a short action on his rifle, and he bolted cartridges about as fast as I worked the lever of the Winchester.

We kept on shooting until the sun had moved far across the sky. It would be dark if we kept it up much longer, and then DuSang would be able to slide away from where he was. Maybe that's what he was trying to do: to wait me out until dark. And then when I came

143

down from the rocks, he'd be there to kill me. Mayb
he'd be able to do that. It depended on how bad hi
wound was.

I crawled away from my shooting position, trying t
figure my chances of making my way to another plac
where he would be exposed to my bullets. There was
sharp drop to a lower level of rock. Jagged ice covere
everything. No climbing was possible; it would have t
be a sudden drop. I didn't know how deep the snow wa
on the lower rocks; if I hit too hard I could break a leg
maybe both legs.

Sensing that I had moved away, DuSang fired, tryin
to make me return his fire. Instead of doing that,
crawled closer to the drop, and when I got there I lay o
the ice and looked down. It looked like a place where
man could get crippled or killed.

Now DuSang was walking his shots along the top c
the rocks, spacing them out, taking his time about how
he did it. I looked down again, balancing one set of odd
against the other. If I didn't make up my mind fairl
soon, I knew I was going to be sorry for it. Here goe
nothing, I thought. I stuck the Winchester into my bel
and hung over the drop as far as I could and let go. I fel
like a stone. The fall jarred me all the way up to my teeth
then I stumbled backward and hit my head on the roc
and I blacked out.

I don't know how long I was unconscious. A fairly lon
time, I guess, because when I opened my eyes the sun wa
lower in the sky. A triphammer beat inside my head. Th
pain was so bad that I could barely see. My body hurt i
the places that hadn't turned numb with cold. I felt fo
the Winchester and it was still inside my belt, but th
buttons of my coat had torn loose and there was a goo
chance that the innards of the rifle had frozen. There wa
no wind now and it was dead quiet, and I couldn't jac
the lever of the Winchester without giving away m

144

position. DuSang might be long gone by now. Or he might be crawling up, wounded or not, to look for me.

There was only one way to find out, so I crawled out onto the rocks that looked down into the pass. There I could see the rock where DuSang had been hiding. As luck would have it, he picked just that moment to show himself. I raised up to fire but the lever of the Winchester didn't want to work. DuSang shouldered the bolt action and fired up at me and missed. I yanked down hard on the loading lever and a bullet went into the chamber. DuSang was bolting another round when I fired. The bullet went wide of the mark and DuSang tried to dive back behind the rock, but his feet went from under him on the ice and the rifle clattered far away from him. I jacked another round and aimed the rifle straight at his head.

"Stay where you are," I shouted. "I'm coming down."

ELEVEN

I held the rifle steady on DuSang as I came up close to him, and he looked from where I was to where his own weapon lay on the ice. He was calculating how much of a chance he had of getting to it before I shot him. I could see that he was in much better shape than I was. He looked again and I raised the Winchester and aimed at his head.

"Try it," I said. "There's your rifle, go get it. Crawl fast. Maybe you'll make it. You're good at killing women. See how good you are at killing me."

When he didn't move I went around him until I reached the rifle. Then I picked it up, still watching him, and went back to a safe distance. His black eyes followed me, still not wanting to believe that he was finished as a manhunter.

"Why does Smith want the body?" I asked him. "You work for Smith, so you have to know."

"I don't know," DuSang said. "Smith didn't tell me

146

his reasons. He never does. Get the body was all he said. That's why I'm here."

"You're here because you're a stinking halfbreed killer. Only you've done your last murder."

DuSang said, "Let me go and I'll give you all the money you want. What I don't have I can raise. The man you want to kill is Smith, not me. I'll give you more money than you're getting now. You can't be getting more than I can give you."

"All you're going to lose is your life," I said. "It belongs to me now. You're already dead, halfbreed."

DuSang showed his teeth, half snarl, half smile. "Smith will get you anyway. You can run for a while, but he'll catch up with you."

"You won't be there if he does."

"You'll be just as dead."

His right hand twitched and I put a bullet through his wrist. A knife dropped out of his sleeve and lay beside him. I went close enough to kick it away. He turned his head to stare at his shattered wrist. There was no sign that he felt any pain.

"There's nothing I can buy you with?" he said, grinding out the words through clenched teeth. "You're crazy not to take the money."

"All I want from you is information. What about Smith?"

I didn't know whether he didn't know or wouldn't say. Then I thought, the hell with Smith's reasons. If I got the body back to the States, Smith's reasons wouldn't matter.

"Turn over on your belly," I ordered. "Try something and I'll stop you. I'll put a bullet in your spine. It'll take you some time to die."

I tied his wrists and ankles with rawhide and turned him over with his face looking up at the sky.

DuSang lay in the snow with his hands tied behind his

back. At first he struggled, but that just made the rawhide cut deeper into his flesh. I knew the halfbreed wasn't afraid to die, but he sensed that what I had in mind for him was worse than anything he had ever imagined. Now, having tried to bargain for his life, he wanted to bargain for his death.

His glazed ham face looked strange in the sunlight. "You're going to kill me, isn't that enough? What else can you do to a man?"

"A lot," I said. "You know what the trouble with you is? I'll tell you. You think a life for a life makes it even. But you're forgetting that your life isn't worth a pile of shit. You kill a fine woman that never harmed anybody in her life. You think your stinking, thieving, murdering life makes up for that. A nice merciful bullet squares everything, is that what you think?"

DuSang squinted against the glare of the sun. "I'll give you a lot of money to kill me quick."

"I can take your money when you're dead. I can take it any time."

"No. A lot of money, Saddler. Everything I have. The trading post. Money in the Skagway bank. I have paper and pencil. I'll write and sign it. You won't have any trouble collecting. I'm worth fifty thousand dollars. A quick bullet for fifty thousand?"

"Not for a million," I said, unwrapping the last of the fatty bacon. "Not for ten million. Not for the Denver Mint."

"In the name of God, please kill me." DuSang's nerve was breaking. I was glad to see that. I wanted him to suffer.

"God's gone fishing," I said. "And won't be back in time to help your case. You have to pay for what you did, DuSang. There's no way around it."

DuSang lay still. "You and that dirty Swede whore," he said.

"A lady from Finland," I said. "Nothing you can say will make me kill you quick."

I kneaded the greasy bacon between my hands until there was grease all over them. DuSang tried to jerk his head to one side when I bent over him with the chunk of bacon. But I grabbed him by the hair and rubbed the pig fat all over his head, all over his face. I gave his face extra pork fat.

His body stiffened when he heard the first wolf howl, and he knew then how he was going to die. The sun was going down—and he knew. I was glad he knew. There was daylight left and the wolves wouldn't come for hours, but they'd come.

I smeared his parka with bacon grease, working it in deep; and then I started on his pants. Last to get a coating of bacon were his boots. By the time I got through there wasn't much bacon left. What there was left—a scrap of meat—I shoved under his shirt. The wolves would have to dig for that. They would.

The wind rattled in the pines and the wolf howls sounded again and they seemed to be closer. DuSang knew this country, knew what wolves were like. Usually they didn't attack humans. At first they would be afraid of him, but they would be drawn by the smell of bacon. The leader of the pack—the boldest—would make a run at him with snarling teeth. DuSang would yell or scream and that would drive them off for a moment. Then the wolves would see that he was helpless, for all his yelling. And then they would attack.

They'd go at his face first because his face was exposed. They would fight over him as they tore him to pieces. I didn't want to be there when it happened, but nothing on earth would have changed my mind. It was the least I could do for Hella, and if I could have thought of something worse I would have done that, too.

I wiped my hands on DuSang and made sure the

rawhide thongs were secure. As I got ready to move out DuSang began to curse me, calling down all the devils in hell on my head. At times he broke into French. He was a tough man all right; I'll give him that.

His curses followed me until I couldn't hear them any more.

Now I was free of DuSang and his killers, but the mountains still had to be crossed and my strength was going fast. I didn't even feel like eating, always a bad sign when a man is coming to the end of his rope. I had to do something about my sinking condition. I started talking to myself, another bad sign that didn't seem so bad at the time, because when you're starting to go crazy you aren't aware of it. In the days—and nights—to come, I was to hold many conversations with myself. And there would come a time when I'd hold lengthy conversations with the judge.

But for now I just kept on going. And I did look after the dogs, resting them, feeding them. I knew the wolves would be after me when they finished with DuSang, with the others I had killed. A wolf stays hungry no matter how much he eats. Food for the dogs was starting to run low. I was feeding each dog about a pound less at the end of every day, and it was beginning to tell on them. If I didn't shoot some meat soon I would have to kill one of the dogs and cut him up for the others. I didn't want to do that, not because I'm sentimental about animals, but because it would slow me down even more. Besides, one dog wouldn't go far among five.

It was getting on toward night—the day after I'd left DuSang—when I saw the she-deer. At first I thought my eyes were playing tricks on me, as they do at that time of day, but when I blinked away my fatigue, the deer was still there. It was a big one, and old, and it was a wonder it hadn't fallen prey to the wolves. Maybe it was injured; it was moving very slow. With trembling hands I took

DuSang's bolt action rifle from its sheeplined scabbard. It was loaded and all I had to do was line up the sights and fire. But it was a big rifle and right then it seemed to weigh a ton. The deer, unused to humans, was moving away without much panic. I was a lot more panicky than the deer. In fact, as I tried to hold the rifle steady, I was close to frantic. I don't know if I prayed for this one shot. I might have. You break down and pray at times like that. I steadied the rifle and squeezed the trigger.

The deer jerked to one side and began to run. Cursing, I bolted another cartridge and fired. The deer kept running. It disappeared behind a scatter of rocks. Alarmed by the shooting, the dogs threatened to overturn the sled in their wild scramble to get away from the noise. Shaky though my first shot was, I was sure I'd hit the deer. That didn't mean it couldn't travel miles before it died. I left the dogs and climbed up into the rocks and there was blood in the snow. Pasted against a rock was a scrap of flesh mixed with fragments of lead. The high-powered bullet had gone right through the deer.

I followed the trail of blood and that took me down into a snow-choked draw. There I found the dying animal hopelessly bogged down. I raised the rifle and put a bullet through its head.

"Sorry, old girl," I said.

Yes, I talked to deer, too.

Weak as I was, it took me a long time to drag the carcass back to where the dogs were. If I'd been thinking straight I would have butchered the deer where I killed it. The dogs barked wildly when they smelled the fresh blood, and they kept on barking and growling while I skinned the deer, doing it carefully so nothing would be wasted. I separated a haunch, cut it into chunks and gave the meat to the dogs, and the meat was still warm when they tore into it, the blood dripping from their muzzles.

And when they finished they wanted more. I gave it to them. I fed them deer meat until they were sluggish and sleepy, then I cooked two big deer steaks for myself. I let them cook for a long time because the meat was fresh-killed and therefore tough. There was nothing to go with it, no coffee, no beans—nothing. There were no plates either, but none of it mattered. When the meat was fit to eat I grabbed up a steak and ate it with my hands. I ate the meat like a savage. Why not? I was turning into one.

Nothing in my life tasted better than the meat from that old she-deer. I ate so much that I began to feel sleepy like the dogs, but this wasn't the time or the place for sleep. Instead, I roused myself and set about cutting up the rest of the meat. I saved everything but the guts and the head. The rest froze as soon as it was cut, and I packed it on the sled behind the coffin, and then I moved on again, climbing higher into the pass. Now the dogs had to work harder than the previous days. I kept wanting to sleep, and I had to fight hard to keep from just lying down in the snow. I knew if I did that I might never get up again. I cursed myself for having left the coffee pot behind. Like they say, I wanted hot coffee so much I could almost taste it.

The pass dug deeper into the mountains and in places it was narrow and all but choked with rocks. There was one point, worse than any of the others, where I had to unload the coffin and take it across on my back. Then I had to unhitch the dogs and drag the sled to the other side. My muscles were trembling by the time I got finished and I had to sit on the coffin before I was able to go on.

As I toiled upward the wind grew stronger and the pass became a giant chimney that sucked all the wind down from the peaks. It remained clear but the temperature was far below zero because of the howling wind. My face burned with frostbite and it continued to burn even when I rubbed it with snow and wrapped my scarf tightly around it. The glare of sun on snow hurt my eyes and there were times when I could hardly see at all. I was close to the timberline now and I made the last big fire I was going to have. Dusk was still an hour away when I made camp in the shelter of an overhanging rock. It didn't give that much protection from the wind, but it was better than camping in the open. I fed the dogs again and made a roaring fire that was better than food, better than anything. Here most of the trees were dead; as dead as I felt. I cooked deer meat on a bed of coals raked to the side. It was black and burned, but I tore at it like a husky.

After I heaped the fire high with wood I crawled into the sleeping bag and slept between the fire and the rock wall. The rock reflected the heat, and it was the first time I'd been warm in days. It was dark when wolf howls woke me up and at first, still drugged with sleep, I didn't know where I was. I fired a shot and the howling stopped and I went back to sleep. I don't know what time it was when the wolves started howling again. By now the fire had burned low and the wolves were closer than they had been before. Now that they had eaten DuSang they were getting over their fear of humans.

With my head still groggy from fatigue, I built up the fire and prepared to stay awake until morning. That was when I began to talk to the judge for the first time. I started by talking to myself, going over my thoughts in my head, then talking out loud.

"Saddler," I said to myself. "Of all the damn fools ever born you are the worst."

Then I added, "Isn't that right, Judge? It's all right if you don't answer, your honor. I know how it is."

Of course I knew the judge was dead—I wasn't that crazy; still, I kept on talking to the corpse as if we were the best of pals. I'm not sure what else I said, but it must have sounded pretty reasonable at the time. I think I must have talked about politics, a subject in which I haven't the slightest interest. Come to think of it, that's probably why I talked about politics. When your mind starts to wander, usually it ends up in strange places. Mine did, that night.

I must have been dozing when the leader of the wolf pack made a run at the dogs. The barking of the dogs rose to a screaming frenzy and I fired at the lean gray shape that darted into the firelight. The wolf went down in a snarling fury and I fired again and killed him and he was hardly dead when the dogs tore him to pieces. I didn't try to stop them—the wolf was meat.

I was never so glad to see dawn as I was that morning. During the night the rest of the wolf pack had kept their distance, howling in their mournful way, as if trying to bring back their leader. But there was nothing left but a few patches of gray fur; even the blood in the snow had been licked up by the dogs.

The team was in fine shape when I started out after a breakfast of burned deer meat. I rubbed grease on the frostbite patches and they didn't burn so much after that. What was left of the deer meat would have to see me over the pass. I knew there were scattered trading posts and way stations on the other side where I could buy food for the dogs, food for myself.

The wolves followed along until I reached the top of the pass. Then one night they were gone, retreating to their own territory, as all wild animals do. There was deep, soft snow on the way to the summit and I had to rig up the shoulder harness to help the dogs. I was so busy hauling the sled that I didn't know I had reached the top. I straightened up to take a rest and found myself looking down the other side of the mountain. Nothing stirred in all that expanse of snow and ice. I was too far away to see the sea, yet I thought I could smell salt in the air. The dogs barked when I let out a whoop. The deer meat was gone and they were hungry and that made them vicious, especially the big dark husky called Siwash. The brute kept snapping at the others, and I decided he'd be the one to get a bullet, if it came to feeding the others. More than once I had to lay into him with the dog whip, though I hadn't used the whip since the start of the journey.

The dogs were dragging their feet and so was I. All my movements slowed down and every little chore was torture. Cold gets to you fast when there's no food in your belly, and looking at that goddamned Siwash, I began to wonder how dog meat tasted.

Now we were coming down from the top of the pass, and hungry or not the dogs were pulling their weight. On toward sunset of that day I shot a big snow rabbit and gave it to the dogs. It disappeared in about a minute, head, tail, fur, everything. If anything, the small meal made the dogs crankier than they had been. Siwash kept trying to get free of the harness and when I hit the bastard with the butt end of the whip he lunged at me with snapping teeth. I was so weak that he knocked me over and I fell hard and skidded away on a patch of ice. The harness and the weight of the other dogs kept Siwash from getting at me, and I grabbed up my rifle in a rage and shot him through the head. I expected the other dogs to turn on the dead husky; all they did was lie down in the snow and howl. But the howling turned to expectant barking when I freed the carcass and began to cut it up. I portioned it out as best I could, keeping only a piece of the haunch for myself. I roasted the meat on a stick and ate it with the grim determination of a starving man ready to eat anything.

Having eaten their brother, the dogs lost some of their crankiness, and we moved on down the mountain. It was an easy descent, but I still had no idea how far I was from Valdez. I guessed about a hundred miles. It could have been twice that distance. I just didn't know.

It took another day to get down from the mountain. The dogs were hungry again and I was weak in the legs, hanging on to the sled as much as guiding it, and I was still on high ground when I thought I saw a light in the distance. With the dry snow blowing it was hard to tell at first, but as I moved on into the dusk I knew I'd really seen it. Every time the snow blew hard the light disappeared; it came back when there was a break in the wind. I yelled at the dogs and my excitement got to them, and right then I loved those dumb brutes.

The light grew steadier as I pushed on through the wind-whipped snow. "We're all right now," I told the judge. "We'll have food and we can sleep, the two of us. No wolves, no DuSang, just food and sleep. I told you I'd bring you home, Judge."

I yelled for the joy of seeing that light. Now there was only a few hundred yards to go, and I was still yelling when a door opened and light from the cabin flooded out onto the snow. The man in the doorway had a rifle—with a round in the chamber, I guess—and he stepped out of the light when I got close. I was so happy to see him, he might have been the older brother I hadn't seen for twenty years. I didn't blame him for holding that rifle at his hip. I was so glad to see him, I didn't even think about it.

He lowered the rifle when he saw what I looked like. I staggered toward him and he kept me from falling. "Sweet Jesus Christ," he said. "Who are you and where did you come from? Am I going crazy or is that a coffin on the sled?"

"The judge," I babbled. "Judge Slocum. I'm taking him back to San Francisco. How far is Valdez? I have to get the judge to Valdez."

He was a big man with the gentle manners you often find in men who don't have to prove how tough they are.

"Easy does it, pilgrim," he said. "You look all in. Never mind about getting to Frisco just now. Come on in and get some good hot rabbit stew in your belly. Hot stew, hot coffee, then you can tell me the rest of it. While you're eating I'll see to your dogs."

McWilliams was his name and he gave me enough rabbit stew for five people, and after he fed the dogs he came in and sat across the table from me. I was so busy eating I hardly noticed him.

"You mean you crossed the mountains?" he said after he put a dollop of whiskey in my coffee. "And you brought this judge—what was that name?"

I said Phineas Slocum.

"Never heard of him," McWilliams said. He slapped the table with a calloused hand. "God Almighty! You brought a coffin and a body over the mountains. I swear I never heard of such a thing in my whole life."

McWilliams was a lonely man by choice, but like all such men he talked a blue streak once he got going. He kept plying me with food and coffee until I was ready to bust. What was going on in the rest of Alaska? he wanted to know. Was it true that the Mounties were expelling Americans from the Yukon? What did I know about the new gold strike to the far north that was rumored to be bigger than anything in the Yukon?

The man was so starved for news of the outside world that I tried to give him civil answers, but all the while my head kept nodding, craving sleep. Finally, I fell forward with my head on the table. I was through talking for a while.

I must have slept for eighteen hours because when I woke up again it was the next night and McWilliams was beside my bunk with a plate of food and a pot of coffee. The knot of tension had faded from my head and I was able to see him straight for the first time.

"Feeling better?" McWilliams asked. "I guess you are.

Stay as long as you like. I'm glad to have the company. I just fed your dogs and they're in fine fettle. If you don't mind me asking, what would your name be?"

I told him and we shook hands.

"How far is Valdez?" I asked.

"About eighty miles, give or take a few," he said. "That's the distance near as I can make out, though I don't go there any more than I have to. I trap my furs and mind my business. You want some whiskey to open your eyes?"

The Scotchman's whiskey opened my eyes and the floor felt solid when I put my feet on it. McWilliams had made a lot of breakfast for both of us, and not much talking was done until I had eaten all I could hold. I asked him about Valdez and he said the ore ships made regular calls there.

"They ought to be able to accommodate you and the judge," he said. "Seeing as how he was so important and all. You're going to be famous, Saddler."

"I'd just as soon not," I said.

"They'll make you famous whether you like it or not," McWilliams said. "Nothing you can do about it."

"I can hide," I said.

That was exactly what I planned to do when I got back to Frisco. If Cynthia wanted to talk to the press that was all right with me, but I didn't want any part of it.

The long sleep and McWilliams's good food had revived me and now I just wanted to get the rest of the journey done with. This, I sincerely hoped, would be my last trip to Alaska. From now on, barring some strange turn of fate, I was going to stay in the sun as much as possible.

McWilliams loaded me up with supplies for the rest of the journey to Valdez. I insisted that he take a hundred dollars. If he hadn't been there I wouldn't be writing this story. To get to Valdez all I had to do was follow a frozen creek that wound its way to the sea. Valdez wasn't much of a place, McWilliams said, but I could find just about anything I wanted there. He said I might have to wait for a while before an ore ship pulled in, but there was a boardinghouse run by a man named Webberly.

"Tell him I sent you and he'll look after you," McWilliams said. "Wish you could stay on here a few days. It's been nice talking to a human after so long."

I said goodbye to McWilliams and headed out. The dogs had recovered from their ordeal and I was feeling a lot better myself. It would be a while before I got back to what you'd call normal. That wouldn't come until after I delivered the judge.

There was no hurry now and so I didn't hurry the dogs. Following McWilliams's directions I picked up the creek and followed it. There was no snow, and so close to the sea the cold was much milder than it had been on the other side of the mountains. Fifteen miles from McWilliams's place I passed another cabin with halfbreed Indians living in it. They came out to stare at the coffin, but didn't speak. I guess the shiny black coffin frightened them a little.

It took me three days to get to Valdez. I could have made it in two, but there was no need to hurry. I camped out for two nights and reached the outskirts of the town at dusk on the third day. I smelled the sea long before I came to the town. It looked slate gray in the gathering darkness. The town itself wasn't much more than one street, with warehouses taking up most of it. Long piers had been built for the loading of the ore ships; right then there was no ship in the harbor.

I went to look for the boardinghouse operated by McWilliams's friend. It was a small building overshadowed by a huge warehouse; on the other side of it was a saloon called Blackie's. Not being a gold town, Valdez was quiet, nothing like Skagway or Dawson. Men came out of the saloon and gaped at me as I went by with the coffin. It must have been quite a sight. The funny thing is that I didn't think anything about it. By now hauling a coffin around seemed the most natural thing in the world.

I found Webberly, a short round man, eating his supper in the kitchen. "You what?" he said, all but dropping his knife and fork. That was the reaction I would get from a lot of people in the days to come. At first Webberly was inclined to get mad at me, thinking it was a joke; the only way I could convince him was to take him outside and let him look at the coffin. But he balked at letting me bring the judge into the house, saying that he'd do fine in the woodshed at the back of the house. That suited me fine because I didn't want the judge to thaw out.

Webberly made me an offer for the team. It wasn't as much as I'd paid in Dawson, but I didn't feel like arguing about money. I put the judge away and was glad that I was nearly done with the whole business. Webberly said there was an ore ship due in three days. It would stay in port for two days, then sail back to the States. It could take me as far as Seattle; there I would have to switch to another ship. For the moment there was nothing to do but wait.

I walked around the town and didn't see anything out of the ordinary. Word had spread about me; I guess the judge's coming was the most interesting thing that had happened in Valdez for a very long time. There didn't seem to be any rowdy element in Valdez. It had the look of a workingman's town. I guess the mining companies owned the town and most of the country around it. All that was fine with me. The last thing I needed was more trouble.

I dropped into the saloon and even got into a very low stakes poker game with some men who were waiting for the ship to arrive. They wanted to know all about the judge and I told them some of it, leaving out Hella and DuSang. As far as I was concerned, it was all in the past. It was good to be back in civilization, that is, if you could call Valdez a civilized place. Whatever it was, I was happy to be there, drinking fair whiskey and whiling the time away in penny-ante card games.

After playing for four hours I was twelve dollars ahead and I told the bartender to spend it on whiskey for the men I'd been playing with. I had a drink with them before I went back to check on the judge. Nobody had disturbed the old geezer, so I went to bed.

I thought I didn't have a worry in the world.

TWELVE

The next day was just as quiet, with nothing to disturb it but the rattle of ore wagons making their way to the dock. That woke me early, but I slept through the rest of it. Webberly gave me breakfast and a month-old Seattle newspaper. Webberly said there was no need to check on the judge. He said he'd done it already. I guess he didn't have any idea why I kept checking on the judge. To him, as to the other men in town, he was just an old man in a coffin, on his way home. Like I said, this was a workingman's town and no one there had ever heard of Judge Phineas Slocum.

I hoped to keep it simple: to wait out the days and be gone forever from Alaska. The newspaper took me through a long breakfast, and when I finished I went to the saloon to look for a game, but there was nobody there with any time to play. Men who worked for the mines came in and went out after their morning eye-opener. It started to rain and kept on right through the day. The frostbite patches on my face were beginning to heal; the bartender, a runty Irishman, gave me some salve that helped a lot. There were a few whores working at Blackie's Saloon and I thought why not try one or more of them to wile away the time I had to wait. I knew Hella wouldn't have minded. Anyway, she was dead. I still felt sad about her, but there was nothing to be done about that. The girl I took upstairs with me was young and slightly hardbitten. But her hard smile softened when I gave her extra money that didn't have to be split with the proprietor. She put her heart into it because of the money. I fucked her in a small, bare room feebly heated by an old kerosene stove. After I came she fed me whiskey and a little later she sucked me off. It was nothing like it was with Hella, but it was all right. She had pretended to come, but I knew she hadn't. That was all right too, because after it was over I had gotten rid of a lot of the tension.

The rain kept up, turning the one street of the town to ankle-deep mud. All day and far into the night the huge ore wagons rumbled down to the dock. The second day passed like the first, meaning that nothing happened, and sometimes there was nobody in the saloon but myself and the runty Irishman, who drank about as much whiskey as he sold across the bar. So we drank together and I half-listened to his endless stories about all the places he had worked before he scraped up enough money to open a place of his own. How he had come to own a saloon in Valdez remained one of those mysteries, for he talked about everything but that. Somehow, though, I got the idea that he had a nagging wife back in the States. Not everyone in Alaska goes there to dig for gold.

There was no trouble in sight, but I cleaned my guns just the same. Anyway, working on my guns is something

I like to do. I still had DuSang's bolt action English rifle and I worked on that, too, not that there was very much need. But I cleaned all my weapons and then I cleaned them again. It gave me something to do.

I got up early on the last day, hoping to see the ore ship when I went down to the dock wearing a yellow slicker I had borrowed from Webberly. Too early, a man on the dock told me, so I went to the saloon and drank whiskey with the Irish proprietor, who never seemed to sober up completely.

"The boat'll be along some time today," he said. "Unless of course it got sunk on the way. But don't you fret, Mr. Saddler. And if not that boat, there's sure to be another real soon. Drink your drink now and don't get too anxious."

I wasn't anxious at all: I just wanted to get the hell out of Valdez. Bringing the judge home had taken too much out of me. I had been too long with the dead and I wanted to start living again.

The bartender and I were playing Liar's Poker, that is, matching the numbers on dollar bills, when a man came in and said there was a steam yacht coming into the harbor.

"Big damn thing, fast-looking thing," he said. "Cuts the water like a knife. What the hell you think it's doing in Valdez? Give me a quick big one so's I can go back and see for myself."

He had gulped his drink and was turning to go when I grabbed him by the arm. "What color is this steam yacht?" I asked him.

"What?" he said. "Oh, sure. It's bright yellow. Sort of like a canary bird color. Come on down and take a look if you're so interested."

I didn't have to look at the fast steam yacht to know that it belonged to Soapy Smith. I had seen it in the harbor at Skagway—the only boat of that color—and

Soapy had boasted about it during our conversation on the first day I arrived in Alaska.

There was nothing I could do but make a fight of it. After all I'd been through I wasn't about to give up the judge no matter what. All I had was my belt gun and I ran back to the boardinghouse to get the rest of my weapons: the Winchester and DuSang's big rifle. The judge's coffin hadn't been disturbed and I laid it flat and covered it with cordwood before I went upstairs. Webberly was alarmed when I came running in and I told him to get the hell out of the way because there was big trouble on its way. I didn't explain but he ran like a bastard.

I filled my pockets with ammunition for the Winchester and the bolt action, still not knowing what I was going to do. There could be any number of Soapy's men on the boat. If there were enough of them I didn't see how I stood a chance.

There was a backstairs to the boardinghouse and from the top I could see the harbor and the sleek yellow steam yacht sliding up to the dock. I made too good a target in the yellow slicker so I threw it away. The rain beat down on me as I went down the stairs, still not knowing what I had to face. All I could do was fight them as best I could. Use everything I had learned in fifteen years of staying alive when the odds were bad. I wasn't brave, but I was ready to die—there's a difference. I hoped Soapy had come along so that I could kill him. I didn't know how likely that was; Soapy liked to stay in the warmth and safety of his back room in Skagway.

I stuck the Winchester through my belt and climbed a muddy hill that looked down on the back of the boardinghouse, and when I got to the top I could see the woodshed where the coffin was. I bolted a round into the chamber of the English rifle and lay in the mud, waiting for them to come. I could see the dock and even before the yacht was secured five men jumped off and came up toward the town carrying rifles. They spread out over the dock and then one of them turned and waved another man to come ashore. I knew that it had to be Soapy, careful as always, wanting to cover all his bets. I'm pretty sure I could have shot him at that distance, but that would just make the rest of them run for cover. Then I'd be in for a siege that could end only one way. What I was hoping to do was to get two or three of them after they crept up on the woodshed, after they asked questions at gunpoint and learned where the coffin was.

While I watched, Soapy's men closed around him, a wall of men that would prevent anything but a head shot. They moved up from the dock, walking fast with Soapy in the center of his bodyguard. The King of Crime had come to Valdez to claim what he considered his.

I lost sight of them for a while. First there was the huge ore dump and after that came a string of warehouses. I pulled the Winchester from my belt and put it beside me in the mud, laying it down carefully so the action wouldn't get fouled. I saw them for a moment when they came out from the cover of the warehouses. Past that point I couldn't see them at all.

Five minutes passed and then I felt rather than heard them coming up the street. The rain pelted down harder than ever; a bone-chilling rain that made all the world look gray and dead. I pulled back from the crest of the hill, cold and wet and covered with mud. Then I saw the first of them, just a face at the corner of Webberly's house. It looked out and ducked back. There was no sign of the others and I wondered if they had figured out where I was—where I was planning to shoot from. The face looked out again and I held my fire, because killing one man wouldn't get me anywhere.

Two men ran forward and another followed. I let them get into the woodshed. The third man stood with his back to the wall of the shed, looking up the hill without seeing me. I let the first two bring out the coffin before I opened fire killing the guard with a bullet in the head. The others dropped the coffin and tried to make a run for it. I killed one man and the other nearly made it to safety before I killed him with a traveling shot that brought him down hard. He tried to get up and I had to shoot him again.

Now they knew where I was and Soapy's last two men opened fire from the corner of the boardinghouse. Soon just one man was shooting at me and I knew the other was trying to work his way around behind me. Soapy—smart man—didn't show himself at all. So far he hadn't, but that didn't mean he wouldn't get into it, if he got desperate. Getting off that hill was foremost in my mind, so I left the bolt action where it was and let myself roll in the mud until I reached the bottom, and I stopped just short of the deep pit where Webberly dumped his trash. Rusty tin cans scraped against my legs as I went into the pit, inch by inch, trying to make as little noise as possible. Hunkered down, I heard Soapy's gunman coming up the other side, running and bent over, trying to show no more of himself than he had to.

He made an easy kill when he straightened up and waved. I shot him in the side and shot him again while he was clawing at the wound, and when I fired again I missed him because he was already falling. Just then the steam whistle of the ore ship sounded. It echoed across the harbor and far back into the hills. One more bullet came at me and that was all. Now it was my turn to go on the offensive and I came out of there like a man who knew what he was doing.

I rounded the corner of the boardinghouse and Soapy was running fast for a man of his age. The last gunman alive turned and fired at me, throwing bullets at me with the desperation of a man who knows he's going to die. He fired fast and wild and even when I threw myself flat he kept on firing. I fired at him and brought him down with a bullet in the leg. His rifle went flying into the muddy street and before he had a chance to crawl after it, I was all over him like crabs in a basket. Soapy was gone, but I wanted some answers from the man I was going to kill.

He was reaching into his coat for a handgun when I stomped on his arm, breaking it like a stick. I took the revolver from his pocket and threw it far away. Then I slammed him against the wall of a building and back-handed him across the face until he was bleeding from the mouth.

"What's been going on, my friend?" I said in a dull, tired voice. "Tell me what you know—your only chance to live. I mean that, friend." I put the muzzle of the rifle under his chin, to show how much I meant it. "Start with Sullivan."

He spat blood before he spoke. "Sullivan knew Soapy wanted to kidnap the judge's body and wanted it for himself."

"Kidnap the body?" I said.

"For a million dollars," the gunman said. "Soapy was going to send a message to the Slocums and the widow. Sullivan planned to beat him out of it. Sullivan left Skagway and hasn't been heard from since. The Slocums sent their own men. Nobody knows what happened to them. That's the truth as I know it. I swear it, Saddler. I just work for Smith. You can't shoot me for that, can you?"

I shot him in the head as a way of answering his question, and when I went to the end of the street and could see the harbor, Soapy's steam yacht was heading out to sea at a fast clip. The ore ship was tying up. It was one of the big new steel-hulled ships with sail as well as steam. I left the dead gunman in the street and went down to talk to the captain.

They were unloading supplies for the mines when I reached the dock. I found the first mate and he directed me to the captain's cabin. He was one of those Yankees who leave home early and never go back, and he talked the way Yankees are expected to talk, which was hardly at all.

"Guess I can fix you up with some space," he said after I explained the situation to him. "Have to charge you for the freight, understand? Them's the rules. You just pack the judge in ice and we'll keep him on deck for the whole voyage."

He didn't whistle when I said I'd brought the judge over the mountains. Yankees think they can do anything, so what was so great about what I'd done?

"You look like you need a tot of rum," he said to me. "Been sailing this coast twenty years or more, and I never seen a man needed a drink more than you do."

The captain, a man named Grinsted, sent three of his sailors to help me with the coffin. The dead men lay where they had fallen, but the sailors just looked at them and then at me with mildly inquisitive eyes. We picked up the coffin and carried it down to the ore ship, where the ship's carpenter made a container for the coffin, leaving plenty of space to pack it with ice. He was a Yankee, like the captain, and didn't have much to say.

Two days later, with the coffin lashed tight against heavy seas, the ore ship *President Hayes* sailed out of the harbor at Valdez. Soapy had long gone back to Skagway, no doubt to escape the wrath of the mining company, for if you know mining companies then you know they have their company gunmen that are a lot more dangerous than any law. The captain fixed me up in a cabin usually reserved for company officials, and I ate the same food he did. I laid in my own store of whiskey for the voyage back to Seattle, and it was a good thing I did, because the Yankee captain didn't drink.

The *President Hayes* was a fast ship and we made Seattle in a third of the time it had taken me to get to Alaska. Now and then I visited the judge on deck to make sure he wasn't thawing out.

In Seattle the captain arranged the transfer to a ship sailing to San Francisco. I told him I didn't want to attract any attention, but one of the crewmen must have talked. Before I was rightly aboard the Frisco boat a horde of newspaper reporters were down at the docks looking to get my story. I knew then I wasn't going to get off that easy; it would be worse in Frisco. The only consolation was that it would soon be over.

The boat I boarded was a passenger boat, and I had to stay in my cabin to get away from all the people who wanted to shake my hand and hear my story and otherwise drive me crazy. But they came to my door anyway. One portly gent owned a company that sold snow country supplies. That one wanted me to sign a paper stating that the sled I'd used to bring out the judge was made by his factory in Seattle. The money was good—$5,000—but I just couldn't see myself as a newspaper advertisement huckster, especially when it would mean having my picture taken when we got to Frisco.

Whores came too—all the coast boats have them—offering to do this and that for me. A whore with a French accent arrived to ask if I'd like a "trip around the world." I told her I'd just had a trip around the world and didn't feel like another one so soon.

Other women turned up with marriage or money on their minds. It had been going around the ship that I was the millionaire judge's long lost son, and that drew them like flies to honey. Still other women just wanted to get in bed with a "hero."

Me, I just wanted to be left alone.

In Frisco I stayed on the boat until the other passeners got off. Then I went ashore to hire a wagon to take the judge up to his fine house on Nob Hill. Crewmen helped me to load the coffin, but by then a crowd was gathering and it got bigger as the wagon rattled away from the dock. There was plenty of noise by the time I reached the house.

Cynthia opened the door and stared at me in absolute amazement. "I was beginning to think you were dead," she said.

"Got a delivery for you, ma'am," I said.

In the hallway, with the door locked, Cynthia hugged me so hard she threatened to break my ribs, and I sat down in the first chair I came to after she let me go.

"What I need is a big drink," I said. "A lot of whiskey and some peace and quiet."

With a drink in my belly and another in my hand, I told the story for the last time. Wild horses wouldn't have been able to drag it out of me again. I asked her about the Slocum brothers and she said they'd been acting pretty cocky, as if they didn't expect me to get back.

"They came close to getting their way," I said. "So did a lot of people."

I asked Cynthia if she'd do me a favor and she looked puzzled. "Anything you want, Saddler. Just tell me what it is."

I gave her a weary grin. "Promise to make your next husband die at home in bed."

Cynthia smiled too. "No more husbands for me, Saddler. From now on I'm going to be an elegant widow."

"But you'll manage to enjoy yourself just the same?"

"You know me, Saddler. I always manage. How would you like to be an elegant widow's companion?"

"Maybe later," I said. "As of this moment I'm too tired to think about anything but sleep and whiskey."

The very thought of sleep made me yawn and I went
upstairs like a man with lead in his shoes. I lay down on
the bed without taking anything off and slept through to
the next day. When I woke up I was aware of a lot of
activity in the house. I figured Cynthia was busy with
lawyers and undertakers, getting ready to bury the judge,
putting the judge's brothers in their place. I was out of it
now and wanted to stay out of it.

In the afternoon the undertakers took the judge's
coffin away so they could thaw him out for the lying in
state. I wondered what the old bastard would look like.
I'd never seen him thawed out.

It was the damnedest funeral San Francisco ever saw.
The governor was there among all the other politicians.
There was fog and heavy rain, but that didn't stop them
from turning out to pay their last respects. The story—
and my name—was all over the newspapers. Reporters
camped on Cynthia's doorstep, trying to get me to talk to
them. But that didn't stop them from writing and
publishing everything I hadn't said. The stories got
wilder and wilder. Not only had I battled wolves and
grizzly bears, I had also fought my way through "hordes
of savage redskins" and eaten some of my dogs in order
to stay alive. I was a real living legend. The newspapers
wanted to take my picture, and when I said go to hell
they cooked up drawings that made me look like a cross
between Buffalo Bill and Abraham Lincoln. In one
drawing I was dressed in buckskins, with long yellow hair
and a flowing mustache. They said I carried a brace of
ivory-handled Colts, a present from the President himself. One scribbler got carried away and said I was the
only man who had escaped the Little Big Horn massacre
back in '76. I liked that one better than any of the others.

I don't recall what else they said about me. They said a
lot, and most of it was a lie. The mayor wanted to give

me the key to the city, and sometimes I wish I'd taken it. It might have unlocked the city treasury.

Cynthia grieved in public and laughed in private. This was an unseemly attitude, to be sure, not that I blamed her for it. Now that the judge was back where he belonged, there was no disputing her claim to all that money. The only time she didn't laugh was when I told her about Hella. Cynthia is a tough gal, but there are certain things she knows about.

"I'm very sorry," was all she said, and that meant more than if she had gone into a song and dance.

I must say I drank a lot in the days before the funeral, while the judge was lying in state in the federal court building and Cynthia was receiving callers who wanted to say how devastated they were by the old boy's passing. Naturally they all wanted to meet me, but I wasn't having any of that. Instead, I drank in my room. So far Cynthia and I hadn't resumed our sleeping arrangements.

There was nothing Cynthia didn't want to do for me. All I had to do was yank on the bell-pull and the household staff would come running with liquor, food, anything. I just wanted to get away from there, from all the hoopla, but Cynthia urged me to stay. And so I did because I was too tired to do anything else.

"You look terrible, Saddler," she said, and I guess I did. There still were patches of frostbite on my face, but the doctor who looked me over said I wouldn't be marked up after all.

I thought of Hella, what was left of her, out there in the Alaska mountains, and I decided maybe she was better off. The city would not have suited her: she was where she had always wanted to be.

Would you believe it! It took them nearly a week to get the judge into the ground. Not into the ground exactly; they put him in the family vault.

I didn't go to the funeral with Cynthia, though she tried hard to persuade me to attend. But I said no. Besides, I was too drunk that day. But I did go by myself, standing well back in a crowd of ordinary citizens, and not a person there knew my face. So much for being the only man who survived the Little Big Horn.

It was as solemn as all get-out, with a guard of honor and all the dignitaries in their glossy black hats, and the hearse they put the coffin in must have weighed twenty tons. It was drawn by black horses with purple plumes. Cynthia wore a heavy veil and I'm sure she was smiling under it. Maybe she wasn't; she had liked the judge in her way.

The hearse moved away and I said, "So long, Judge."

I was packing my few things when Cynthia came back to the house after the funeral. She came into my room and threw her hat and veil in a corner.

"Where the hell do you think you're going?" she said. Before I answered she took a swig from the bottle of bourbon on the dresser.

"Back to Texas," I said, taking a swig myself.

"Not today you're not," Cynthia said. "I'm not going to try to make you forget that girl. But I am going to bring you back to life." And saying that she pushed me onto the bed and started by taking off my boots.

Well you know how it is. You get over everything if you give it enough time. But you've got to have help, and that's what I got from Cynthia. She helped me every way she could; she knew exactly how to do it. I'd done a lot for her, and now she was doing a lot for me. I lay on the bed grinning while she unbuckled my belt and pulled my pants off, and when she finished she rolled me under the silk sheets and got in with me. I was in bed with one of the richest women in San Francisco, but money wasn't a consideration at the time. After many weeks of cold, hunger, misery and danger, I needed a warm woman more than anything else.

Cynthia was warm, she smelled good, and she was all woman. I was tired but she stiffened me up like the bed expert she was. After a while I wasn't tired at all, and I went into her like a bull. I went at her so hard that she gave out little cries of surprise. She lifted her legs until they were over my shoulders, making it possible for me to penetrate her to the fullest. She was wet and warm and I drove in and out of her like a piston. I must have been more desperate than I thought because even when I came I didn't get soft. Cynthia cried out again when she found that I was still hard, still ready to go on with it.

And that's what we did all through the afternoon of the judge's funeral. Winter rain beat on the windows, but it was warm and friendly where we were, and Alaska began to fade from my mind. The only time Cynthia got up was to get whiskey for both of us.

Finally I slept and when I woke up hours later she was still there and just as eager to please as she had been. Her fingertips touched my battered face and she smiled at me. "You've done a lot for me," she said. "I don't know how I'm ever going to make up for it."

"You just did," I said. "Let's not be talking about what we owe each other."

"I feel bad about that girl you liked so much."

"Don't be like that. Talking like that is a waste of time."

"I wish you'd think about becoming an elegant widow's companion. It wouldn't be like . . . well, like it is with other people. We've known each other too long for that."

"Maybe that's why it wouldn't work," I said. "You're as restless as I am. You've got a place here in Frisco and I just wouldn't fit in. I am what I am and there's no changing me. You can take the boy out of West Texas but you can't—and so on. Let it go, all right?"

175

Cynthia said, "You're from the shitty end of Texas. Where the hell do you think I'm from?"

I said, "Makes no difference where you're from. You were born to live like this. 'Fess up now, you know it's true."

Cynthia gave a breathy sigh. "I like it fine, but there are times when I get sick of it. Goddamn but didn't we have a good, wild life in the old days?"

Some of that was true, too; on the other hand, Cynthia was looking at the past from a distance, and that made it seem better than it was.

"You can't have it every way," I said. "You got what you wanted. Better make the best of it."

"Damn right I will," Cynthia said, reaching down between my legs. "But I'd like it more if you stayed around. What in hell do you want anyway? How about a gambling house? You're a gambler so how about running your own place right here in San Francisco? If it's the money you're thinking about you can pay me back when you like."

"Be quiet," I said, drawing her close to me. "If I think of something else I want after this, I'll let you know."

It took me a long time to get back to Texas.